Maggie's
PLACE

Maggie's PLACE

a novel

Annette Haws

Covenant Communications, Inc.

Cover image *Women with an Umbrella* © Sguler, iStockphoto.com

Cover design by Christina Marcano © 2019 by Covenant Communications, Inc.

Published by Covenant Communications, Inc.
American Fork, Utah

Printed in the United States of America
First Printing: November 2019

26 25 24 23 22 21 20 19   10 9 8 7 6 5 4 3 2 1

ISBN 978-1-52441-016-2

To my darling Aunt Maydae, who understood
family better than most.

Acknowledgments

My FAVORITE AUNT LIVED THE last ten years of her life—her happiest years—at the Eagle Gate Apartments. During frequent visits, I met her delightful collection of neighbors who played Scrabble, shared late night pizzas, visited back and forth, made shopping expeditions to Harmon's and City Creek Mall, and most importantly, cared for each other. They embraced the third act of their lives with humor and courage, and I am thankful for their example.

Writing a book is not a solitary endeavor; it is a collaboration of friends, and so, many people deserve my gratitude. First the writing goddesses, Terrell Dougan, Kate Lahey, and Sally Robinson, for years of laughter, valuable insights, and lessons about the craft. As this is a book about friendship, I am grateful for the inspiration of lifelong friends: sweet Sue Kaelin and Jan Smith. Julie Markham and Randy Haws read early drafts, spoke honestly, and changed the shape of the novel. Shawna Wilde, Kathy Peterson, Kathy Merkley, Kim Jones, Steve Dunn, Dorothy Watts, Kris Groll, and Janet Jensen have offered unwavering support. The world's greatest cousins, Georgia Miller, Laurie Priano, Karen Therios, Rosanne Nieto, Mary Elizabeth Cannon, Susan Forsberg, and Sid Kimball, have cheered me on from the sidelines. For twenty-five years, Sid Groll has happily offered his expertise on law enforcement and the dark side of human behavior; he certainly deserves a large thank you. Kristy Black deserves a special thank you for sharing funny stories that have made their way into these pages, but more particularly, for teaching me how to laugh and smile in the face of perilous situations. I would also like to thank my editor, Ashley Gebert, as the first person to see the novel's possibilities. I'm grateful to her and the wonderful Covenant Communications family for their professionalism, patience, and kindness.

And where would authors be without ladies who read, think, and discuss? Sincere thanks go to friends in my book clubs: Martha Blonquist, Lynne Carlquist, Sally Larkin, Phyllis Griffiths, Clytee Gold, Liz Gloeckner, Kathy Newton, Jo Ann Miner, Kaylynn Nielson, Jenny West, Liz Goodell, Karla Wilson, Tracy Bigelow, Deanne Curtis, Penelope Harris, Nancy McDonald, and Carol Haymond.

A big thanks to my wonderful kids, Pete, Andy, Betsy, and Charlotte, who are always so pleased (and a little surprised) when their mother does something out of the ordinary. My first reader and best friend is my husband, Charlie, who willingly tosses aside his golf magazines in favor of a red pen. And to the two people who always encouraged me to color outside the lines—thanks, Mom and Dad.

Part One

Chapter One
A CLEAN SLATE

SEVEN YEARS AGO, MARY MARGARET Sullivan changed her name and moved into the Eagle Gate Apartments where becoming elderly was not something discussed, as it had already occurred and couldn't be unwound. Residents could conveniently forget troublesome pasts they didn't wish to remember and attribute the memory loss to age; in other words, moving into a one bed, one bath apartment on the seventh floor had been a fresh start, a clean slate, for Maggie Sullivan, and she was happy about it, even seven years later.

Thanksgiving was a week away, but only an old horse, which wore a pilgrim's hat while clomping along behind a carriage, seemed to understand Thanksgiving was still a holiday worth remembering. Christmas carols playing in sync with the fountains at City Creek Center reached Maggie over the congestion of five o'clock traffic. Twinkling lights, mannequins dressed in holiday finery, toy displays in the Disney Store, and the eclectic merchandise in the menagerie of shops were already drawing shoppers into the heart of downtown. In a week or two, Maggie would wander over to Temple Square in the evening to smile at families with red-cheeked children, who would bob along in hats and mittens and point with awe at the millions of tiny colored Christmas lights decorating the century-old trees.

But on this particular evening, distracted by thoughts of small children and Christmas and spare money for gifts, Maggie bumped into a couple walking toward her. Heat rose in her cheeks, and she muttered apologies to the stylish woman and to the woman's companion—a bearded, white-haired gentleman steadying himself with a brass-headed cane. His Christmas tie was covered with miniscule red-cheeked Santas who looked as ridiculous as Maggie felt at nearly upending a disabled man. She was turning away when the gentleman reached for her arm.

"Maggie?" he questioned. No last name was mentioned, but the warmth in his voice suggested she might be more than a familiar face to him and was, perhaps, an old friend.

Startled, she stepped back. No reluctance in his face. No hesitation. He didn't avert his eyes. Maybe he was a high school classmate who'd lived in Nigeria or Madagascar or some other far-off place for the past fifty years? Separated from newspapers, laptops, and the six o'clock news? But how could he know her if she didn't recognize him? "Excuse me," she said. "Have we met before?"

His bright eyes searched her face as if he sought a different reply. When she didn't speak, he straightened, as though his cane were just a prop, and said, "Forgive me. I mistook you for someone I knew years ago." He noticed the Campbell soup cans she was carrying—she couldn't afford free weights—and the duct-taped hole in the toe of her Nikes. His jacket shouted, *Armani*, and her coat said, *better luck next time*, but shame didn't count for much, not anymore.

"No harm done," she said, but that wasn't quite true. She felt intruded upon, somehow discovered, and not quite herself. Something about this elderly man made her feel exposed.

Dipping her head, she quickly stepped past him and spotted Jan waving in front of the Joseph Smith Memorial Building. She needed a joke, something simple to push worn thoughts aside. *Maybe it's the season, but I feel like I just met Santa and he's been on a diet and trimmed his beard.* Not too funny, but that's what she thought and then said, as she jerked a thumb in the direction she'd just come, and Jan laughed and took a look over her shoulder for the skinny Santa.

"The guy acted like he knew me," Maggie said, thinking this was the last thing she needed.

Jan sang, "*He sees you when you're sleeping. He knows when you're awake.* Of course he knows you."

The crust of ice crunched beneath their cross-trainers, and the drizzling, low-hanging clouds turned Maggie's silver hair into a frizzy mess. Her damp scarf hung limp around her throat. The streetlights glowed in the mist as the two friends lapped Temple Square and the adjacent block to the east—the perfectly landscaped heart of their city—for the third time.

Jan clasped five-pound weights, and, moving in concert, the two women began their fourth set of arm exercises. Jan lifted her weights and Maggie raised her cans of chicken soup—palms up and arms extended for forty counts. Their lips moved silently. They passed the west entrance to Temple Square with their palms down, forty more counts.

Scanning the crowd over her right shoulder, Maggie watched for the bearded man with white hair and replayed the ten-second encounter in her head. He knew her. No question. But whom did he know? Which Maggie? Past or present? And that's when she noticed a couple of stragglers following at a safe distance and trying to mingle with the late-afternoon crowd. Whoever they were—two faceless transients or harmless young lowlifes—they'd stumbled into her peripheral vision yesterday and the Friday before.

Maggie nudged her companion. "Our boys are back."

Jan peeked over her extended arm. "Same guys?"

"Same limp. Same size." Short, stocky, and wearing worn clothes that looked like they'd been plucked from the fifty-cent bin at Deseret Industries. With scarf-covered mouths and hats pulled low over their foreheads, only their downcast eyes were visible in the twilight. One tugged on the other's sleeve before they made a quick right and headed through the north gates into Temple Square. Did they know they'd been spotted?

"Maybe they get off work the same time that we walk," Jan said. "Coincidence?"

Were they just strangers weaving in and out of the crowd or two punks working hard at being inconspicuous? Maggie shrugged as she noticed a blind man—looking like a shapeless pile of rags and worn blankets—with a bit of cardboard propped beside him next to his dog.

"Hey, Sam." She slipped a bone-shaped biscuit out of her pocket and fed it to the black-and-white mutt. "How's business?"

"Slow."

She squeezed his shoulder. "Don't stay out too late."

Out of earshot, Jan muttered, "There's help for people like him."

"But none he's willing to take." *Public disgrace is a strange thing*, Maggie thought. Most people assumed clean sheets and a bowl of beef stew served in a converted warehouse must be preferable to a perch on frigid concrete, but Maggie understood Sam's reluctance. Independence was hard to come by.

The clouds released more drizzle as she and Jan took a last right onto State Street, and Maggie noticed their two lumpy shadows had returned, one with a pronounced limp and a mud-colored scarf covering most of his face. He straggled behind his companion as they tried to blend into a cluster of secretaries popping umbrellas as they exited the Church Office Building and hurried toward the bus stop.

With the Beehive House on her right, Maggie slowed her pace and tugged on Jan's sleeve. Two additional shrouded males, one lanky and one not, stood waiting on the pavement near the crosswalk, striking an easy, slouched pose, feigning nonchalance. His ankle-length coat flapping in the breeze, the taller of the two flipped a cigarette butt onto the sidewalk and then lit another. Wearing fingerless gloves, he pinched his cigarette with a gesture that seemed oddly rehearsed and almost effeminate. The two boys who had been following Maggie and Jan passed them on the left and joined the other two near the crosswalk. No one spoke, but the four young men formed a loose group. The *chirp-chirp* of the crossing signal gave pedestrians permission to walk, but Maggie nudged Jan's arm. "Let's wait. See if they go on their way."

Maggie glanced at the *Visitors Welcome and Free Tours* placard near the front entrance to the Beehive House before pushing open the iron gate and easing herself onto the wooden porch. *I'm being silly,* she told herself and sat forward, her feet planted on the step. Still, life had taught her to be wary, and like it or not, her sprinting days were over.

"Okay." Jan sat beside her. Her tone implied *what now?* Jan wasn't intimidated by adolescents—or anyone else—which was likely a result of being a high school principal in her past life.

The same could not be said about Maggie. Unwelcome memories flitted in and out of her consciousness as though a rearview mirror were permanently attached to her mind and looking forward was no longer a possibility. Zipping her coat up under her chin, she shivered and remembered waiting for her husband at the top of the Snake Creek lift on a wintery afternoon. A layer of frost coated the giant fir trees and a bank of low clouds draped the top of the mountain, casting the afternoon in an eerie light. Snowboarders—maybe five or six—lingered on a snowbank, quiet, unsmiling, blending in with the mist. Late in the day, with snow sifting out of the fog, she had felt then as she felt now; they weren't boys. With ice crystals sprinkled on their clothes and cheeks, and eyes keen and glittering, those snowboarders were a pack, a wolf pack.

Now the leader of this crew waiting near the crosswalk stood a little straighter, pitched his third cigarette into a storm drain, and then arched his head back, searching the evening sky. If he'd howled, Maggie wouldn't have been surprised, because these boys were a pack too—hungry young wolves, alive and hunting, and deliberately ignoring the two women sitting on the damp planks of the Beehive House porch. Dodging pedestrians, the four boys milled around the pavement, occasionally muttering in low voices Maggie couldn't hear. The freezing drizzle soaked the boys' hair, drenched the shoes on their feet, and darkened their shabby garb into a blur of black and gray.

Maggie thumped her fist on the wooden plank. She wanted to pitch her can into their midst, a grenade of exploding chicken soup, to splatter them, to mark them with thick yellow glop, before stomping her foot and chasing them away. *Get a grip.* She waved a mittened hand at the security camera tucked under the eaves before she mouthed in its direction, "Send one of the suits. We could use a drive-by." Maggie liked to think of herself as an urban oldie—cool and competent—not gray-haired prey, not a wounded elk struggling across a meadow, waiting for that first nip on her Achilles tendon. She was nobody's victim, not anymore.

"Pluck the ringleader out of the middle"—Jan gestured as if she were extracting a coin out of her gloved palm—"and the followers fade into the woodwork. Gangs are harmless without a leader. Age makes no difference. He's the paterfamilias, Peter Pan with his crew of lost boys." Her tone was matter-of-fact. "Three-year-olds in great big bodies. Let's go home."

"I doubt Greta Vanderhoff would think of them as lost boys." Lost boys were cute kids who wore pajamas and somehow looked endearing when airborne.

Greta . . . Had it been just a year ago? That October afternoon, the sun had been shining, and dry leaves strewn over the concrete rustled as people strolled by. Greta, a stout woman had been hurrying toward the front entrance of the Eagle Gate, a shopping bag tight in her fist, and her black patent purse slung over her arm.

In a move choreographed with absolute precision, a youngish man with a baseball cap pulled low moved in from the right and slid into her, another kid drifted over on cue and stooped in front of Greta to tie his shoe, a third crashed into her from behind—and Greta lost her balance—but she didn't fall, not Greta. Arms flailing, she reared back. Her bag, containing a twenty-pound wedding present, clobbered the kneeling boy upside the head. He toppled over, knees pulled up to his chest, stunned with one foot twitching.

The fourth member, a lanky conductor standing under the trees, swooped in and snatched Greta's dropped purse, fished out a credit card, and skidded the purse across the pavement in one deft motion as though he were skipping a stone across a lake. By the time a police car rolled over the curb with lights flashing, the long-limbed conductor was back under the trees, but he sidled up to the officer when the opportunity came. "That old woman assaulted that kid." He pointed to the inert body. "He was just tying his shoe." A half smile on his face, he drifted into the crowd of onlookers and then briskly walked away.

Lori Rice and her handsome son, pulling up to the curb in his BMW, saw the whole thing. "It was rehearsed. Not an accident," Lori insisted first to the officer making notes and again that evening in dramatic detail to the gathering of indignant friends from the sixth and seventh floors who wandered in and out of Greta's apartment. "They'd practiced a hundred times," Lori huffed. No doubt falling and bouncing back up with bones that weren't brittle and joints that worked smoothly.

The cold from the porch planks penetrated Maggie's backside and pulled her back into the present. "I bet not one of those clowns could spell *osteoporosis*," she hissed.

"Why would they want to?" Jan's lips curved in a thin smile. "I'm not going to be intimidated by a bunch of kids."

Had Maggie been seeing things, misreading things? Something here didn't make sense, something she'd skated past. Neither she nor Jan was carrying a purse or wearing a fanny pack. They had nothing worth stealing. Why were those boys stalling? Were they waiting for two women to push past them to the crosswalk? Or were they just waiting for friends, passing a few idle minutes, on their way to the movies at The Gateway?

A fine haze was haloing the streetlights, and the air was freezing and damp, the kind of damp that settled in her bones. Maggie patted Jan's hand and shivered. Across the street, home was waiting, that massive yellow brick building with security guards, elevators that always worked, a closeted furnace that kept her apartment at a toasty seventy-two degrees, and her delightful assembly of eclectic friends, some slightly demented and some not. Lights in the windows beckoned her, welcomed her. Through fourth-floor windows, she could see Phyllis MacGruder's silhouette. She was probably fixing packaged soup and a cheese toastie, a dinner Phyllis would happily describe if anyone slowed long enough to listen. The new tenant in 8-B had strung icicle lights along the railing of his terrace, though it wasn't much of a terrace, more of an architectural detail decorated with wrought iron painted white.

"Icicle lights? And a tree?" Maggie whispered. Her breath came out in a cloud.

A string of colored light was one thing, but the tree glittering in the penthouse with thousands of twinkling lights seemed a bit much.

"You haven't met 8-B?" Jan's gloved hand pressed lightly on Maggie's elbow. "Rosie said he arrived without a moving van. Everything was delivered the day before, brand-new. And it came from Restoration Hardware, not RC Willey."

"If you believe half of what Rosie says, you're being generous."

"And she said he's a widower," Jan added, rolling her eyes.

"Those old coots. They all want the same thing." Maggie laughed. "A nurse and a maid and a cook." And a companion—someone to wrangle with over the remote, or to plump a pillow before bed, or to extend a wrinkled hand to clasp as the evening sky darkened.

Nodding, Jan looked past her to the young gray-clad strangers. The boy's limp was more pronounced, and his grimace reached his eyes each time he bore down on that foot. And then the pack was moving, melting into the five o'clock crowd on the sidewalk, moving toward City Creek Center, toward florescent lights, fast food, and out of the cold, but one man peeled away from the group and waited in the shadows.

Maggie noticed him, that solitary young man, a woolen scarf over his mouth, a baseball cap pulled low over his forehead, and his shoulders hunched against the cold, who stood watching them long after his boyish companions departed. Why was he waiting?

"Let's go," Maggie said, feeling stiff as she rose and walked toward the crosswalk, chatting about the ostentatious display on 8-B's window.

Chapter Two

DANGEROUS HOOLIGANS

CARLY NERVOUSLY FINGERED THE ROLL of blue masking tape she'd just lifted off the shelf at Home Depot when the clerk's back was turned. She stood at the intersection staring at the decrepit apartment building that looked exhausted, like a wrecking ball would be a relief. There was an alley on each side with no sign of grass. Some optimistic landlord had painted the building slate gray in 1928—the date and the name, The Oxford Arms, were announced in chipped Italian tiles over the main entrance. Not much upkeep had been done since. A couple windows on the main floor were covered with plywood, and some budding artist with a talented finger had spray painted gang signs mingled with stylized flowers and rainbows on the boards, but overall the effect was grim. What would her dad say if he could see where she was living? See her. His heart would break, and then he'd let her have it—both barrels. She wiped a stray tear with the back of her hand. She was surprised she had any tears left.

According to Lemon's stupid plans, she and Terry were supposed to be cagey and approach the building one at a time in fifteen-minute intervals. It was a big deal, at least to Lemon, who implied that if the manager or any of the other tenants knew six bodies shared the fourth-floor studio, their stuff would be chucked out on the pile of dirty snow in the alley. Carly touched the thumb-sized canister of mace she kept deep in her pocket. She'd picked it up at the Women's Rescue Center, not that it would do much good now. All her stuff had been stolen in a homeless shelter while she and Terry were sleeping—a crucial point Lemon forgot while he went off on a rant, and besides, the building manager was a drunk. They could arrive playing trumpets and kettledrums, and none of the residents would do anything except shout obscenities and slam warped doors. And so far, only four other people crashed on the floor, one comatose body for each finger on her hand. Not difficult to keep track. Number six was a no-show.

Carly climbed the four flights, shoved open the door, and started taping layers of newspaper over the windows. Maybe it would cut down the frigid draft that blew in at night.

Terry edged next to her and whispered, "When the weather gets warm, we're out of here."

"No kidding. *Adios* to this bunch of druggies."

"We should have checked out Utah winters before we left Eureka."

They should have checked out a lot of things. She pressed the blue tape against paint flaking off the windowsill before she gave him a half smile and nudged him with her hip. The boy next door, Terrance Romero, best friend since third grade. He was skinny and shy, and in the closet, but not far enough in the closet to avoid getting smacked when his dad had been in a foul mood—which was all the time before they'd left. Terry's preferences were not something they mentioned to the odd collection of *compadres* they'd been living with since the end of October.

Compadre was Lemon's word. *Really weird family* was how Carly thought of them. For the most part, they left her alone because the other guys assumed she and handsome, dark-eyed Terry were a couple, not just refugees from Northern California. Except no one left her alone the day she'd dumped a half liter of Diet Coke into the toilet bowl to dissolve the disgusting layer of scum, and the apartment exploded in unison, "You just poured Diet Coke down the john? Are you out of your mind? That costs money!" She didn't care. That bathroom was so filthy she almost hurled every time she backed in and shut the door. The kitchenette was worse. A couple of days ago, she'd slipped a bottle of Pine Sol under her coat at the market, but hustling down the aisle, a cute guy in a red vest shook his head at her, and she'd shoved the bottle back on the shelf of dry cereal with both hands. He'd tailed her until the automatic door closed so fast it almost nicked her ankles. Grocery stores were tough. A bar of soap and candy bars were easy, but it's hard to tuck a loaf of bread, or a quart of milk, or a bunch of bananas inside your jacket. Too bad because she was hungry most of the time.

Filth didn't bother anyone else. A hundred years of stale cooking odors permeated the walls, and embedded soot and grime covered every flat surface. Maybe she was doomed to a life of cleaning up other people's mistakes. She thought back to that hot afternoon, to that last straw, to that house no longer her home. Cleaning up after Dale-Call-Me-Dad and his joint-custody kids, that's what caused the last major blowup before she took off. Carly had had it, and the day her mother's recycled husband left a two-page contract on her desk pretty much spelled out the end. She'd given the contract the once-over and then penciled a note on the top: *Didn't get a chance to read this. Hope you didn't spend hours writing it.* Ballistic, red-faced, and beyond furious, he corralled Carly in her bedroom. One hand clutching her neck, her mom stood in the doorway. The contract twitched in Dale's stubby fingers as he read his masterpiece out loud.

"Call me stupid, but this feels a little lopsided," she'd said, twirling a pen in one hand. "You want me to tend to your brats Friday and Saturday nights, do four hours of light domestic servitude every week, do three hours of directed yard activity on Saturday, and maintain a 3.5 GPA." She clicked her tongue stud against her teeth. "Reciprocity? What does the Party of the First Part receive by way of compensation?"

Dale-Call-Me-Dad spit words on the floor: "A roof over your head and food on the table."

"Sorry, but Dad's life insurance paid off the mortgage. So technically this house belongs to Mom and me. Not your bargaining chip. Too bad." Her tone said, *Sucks to be you.*

A dark look crossed between her mother and Dale, sort of like a trip wire, before her mother landed a sharp punch to the gut. "That's not *technically* the case." Her mother couldn't look Carly in the eye—total betrayal does weird things to mothers. "We chose to co-mingle our assets."

"Hold on here, Mom. You get hit by a truck tomorrow morning, and my dad's house belongs to this joker?"

"Dale and I own it jointly, but this will always be your home. You know that."

No. Carly didn't know that. Didn't believe that. Not for a second. The only thing she knew for sure was that she hated this slime ball.

"I'm seeing an attorney. This stinks. Dad left a will."

"Calm down, Carly." Her mother had that mulish look, like she'd dug in her stiletto heels.

"Dad knew you. He knew you'd turn into a spineless wimp. He would have protected me. He loved me. He wouldn't have rolled over and played dead." But, of course, he was dead. Four years dead. And here was Dale-Call-Me-Dad standing on her father's beige carpet, in her father's upscale, three-bedroom ranch, looking out her father's wood-wrapped windows at shade trees her father had planted in the backyard. With his arms outstretched, Dale made fists with his meaty hands like he was about to part the Red Sea. All he needed was a cloak and a cudgel. So lame. This was all so lame.

"Pack 'em," he sputtered, standing next to her red-cheeked mother.

"Are you really this dumb? Who do you think you are? Vin Diesel? 'Pack 'em'?"

"Your bags. Pack your bags, or I'll dump all your crap on the front lawn: the year's supply of Junior Mints, and the dirty laundry, and the magazines, and your paperbacks. Your choice." His hands waved in larger and larger circles, like he was imitating a helicopter about to take flight.

Another major chest heave, then her mother spoke, "No one's going anywhere. No one's packing anything." Fingers outstretched, she inched toward her iPhone, toward her best friend Marcia's voice, her mom's go-to person in times of crisis. No doubt Marcia, who'd listened to the shouting matches drifting over the hedge the past two years, had already recommended another family therapist that somebody or other had suggested—a real gem, Northern California's finest. Then words stretched out of her mother's mouth like a string of drool. "We just need a little counseling."

Right. One more blank-faced woman with a notepad on her lap and a pen poised to write, *These people are making me crazy, and I'm the one who's supposed to be sane.*

"You think you can hire someone to fix this mess you've made." Carly glared at Dale, itching to point out the tufts of hair growing out of his nose and ears and the CPAP machine next to the nightstand in her mother's bedroom. "Did you really think this man was better than no man at all?" Now they were both fuming, and if Carly had gone too far, she didn't care.

He was Mr. Ancient Nice Guy until her mother tied the knot, and then he turned into a thrice-married control freak, bullied her mother, and tried to bully Carly. Nine o'clock curfew. No friends in the house. One hour of screen time if she got her *chores* done. He cut off her phone if she gave him any attitude, and her mother took his side every stinkin' time. But the worst was how he mimicked her protests when her mother wasn't around and muttered *Cinderella* or *Miss Piggy* under his breath when he surprised her munching a cookie in the kitchen or when he hugged the wall when she passed him in the hall like she'd squash him flat as she rolled by. It stung.

When Terry's macho jerk of a dad kicked him out the last week in April, she and Terry met at the fence, laughed a little and cried, and then spent a solid hour conspiring under Carly's favorite Norway maple. Cutting herself off from her supply line wasn't in Carly's nature. She enjoyed cooking and liked to know where the kitchen was located at all times, but not anymore. She and Terry pooled what little cash they had and talked Terry's older brother into renting a car they could drive to Utah. Carly didn't know if the brother felt sorry for Terry, or if he was thrilled to wave good-bye to the family's identity crisis. Whatever. They were on their way. Her mom and dad had grown up in Utah, and Terry said anyone could get a job at the resorts loading skiers on the lifts. While they were waiting for snow to fall, they found jobs at a Wendy's on Fourth South until they failed the drug tests—*Pot, are you kidding? Who doesn't smoke weed?* Her blue Mohawk and the stainless-steel rings in her nose and eyebrows didn't help. In a matter of weeks, they'd gone through their cash, and boom, they were out on the street. AT&T cut off their phone plans, and Terry's thumbs went into withdrawal. So third world.

Trouble that seemed huge in April sort of shrank. It was tough to keep a good burn going when they were sleeping in the park. She was thinking hard about going home, and then they met Lemon. Admittedly he was weird—on a scale from one to ten, he was definitely an eight. Six-two and razor thin, he'd tossed five bucks in their *Will Sing for Food* can and told them panhandling was a losing game for anyone who looked as healthy as they did.

"You need a skin disease or a missing limb," he'd said, but they weren't inclined to saw off their fingers. "Or you can share my space. Fifty bucks a month. Each. Potential employment. Entertainment's free."

And Lemon was entertaining. She never heard his first name, but Ichabod would fit. When he laughed, all she could see were six inches of pink gums. His white-blond hair looked like someone cut it with toenail clippers. His claim to fame was that he'd been cast in *Revenge of the Sith* right out of UCLA, until he showed up on set "slightly indisposed" once too often. She didn't buy it. Lemon *never let the truth get in the way of a good story*, a phrase she remembered her grandmother saying. She didn't remember much else about the woman who smelled like Endust and dish soap, but her grandmother's phrase came to mind every time Lemon went on a roll, and she had to admit, heroin addicts were pretty reasonable people, even funny, as long as they got their fix.

So here she was in a rat trap in Salt Lake City, and Thanksgiving was a week away, and she had no money for food. Dinner at the shelter was a given, and for the first time in six months—well, maybe not the first time—Carly missed her mom, felt guilty about leaving home without a word, and thought about the senior year she wasn't having. Homesick? Hard to admit, but maybe she wasn't the only one feeling this way, because sitting next to her, Nolan, another one of the *compadres* who was no more than sixteen, was habitually silent. Never said a word.

Lemon and Burt were horsing around, distracting everyone, putting on a show. "So, this old biddy absolutely loaded with loot is marching across the plaza in front of Fort Knox. Glasses half an inch thick, and her dress was right out of the fifties. A real charmer." Lemon paused for the canned laugh. "Bill moves in from the left and gets her off balance. Burt stoops right in front of her to tie his shoes, and then Nolan crashes into her from behind. She's supposed to go down like the Titanic, but instead, she clobbers Burt with a twenty-pound Vita Mix. Knocks him out cold." He mimed the fall, sprawling across the floor, tangling his feet and hands in a dirty blanket. He struggled to stand and fell over again with his legs spread. Carly laughed, couldn't help herself. "I snatched the old broad's purse, pinched a Visa card, and in the next four hours, we hit five grocery stores—stocked up on all the essential items—and bought four toasty sleeping bags at Kirkham's Outdoor Products. Planning ahead. Thank you, social security. Your government dollars at work." He took a deep bow.

Looking out the corner of her eye, Carly thought Nolan, something of a troll, might be smiling, but it was hard to tell since his face was such a crust. She cheered instead, "Hooray for American ingenuity!"

Lemon grinned. "I think of myself as a hedge fund manager—just theft on a smaller scale."

Lemon liked to cook up schemes, and they all played along because it felt like a game, cops and robbers on a weed-strewn playground on the dark side of town. But their stomachs ached when the cupboard was full of nothing but trash, and the apartment was cold when the gas bill sat forgotten on the top of the fridge. So if Lemon's schemes included cash and excitement, they were all in.

She spent the next afternoon at the city library, warm and dry, scrolling through employment opportunities for a high school dropout with no references. She would have been discouraged, except she loved the library with its open ceilings and the dusty smell of thousands of books. She'd tucked a copy of *Eleanor and Park* behind a shelf full of self-help titles, hidden it actually. It was the story of two outcast teenagers, and she was loving every word. No one told her to *move along* if she was reading a book, and there was a nook and an easy chair in the corner of the third floor she thought of as hers. Her dad always had a book in his hand and an idea to share. Four years gone, and she missed him more now than she did the week he died.

Her eyes blurred as she stared at the computer screen. She needed a job and a new place to live. She tried to ignore the bad smells in the apartment, the ever-present hunger in the pit of her stomach, and Lemon, the human scarecrow, but had no luck doing it. Her luck had run out.

Chapter Three

TRUE JOKES

MAGGIE LOOKED BACK FONDLY TO a particularly hot day the previous August. Jan—although at the time Maggie thought of her as 7-A—had leaned against Maggie's open door, not long after lunch, and mentioned she was looking for an exercise partner to join her on power walks with weights.

For weeks, gossip had concluded that 7-A must be recently widowed or divorced, estranged from her adult children, a vegetarian, and possibly a democrat. One item everyone could agree upon was that the sixtyish woman had moved in on the twenty-fourth of July—Didn't she realize it was a holiday?—and created a traffic jam on the seventh floor. The congestion of Pioneer Day and the throngs of downtown visitors—including children primed to race into the street to collect candy tossed from floats—were crazy enough. High school bands belted out the themes from *Rocky* or *Star Wars* as they marched down South Temple in the sweltering heat. The pounding of their drums filled the building. Extended families wanting to view the parade from the vantage of the south apartments had to sidestep Jan's possessions, which were being muscled through the west entrance by a couple of burly men, who bore no resemblance to the new resident of 7-A. Paulo Ferrante, the security guard assigned to nights and holidays, directed disgruntled residents past the stacked boxes labeled *kitchen*, matching love seats upholstered in blue corduroy, an oak dining table, and a king-size mattress and box spring. Then there were the skis, the mountain bikes, a couple of tennis rackets, a mound of boxes, and suitcases tagged for the basement storage unit. By the end of the day, the bustle up and down the seventh floor hall was over. No one saw much of 7-A for weeks until people were starting to whisper *recluse* and *grief* and hurry past 7-A as though the sadness inside could attach itself to residents who didn't want to revisit places most had already been.

When 7-A arrived at Maggie's door that August afternoon, Maggie was surprised. The purple circles under the woman's eyes looked like they'd been painted with a brush, but a web of white wrinkles fanned out from the corners of her eyes, suggesting time spent smiling in the sun. 7-A was quick to smile and her eyes were blue. *Resolve* was what impressed Maggie as she invited the woman in for a glass of powdered lemonade spooned out of a box. *She wants to move forward*, Maggie thought, dropping ice cubes into a couple of glasses that actually matched. She liked 7-A immediately.

More agile than most and still in possession of her original knees, Maggie had been flattered to be asked if she would be 7-A's exercise partner. A power walk? Why not? She'd only lost an inch—gone from five nine to five eight. She preferred *lost* to the other term she frequently heard, *shrinking,* which sounded like a magic trick or a glimpse in a mirror that deceived.

"I have a part-time job." Maggie lifted her chin and smiled. "Two mornings a week and Thursday evenings. Afternoons are better for me." And so late afternoon was the agreed upon time. Neither woman spoke of the hours that stretched long when noisy children didn't come home from school or basketball practice, when a husband didn't breeze home from work or a golf game to consult about dinner, when the phone didn't ring.

After the time was agreed upon, Maggie had plowed into the back of her closet, past sacks of yarn and albums stuffed with loose snap shots, until she found ancient cross-trainers with tattered laces. That same August afternoon, pounding along the hot pavement, arms extended for a count of forty, they didn't confide any of their life junk. Oh no, Jan talked about brain oxygenation and bone density and conserving muscle mass. *Caffeine is the enemy to good sleep hygiene.* This was an admonition Jan repeated at least once a week as the leaves started to turn. How did she know Maggie didn't sleep?

Afternoon walks became a welcome pattern, and they strode around Temple Square as if they owned it and then marched into fall. No awkward moments or unsettling questions. All had been pleasant until the last days before Thanksgiving, when a cold front lingered in the valley, and Maggie had the uncomfortable sensation they were being watched.

Their breath quick bursts of white, Maggie and Jan waited at the intersection of State and South Temple for the light to change. Yesterday's drizzle had given way to snow, four or five inches, in the pre-dawn hours. Now clouds and the fog were banished to the tops of the granite mountains. Cleared of sooty particles, the air felt clean and smelled clean. Cars honked at them—as a warning or a reproof— as Maggie ventured off the curb seconds too soon. But before long, they stood in front of the Beehive House, surrounded by well-dressed women and men hurrying home, or hurrying to meet friends, or hurrying for the simple sake of being in a rush as Maggie and Jan waited for the light to change. There was no sign of the lost boys from the previous night. Soup cans clenched in her mittens, Maggie experienced relief that didn't feel justified.

She frequently rehearsed bits of conversation, stories from the news, or a thought from a book she was reading—something intelligent she could share with Jan since

Maggie didn't like playing the part of a mute sounding board. This afternoon, however, her thoughts were scrambled and ill defined. She'd been awake at 3:00 a.m. with a sense of unease, and now she glanced over her shoulder two or three times as she extended her arms. The words that tumbled out of her mouth next were something of a surprise.

"Have you ever been robbed?" Maggie spoke abruptly, then cleared her throat and spoke again. "It's such a violation." The shadows from the previous afternoon needed to be chased into the fresh air.

"Petty theft. At school things vanished off my desk." Jan shrugged. "Mementos, stuffed grizzly bears, painted rocks. Nothing important. Irritating, but no reason to call the police."

"A guy walked into our house once. Came right in the front door." Maggie didn't name her old neighborhood, Fremont Park, an uninviting address. "My daughter was home alone." Maggie had just left to take Henry to scouts—pale, little ninety-eight pound Henry—and the last words out of Maggie's mouth had been *lock the door.* But because that's what she'd always said, she had been ignored. "He was massive. Kristen caught a glimpse of him trying the door and then rolled under her bed. She hid there while he rifled through the house." When the glassy-eyed creep didn't find a solitary thing worth stealing, he'd dumped a gallon of milk on the kitchen floor and urinated a smelly stream on the only good rug she'd owned. "He'd been watching us, saw me leave, and probably didn't think anyone was left at home. Thank heaven." All the color had washed out of Kristen's face, and her wide eyes had finished the story as Maggie held her tightly against her chest, but the girl never cried and didn't make a sound—not for days.

"How old was your daughter?"

"Fourteen." And never the same. It was as though that man, whoever he was, had chipped off a piece of Kristen, like a broken front tooth or a slice of her ear, and changed her appearance forever, made her timid, reluctant, and slightly hostile.

"You're lucky it wasn't worse."

But Maggie hadn't felt lucky at the time.

Without speaking, the women marched past the executive office building and the Joseph Smith Memorial Building before Jan lifted her weights to shoulder level. "So," she raised her eyebrows, "what happened to Greta Vanderhoff?"

The end of a story no one liked to remember. "The surveillance video showed a couple of kids horsing around, tossing a Frisbee. One got tangled up with Greta, and she belted him with her granddaughter's wedding present. At least, that's how it looked. She had a stroke a couple weeks later."

The residents of the seventh floor had made outraged calls to the police and muttered among themselves about the sorry state of today's drug-addled young people, but none of that prevented a clot from wending its way up Greta's carotid artery and lodging in her brain at two in the morning. The paramedics took her away on a gurney. That was everyone's worst fear, being strapped on a gurney. *A wheelchair*, Maggie had thought at the time, *if you left in a wheelchair, there was some chance you'd come back.*

A wizened cardiologist down on three had grumbled to his wife and anyone else who would listen, "Undiagnosed atrial fibrillation," but no one believed him, certainly no one up on six, seven, or eight. No, the trauma of getting mugged had done Greta in—no question.

"She was hospitalized for a couple of weeks and then went into extended care and died on a Tuesday," Maggie said to Jan. The day of the week felt significant to Maggie, as though Greta's death didn't merit a weekend or a disruption on a Friday night. "No one knew her credit card was gone until the bills were sorted out a couple of months later."

Jan rotated her left arm in a series of stretching exercises. "Did they track the credit card?"

"Someone charged a couple of thousand dollars at six different grocery stores and then bought four mummy bags at Kirkham's. Not much of a spending spree. It was just petty theft, a misdemeanor. When the funeral was over, her kids didn't want to prosecute over food and sleeping bags, plus the chance of catching the perpetrators was nil, according to the detective assigned to the case."

Maggie and Jan exchanged a significant look.

As horrible as the assault had been, Greta didn't have to die by inches with some exotic breed of cancer, or gradually forget the names of her grandchildren, or wander the halls in her pink nightgown. When Maggie was searching under the couch, or the dust ruffle, or the back of a kitchen cupboard for her key card, her wallet, or her size eight knitting needles, she occasionally wondered if she might happen upon the mind a previous resident had lost, a mushy lump or maybe a withered mass the size of a grapefruit. Would a lifetime of memories be locked inside? How did that all work? Did the neurons shut down in sync or one at a time? Best not to think about it.

Maggie inhaled through her nose, and her lungs filled with frigid air. "Rest in peace, Greta. What a woman."

Silent amidst the sounds of afternoon traffic, they both forgot their overhead arm extensions for a good five minutes. "Arms up," Jan finally muttered, and Maggie tried to smile. They picked up their pace as they passed the statue of Brigham Young for the third time; he always seemed to have that effect. "So you have a son and a daughter?" Jan asked.

Maggie hesitated. "Kristen and Henry. He's a CPA." Funny Henry, the accountant, who called on Sunday mornings the same time each week. If she wasn't there, he left a pleasant message on her machine but didn't call back. "He lives in Norfolk, Virginia," where having Memmott as a last name didn't mean anything to anybody. "Henry's a contract civilian for the Navy. Whatever that means." She forced a quick laugh that felt more like a cough. Two weeks before high school graduation, Henry, waylaid by a recruiter, signed up to see the world. With a hug and a kiss, her little boy as good as vanished in a puff of smoke, and so, Sunday mornings when she hungered for the sound of his voice, she lingered in her apartment, showering, dressing, and getting ready for church, until the telephone rang.

"Norfolk," Jan exhaled. "That's not next door. Do you see him often?"

"Well, there's a slight complication." Maggie's tone implied webbed toes or a borderline personality disorder. "His wife was an adorable blonde when he married her, and now she's an adorable Southern Baptist—dyed in the wool."

Jan nodded. "I get it."

"Bobbie has three sisters. They're very tight." Peas in a pod. "Her parents rent a house on Virginia Beach each summer. The grandkids play in the sand, cook hotdogs, play video games, tell stories. But that uses up Henry's vacation; plus, flying four people out here costs an arm and a leg." *Close your mouth,* Maggie told herself. *Let go. Don't be toxic.* She felt a bit exposed and vulnerable—something she avoided.

"I don't remember being a pain for my mother-in-law." Jan was deliberately vague. "But I probably was. There's a reason for stereotypes and the jokes, the endless jokes."

"True jokes." Maggie sighed.

"What's the difference between a joke and a true joke?"

"A true joke is something ridiculous that actually happened."

Jan's laugh was complimentary. "Outrageous equals funny?"

"Doesn't it?" Maggie said. "Isn't that what black humor's all about?" Palms down, she clutched her soup cans in the chill air and started the count. Two laps later and aware that her fingers suddenly felt like ice, she said, "Let's go home." Skirting a puddle of slush, they walked to the light pole and pushed the button. A black Mercedes splashed frigid water in front of them before it rolled to a stop. Maggie shuffled from one foot to the other. "We're like the Marching Mothers."

"Another true joke?"

"That's what my little boy called the ladies who walked along Bountiful Boulevard. They exercised with a vengeance. Bless their hearts. The Marching Mothers." She smiled. "He was a funny kid."

"Henry?"

"No. David." Little boy lost.

Jan didn't question her about two children who had suddenly become three. Silence separated them as they walked to the west entrance of their building next to the fifteen-minute unloading zone. Maggie passed her white keycard over the scanner, and the heavy door, an electronic marvel, swung open without making a sound.

Chapter Four
MEMORIES WAREHOUSE

It was past five and nearly dark when Maggie set her damp shoes in the closet. The Alta Club directly across the street had artificial candles, red bows, and evergreen wreaths in each stately window. She owned several strands of multi-colored Christmas lights. She should string them around her sliding glass door to welcome the season, set out her stuffed Santa, and hang her quilted advent calendar on the wall. But the box labeled *Christmas* was in her storage unit, two floors beneath street level, and could only be accessed by the service elevator. The first basement level contained the building's innards, heart and lungs, pillars and pipes, chugging air conditioning, mechanical devices only a gray-haired wizard could control, and the cluttered security office at the end of the hall.

After deciding the decorations were worth the effort, Maggie made her way to the elevator and hit B2. The door opened on the bottom level, twenty feet underground. Single bulbs in stainless-steel baskets lit the rough concrete floor. Maggie felt like she'd wandered onto a movie set for a film about a prison escape; Clint Eastwood might appear any minute, forty years younger and wearing a denim work shirt and his artful sneer.

A thick steel door faced the elevator. Maggie turned her key in the lock, held her breath, and stepped inside. Washed in harsh florescent light, the low-ceilinged room contained wire storage units—one per apartment—five feet wide and fifteen feet deep. She would have preferred a few shadows, a bit of gloom where she could hide. Pine boards and chicken wire closets with padlocks didn't protect the contents from much. A sturdy wire cutter would give a gloved criminal access to every conceivable bit of life debris from surf boards to ski equipment, cardboard boxes, and well-used suitcases—all covered with a fuzzy coating of beige dust. The belongings waited for the elderly owners to visit the gym, build up a little muscle mass, and shed a few years before they returned to the slopes, or the surf, or booked an excursion up the Danube.

Cold penetrated the soles of her shoes, and every footstep echoed. She half expected some scaly creature to leap out at her and scare her spitless, but all was silent as she walked down a corridor with a combination on a scrap of paper in her fist. She stopped in front of her own chicken wire unit. *Sullivan 7-B* was printed on a 4x6 card and tied to the wire with a bit of twine.

She tumbled the lock and stepped inside. One battered black suitcase and a dozen boxes sealed with strapping tape were stacked in the back as if they were waiting for more household goods to be delivered, but nothing more was coming. Not much to show for seventy-four years, at least not much that could be packed in a box. Buttoning her cardigan, she eased herself down on the cardboard box marked *Christmas decorations* and pulled a tissue out of her sleeve.

When she'd put that little bungalow in Fremont Park on the market, Henry and Kristen had collected their possessions from her basement, commented on the smell of mold, and loaded this and that, an odd lamp or a picture frame they could use, into their cars—and didn't look back. Best to leave some memories behind. But David's things had moved with her to the Eagle Gate. Three boxes of his yearbooks, his high school diploma, a couple of baseball trophies, sweaters she'd knitted, his baby clothes and stuffed animals, and another box of pictures. She didn't need to rip off the tape; she'd memorized each image and could play the photo gallery simply by closing her eyes.

In Maggie's head, Davey was a composite of all his wonderful selves. He wasn't always a gangly adolescent, some days she remembered a toddler with thick curls too precious to cut and long, dark lashes that rested on his cheek when he napped. Maggie took artsy photos when he slept in his crib. Strangers stopped her at the mall, *goo*'ed and *gaw*'ed at the little boy, and commented on his large brown eyes and chubby legs. He'd been such a mama's boy; he'd reach his plump little arms for her every time she'd walk into the room. And of course, she'd swing him up in her arms and give his soft cheek a quick kiss.

An Ensign Stake softball star, she'd been the one to teach him how to pitch and throw. They'd played catch on the side yard until they'd worn a path in the grass and home plate became a muddy puddle when it rained in the fall. When Davey was a little older, Finn O'Hara and Matt Johnson would play hot box on the side yard. Leather mitts on their hands, they threw the ball back and forth, until the boy in the middle had nowhere left to go. Out. Making the all-star team was all the boys talked about on those warm summer nights when early clusters of stars dappled the pale sky. Henry would toddle into the kitchen dragging a blanket and his ragged Buffy Low. And where was Kristen's six-year-old self? Fresh from her bath dressed all in pink.

Sitting in her chicken-wire unit, Maggie swiped the tissue under her nose. Fifteen years ago, or maybe twenty, her friend Rose had phoned her on a rainy afternoon. "Sister Obermeyer called me this morning. Third time in six months." And Maggie had sighed. She knew what was coming. Every neighborhood had at least one Mrs.

Obermeyer, a robust woman who reported on miscreants when she wasn't busy raising children who wore bug-like glasses and had wisps of errant blond hair. If Maggie thought she'd escaped Mrs. Obermeyer's keen sense of observation when she moved to Fremont Park, she was mistaken. Maggie's move, and the reasons for it, only whetted the woman's appetite for gossip.

But that long-ago afternoon, Rose had been totally exasperated. "No more lurking around the neighborhood," she'd complained. "I know you're not a robber checking things out, but Obermeyer is talking this up and making people nervous, like you're some kind of crazed stalker seeking revenge. The neighborhood watch is going to accost you, and then you'll be embarrassed, and I'll have to defend you, and honestly, I don't understand the self-flagellation. Why do you keep beating yourself up?"

"I'm not hurting anyone," Maggie had sputtered.

"You're hurting yourself."

The phone cord wound around her hand, Maggie had taken a deep breath and counted to twenty before she said good-bye. Maybe Rose was right. Maybe it was time to leave and not go back. Maybe pain was a knife, and sooner or later, it cut out your heart. That would be a relief.

But if the evening was lovely—and sometimes when it was not—Maggie just gravitated out the front door of the humble little bungalow. Her car keys magically appeared in her hand. And the car seemed to drive itself to her old neighborhood. A pilgrimage of sorts.

In the gathering darkness in her rusted Toyota, she'd park on the side of the road, two or three houses above the white Cape Cod with speckled rock on the front, a broad porch, and two windows on each side of the front door. The maple sapling she and John had planted had grown into a spectacular tree and now boasted a tire swing and a tree house. She'd roll down her window and listen to the sounds drift up the hill of children enjoying those last stolen minutes before mothers called them in for a bath or to finish homework. She sat staring at a stranger's window a half block away—her bedroom window—until she felt like a voyeur.

Maggie didn't bother a soul, didn't honk her horn or call out, "Give that little one an extra hug tonight." She just sat behind the steering wheel and felt the canyon breeze on her cheeks, felt it ruffle her hair. "Read more stories," she'd whisper. "Laugh more." And then she'd wait for a small crack in the universe to appear, a crack she could slip through and become thirty years younger, standing at the kitchen sink washing up the remnants of mac and cheese or spaghetti. If she stared at that house long enough, more years stole by, and a for sale sign would appear in the parking strip between the Hawthorn trees. *Leave*, she'd whisper to herself, but if she left, she couldn't reshape the past, and all those stars in the evening sky couldn't align properly to give her a second chance. That's all she wanted, a second chance.

What had she done wrong that everyone else had done right? She didn't know, but it must be something, a hundred somethings—large sins and small. The neighbors all knew. They'd made lists of her shortcomings, justifications, reasons not to let their children attend Henry's ninth birthday party. But how unfair. If there was a punishment, she needed to bear it herself. She'd wanted to run out onto the front lawn and beat on her chest. *Be kind to my children.* How foolish was that? More drama for the invisible, whispering audience.

Long ago, the night after the boycotted birthday party, her husband had come home late, a gift in his hands, but Henry was asleep with his covers kicked aside.

"Too late," she said. "We needed you today."

Thin shouldered, he stood next to their bed, cheeks pale under dark stubble and the hollows under his eyes looking like bruises.

Maggie was too tired to shout, so she whispered, "We need to pull together. Be a family. Get through this."

But he turned away and kicked his shoes in the direction of the closet before he spoke to the lamp on the dresser, the strain in his voice stretched tight as a wire. "I hate walking into this. You ratchet up the pressure."

A vein throbbed in her forehead; her mouth was so dry, she couldn't swallow.

"I'm working hard to straighten out the mess," he said, "but when I walk in this house, it's like all the oxygen gets sucked out of my body." And that's how he looked, just a brittle shell of the man she loved wearing expensive gabardine slacks and a starched shirt that looked like it had been crushed by shadowy hands.

"What a luxury—to leave. You didn't have to see Henry's face," she muttered, "when Chris Thorndike was the only kid who showed up for his party."

"You called. We've been over the party. Remember?" He stood in the half-light.

"You don't understand how hurt he was." Her voice cracked.

"Do you need to slice me open and see the pain? Would that be enough for you?"

"You've walled us off. The kids feel it too."

"I have to survive. I have to get up tomorrow morning, polish my shoes, plaster a smile on my face, and talk to furious investors who want their money back like I have pockets stuffed with thousand-dollar bills. I have to look great and be clairvoyant. I can't jump down the black hole with you. I can't fall apart. I can't wail and grind my teeth and examine every single mistake we made in the last five years."

With sheets puddled around her, she sat dazed until he rapped on the headboard like maybe he didn't have her attention.

"I could get indicted, Maggie."

She gasped as though he'd slapped her.

"Sort of puts birthday parties in perspective, doesn't it?" Anger and fear—the air was thick with it. He shrugged out of his clothes and stood at the foot of the bed, staring at her. His mouth twisted. "We owe everyone, Maggie. I don't know how much. I've lost count." He could imbue her nickname with tenderness, but he could also sound like a stranger spitting out that *M* like a bad taste in his mouth.

***

Maggie raised her head and glanced unseeing at the scores of chicken-wire storage units and the concrete walls. This place was a warehouse for memories. She shivered. The heat was kept at forty degrees. Too warm to freeze, but too cold for hope. One day soon, Kristen—because Henry couldn't organize his time to come—would haul these boxes to a paper recycle bin, and then all evidence of Maggie's life would be shredded, and bits and pieces of Mary Margaret Sullivan would become cellulose insulation and would be sprayed into new construction. *Ghost* took on a new meaning.

She stood and wedged her toe under the box of Christmas decorations, lifted one corner, and then grasped it with her hands and heaved. She didn't stop to lock her gate. *Thank Heaven for elevators,* she thought and hit the up button with her elbow.

Chapter Five

OLD FRIENDS

THE CARDBOARD BOX LABELED *CHRISTMAS decorations* was waiting in the middle of the living room floor when Maggie woke the next morning. She was quite sure she hadn't tied the strings of lights in knots before she tossed them into the cardboard box last New Year's Day, but sitting in a mess of tangled wires, she knew someone had sabotaged her decorations. She looped one strand over the end of the couch and was starting on another when she heard familiar voices in the hall that sounded like more fun than a mess of lights. She stood slowly, both knees feeling the ache.

"More snow tomorrow," Rosie sang. "We're headed to Woolworth's." Rose was stuck in 1965. Some mornings were like that. Evenings too.

Jan trailed Rose into Maggie's apartment, pulling a collapsible wire cart on wheels. "Harmon's," Jan corrected, "while the sidewalks are dry."

The previous storm was a warning that serious weather was barreling toward them on the jet stream. Then in one of those temperate reversals, the thermostat jumped to fifty, and all that glorious sunshine melted the piles of snow. The sky was a brilliant blue. Since the store wasn't more than a block away, the walk through the scattering of soggy leaves would be *invigorating*, one of Jan's favorite words; plus, the store was new, brightly lit, and the fruits and vegetables were artistically arranged as if they were a backdrop for a school play. Even if Maggie didn't buy a single thing, inhaling the smells from the meat counter and the in-store bakery made the trip worthwhile, and the staff was so obliging that their smiles looked like they'd been stitched onto their faces. The exterior resembled a tin can with windows, but not much could be done about that.

"This wind is bringing a storm." Rosie laughed, circling her hands. "A huge storm. We'll have to call this brick box the Snowed Inn." Then she hummed a cobbled medley of *Over the River* and *Jingle Bells*.

"Lists?" Jan asked.

What was it about retired school principals and their need to organize everyone? Jan's shoes were always sturdy—no exceptions—and she had a pair of no-nonsense hips. A green fleece scarf hung loosely over her shoulders, ready to wrap around her neck at the first suggestion of an unruly breeze.

Maggie tapped her forehead. "My list's inside." It never varied. Two cans of tuna (she was past worrying about mercury poisoning), a half-dozen eggs, one loaf of whole wheat bread, a barbecued chicken in one of those cardboard-and-cellophane containers, butter, OJ, a quart of milk, five bananas, a box of oats, two apples, some carrots, and a handful of green beans if they were in season. And three miscellaneous items. Anything she wanted. Anything at all. Some days she just took a deep breath and let her nose guide her to lemon curd she could eat with a spoon while she watched British comedies, or to a carton of clam chowder and a box of oyster crackers, or to something chocolate and gooey.

Sue, who lived in 7-F, had recommended a book a month ago, *Reinventing the Body, Resurrecting the Soul* by Deepack Chopra, and swore it would alter Maggie's life, her aura, her karma, her inner sense of self. Each month Sue took a new path to an expanding cosmos, and she was always looking for recruits, but she was never boring, not Sue. "The physical body is a fiction," she'd say, extending all eight polished fingers and both thumbs as though she were embracing her and her friends' collective consciousness. "Really Maggie, welcome every day as a new world. Focus on relationships instead of consumption." Then she'd give Maggie a stiff-backed hug, the best Sue could manage. Well, this "fictional body" Maggie inhabited needed a slug of chocolate every week or two, and today might be one of those days.

"Did you invite Sue?" Maggie asked as she tied a shoe. The three of them knew Sue's groceries were delivered by a personal shopper from Whole Foods, and so neither Jan nor Rose bothered to answer her question.

Maggie unfolded her own cart from the closet and buttoned her good wool coat neatly under her chin.

"You'll want a hat," Jan said. "There's a real nip in the wind."

Someone else in charge? It was relief. Unlike Jan or Sue, Maggie didn't have the energy to pull other people along with her opinions or her ways of doing. She was more of a follower, always had been, which had been difficult when there was no one around she was inclined to follow. Jan was already zipping her coat, adjusting her fanny pack, settling her shoulders. A lump in her pocket suggested a large potato or a yam, and Maggie had to ask, "What is that?" directing her finger at the bulge. Jan yanked a man's sock filled with dried beans out of her pocket with an exaggerated air of duty. The end was tied securely in a knot.

"Desperate times."

Maggie laughed, couldn't help herself. "Give me a minute," and she pulled open the top drawer in her bedroom bureau and grabbed a pair of size-ten knitting needles. "Okay, Jan. If someone lurches at you, whack them with your sock, and then I'll stab them with this."

Rose examined the metallic green needle Maggie handed her, then she paused. "I thought we were going shopping." Not going into battle armed with a sock full of beans and knitting needles.

A year ago, Maggie and Rose would have collapsed on the couch, laughing at the image of Jan clobbering some punk with her loaded sock, but Greta Vanderhoff was hovering around the edges of their conversations, a cautionary tale that didn't bear repeating. Maggie and Jan grinned at each other, teeth showing, with fixed determination.

Her door always open, Sue Carlyle heard the loose talk, glided down the hall, leaned against the doorjamb in her dark-teal turban, and surveyed the weaponry. "Is the Alta Club launching an assault?"

"Zero tolerance," Jan hefted the sock in one hand, "for purse snatchers."

"Safety in numbers. I'll come with you," Sue announced. "I'll grab my poncho."

Rosie warbled as they cleared the front door, "*Oh, the weather outside is frightful.*" Rosie paused and got a better grip on the handle of her cart before she shoved her knitting needle through her belt as if it were a scabbard. "We'll have to call this old brick box the Snowed Inn." She laughed.

Maggie suspected they all did a bit of rehearsing before they left their apartments, but she'd found the slips of paper where Rose actually penned her remarks. Rose tried to memorize them and then repeated what she'd rehearsed—over and over again. They all did it, this repeating business, but Rose's cycle was getting shorter by the day. She didn't know when to be still, when to speak, or what she'd already said; it was as simple as that.

A half an hour later, the four ladies were standing in the aisle at Harmon's, holiday music alternating with soft rock, and Jan was re-shelving twenty cartons of yogurt Rosie had swept off the dairy section into her cart while Maggie was examining a barbecued chicken. With a gentle hand on Rosie's arm, Sue directed her attention from the yogurt to the bananas. "You love bananas. These are perfect. Not too green."

Rosie bobbed her head, her dangling earrings swinging beneath her mop of curly white hair. "And a carton of cottage cheese." Rose glanced over her shoulder at Jan lining up the cartons of yogurt according to flavors, then she gave Maggie a deliberate sideways look. "I know what you're up to," she said, as though Maggie were the leader of a conspiracy.

"You'd be drowning in yogurt, swimming in the stuff. And what about a couple of Marie Calendar's potpies?" Maggie pushed their carts toward another aisle. She grabbed two bags of baby carrots and tossed one in her cart and one in Rosie's, then she whispered to Jan behind the flat of her hand, "She forgets to eat."

But over the last few months, Maggie had discovered when Rose wandered into her kitchen, she grabbed whatever was in the front of the fridge, so Maggie routinely boiled a dozen eggs and put them in a dish at eye level, and she left Rosie's dry cereal opened on the counter. She could never think of Rose as a problem; it was just that the rooms in her mind were closing and the drapes were being pulled. But some days, some mornings, light filtered in the windows, and for a moment or two, Rose was her old self, a hilarious white-haired woman not more than five feet tall.

"Do her kids know?" Jan said as they paused by the paper plates, napkins, and Ziplock baggies.

"They know she's foggy, but if she's not losing weight and she doesn't take a fall, they won't do anything."

Jan's cheeks drooped. *Do anything*. They all knew what that meant: Highland Cove Senior Facility, memory care, the off odor of Depends that needed changing, and overcooked peas and a few bites of chicken or beef hash for dinner and lunch. Vacant souls shelved like the coconut yogurt.

Pulling their wire carts with the sunshine on their faces, and Jan gulping mouthfuls of fresh air, they chatted as they walked up State Street about the newcomer in 8-B, the only single man on their side of the building. A novelty in zippered pants, that's what he was. Someone new to discuss. A mystery who leaned heavily on a cane. Aleph, one of the security guards, buzzed the ladies in, and their intriguing conversation—that would continue for days—was interrupted.

After depositing her groceries in her own apartment, Maggie arranged Rosie's groceries in the fridge, then put a potpie on a cookie sheet and shoved it in the oven. In minutes, the delicious smell of baking wafted through Rose's apartment. She organized some boxes in the cupboard and listened to the comfortable noise of eggs tumbling in boiling water.

Heaven knew her life wasn't perfect, but for seven years, Maggie felt like she'd grabbed something out of thin air, something indefinable, something as intangible as warm steam above the pot of eggs: happiness. She sat next to Rosie on the couch and patted the back of her hand. They had a matched set, raised veins and age spots. "Do you remember that afternoon we tried on hats in Dillard's? Easter hats with wide brims?" She started to laugh. "Ridiculous fake peonies?"

Rose turned her head and smiled. "They were pink."

Chapter Six

GANG OF THIEVES

NEAR SIX O'CLOCK, CARLY WRAPPED a scarf around her neck and stuffed her hands deep in her pockets before she headed out onto the slush-covered streets, the library behind her. Her breath crystallized in the cold air as she glanced at the Christmas displays in store windows and thought about Thanksgiving preparations at home that hadn't really been home since Dale-call-me-Dad had inserted himself like a bad joke with a stupid punch line.

Hauling herself up the last flight of stairs in the dilapidated apartment building, she could hear Lemon performing behind the closed door. Wishing she had anywhere else to go, she paused outside the door. Nothing to eat since she'd shared a stale bagel with Terry that morning, she felt dizzy with hunger, but not Lemon. He was in fine form—he'd obviously had something to eat—and was pitching a new plan that involved some sketchy scheme to invade Fort Knox.

"They're sitting on a pile of cash and jewelry. And they're old, very, very old. Their minds are gone. They don't remember what they've got." He tapped his forehead with his skinny finger. "Let's see. I used to have a diamond necklace, but where did I put the darn thing?" He mimed groping his pockets and pulled out a bit of string and a gum wrapper. "Mislaid? Stolen? They're not about to admit incompetence, because their beneficiaries will swoop in and cart them off to the death factory, so they'll say nothing. I guarantee it." He sliced a quick hand across his chest.

Nolan passed a joint to Burt and then nodded to Lemon as if to say, *Continue*.

"Plus, it's Christmas. They're too old to shop, and they don't know what to buy. They're not sure who's going to stop by, but they want to be sure whoever comes doesn't leave empty handed. Best way to ensure a visit next year are crisp fifty-dollar bills in little white envelopes with poinsettias printed in the corner." He clicked his tongue. "Merry Christmas. Here's a little something I picked out—just for you."

"That's pretty pathetic." Too tired to stand, Carly slid down the wall until she was sitting on the stained mattress, their stand-in for a couch.

"Sad but true. Family interest in old folks only goes so far."

She stifled a cough. Her eyeballs felt like they were on fire. She was catching something. She whispered to Terry, "What's the bottom line? What did I miss?"

"He wants to infiltrate an apartment building where a bunch of old people live."

"What?" What a jerk.

"Just roll with it." Terry smiled, his eyes glazed.

"Merry Christmas," she muttered.

Lemon had moved on to the building's security personnel and the location of hidden security cameras. *Too much time at the movies,* she thought. Then it was like he was describing a ballet, a dance that involved filching an old woman's keycard, but it absolutely could not look deliberate. No one could know the keycard had been lifted because it took security less than an hour to issue new cards and enter new codes, and then what was the point? No one wanted to hurt the old lady, just jostle her enough so she'd stay home a couple of days. A couple of days when she wouldn't notice her keycard was missing. They could let themselves in, wander the halls during church, find a few unlocked doors, and then get out of there in minutes with a pile of cash, which equaled food, heat, and a high to last through the holidays.

Carly's head ached. She was having trouble keeping all this straight. Maybe she should take notes, but that would require a pen. "So where is this amazing place?"

"The corner of State Street and South Temple. The Eagle Gate." Lemon raised his eyebrows suggestively as though he'd just smooched his own private golden goose, and it was ready to deliver a solid gold egg.

"You're barking up the wrong tree. I knew a lady who lived there, and she was strapped," and then Carly stopped, sorry she'd spoken, because what happened next was kind of extraordinary; Lemon quit talking. Grinning, he stared at her like she'd grown an extra head and he could charge people a nickel for a look at a freak.

Lemon beckoned with his fingers. "More, give me more."

She felt wiped out and speechless. "Maybe she lived somewhere else. I don't remember." She hadn't been to Salt Lake since she was little, and there were a ton of old apartment buildings bunched along the lower Avenues. Carly couldn't remember the buildings' names. "She wasn't rich. She didn't have two nickels to rub together."

"Who?" Lemon's eyes roamed the ceiling. "Who wasn't rich?"

"Some relative. My mother's aunt." Carly felt like she was being sucked into a quagmire, a filthy, stinking swamp.

"A great-aunt?" Lemon's phony smile vanished. Show over. He slid one skinny size 13 foot in her direction and shifted his weight. "Happy day, when I met you. Where is she now?"

"I don't know. Dead. Not dead. In Cedar City maybe. We," and she tripped over *we,* "haven't seen her in years." Her great-aunt had sent Carly birthday cards when she was little with pictures of fluffy kittens and puppies with funny captions, but that was years ago. Elementary school.

Lemon's pale eyes traveled over her face. "But maybe not. Maybe she's still there. Auntie might be the key that turns the lock."

"She's got nothing worth stealing. And she's had a miserable life. Her husband plowed into a tree going ninety."

"Sounds like *some relative* has quite a story." Lemon tilted his head, half his mouth in a grin.

She could see where this was going. "Sorry. I'm not taking advantage of an old lady who's had her guts kicked out." Carly stuck out her chin and tried to feel more assertive instead of just hungry.

The apartment door swung open, and a guy with a three-day beard—maybe thirty years old, maybe not—stood in the doorway and surveyed them all. The stubble couldn't hide his pitted acne scars, but his shoes were tied neatly, no knots in the laces. He had two boxes in his hands, large pizzas, and the smell made Carly feel faint. The guy was ham-fisted; he probably couldn't lift a wallet if his life depended on it. Where did he get his money? Pizza wasn't free.

"Bill," Nolan whispered. It wasn't a greeting, more of a grudging acknowledgment, or maybe a warning. His arms crossed over his stomach like he needed to protect his vital organs. The absentee roommate, number six, had just arrived.

"Bro Lemon, have you explained our plan?" His broad smile didn't make it up to eyes that were small for his face, too close together, and almost concealed by the thick wedge of eyebrows low on his brow. Nothing was wrong with those eyes that could be surgically corrected; they were just intense, mean. Carly didn't just shudder, she almost convulsed. *Sociopath,* a word she'd tossed around before but never intuitively understood until now. She'd never seen this guy before, but the easy, stoned companionship shifted. Nolan was afraid, fear plastered right there on the kid's face. Lemon fluttered around making room on the counter for the pizzas and rummaging for a dull knife in a drawer. He thumbed in her direction.

"A new wrinkle." Lemon gave her an exaggerated wink. "An aunt. Maybe dead. But then again, maybe not."

Chapter Seven

MAGGIE AND ROSE

THEY HADN'T COME FULL CIRCLE, so the ending wasn't clear—but for thirty-four years the only constant in Maggie's life had been Rose, the friend who instinctively knew when a phone call was needed or a pot of fresh basil or something as simple as a hug or a smile. The petite blonde had been Maggie's next-door neighbor in Bountiful back when Rose wore a retainer each night to keep her teeth from crowding, back when a new dress or a pair of shoes was an event worth sharing, back when Maggie's three little children rolled in the grass or made angels in the snow. Kristen and her family had been gone less than six months when Rose called.

"Listen, Maggie, don't turn into that weird old woman with twenty-nine cats that eventually eat her dead body."

"That's a terrible thing to say." Maggie started to laugh. "You're safe. I'm allergic to cats. Maybe I'll get a puppy," she shrugged, "but then again, maybe I won't."

Rose's voice dropped an octave, "Listen. 7-B's vacant. Two doors down from me." She stretched out the word, "Perfect." Then she sighed. "No one on the seventh floor waits around chewing their nails for their children to call. We have a great time." But nothing in Rose's voice said *great time*. Her tone said *worried*.

"Rosie, I can't afford the Eagle Gate."

"What are you paying now? What's your house payment?" After Maggie answered, Rose exclaimed, "Rent on 7-B is a hundred dollars less. Sixes."

"I can't believe that."

"It's true. Everyone wants the two bedrooms, so the one bedrooms are cheap."

"Are you sure?"

"Trust me." Then Rose had whispered, "You can't stay there. Absolutely cannot. Not by yourself. I'm going to see the building manager and start the paperwork." Then after two minutes of chitchat to fill the uneasy break in their conversation, Rose had said good-bye.

Maggie glanced around the room at her meager possessions. She'd lived in the dark red brick bungalow for almost three decades. Her mother, tall, slender, and serious, had given her a warm hug and the down payment. "A home is what you make it," she'd whispered. Maggie could almost hear her mother's voice and wondered if she'd been a disappointment, the pretty daughter who wasn't much else, but her mother never criticized—that wasn't her way—but still, Maggie wondered.

She'd felt like her life was finished that April afternoon. Moving day. The crew from the elder's quorum set the last box on the living room floor and backed out the front door. Sweaty and relieved, the elders quorum president extended his hand. "Good luck." That was all. Now she was someone else's problem. She should have ordered pizza or a case of soda, but that would have extended the uneasy silence. They'd all lost money, some more than others. The men—they used to be her husband's friends—were glad to return to their wives, shaky mortgages of their own, and the noisy chaos of Little League games. Almost to his car, the president turned and walked slowly back up the steps. He gave her a hug and whispered, "No one blames you, Maggie. Not for a minute. If you need anything—and I'm dead serious—give me a call." It's what she would have said in his place, but she'd never call. They both knew it.

If she didn't count her marriage, Maggie had been robbed twice—once during the night when they were sleeping and once in the light of day—before she realized watering her lawn marked the small house as affluent. She'd stopped sprinkling the grass, let the terra-cotta pot of red geraniums die, and melded into the neighborhood.

***

Sixty-seven years old and sitting alone at her kitchen table, Maggie had stared at the sheet of paper on the mottled Formica. She'd done the math twice and then a third time. The scant equity from the bungalow wouldn't last forever, and social security could only stretch so far, but she wouldn't last forever either. If she was frugal, her savings might last until she was eighty, and then who knew? She'd tapped a pencil on the tabletop.

She'd had long complicated conversations with the Lord. At the first sign of cancer, or a heartache that required a stent or surgery, or when the balance in her bank account registered ZERO, she would slip quietly, peacefully away. She'd pocketed the brown bottle of morphine from Lucy Beth Meacham's bedside before the dear woman's body was cold. "You take this," Lucy Beth had spoken so softly Maggie had to put her ear by her friend's mouth, "after I'm gone. No virtue in suffering."

It wasn't hard for her to imagine the postmortem whispers or the phone calls to Maggie's children. *It was a blessing. She passed in the night. No sign of a struggle. She was eighty, after all. She lived a good life. Everyone loved her.* Everyone? Maybe just Rose. Maggie had shrugged and signed the lease with Rose peering over her shoulder. Eagle Gate Apartments. 7-B.

***

Now her old neighbor became her new neighbor and visited every day—not just a nod as they passed in the hall. Before Maggie had unpacked a single cardboard box, Rosie arrived in the doorway with an application in her hand. "You're going to be a docent at the Church History Museum. You can be my assistant. I run the puppet show."

Then she grabbed Maggie's shoulders—not a simple gesture for the compact woman who only stood at five one—and looked her in the eye. "Happiness is a choice. It's not a circumstance. It's not about money, or kids, or a perfect past. It's about right this very minute. And right this very minute, we're going to be happy. You and me."

Maggie had eased herself down on a large cardboard box.

"And we walk everywhere," Rose said. "That's the deal. Exercise. It forces oxygen into your brain."

Maggie nodded, feeling a bit overwhelmed. Rose could have that effect.

"This is just the beginning of our third act," Rose had said, "where everything is wonderful and there are usually a couple of weddings to tie up loose ends." Maggie's laugh made people down the hall smile.

For seven years, Maggie had been Rose's accomplice. They were regulars in the water aerobics class in the pool on the main floor. They begged tickets to the symphony's dress rehearsals from the man in 3-C, an usher when his health permitted. They'd sit in the back of the symphony hall with balled tissues in their fists, tears rolling down wrinkled cheeks, and listen to Paganini or Rachmaninoff or Mahler's *Seventh Symphony*. Arriving on TRAX, they'd audited a class on primitive Mesopotamian cultures at the university, and one spring they signed up for flower arranging at the YMCA. They'd strolled over to the city library and cajoled teenagers to teach them how to use email and watch YouTube videos on the bank of computers on the second floor. They'd watched old movies on Rosie's TV (she could afford cable), and in a moment of absolute audacity, they'd tried on emerald necklaces at O.C. Tanner until the well-dressed clerks realized they were just a couple of crazy old ladies wringing all the happiness they could out of every single day.

And then this September, an unwelcome day arrived at the puppet show in the form of Sister Eliza Wood, the director of volunteer services at the museum. She had a lovely certificate with a gold border and Rosie's full name written by someone who knew her stuff—calligraphy.

Rose was being thanked for eleven years of wonderful service. Dismissed. Let go. How could a person be sent out to pasture when that's already where they lived? Next stop, the glue factory.

Maggie had followed Sister Wood to the elevator door. "Can't she stay with me? Be an assistant? No one can do the wolf voice like Rose."

"We love Rosie too, but she wandered into the rag doll demonstration last Thursday and told thirty fourth graders that crafts are crap."

"Just a slip of the tongue."

"And what about telling that group of Baptist ministers that Mormon crickets were one of the seven plagues of Egypt?"

"Seems like a small mistake." Or an incidental miracle left unrecorded.

Sister Wood spoke about self-respect and cycles of life with all the warmth of an appliance repairman discussing a faulty plug before she patted Maggie's arm. "It's time. It happens to us all, and it's Rosie's turn. She's lucky to have you as a friend, but we can't have her as a docent."

Maggie sighed and glanced down at the floor. Sister Wood's socks didn't match—one was striped and the other was solid blue, but Maggie decided not to mention it—instead, she reached behind Sister Wood and pushed the elevator button. With a quick nod of her head and her purse gripped in one hand, Sister Wood vanished behind the closing doors. That was two months ago, and Rosie wasn't improving.

Chapter Eight

SCRABBLE AT ONE

AT ONE O'CLOCK SUE ARRIVED for the Tuesday afternoon Scrabble game. She was never late, something Maggie admired, and Sue never knocked—that would interfere with her entrance, and Sue was all about making an entrance. Her champagne-colored hair curled over one of the caftans she habitually wore, even though Maggie had glimpsed the interior of a closet stuffed with pastel silks and pressed linen.

Maggie was fussing in the kitchen as Sue stood over the table flipping Scrabble tiles as she spoke. "I didn't see you in Relief Society, so I signed you up to bring two pumpkin pies." She nodded at Maggie. "Bake them. Buy them. No one cares." Thanksgiving. This week, and of course, it was always on Thursday. An odd assortment of misplaced people collected in the party room off the lobby to share a meal on collapsible tables with recycled centerpieces, fake autumn leaves, and yellow mums that would pass for festive anywhere else. Someone, no one could remember who, had dubbed this elderly group the Holiday Orphans. The name stuck, and they were stuck with each other because their families had—for one reason or another—decided their company was no longer worth the inconvenience of having the upholstery cleaned.

"I'm not sure I can endure another of those lunches." Maggie sighed. Sue would be on her right, but on her left, Maggie would invariably be seated next to someone who drooled gravy out the corner of his mouth or dropped cubes of stuffing in his lap, while Sue's end of the table roared with laughter. Maggie felt drowned in a tide of insignificant things she preferred not to notice. Was she being a snob?

Maggie hadn't mentioned her own holiday menu to anyone: a whole chicken cooked with fresh sage, a three ounce can of cranberry sauce, two potatoes to mash, an orange for a garnish, and all the fixings for one spectacular pumpkin pie. She'd checked out three movies from the library, *The Big Chill*, *A Room with a View*, and *Ben Hur*. Charlton Heston never disappointed. So handsome, the man simply exuded virtue. It didn't matter that he was dead. She planned a relaxing day with her feet up on the ottoman, smelling the diminutive turkey roasting, and watching old movies. A perfect day. A quiet, completely self-indulgent day. Lunching with the Holiday Orphans was not part of her plan.

"Don't be silly," Sue said. "Of course you're going. We had a marvelous time last year." As Sue turned the last tile and bit down on a chocolate mint, she insisted, "We'll go together." A crumb of chocolate escaped her mouth and landed on an *E*.

There were unmentioned women on other floors—and actually a couple on seven—who droned on and on about the successful children they'd birthed, molded, and shaped. Women who drove a twenty-year-old Mercedes or an Accord with low mileage to Bountiful or Midvale or Park City to be the guests of honor at family feasts. Those women might be drawn to the laughter behind the closed door on Tuesday afternoons, but they weren't invited inside.

Sue had no children. She did have several large diamond rings—a carat or two each—that slid over long fingers and smooth joints. Lovely works of original art covered the walls of her living room—not crowded on the walls, but artistically arranged and well lit. There had been several husbands, but none currently in evidence. When pressed to rudeness by curious people who chose not to understand obvious non-verbal cues and questioned her childless state, Sue would glance over the top of her tortoiseshell glasses and reply, "I've never understood the need to populate an already crowded planet with little ruffians. It always struck me as genetic megalomania." Invariably, the interloper huffed away as though Sue had criticized their progeny as *small grubby things with untied shoes and sticky fingers*. Maggie edged next to Sue in a crowd to listen to her imperious put-downs and then howled with laughter when she was home alone.

Maggie's pretty diamond solitaire had been sold years ago to pay for Henry's amazingly crooked teeth that caused the orthodontist to twist more wires and shake his head. "Never seen anything like this kid's mouth." For years the only ring on her finger was the worn wedding band with three small diamonds that had belonged to her mother. It was a connection she needed, a connection that couldn't break, vanish, or make other life choices. After degenerative arthritis arrived, making Maggie's knuckles swollen and sore, the ring rested in a faded blue velvet box in the top drawer of her dresser, and she glanced at it every now and again and smiled, remembering her mother's quiet hands.

Unzipping her puff parka, Rosie wandered in at a quarter past the hour, her mass of white hair poking out in odd directions. Jan arrived last and shut the door with a firm click.

"Nothing's more irritating than interlopers who watch over your shoulder and gasp when you miss a triple-word score," she announced in a superior tone, as though dozens of women were clamoring for entrance and would shove their way in and snatch loose tiles if the door were left ajar. Jan settled herself in a dining room chair, happy to leave non-combatants down the hall.

At a quarter to three, Rosie was a hundred points ahead because no one had the heart to challenge *oronge* on a double word score or *chepter*. "You know, like a *chepter* in a book," she explained, as she paused and took a sip of lukewarm peppermint tea.

Jan propped one elbow on the edge of the table and arranged her tiles, frowned, and arranged them a third time. "You realize we're being stalked? I saw those kids again loitering outside the building. I made the descent down to Aleph's office—in the belly of the beast—and got no response. He's hibernating down there surrounded by mountains of Cheetos. A two-year supply."

Building security was outsourced, and the result was two security specialists: Paulo, a universally admired young man who still lived with his mother, and Aleph, an aging junk food connoisseur.

"What did you tell him?" Maggie asked. It wasn't hard to imagine Jan lecturing poor Aleph.

"That a gang of thugs is following us."

"Let me guess." Sue slid four tiles across the board. "He can't call in a complaint about something that hasn't happened. A crime not yet committed. Bones not broken. Purses not snatched. No harm. No foul. Put me down for twenty-one points." She glanced up with a pleased half-smile on her face. "Wait until eight and talk to Paulo. He's the only one with more than two functional neurons." The handsome young man was headed to graduate school in two or three years, and they were already mourning his loss.

"I thought preemption was the new national trend. Attack before we're attacked," Jan said. "What we need is a petition. Put a little pressure on the board. Maybe they can pry Aleph out of his lair in the basement."

Not a lair, Maggie thought, *a cave with five screens, one for each exterior door. How boring, watching those screens for an entire eight-hour shift.* She didn't begrudge Aleph his Cheetos or his video games.

Jan folded her arms across her chest as if she'd been waking up at three a.m. to worry about delinquents and was prepared to go on the offense. Man the barricades. Fortify the doors. "Really, if someone, anyone in a uniform marched up and down the street a few times in the late afternoon, those kids would be scared off."

No one answered. The clock on the wall chimed three times. Greta Vanderhoff's case was closed. Did anyone care? Anyone under seventy? If it had occurred to Jan that she was Greta's replacement at the Scrabble board, she didn't mention it.

Maggie rearranged the letters on her tray: O R Q P A U T. Nothing came to mind. She juggled the vowels. There was an available T on the board, but she'd need an extra R to spell *rapture.* She dropped O and R in front of the T and waited for the challenge.

"Ort?" Jan said. "Never heard of it."

"I almost had *rapture,* but I didn't have an extra R."

Rosie started to laugh and rolled *rrrrr* off her tongue.

"Ort." Sue smiled. "What an elegant little word. A small morsel of food."

"Typically lurking in the back of a fridge. Three bites." Maggie raised her eyebrows.

"And what's the word on the elegant Mr. 8-B?" Sue asked, as though any suggestion of rapture must include someone specific, not the male species as a whole.

"There's a line outside his penthouse." Jan threw a glance toward the door, as though the fluttering clutch of would-be Scrabble players had suddenly elevated up a floor and were lurking in the hall, waiting for Mr. 8-B to hit the down button on the elevator to collect his mail in the lobby. There was always a crew of plump smilers waiting to pounce on the poor man with a plate of signature cookies or a loaf of fresh bread or tickets to some inspirational program at the tabernacle on a Thursday evening.

Rosie was paying more attention than anyone realized. "Why would anyone want to take on a new man?"

Maggie started to laugh.

"Why indeed?" Sue said, before she thoughtfully arranged a half-dozen mints on her wooden tray as though they were vowels. "But I have to say 8-B has kind eyes."

Maggie winked at Rose. For years Sue had entertained them with stories of the "villains," her collection of ex-husbands, so of course, Rose had assigned them all nicknames.

"Wouldn't it be lovely if Darth is getting up several times a night with plumbing issues?" Maggie laughed.

"We can only hope." Sue feigned a yawn.

"Darth?" Jan said.

Sue hung an elegant arm over the back of her chair. "Darth Vader, husband number three."

"Or Puke." Maggie smiled.

"As in Puke Skywalker," Sue added. "Number Two."

"Or Geng." Rosie nodded.

"As in Khan."

"Or sweet Benny." Maggie laughed.

"As in Arnold."

"Or Johnny?" Jan volunteered that maligned king of England, not knowing John was a name never used. She knew in a second she'd said the wrong thing. "You know, Robin Hood's foil."

Sue answered too quickly. "Who was such a despicable king that he probably wore his pointy crown upside down."

"I liked John," Rose muttered. "In the beginning." She'd lost the thread of the conversation and wrinkled her nose at Maggie. "So did you. You loved him." She wasn't referring to King John, dead for eight hundred years. She was talking about Maggie's husband. The four women were silent as Maggie studied her thumbnail intently. Of course she loved him, thought of him, ached for him. Each night her eyes lingered over his face on the nightstand before she knelt beside her bed.

"You were the perfect family, perfectly, perfectly perfect," Rose said, but the edge in her voice implied something else. "Johnny was in the bishopric, and Maggie was the primary president. They were the family everyone wanted to be."

"Do you remember the day our dog died?" Maggie's voice cracked. "I thought I was fine, but I wasn't. My counselor rushed up. Georgia Archibald, wasn't that her name?" Maggie glanced over at Rose, who'd been playing the piano that day.

"Sylvia," Rose said. "A pretty red-head. *My Grandmother Dear has a Garden.* That was the song. I'd just finished playing, when your face turned into a flood." A teary wash of mascara and make-up. "We thought John had gone AWOL." Rose laughed.

Maggie didn't know that, not until this very minute. Why would anyone think that? Leap to that conclusion?

Sue clicked her long nails on the table. "Men." She rolled her eyes. "Who needs them?"

"She died in Brazil," Rosie mused.

"Who died?" Jan asked.

"Sylvia Wood. Not Georgia. Georgia was her cousin. She was a year behind me at Bountiful High. It was very sad. Her husband was a mission president out in the jungle somewhere, and her cancer went undetected too long. She had her homecoming in a box—with lots of red carnations on top."

"Who? Sylvia or Georgia?" Jan raised her voice.

"The *who* doesn't matter. She's dead." Sue arranged four tiles on the board. "Knive."

"Won't work," Jan said. "You need an *s*. *Knives* is the plural of *knife*."

Everyone talked. No one listened. Rosie's long-term memories weren't always in sync with what Maggie chose to remember, and Maggie felt like a piece of fabric stretched on the bias. Nothing in her mind stayed put. Stray thoughts intruded, thoughts she'd put away, boxed up, labeled, and stuck in a dark corner of her storage unit. Now they were out on the table ready to be challenged, scored, and tallied up at the end of her life.

Maggie stood. "More peppermint tea?"

Sue reached over and pressed the back of Maggie's hand. They heard bits of snow pelting the windows. The storm had arrived with a vengeance.

"I knew Mr. 8-B a long time ago," Rose said, pressing her fingertips against her temples, her forehead wrinkled. "And he knows you. But for the life of me, I can't remember his name." She gave an audible sigh. "He's tucked away somewhere in an old yearbook. Or a snapshot." She frowned at Maggie. "He asked about you at church. He wanted to know if you were Maggie Memmott before you remarried."

Sue had a mint halfway to her mouth and paused with open lips. "Who is he?"

Jan was mouthing *Memmott*, trying to pin down a thought.

"I never remarried." Maggie tried to stay calm, pressing damp palms against her thighs. "I took my maiden name back after John died. It's a perfectly good name, and it belongs to me."

"That makes absolute sense. Don't apologize. I use my maiden name too." Sue stood abruptly, placed the mint back on the tray, and turned toward Rose. "And how did you respond to mysterious 8-B?"

Rosie smiled and nodded. "I told him a rose by any other name would smell as sweet, but of course I wasn't talking about myself. I was talking about our Maggie."

"Perfect," Sue said. "Shakespeare never faileth."

"Who won?" Jan stretched her arms above her head.

Sue poured the tiles into the box. "I would have to say Rose bested us all this afternoon."

Chapter Nine

CALL YOUR MOTHER

No question, Maggie's daughter knew the hour before sleep was the time to pick up a novel, adjust a blanket, coordinate schedules, whisper little innocuous things about the day, respond to a lingering kiss behind her ear, and finally plump her pillow and drift off to sleep. It was not the time to watch CNN or have an angry whispered exchange. Tense discussions at ten o'clock ensured that neither Kristen nor her husband, Blake, would sleep particularly well because Blake kept waking up to have the last word like there was an alarm in his brain. Being married to a man whose moral high ground was up there in the clouds, around thirty thousand feet, wasn't easy. She'd felt oxygen deprived more than once.

"Did you call your mother?" Blake murmured, safe behind the current copy of the *Ensign* held close to his face, like a mask or a shield, she wasn't sure which. *Here we go*, she thought as she climbed into bed beside him and pulled the quilt up over her shoulder. *Call your mother* were fighting words in their small corner of the universe. And honestly, she didn't know any man who loved his in-laws the way Blake loved her mother.

She waited for his next line, *Once a year it might be nice not to have one of those plastic pies,* delivered in his pleasant, non-confrontational tone that he'd rehearsed in the car driving home. *Plastic pies,* that's what he called them, in a box courtesy of Marie Calendar or Sara Lee, but Kristen wasn't fooled, he didn't care about pies, he was talking about her absentee mother who incidentally whipped out pumpkin pies that made everyone at Thanksgiving dinner drool.

He'd wondered out loud that very afternoon—when he saw the boxes coming in from the car—if Marie Calendar and Sara Lee were actual people or if they were invented during some marketing session with a dozen men in suits in some high-rise office building off Madison Avenue. That first observation led to another. How many chemists collaborated on the pie content? How much actual pumpkin, or a chemical equivalent, was required for the typical housewife to plunk down the targeted pricing? Blake had droned on that the crust has a dual function. After choking down the filling, they could wash out the crust and use it as a Frisbee on the back lawn after dinner with the cousins.

Surrounded by groceries on the counter, Kristen had huffed, "How about *you* plant, water, and harvest a real live pumpkin in a backyard garden—which we don't have—and I'll learn how to stew the stuff and bake you the most fabulous pie ever." *Better than my mother's*, but she hadn't said that, not out loud. Her family would just laugh.

She flipped her pillow over and gave it a resounding thump. Call her mother? She mumbled, "I'm going to. In the morning." Maybe. "Mom's happy. Isabelle recruited her to work on Black Friday and Saturday." Busiest knitting days of the year. All hands on deck.

"Did she tell you that before or after you told her that no one was coming to collect her?"

A direct hit. Kristen tugged the sheet up around her neck. She felt a slew of converging emotions at that particular moment, but shame wasn't one. "She loves that job," she fired back, "loves every minute she's in the store. She's the ultimate authority on knit and purl. And everyone loves her; she's everyone's favorite grandmother."

Blake carefully positioned his magazine on the nightstand and studied her with a look of real concern, like he'd just discovered he'd married an atheist. "She's the favorite grandmother around here too."

Did he think she hadn't noticed? She knew her next line perfectly because they'd had this same argument at least a couple hundred times. She and Blake had five basic disagreements: why wasn't their oldest son getting married; they needed to save more money for retirement; the dog was destroying the backyard; the kids needed to help more with housework; and her mother. Sometimes she wished they could just shout out a number, *Four!* and then hold their breath. Whoever passed out first won the argument.

Tonight he'd fired the first shot, hiding behind his *Ensign*, but she was too tired to return the volley, so she rolled over and gave him her backside. He was not deterred.

"It would have killed you to miss Jenny's musical." He kept his voice low, but she wasn't fooled. He wasn't going to quit, not Blake. He was just going to keep ratcheting up the ante in this war of attrition until she dragged her exhausted body up to the balustrades and waved her white pillowcase. "How do you think your mother felt?"

"Could we make an appointment to discuss this later? Maybe Friday at three? Or Sunday afternoon. We could go for a walk." And duke it out in the street in front of all the neighbors dragging pine trees home to decorate.

"Those life events only happen once," he whispered.

"I ordered the DVD."

"It's not the same thing. Not like being in the audience and going backstage after."

Kristen squeezed her eyes shut. The truth was she didn't want her mother in the audience. She didn't want to share the moment. She wanted her daughter to turn to her for approval, to turn to her to fix the hem of her costume or glue down the stray lock of hair with industrial-strength hair spray. She wanted to be the one to reassure Jenny that her singing was perfect and the click of her heels during the shop scene was electric.

For seventeen long years, Kristen had worn the bad-cop uniform. She had been the enforcer of familial edicts. The killjoy who made sobbing little children choke down vegetable sludge and enforced a seven-thirty bedtime. The scrooge who wouldn't fork over the cash for summer blockbuster movies. At least once a week during family melees, her mother sat on the couch with her lips pressed together like she'd just chomped down on a sour pickle. *No* never passed those wrinkled lips. Did her mother think hearing that word would damage her grandchildren's tender psyches forever? Ryan, Kristen's oldest, had violated curfew when he was fifteen. It scared Kristen to death, and she sent Blake out driving past midnight while she clutched the phone in her fist calling her son's friends, waking their parents, and muttering her apologies. He was grounded for a month, that was the consequence, a punishment carved in stone. Wide eyed and serious, her mother sat on the couch the next afternoon with a picture book in her hands and Lizzie in her lap. Just before the mean fairy on page thirteen turned into a fire-breathing dragon, her mother paused mid-sentence. "I never thought grounding a teenager was a particularly useful punishment."

The retort had been waiting on the tip of Kristen's tongue for ages, "That's because Henry and I grounded ourselves." For four years. "That neighborhood was so rough, we were scared to walk out the front door." Self-imposed exile for sins Kristen hadn't committed. Her mother cleared her throat and turned the page so the prince could stab the dragon in the neck with his magic sword.

Perfect grandmother-hood had started in the hospital on day one. Bleary eyed, Kristen was holding the new little person in her arms, the world's most adorable Christmas present, when her mother arrived hiding behind a gigantic stuffed bear, the equivalent of an entire week of her mother's salary working at Bethlehem Interstate Trucking. The owner had known her dad and had given her mother a job out of genuine heartfelt sympathy; unfortunately, his sympathy didn't extend much beyond minimum wage. How her mother got two weeks off in a row was hard to imagine, but there she was, holding that bear with both hands, a newborn binky in her purse, and determined to be useful.

After a solid week in the tiny one-bedroom apartment, Kristen was ready to commit matricide. Her nipples were a fiery red and so sore that every time she heard the baby cry, she started crying herself. Each time the baby whimpered or fussed, her mother changed him, wrapped him tightly in a receiving blanket sprinkled with fuzzy lambs, and then she'd say, "I think this little man is hungry." Same exact phrase, every time. Never varied. Kristen had swallowed her screams.

Five babies. Seventeen years. Nothing changed. When they all lived in the same zip code, her mother came over after work, two or three times a week, her forgotten name tag swinging around her neck. She caught up the laundry and fixed dinners that always tasted better than anything Kristen could mash or peel. Her mother read stories until her eyes were bloodshot, and she never tired of building Lego towers or spaceships or drawing pictures of smiling green aliens with large almond-shaped eyes. Laughing, she'd hide under imaginary forts made of blankets thrown over kitchen chairs and the back of the couch. She proofed essays. She corrected math homework that the poor woman struggled to understand herself. She never admitted she was so exhausted that her arms were going to fall off, not her mother. Those ancient knees cracked without a word of complaint. What a sham. It was like Kristen's family was the penance a depraved priest had assigned her mother. Four thousand Hail Marys, a million cookies, forty-six handmade Halloween costumes, thirty gallons of beef stew, and that perpetual, never-ending, ear-to-ear smile. When Southern Utah University had offered her husband a cushy job in student services, Kristen had started packing her bags before he hung up the phone.

"She is not coming with us." She'd introduced a new variation of Conversation #5. "Rose and I have talked about this. A dozen times. Mom needs her own life. Her own friends. Granny Nanny is a dead end."

"When are you going to forgive her?" Blake had said, both feet planted firmly on the kitchen floor. "Of course she's coming."

Twenty more years of smother mother? "Oh no. She's not." Round and round and round. Until an invisible referee rang a bell.

She didn't owe her mother another minute. She didn't owe her anything. Not after the way her parents had behaved. Okay, so their family had taken a direct hit and spun out of control with all engines on fire, but they could have made a crash landing, walked away from the wreckage, or parachuted to safety. But that didn't happen. Her dad had ejected from the cockpit and abandoned the four of them to implode on their own. Every man for himself, only she and Henry were just kids, and her mom was a mess, a certifiable mess. Some straight-laced official from the state office for dysfunctional parents should have scooped up the remains of Mary Margaret Sullivan Memmott and locked her in a padded cell. Foster care would have been a relief.

There had been so many other choices. Blake was the bishop. She knew how this worked. Families got knocked to their knees, and the bishop saved the day, paid the rent, sent in the Relief Society president with a food order and cash for school clothes. Kristen remembered the Bountiful bishop, a kind elderly man, sitting next to her mother on the couch and offering more than just sympathy; he'd offered serious help. Their adorable Cape Cod had to go; Kristen had known that even when she was a girl, but with their bishop's assistance, they could have rented a modest apartment, something small, two bedrooms and a closet. It wouldn't have been great, but it would have been better than Fremont Park. But her mom was too humiliated to stay in the neighborhood the world's greatest dad had robbed blind.

Anywhere in Bountiful would have been better than Fremont Park. She and Henry could have stayed in the same schools, safe schools, a school where skinny little Henry wasn't hefted onto the drinking fountain every single day or stuffed in a locker and left there to rot until some hall monitor heard him banging against the door or, worse, crying. No one noticed the burly morons who sauntered up to Henry in the hall. "Hey, Wimp, let me see what you got." A pencil, a pen, a half-eaten tuna sandwich, a geography assignment, it didn't seem to matter what. They grabbed everything, ate it, pocketed it, or ripped it in shreds and scattered the pieces on the floor. Henry lost weight, tried to vanish, hid in the library, and threw up before he left for school every single morning. He tried slurring his words, used atrocious grammar, inked a grainy tattoo on his forearm with a sharpie, quit handing in homework, and slouched around in clothes that reeked of an odd mixture of dog urine, cumin, and dirt, a concoction he'd tossed in the blender on the kitchen counter. He'd hoped the smell would repulse his tormentors.

"Dog urine?" she'd quizzed him the first time he brewed up the potion. "So how did you convince that rottweiler next door to pee in a cup?" Henry's face had flushed. He was embarrassed but also determined, so they'd slipped out the back door and diluted the foul-smelling stuff with the garden hose before she grabbed an old paintbrush she'd found in an ancient cupboard in the detached single-car garage. With her left hand holding her nose, she'd slopped muck over his clothes that were hanging on a line in the backyard. Henry rolled in the grass, laughing, while a couple of souped-up cars thundered down the street. The night air was soft and breezy, windows were open, and the neighbors were at it again. *Rosa, you witch* started every sentence, every single one. Their arguments were always about sex and food and money, but not in any particular order. Henry could mimic Mr. Padilla perfectly, and so they were careful to smile politely and keep their mouths shut when they encountered Mrs. Padilla, and in spite of the fact that the woman always told them to call her *Rosa*, they never did.

More often than not, their mother fell asleep on their dump of a couch with her swollen ankles propped on pillows, so she never noticed Henry sitting up late at night, fresh from the shower, with a legal pad on his lap, devising junior high escape strategies and elaborate plans for retaliation. But nothing he wore could disguise the way he spoke, his curly blond hair, or his intelligent green eyes. Nothing worked because his heart wasn't in it. Henry was just an inherently nice kid, and at Ensign Peak Middle, he was a marked man.

Kristen had tried to help in her own dispirited way. She fashioned a secret pocket in the lining of his worn jacket where he could stash food. She held up a finger to her lips when he started to complain within earshot of their mother. Instead they played pretend games. *Let's pretend that we're in the Battle of the Bulge, and we're stuck in a fox hole, and the ruthless enemies around us are about to be blown to bits. Let's pretend we've infiltrated a terrorist cell that's planning to blow up the cafeteria in the middle of lunch.* Henry was ready to blow the whistle on the terrorists and imagined all those beefy bullies who delighted in making his life miserable being carted off to prison camp and being forced to eat tuna sandwiches until their insides exploded or until they got mercury poisoning.

But there was one game they never played: *let's pretend Mom's normal and Dad didn't die.* There were only so many places fantasy could take a person, even when she and Henry were on a roll.

Kristen's life had been easier, but she could still sympathize. At West High her auburn hair was suddenly considered disgustingly *red*, unattractive, and fodder for jokes. Bright red hair out of a bottle was cool. God-given red, from the roots out, was an embarrassment. But relatively speaking, a few mean-spirited catcalls were pretty benign. The real trouble dropped out by the beginning of her sophomore year, and instead, those guys hung out in the parking lot or loitered across the street, smoking and trying to look manly. Mumbling delinquents weren't much of a problem in classes or the halls because those losers weren't allowed through the front doors. There were still gangs and nasty cliques, but Kristen was quick, greased lightning. A puff of smoke. Invisible. She skipped out on graduation and left her mother sitting alone in the stands on the football field. Done. She was so done.

She'd married the world's most forgiving man from the world's most ordinary family, completely vanilla. The Anderson's idea of a serious problem was being shorted five bucks on a tax return. Blake's brother ran a tire store in St. George. Big O Tires.

"Kristen," he'd say, "you need to check the depth of the tread on those tires of yours. The last thing you want to do is hydroplane in a car with five kids." He could regale Kristen with anything she ever wanted to know about treads, length, width, depth. Fascinating stuff. He, Clarisse, and their three rambunctious kids were arriving tomorrow for Thanksgiving. They would be delighted with the plastic pie she sent their way. After dinner, there was always some rowdy outdoor game, touch football, ultimate Frisbee, soccer. It didn't matter. All that laughter, all that hustle and bumping around was a symphony to her ears. Normal, so completely normal.

She talked to Henry every year on his birthday. It took a couple of calls before she connected, but she didn't give up; she kept pressing his number—listed in her favorites—until he caved in and picked up. She didn't know his little girls. She'd only met them a couple of times. She asked for pictures that never came.

More than once she tried to have an adult conversation with Henry about the Fremont Park years, or leaving Bountiful under such a black cloud, or their mother who was slowly aging. She tried to sound lighthearted, not like two damaged adults trying to piece together their crumbled past, but grown-up Henry didn't resemble the boy she loved, the kid who splashed foul-smelling muck on his jeans and T-shirt to protect insides so hurt and raw that every dirty trick or cruel remark pierced him to the heart.

"Honestly, Kris," he'd say, "the four or five years in Fremont Park were awful. I don't want to walk down that particular memory lane. It's all a blur anyway," he'd lie, "and Bountiful? I remember the day the police came to tell us about Davey. After that, the next two years are a blank."

Then the doorbell would conveniently ring, and she was pretty sure he'd opened the door and pushed the button himself.

Chapter Ten
4TH STREET CLINIC

CARLY'S FACE FELT LIKE IT was stuffed with damp cotton, her head throbbed, and all her joints—even her knuckles—ached. Terry had grabbed a handful of paper towels from a gas station, and when she blew her nose, that paper rubbed against her raw skin like sandpaper. Sitting on prehistoric folding chairs, they waited for the receptionist at the free clinic to call out the fake name she'd given, Janette Robinson. It had a nice ring.

If she were home, she'd be wrapped in an old quilt in front of the TV watching movies and drugged with decongestants. Her dad used to read to her out loud when she was sick. He was never too busy, not her dad. One long leg over the arm of his easy chair, his deep voice rumbling, he'd read whatever was on her nightstand. He didn't care what—*People* magazine, a dog-eared novel, her AP Lit anthology. Her mom would come home early from work to *push fluids* and flutter around trying to make her feel better. Her mom. Home. Hot soup. A bed with clean sheets. One lousy phone call is all it would take, and a plane ticket would be waiting in the Delta kiosk at Salt Lake International.

The exam room was Spartan and reeked of the antiseptic hosed on the beige walls and the drab linoleum floor. The walls were bare—no charts and no disgusting pictures of bodies minus skin. The doc was an older guy with white hair thinning on the top of his head, but his glasses were cool, rectangular and metallic.

"You've got a bad case of the flu," he said.

No kidding. She'd walked five blocks to hear that bit of news? The cuffs on his starched blue shirt were rolled up to his elbows and the backs of his hands were webbed with raised veins. He made sure the stethoscope was warm before he touched it to Carly's chest.

"No bronchitis," the old doc said, "at least not yet. But you've got to stay off the streets or this will be pneumonia." And then he sat down on the stool, rolled back a few inches, and studied her face as though seeing her for the first time. "You're not even eighteen, are you?" He sighed like the world was too heavy. "I've seen too many kids like you."

"Can I leave?" She didn't come for a lecture. "Do I get an antibiotic?" Preferably free.

"And where are you going when you leave here? Where's home?"

What's the rush? Is that what he meant? Carly shrugged.

"Where did you live the first sixteen years of your life?"

"Eureka, California." Where Dale-Call-Me-Dad was lurking around, poisoning her mother's fragile mind, and waiting to negotiate the screwed-up prodigal's return. She hadn't answered his half-dozen snarky emails. She could just see his smug face through the glass on the front door, his hands holding his stupid contract tied with a red bow. Merry Christmas.

The doc shook his head slowly before reaching for a manila folder next to the sink. "You're underweight, you're sick, running a fever. You probably won't take it, but I'm going to give you the best advice you're ever going to get." He pushed his glasses up the bridge of his nose. "Go home. I'll even take you to the bus station and buy your ticket."

She shook her head, but *underweight* caught her attention. Was he kidding?

He pulled a grainy eight-by-ten photo out of a folder and held it in front of Carly's face. "This is you in four years. Take a good look. This girl was pretty, not as pretty as you are, but close."

She didn't want to hear his spiel, but she gave the picture a sideways glance. Maybe if the girl in the picture had more teeth, it wouldn't have been so startling, but the girl was missing a front tooth and three on the bottom. Purple scabs pocked her skin, and she had bald splotches on her head where hair should've been. And she was filthy. The camera caught it all.

"Classic meth addict," he said. "Kids think they've got insects crawling under their skin, so they try to dig them out with their fingernails. She's only twenty-four, but she looks forty."

"I don't do meth," Carly muttered.

"Yet." He spoke with sadness that went all the way to the bone.

She struggled into her jacket and barked another cough. "So why are you here? Why aren't you off playing golf in Maui?" He was probably sitting on a pile of money, but he volunteered here because he couldn't quit telling people what to do. Everyone knew doctors were rich. Dale-call-me-Dad whined every time he opened a bill.

The doctor's back straightened at the edge in her voice. "My wife died a year ago, and Hawaii sort of lost its appeal." He rolled back on the stool and rapped the edge of the folder on the counter. "Have Lauren give you some juice and Tylenol before you leave. And get rid of the hardware until spring. It just makes things worse." The skin around her nose ring was inflamed, sore to the touch, and her lips were chapped. "Germ magnets," he called after her as she exited the exam room.

Terry was sitting on a folding chair, elbows on his knees, head in his hands. She dropped down next to him and coughed into her sleeve.

"Janette?" A broad-shouldered woman in faded pink scrubs handed her a paper cup and offered a couple Tylenol pills in her palm. Then the woman walked behind the counter, picked up a clipboard, and called out another name. She nodded at Carly and whispered behind her hand to a woman working at the computer, "Same girl. Different face."

A remark Carly was supposed to hear. Their whispering didn't fool her. Maybe they thought they were doing her a favor, giving her a wake-up call, like she didn't know she was screwed, like she wasn't sick and so miserable she could curl up on the floor right there and not move for a week.

"We've got to get out of here," she mumbled.

Terry raised his eyebrows. After insisting she see a doctor this morning, he hadn't said much else.

"Out of Salt Lake. Out of the cold." She stared at the linoleum. Her socks were damp, and her feet were freezing. "If we had a little money, we could get to San Diego. Somewhere warm. Be professional dog walkers or something. Get our GED's."

He put his arm around her shoulders, and they walked east into the wind, past clutches of weary men wrapped in dirty blankets or sleeping bags, some talking, some mumbling incoherently. No one had anywhere to go, nowhere to be. Their clothes were crusted with grime. Soon they'd wander down to St. Paul's for their only meal of the day. She'd seen them before plenty of times. They ambled up to her at lunch, sat at her table, and murmured their stories with a dry baloney sandwich clutched in their hands like someone might steal it. Half were vets. Most were addicts or alcoholics. They all were crazy.

"You want to go back to the apartment?" Terry asked.

Carly's wet cough had kept everyone awake last night. "No. The library."

He slipped three dollars into her hand.

"Where did you get this?"

"Tip jar at Starbucks. Get some juice at that vending machine."

Carly rolled her eyes.

"Hey. Some woman spilled scalding coffee on her friend. Caused a frenzy."

"With help?" Carly was sure he'd jostled the woman's elbow.

"Maybe a little." He nudged her shoulder instead of giving her a wink. Two or three times a week, Lemon taught spontaneous courses in petty thievery. Now it was almost automatic to look for an open purse or diaper bag slung over the back of a chair, or a tip left on a table, or a credit card in plain sight. A tip jar by a cash register was a gift. A quick distraction was all it took.

Shivering and chilled, she stood at the library's main entrance a few minutes later and watched her only friend meander off down Fourth South. The gay kid and that fat girl. That's what they'd always been called at school—it was like they didn't have names. Terry looked so desperate she wanted to cry. He'd almost quit talking. He blurted chopped phrases or said nothing at all. She'd always been the brains in this operation, and she needed to do something. Make a plan. But she felt so lousy. She'd worry about him when she felt a little better, maybe in a day or two. She made her way to the third floor, eased into her chair back in the stacks, propped a book in her lap, and fell asleep in a square of pale sunshine.

The chirp of a voice woke her. She couldn't be a face the librarian remembered, so Carly slipped out of the chair and made her way to the restroom, one quick right turn past the elevator. She hid in a stall until the sounds of water running in the sink quieted and she was alone. She nudged the stall door open and peeked outside.

But she wasn't alone; a slender girl stared at her in the length of mirror above the sinks. She knew she'd been dropping weight, but startled by what she saw, she dumped her bag on the floor and leaned against the counter, gaping at her reflection under bright lights. Underweight. Who was this girl? She didn't look good; she looked anorexic. Her skin was messed, broken out, dirty. After turning on the faucet until the water ran hot, she pumped liquid soap into one hand and scrubbed at her face until it ached. Three or four inches of new growth was matted over the intricate spirals tattooed on the sides of her head, and that once spectacularly cool, blue Mohawk topped light brown hair. *Weird* was how she looked. Weird and sick, but the doctor said she was pretty. Maybe anyone under forty looked good to someone that old, because no one had ever called her pretty before.

She'd been called plenty of other names: The Whopper. Tiny. Miss Piggy. Fat shaming? That's how she grew up. She remembered cutting out gingerbread cookies with her Dad when she was five, maybe six, and her pencil thin mom stomped into the kitchen and huffed out dire predictions about high school and no dates to the prom. When she was nine, she'd plopped down on the teeter-totter in the playground and catapulted a first grader twenty feet into Pyracantha bushes. A week later the ground crew took the teeter-totter apart, a liability issue was how her teacher explained it. Right.

She was the girl whose books were knocked out of her hands, never the cool girl boys wanted to impress. But that doc said she was pretty. He needed new glasses.

Carly stuck her head under the faucet and rubbed hand soap into her hair. Not much in the way of suds, but it smelled clean—not like the rosemary shampoo she used at home but better than nothing—and the hot water rinsed away a week's worth of dirt. She blotted her hair with paper towels, then sat on the tile floor under the hand dryer and let the hot air blow on her head and neck until the chill departed. She removed the stud from her tongue and took the purple rhinestone out of her left nostril. She unscrewed the steel rings in her eyebrows and took out the nose ring. Then she stood to look in the mirror again. She'd lost her edge, that was for sure. Her eyes were bloodshot, and the skin around her nose was an ugly red. The girl staring back at her was exhausted, washed out, humbled, but not that frightening face the doc held up for her to see. She just needed some money, some money to get out of here and to get Terry out of here. She'd seen the track marks on his arm last Tuesday. Time to go. *Pronto.*

The library's staff break room was empty. She fingered Terry's three dollars and hoped for a vending machine, but there was only a microwave and a half fridge in the corner. No sounds in the hall. The paper sack in the fridge was somebody's lunch, but it was no one she knew, and they'd probably had a decent breakfast—a muffin on their way to work or a bowl of dry cereal sitting at the counter at home out of the cold. She slipped the paper sack under her coat, pressed her arm against it, ducked out the door, and casually sauntered back to her spot in the sunshine.

***

That evening, Lemon was in fine form prancing about. All he needed was a laser pointer to look like a scarecrow lecturing a class full of pumpkins. "A pebble in the shoe," he held up his finger, "and all anyone remembers is the limp. A perfect disguise. Or a bright scarf or a hat. That one detail will catch the eye, stick in the memory. Toss the scarf in the trash, and you're invisible."

But jaunty Lemon never put a pebble in his own shoe. He never snatched a wallet out of a diaper bag. Not Lemon. He waited a half block away and sent Nolan, Burt, Terry, or Carly and then extended his palm for the cash or *rent* as he called it. Pawns, that's what they were. Petty criminals. Her head ached, and she quit listening. She needed to sleep, but Lemon grabbed her attention when he started talking about the Eagle Gate.

Lemon's Adam's apple bobbed, and his gestures were broad. "We need an entree. A key to the city of gold." He turned toward her. "Miss Carly, any more thoughts about the greatest of all aunts?"

Carly pretended to be thinking it over. "No," she finally said. It was one thing to lift a couple of bucks out of a tip jar, but felonies were something else.

The previous week when Bill had arrived with the pizzas, Terry had whispered in her ear, "Lemon knows you're lying. They both know."

"No way."

"You can do lies," Terry had said, "but you can't tell them. You're transparent."

Sitting on the threadbare carpet, she felt transparent now. "I don't know where she is." Which was true. "She might have lived at the Eagle Gate once, but who knows where she is now." But if Aunt Maggie had died, someone, one of her mother's first cousins or an elderly neighbor with Maggie's address book in hand, would have called. Her mother would have teared up and mentioned her favorite aunt, Mary Margaret, the pretty one who'd worn a taffeta skirt at Christmas that rustled when Carly's mother was a little girl and easily impressed. Mary Margaret was the aunt with *The Story*, the hushed aside that was not mentioned in front of small second cousins too young for gossip about total disasters.

On the scent of easy cash, Lemon was not to be deterred. "How about a name? Something as simple as a name will further our cause."

Carly's bout of ragged coughing grabbed everyone's attention, then she took a couple of deep breaths. "My grandmother's maiden name was Sullivan, but my aunt's last name now? Married name? Who knows?"

A muted *bing* caught Lemon's attention, and he glanced at the text on his phone.

Terry looked right and left, then whispered hotly in her ear, "Don't go there. Tell him what you know."

"Troubling," Lemon glanced in her direction, "but surely you remember a first name. Auntie someone?" Lemon strung out the last syllable, and he leaned forward to hear what Carly might say.

A sick feeling turned in her stomach. "Mary. Mary Margaret."

"M and M. Easy to remember. Probably goes by Maggie or Mary or Meg." Lemon turned his attention to Nolan. "What did you discover about the Eagle Gate online?"

"Eighty-five units. Eight stories. No pets. Smoke free."

"Excellent. No yipping dogs. What about security cameras?"

"Five. One at each outside entrance."

It was well-maintained rental housing with elderly tenants—single still or single again. Couples and males would be the exception. A hundred plus residents. How did Lemon think he was going to find a woman named Maggie? Phone books were a relic of the past. Carly fingered the hole on the side of her nostril and squeezed her eyes shut, but there was no stopping this roller coaster about to crest the first peak.

"Anything else, Nolan, that you observed?"

"The UPS man. He went right in the front door. Fingered a keypad on the wall and got buzzed right in."

"Auntie's name is key. Forgive the pun," Lemon added. "Nolan has been useful, but it's time to utilize Terry's considerable talents."

According to Lemon's plan, when an elderly woman, or two or three, exited the building, Terry with all his boyish charm, hair clipped and sporting a relatively clean shirt and woolen scarf, would call out *Mary* or *Maggie*, as though he'd recognized a valued relation.

"The one who turns her head is our girl. Then Nolan will tail her." Carly glanced at the boy sitting beside her. Too bad they couldn't peel off that outer layer of leathery skin to reveal the boy beneath. "And before you know it, we'll have the details of her life." He gave Carly a meaningful stare. "That is when we'll insert you."

Like a knife in the back, she thought. "Why don't I just go to the front entrance— like the UPS guy—scan down the list of residents and announce myself, the long-lost niece? She beeps me in and there you are. Entree."

Dismayed, Lemon closed his eyes. "She'll know she's a target. This isn't about being overt. Your aunt must discover you, trust you." He squinted at her out of one eye, "That ratty blue mess on the top of your head has to go."

"Great," she said, "I'll make an appointment for a day at the spa."

Chapter Eleven

ARTIST IN RESIDENCE

PERFECT. THE PUMPKIN PIES WERE perfect. Tomorrow was Thanksgiving, and the warm smell of cinnamon and pumpkin filled Maggie's apartment as though a hungry crew would arrive any minute to celebrate the congenial holiday. Maggie inhaled and smiled. She did know how to make the perfect crust. She'd learned through the years that a beautiful crust disguised Thursday pie—a jumble of gravy, assorted leftover vegetables, bits of chicken, and a few noodles—as something gourmet to feed her kids, one last meal before she cashed her paycheck on Friday. She wiped her hands on the front of her apron before she undid the ties and tossed it over a straight-backed chair.

Wednesday night, *Midsomer Murders*. She grabbed the remote, settled into her easy chair, rested her bare feet on the worn ottoman, and then lifted her knitting into her lap. Pausing for a second or two, she exhaled slowly, realizing she was perfectly content. Before Rose had become fogged in like a summer day in San Francisco, she'd always said, "Happiness is a choice," like maybe Maggie had been making all these left turns on purpose, but Maggie didn't buy that, not for a minute. Nope. Happiness was a collection of stolen moments: a comfortable chair that didn't need to be new, wonderful smells from the kitchen, a ball of deep purple worsted wool in her lap, and British mysteries on the television.

Telly was how she referred to it when she talked to herself. *Well, Maggie, old girl, what shall we watch on the telly tonight?* she'd say as though the woman who brushed her teeth after dinner was a friendly Brit, and they shared inside jokes or held common opinions about this and that. They obviously had the same face, heart shaped and green eyed; the same hairstyle, soft and silver; and the same clothes, pants and hand-knit cardigans with novelty buttons, unless religious observance forced her reflection into wearing a dress and pantyhose. If she complained into the mirror with "Let's miss The News Hour tonight," the woman in the mirror invariably agreed; she was so obliging. "The news is so depressing." So they settled for murder instead, clever murders somewhere else, in Oxford, in Surrey, in the Lake Country. No tragic real-life dramas. No thugs carousing in fast cars. No random shootings. No hand wringing. Just a couple of tongue-in-cheek deaths.

The colorful stack of hats was growing in the plastic bag next to her chair. Black Friday was in two days, and there was a serious demand for her hats, which surprised her and made her smile. She sold them at Hip and Humble on Ninth and Ninth.

"Whatever you can give me, I can sell," the exhausted owner had said with a smile as she stacked bottles of pricy fabric softener on a glass shelf. Hip and Humble sold an eclectic collection of gifts and was the perfect venue for an artist-in-residence, which is how Isabelle Yanguez referred to Maggie.

A sample hat in hand, Maggie had acted on a whim and stopped at Hip and Humble the last week in June on her way home from Blazing Needles where she worked two mornings a week and on Knit Night every Thursday. On Friday mornings Maggie taught the ten o'clock classes on stocking caps or cardigans with raglan sleeves or colorful stockings in a variety of patterns—the Easy Peasy Socks class. In November and December, the Santa sock pattern was everyone's favorite. On Monday mornings, she sat at the round oak table in the rear of the store and unraveled mistakes made over the weekend. She clucked and encouraged neophyte knitters as she arranged the yarn through awkward fingers. She explained yarn overs and slip, knit and pass. She made friends with fresh-faced women half her age. She laughed at their jokes and smiled wisely when they complained about husbands and money and elementary school teachers who didn't understand how extraordinary their children really were.

If Maggie was a fraud, no one knew it. Three years ago, at Rose's insistence, she'd introduced herself to the owner of Blazing Needles. "I'm Mrs. Sullivan. And I think you need me." Both feet planted on the wooden floor, she'd waited as Mrs. Yanguez studied the sweater Maggie was wearing, a beautiful display of cables and seed stitching in three soft shades of gray with a shawl collar that rolled perfectly against Maggie's slender neck and reflected the silver in her hair. The sweater was her magnum opus, her *piece de resistance*, her impressive resume in merino wool.

Mrs. Yanguez nodded, and the bamboo needles holding her coil of dark hair in place bobbed up and down. "Mrs. Sullivan, I do need you. Can you do a pattern search on the internet?"

"Not yet."

"Well, let's talk." She led Maggie into her crowded office, a galley kitchen from the shop's past life, where the cupboards were stuffed with new inventory encased in plastic and dozens of boxes of green tea. "First name?" She pulled a form out of a two-drawer filing cabinet.

"Maggie. Maggie Sullivan." She twisted her mother's wedding band on her little finger. She'd worn it that morning for luck. The three small diamonds sparkled at her, and if her mother were standing at her shoulder smiling, Maggie wouldn't have been surprised.

"What about two mornings a week? Ten to noon? And Thursday night? Five to eight? Friday you could teach a class. Something simple in the beginning until you develop a clientele. I can pay you fifteen dollars an hour. And if you could come in on Mondays and just be here, that would be great. I think of Monday as fix-the-weekend-disaster's morning. Of course, that's not something I'd ever say out loud." She rattled on, "Help knitters correct their mistakes. Help people select yarn and patterns if you're not busy. I can't teach and sell at the same time." She leaned forward as though she were about to share something secretive. "I really don't have the cash flow to pay you for Thursday night, but I could pay you in yarn. Two hanks. Anything you like."

"I would love that." So pleased, her eyes felt teary, Maggie pressed her hand against her chest.

"Before Monday, decide what your first class will be, and I'll announce it in our online newsletter. Marketing. I hate it, but what can you do?" Mrs. Yanguez stabbed one knitting needle into her hair more firmly. "Would you like a cup of tea? Coffee?"

"Thanks, but I don't indulge."

"No tea, no coffee, no glass of red wine at the end of the day?"

Maggie nodded.

"We get all kinds in here." Mrs. Yanguez smiled. "Young, old, you name it. A tattoo artist is one of my best customers, and Gloria Mayfield, she's a stripper in a club on North Main. She comes in a couple of times a month, says she knits between sets. And thank Heaven for gay men; they love to knit. Honestly, they keep the shop afloat."

"I'm an all-kinds type of person. You don't need to worry about me." Maggie wanted to say that she had spent twenty-seven years living in Fremont Park and had worked as a receptionist for a trucking company—long-haul truckers, some sweet and some decidedly not—but instead she brushed her past to the side. "If you have any reservations, let's have a trial period. Two months?"

The bell on the front door tinkled, and Mrs. Yanguez rose from her chair. "I'll see you on Monday."

Maggie couldn't make herself leave. She ran her hands across the colorful skeins, pulled the yarn through her fingers, drank in the musty smell of wool. Closing her eyes when Mrs. Yanguez wasn't looking, she imagined herself as a figure in a Renoir painting. Never dying because she was fixed forever in oil on canvas in the Museum d'Orsay. A brass plaque on the frame would read, *Woman in a Yarn Shop*. People would sigh, *Oh drink in those colors*. How wonderful. How delightful.

Over the past two years, Mrs. Yanguez had become Isabelle, and she picked Maggie up when the weather turned nasty and always drove her home on Thursday nights after they closed the shop together.

Tonight Maggie turned up the volume on the telly before she reached for a crocheted flower and whip stitched it onto a hat. A hot-pink flower on a dark-purple field. She held the finished product in one outstretched hand and admired the even knitting, the intricate pattern that ended in a pompom. Twenty adorable hand-knit hats. Four hours of knitting per hat. A half hour to crochet the flower. She cleared seventeen dollars apiece.

As the perfect Christmas gift for high school girls or cousins or sisters, the hats were carefully stacked, ready to deliver to Hip and Humble on Friday morning before she made her way to Blazing Needles. She'd need to catch Bus 217 at a quarter past nine, transfer at Seventh East, make her delivery before the store officially opened, and then hurry to the yarn shop. The knitted equivalent of $340 sat in two white plastic bags. She'd sold twenty-three hats already and had the bills tucked inside a brown drawstring bag next to her socks and pantyhose. She didn't know why that bit of cash lightened her mind, made her hold her head a little higher, made her say with a careless toss of her hair, "Why not?" when Sue suggested a matinee at the Broadway.

A quick rap on the door startled her. It was nearly eight, but Rose was getting more nocturnal as the weeks went by. Maggie was prepared to usher her back to her apartment, but it was Jan's face she saw through the peephole in the door.

"Do you have a minute? I know it's late."

"Never too late for a friend."

But Jan was uncomfortable and shuffled a bit from foot to foot.

"Come in." Maggie moved a couple of library books off a chair and nudged her worn shoes under the table.

"I know we're getting paranoid about those kids," Jan spoke as though she were somehow embarrassed, as though age and vulnerability were a character flaw that could be resolved with gritty determination, "but the other day when we were walking past City Creek, I heard someone call your name."

"I remember." The voice had been lilting and clear, and Maggie had glanced around for Lynette Williams, a high school friend with perfect pitch, until she remembered Lynette had succumbed to a virulent strain of pneumonia three years before. People, voices, memories scattered in her head like loose snapshots spread across the living room floor.

"I didn't think anything about it," Jan said, "but Monday morning I was looking out the window at the plaza, and I could swear a kid followed you to the bus stop."

Maggie's toes curled automatically, and she took a sharp breath. At nine thirty in the morning, the people riding the bus weren't the criminally insane; they were just tired people going to minimum-wage jobs that didn't deliver enough cash to make a car payment. No three-piece suits on the bus, no platform heels or expensive haircuts, just the working poor. *Me*, Maggie thought. No thugs.

"He was a little thick, and his skin was leathery, like a farmer, someone who spends days in the sun, but white from the eyebrows up, like he wore a baseball cap all summer." Jan unconsciously made a fist as she added more details. "He wasn't wearing a hat that day, but he was bundled up."

"That morning was cold." Maggie had been wearing boots with a firm tread, but nevertheless, she'd been concerned about patches of ice near the bus stop, not a young man with a pale forehead who was bundled in a nondescript coat.

Jan edged nearer the couch and sat down. "Have you seen him before? Is he a regular?"

People on the bus don't make eye contact, don't chat, don't smile, don't tell funny stories about the previous night. They're exhausted before their workday begins because most are heading to a second job. Maggie thumped the side of her forehead and tried to remember fellow riders. There was a lady who wore a plaid coat, a Latino who wore a white apron under a jacket, and an elderly man who had a distinctive odor that made Maggie turn away, but a boy with a white forehead? No memory of anyone like that. She bit down on her bottom lip, then shook her head.

"Probably nothing." Jan exhaled through her nose. Duty done. Warning posted.

"Are you going to spend tomorrow with your son?" Maggie asked.

"Ah yes. The perfect day. Four meaningful hours. The three of us around a lump of tofu shaped like a bird with a couple of pheasant feathers stuck in its rear end. Always exciting. No butter. No cream unless a cow dropped by to make a personal offering. No eggs. But lots of whole grains, root vegetables, and a variety of nuts."

"I'll save you a wedge of pie."

"With any luck, I'll be back before five." Jan still owned a car and all the freedom that came with an insurance premium.

"I have *Ben Hur*. We could watch it together," Maggie offered.

"Can we rewind the chariot race? Two or three times?"

Maggie laughed. "Of course. Perfect end to the day."

Chapter Twelve

BLACK FRIDAY

BLACK FRIDAY DIDN'T FEEL THE least bit black to Maggie, at least not in the morning. Under her good wool coat, she was wearing her favorite gray cardigan and a starched white shirt she'd ironed the night before. The wind was frigid, but when she climbed onto Bus 217, the driver smiled as she flashed him her senior pass. "You don't look a day over sixty."

"Oh, Mort, you're such a joker." She touched his shoulder as she walked past.

"Not me, not for a minute."

Warm and smelling of diesel, the interior felt muggy; she didn't know why. Maybe wet feet and twenty or thirty people exhaling in unison filled the bus with an invisible cloud that never coalesced into rain. Clutching her bags of adorable knit hats, she sat near the front and looked past the fogged windows at the dirty snow piled along the streets. The lights in Temple Square would be lit tonight, and tomorrow the crowds flocking downtown would make exercising with Jan difficult, but Jan would have a detour planned. No question about that. Humming *I Heard it Through the Grapevine*—the movie *The Big Chill* a vivid memory in her mind from the previous afternoon—she made the transfer to Bus 87 and then exited on Eighth South and walked briskly to Hip and Humble. She left ten minutes later with $340 dollars hidden in the lining of her purse, and those crisp bills felt like a million bucks.

She was, perhaps, not an astute businesswoman, but she was certainly a competent seventy-four-year-old person managing her own life. She straightened her shoulders and walked the eight blocks to Blazing Needles, resolutely skirting the frozen puddles on the sidewalk and ignoring the stiff wind in her face. Bells jangled when she opened the front door, but so early in the morning, the yarn shop was still, the wooden floors were neatly covered with rag rugs, and the smell of brewing coffee filled the back room. Christmas balls hung on silver ribbons in the windows and tinsel was draped over just about everything. Knitted stuffed elephants, pigs, and hippos peeked out from behind yarn displays as though they were children playing hide-and-seek. Red cheeked from the cold, Maggie inhaled deeply in a satisfied way as she hung up her coat. This shop felt like a second home. Wearing her holiday sweater, a delightful hand knit with a green tree and sequins, Isabelle hurried around the corner and gave Maggie a quick hug.

"I have to tell you, today and tomorrow are going to be nuts with people wanting to start a handmade gift that will be impossible to finish before Christmas. The word to remember is *simplify*, or just sell them whatever they want and suggest it would make a lovely gift for Valentine's."

Maggie nodded.

Isabelle swiped her hand across her forehead. "I never discourage anyone from buying yarn. The tax man cometh."

Maggie laughed, lifted a frosted sugar cookie from a tray on the counter, and nibbled the corner. Five minutes later, at ten o'clock, the bells on the front door started ringing and every entering person brought in a whoosh of chill air. *Christmas*, she thought, *is in the air,* and she smiled. She loved the holidays.

The shop had been someone's home in its past life, and the room where Maggie taught her classes must have been a comfortable dining room with a fireplace in the corner. It was never used now, but more knitted animals and pattern books were displayed on the mantle. Some of Maggie's regulars sat around the oak table, chatting and pulling projects out of a variety of bags and satchels or waiting, hands in laps, to learn something new. Most had become her friends—there was just something companionable about knitters—they were a comfortable lot, warm-hearted people without sharp corners or quick words, people who fit nicely in overstuffed couches or chairs.

She passed out instructions for an abbreviated version of the hats she'd been knitting, more of a headband, an excellent teaching tool with increases and seed stitches and a couple of twisted cables down the center. With hands raised to shoulder level, she was demonstrating the intricate twist with rose-colored yarn and size four needles, when a girl shuffled into the shop.

She was a pretty young thing with short brown hair framing her pale face. She tried to stifle a thick cough in the crook of her arm as she sat quietly at the end of the table. Her faded parka hung loosely on her body, and her jeans were dirty and torn on both knees. She didn't have yarn or needles, didn't ask questions, and it was a half hour into the class when everyone else was busy knitting and chatting that Maggie finally had a moment to give the girl attention.

"Have you ever tried knitting before?" she spoke softly.

The girl shook her head.

"Would you like to try the headband? Maybe skip the cables to keep it simple until you get the knack?"

The girl nodded.

"I could help you pick out some yarn." Maggie was afraid for a moment the girl was mute or, worse, left-handed, a knitting teacher's nightmare, but the child finally spoke.

"How many balls will it take? The headband."

"Just one." They stood from the table and looked in the four-dollar sale basket sitting on the floor, because apparently this little waif had blown in through the front door without any notion of what knitting truly entailed. Maggie wondered if what the girl really wanted was a place to get warm on such a cold day, and she regretted the hearth was full of chunky weight Brooklyn Tweed and not a comfortable fire. "If this is for you, that soft teal will look well with your eyes, or maybe this is a gift?"

The girl drifted over to the knitting needles and bit her bottom lip, something Maggie did herself when counting the cost of things she couldn't afford.

"I have a pair of size five needles that I can loan you to get started. I'll grab them from the back," from her purse that she'd hidden under the sink after she'd tucked half of her cash under the elastic of her bra. Not the full amount—she didn't want an obvious bulge. She wrapped a couple of cookies in a napkin and poured hot tea and a rounded teaspoon of sugar into a plastic cup to ease the girl's cough.

When Maggie returned to the table, the girl pulled a wad of grimy bills from her pocket and counted out four as if each dollar were a treasure she was loath to lose.

"I'll put those in the till when I get a minute." Maggie nudged the cookies and tea in the girl's direction. "It's getting close to lunch." She took up the needle and the yarn and demonstrated casting on, unraveled the stitches, and said, "Now let's have you try."

The girl's nails were bitten down to the quick, and bloody scabs covered her cuticles. Maggie took care not to sigh. She threaded the yarn through the girl's chapped fingers before she touched the girl's right hand and guided the needle. "This works just like the tension on a sewing machine."

"I've never sewed."

"No, of course not. No one sews anymore, do they? But knitting is an art. And the feel of wool in your fingers is soothing, all that repetitive motion. I think you'll enjoy it."

But the girl was so awkward it was as though she were holding dozens of prickly needles in all manner of sizes—not just two. She'd only knitted three rows and it was nearly noon when Isabelle glanced in the room with her eyebrows raised and mouthed, "*Help*." The shop was bustling, and a crowd of knitters was pressing around the counter that held the cash register.

"I'll be here tomorrow and again on Monday if you need me." The girl needed Remedial Knitting 101, resource knitting, but she wasn't the first knitter to begin slowly, and if ever a child needed the therapy of wool and needles, this girl was it. "I'm Maggie," she added.

Her arm halfway through the sleeve of her coat, the girl paused and took a long, drawn-out breath before she looked Maggie straight in the eye—the first time that morning—and said, "I'm Carly," with the quiet finality of a judge passing sentence, and then the girl glanced around the room and waited.

"Well, Miss Carly, I think a headband will be just the thing to keep those ears warm." And standing close to her, Maggie noticed a dozen empty holes in her ear lobes, one in her left nostril, and a couple in each eyebrow. The girl looked like she'd been attacked by a miniscule paper punch. She coughed again, a deep, rumbling cough, and wiped a bit of phlegm from her mouth with the edge of her napkin. "More tea?" Maggie asked. "For the road?"

The girl nodded, but when Maggie returned, the girl was gone. The door chimes jingled. The crumpled dollar bills sat on the table. She only counted three, and she knew there had been four. Poor little thing. She doubted she'd ever see the girl again.

Chapter Thirteen

THE BELLY OF THE BEAST

The morning's brisk wind had blown in a blizzard. Exhausted by six thirty and feeling guilty about abandoning Isabelle to restock alone, Maggie eyed the blowing snow through the bus windows and made that last leap between the bottom step and the curb in front of Eagle Gate. Fearful of slipping and breaking her neck—or, worse, a hip—she paused, took a quick breath of freezing air, and made sure she had her balance before she took another step into the falling snow and an unexpected commotion.

Her palm pressed against her mouth, she felt like an extra in one of the British mysteries she loved, except this was startlingly real. Two emergency vehicles, lights pulsing red and white against the snowy darkness, were parked on the concrete plaza. The building's front doors were propped open. Uniformed EMTs hustled in and out. Microphones clipped to their chests squawked. Clutching her purse against her stomach, Maggie stepped cautiously through the inches of new snow to an elderly threesome in hats and coats standing outside in the cold. Snow settled on their shoulders that none bothered to brush away. She recognized the Badgers immediately—they'd lived on her floor for six years—but it took her a minute to place the man standing beside them.

She'd met him the day before at the Thanksgiving dinner in the common room off the lobby. Graciously passing his tray of gourmet hors d'oeuvres—chestnuts wrapped in bacon glazed with brown sugar and speared with a frilly toothpick—he'd waited at her elbow until she had to meet his eye or be unforgivably rude.

"Ed. I live in 8-B," he'd smiled and then paused.

"Maggie," she'd replied.

They'd both laughed; but nevertheless, it was an awkward moment because she'd been surprised to see him. She'd crashed into him last week on the sidewalk in front of the Lion House. He was the man who had spoken her name so warmly. This person was one of the holiday orphans? This man with the thousand-light tree in the penthouse? Cautiously, she'd nibbled on the chestnut he'd offered.

Now here he was again, standing silently with the Badgers in wind-whipped snow.

Gesturing with a mittened hand toward the emergency vehicles, she mumbled, "What's happened?" Her voice was so weak she doubted anyone heard her.

But the man turned toward her, recognized her, and spoke with all the seriousness the occasion required. "A terrible accident." He leaned heavily on his cane as though the weight of the disaster were a physical burden. "There's been a terrible accident."

Flakes of snow turned to droplets on her glasses, and she shivered, before she repeated, "What happened?"

"Down in the storage units, someone dislodged a box, and two other heavy boxes fell on top of her. She couldn't free herself or maybe she hit her head. I don't know. Poor woman laid there most of the day. Paulo found her when he came on duty at six."

Faithful Paulo would have checked for a pulse and then cradled her head, alive or not, in his lap on the chill concrete floor under glaring florescent lights as he waited for the ambulance to arrive.

"Who was she?" Maggie knew everyone in the building, their stories, their symptoms and surgeries, and the names of their children.

He shook his head dislodging the layer of snow on his hat. His eyes flickered away. "I don't know." He was lying.

A gurney—with a uniformed man on each side—rolled through the front doors and across the concrete toward a vehicle with *Larkin Mortuary* in bold lettering on the side. She hadn't noticed it until this moment, the hearse waiting with rear doors open. Mr. 8-B—she couldn't begin to remember his name—knew who was under that sheet. If he couldn't speak the name, it must be someone she loved. She started to weave back and forth. Her knees buckled, and he grabbed her forearm.

"Steady there. Let's get you inside. Out of the weather."

But Maggie couldn't move, couldn't force her eyes away from the gurney, because she knew as surely as if she could see the hidden face. It was Rose. Her Rosie. No point in asking questions, not now. Nothing else mattered. Rose was under that sheet.

Twenty feet below ground level, Rose had dislodged a box of books or kitchen equipment, and an avalanche of her possessions had buried her all day before anyone realized she was missing. Just Wednesday afternoon, Maggie and Sue had hauled up three boxes of garlands, lights, red-cheeked Santas, and an entire miniature village to decorate Rosie's apartment, so why was Rose down in that lonely vault alone? What was she looking for? *Why didn't she wait until I came home?* Maggie thought, trying to piece the fragments together, trying to unwind what had happened, trying to understand a world without Rosie.

Two men lifted the body into the hearse. Rose didn't weigh much.

Falling snow softened the sounds of doors closing. An EMT reached into the cab of the emergency vehicle and turned off the lights, leaving the plaza shrouded in snow and darkness. The hearse moved slowly off the concrete, over the curb, and onto South Temple. The curious drifted away. Paulo closed the front doors. With her feet fixed to the pavement, Maggie stood staring at the place where the hearse had parked as though she could will it to return and Rosie would jump out of the back and laugh at scaring her nearly to death. Her bottom lip trembled, and Maggie brushed a frozen tear with the back of her mitten. Mrs. Badger gave her a hug before she and her husband tottered off to the building, leaving 8-B and Maggie alone in the snowstorm, the cold from the concrete penetrating her feet as if she were standing on a sheet of ice.

No words were needed. He knew that she knew. "Let's go inside. Out of the wind." His free hand on her elbow, he guided her through the snow and past the doors to the lobby and toward the elevator. He hit seven and the button lit. The doors closed with a mechanical whir. He was taller than she was, no stoop in those shoulders. The man had a presence, no doubt about that. A quick impression darted through her head. How did he know she lived on seven? She hadn't mentioned her apartment number when he'd offered her a chestnut the day before.

"I don't want to intrude," his head bent toward her, "but you shouldn't be alone. You've had a terrible shock. Can I fix you something? A cup of tea? Hot wassail? I have some in my fridge I could nuke in a minute."

But at that moment the elevator door opened, and there was Sue flying down the hall, her caftan billowing behind and her cheeks smeared with tears and mascara. "Rosie, Rosie." Her hands fluttered wildly like trapped birds. "Maggie, have you heard?"

Jan called their names through her open door. Neither Maggie nor Sue noticed the man step back into the elevator or watched the doors close with a soft whoosh.

Jan plunked a box of Kleenex down on the coffee table, and the three women sat on the couch sobbing—with bits of talk interspersed.

"Down in the belly of the beast." Sue raised her eyebrows. "Did anyone hear her call? At least for the first hour or two? Did Aleph notice anything? At all?" Sue daubed at her nose with a tissue. "That human blob has got to go."

"There are security cameras down there. At least two. I've seen them," Maggie said.

"What was she getting?" Jan asked. "What was she after? Why was she alone?"

Maggie shrugged. "More decorations? Pictures." Or maybe she'd needed to touch a baby sweater, or her husband's worn golf bag, or a wedding album, maybe her own. Memories. Possessions. Pieces of her life in a chicken-wire storage unit, and then her life ended there, her body slowly growing cold under the jumble of cardboard boxes. All alone, Rosie's life had ebbed away.

"Who found her?" Jan needed details.

"Paulo. The door into the storage units wasn't shut tightly when he started his shift, so he went to look. He called 911, but it was too late. She was gone," Sue said. "Bless that boy."

Her forehead cupped in her hand, Maggie stared at the beige carpet. She couldn't believe any of this. It just wasn't real. Rose gone? How could that be? "We need to go down there and have a look around."

"What?" Jan said. "I didn't hear you."

"We need to go down there and look around."

"Maggie, she's gone." Sue gazed at her sadly as though Maggie were somehow behind schedule. "No bringing her back."

"What was she looking for?"

"It doesn't matter," Jan said. "We're not going anywhere."

Sue sighed. "She was confused, agitated about something. She had been for a few days. A sliver of a memory just out of her reach."

"In a couple of days," Maggie whispered through her tears, "or maybe next week. We need to look. I need to know what took her away from me. My Rose. My precious Rose."

Part Two

Chapter Fourteen

A LOVELY GESTURE

THE NEXT MORNING MAGGIE DIDN'T call in sick, she called in distraught and difficult to understand. Isabelle, the owner of Blazing Needles, was all kindness and understanding and told Maggie to stay home as long as she needed. She'd call her mother-in-law to lend a hand with the holiday rush. Maggie was not to worry. And she didn't worry. She sat on the couch, on a chair, on the edge of her bed, as if she sat very still, she might fade away altogether. She stared out the window at the Alta Club, that solid gray shape that didn't move or change. She didn't pick up the phone. There was no one to call, no magical number to punch, no 1-800-BRING-BACK-ROSE.

For two days, she and Jan and Sue drifted in and out of each other's apartments. If she encountered anyone in the hall, she'd receive heartfelt expressions of sympathy, but Maggie had a hard time understanding their words. It was as if they were blurred or spoken in a foreign language. She focused on faces instead and smiled at the soft touches on her arm. Was she having a dozen miniscule strokes, a platoon of stray blood clots meandering through her carotids? But no rushing to call a doctor, no one yelling STAT in a panic, or roaring for an ambulance. Alone in her apartment, she whispered, "Rose, do you need me to come with you?" but Rose was uncharacteristically silent.

On Tuesday, Sue entered Maggie's apartment with a newspaper clipping in one hand. "The obit. You're mentioned, which is a lovely gesture: *survived by hundreds of grieving relations, and her dear friend, Mary Margaret Sullivan.* And Rose's son called me. Evidently, you're not answering your phone." Over her half-moon glasses—today they were lilac—she gave Maggie a disapproving nod. "They want you to say a few words at the funeral on Saturday."

"Impossible." Maggie shook her head slowly.

"Evidently, Rose left a detailed funeral plan. Flowers, music, coffin, and Maggie delivers the keynote. Five minutes." And then Sue reached for Maggie's hand. She wasn't a touchy feely sort of person, and so the gesture was significant. "Time to rejoin the living, Maggie. Rose wouldn't want you to throw yourself on the pyre."

Maggie squeezed both eyes shut. "What will I say?"

"Who knows? But this is Rose's way to jump start you back to reality. You'll be so freaked out about talking in front of three or four hundred strangers that you'll forget to be comatose."

Maggie felt a smile inching onto her face. *That Rose*, she thought, because of course Sue was right. Maggie was being nudged from the edge of the grave.

"No post-mortem whitewash. Rose doesn't want anything sappy." Sue plunked herself down on the couch. "I did a quick drive-by through the lobby, and everyone's overreacting."

Maggie shook her head. Sue wasn't making sense.

Sue began again, speaking more slowly. "Fifty percent of our fellow residents are sporting something new." She raised her eyebrows. "A thin black cord under their blouses and shirts. Med-alert buttons. In the elevator, collecting mail, in the pool, everyone's talking about relative costs, benefits, and response times of a half dozen different companies. Everyone's telling the same stories over and over like they've lost their minds and not just their hearing."

Trying to cheer her friend, Sue cleared her throat and began theatrically, "A woman in Westbank, Montana, fell over her couch and only the scent of rotting meat would have alerted her friends," Sue raised both hands with a flourish, "if not for the magic of her med-alert button. An elderly stockbroker—in excellent health—slipped on black ice in a parking terrace and was saved from imminent death in the frigid darkness by Alert Response's Sudden Altitude Sensor. In both cases, disaster was averted by the arrival of EMTs in a matter of milliseconds." Maggie just sat staring at her hands. Sue finally rose and moved toward the door. "Have a shower. Jan is meeting us at ten. We're going to check out the basement. See if we can understand what Rose was after. Maybe if we can answer some questions, we can have a little closure." And then she was gone, her ankle-length caftan trailing behind her.

An hour later, wrapped in a towel, Maggie stood in her bathroom pondering all Sue had said. Thirty to fifty dollars a month for a med-alert necklace? What did it matter? And besides, anyone stretching an already stretched budget would gasp at the price tag. It felt like high school all over again. "But, Mom, everyone's going. But, Mom, everyone's got one." Maggie shook her head at the silver-haired friend brushing her teeth in the mirror. *Sorry, we can't afford this particular necklace. You'll have to make do.* If Maggie was absent for more than a couple of hours, one of her friends would start asking questions, call Paulo Ferrante, the newly named chief of security, and organize a search-and-rescue party. At least she hoped someone would notice if she was missing.

The excursion to the subterranean floors felt like a trip to the bottom of a dry well. Maggie tried to tell herself morbid fear had nothing to do with their descent, but the florescent lights exposed them all, every wrinkle, every misplaced strand of hair, every unanswered question. Sue didn't speak as they tiptoed down the silent corridor to Rose's storage unit, adjacent to Maggie's own.

No yellow crime scene tape. The wire gate was open. Colored snapshots lay scattered across the concrete floor. An opened college yearbook rested on top of a box with loose flaps. Two heavy boxes had been shoved to one side. They weren't labeled "the cause of death," but they looked suspicious and were probably the very boxes that had knocked Rose to the floor. Maggie gave one a serious kick. She hoped they'd tumbled unseen from the top of the stack. She hoped it was quick and painless, because this wasn't a fitting end for Rosie. She should have been resting on plumped pillows and should have breathed her last with a smile on her face surrounded by the family who adored her.

Jan turned a page in the yearbook. "Sigma Chi's. 1959."

"Let me see that." Maggie reached for the annual. "That's Carl." She pointed. "Rosie's husband. Third row." One familiar face in a group of thirty self-satisfied faces grinning for the camera. She couldn't believe they'd ever been that young and had such bad hair.

No rhyme or reason for the dozens of scattered photos, many of which were unlabeled shots of the Kimball boys at various ages hamming it up. Sue was scooping them up, stuffing them back into the box.

"She was here for the yearbook," Maggie said. "The snapshots slipped out."

"Or perhaps in a moment of lucidity," Sue suggested, "Rose wanted to organize all these pictures into an album to archive?"

"I doubt it. The last couple of years, she wasn't into organizing." Maggie turned away from the mountain of boxes. "She was trying to trigger a memory." If Rose was true to form, she was trying to help someone, and Maggie had a nagging feeling that someone was her. She touched the yearbook again and flipped back a few pages. Had her life and Rosie's overlapped in some curious way long before their backyards joined?

Jan touched Maggie's shoulder. "Come on, girls. Let's rejoin the living."

***

That evening after the tears had stopped and Jan and Sue had retreated to their own apartments, a rap on her door startled Maggie. Her friends never bothered to knock; they just stuck their heads in the door and called out, "Are you home?" But this was a firm sound, an insistent noise, and Maggie set her knitting on the floor and rose from her couch.

Mr. 8-B was standing outside her door, his cane raised, ready to rap a second time and perhaps a third. He looked armed and dangerous, but the steaming pot of soup in his left hand gave him away.

"You know I'm fairly new here and not sure of protocols, but I've been working in the kitchen all afternoon, and I really don't want to take this home." The gesture was meant to be kind, but his pot of soup seemed oddly irrelevant given the depth of her loss. Perhaps that showed on her face, because he said, "I'll just set this on your counter and be on my way."

Maggie felt uncomfortable standing at the door with a stranger who was behaving like he'd been assigned a task he wasn't keen on doing. Why was he here? The bishop had already visited, and her ministering brothers, Brother Jones and Brother Philden, had been by twice.

Maggie wasn't raised to be rude, and so she took a step back. "Please, come in. I'd love a cup of your soup." Although she'd flushed the remains of a half-eaten peanut butter sandwich down the disposal just ten minutes earlier. She stepped out of her doorway. "Will you have some with me?"

"That would be nice." He was dressed in slacks, a pullover, and a starched shirt—all expensive—that hung loosely on his tall, angular frame, but the lingering cooking odor interested her most. She hadn't consumed anything hot in three days.

The light from a single lamp didn't reach the dark corners of her living room, and the Christmas lights around the sliding glass door seemed a bit garish, all things considered. She saw her shabby furnishings though his eyes, her comfortable couch with a split in one cushion, an ancient television with an electronic contraption on top sprouting cables and wires, and pictures—dozens of framed pictures—of her children and grandchildren propped on every flat surface. A week or two ago, she might have experienced a moment of shame, but not today. Today none of that mattered. Rosie was gone.

A mug in one hand and a spoon in the other, Mr. 8-B and Maggie mirrored each other in mismatched chairs on either side of her dining room table that was cluttered with odd pieces of mail, a program from church, and her ever-present Scrabble game. The soup was unusual, a corn chowder with bits of scallop, and she thought she detected a jalapeño pepper. Interesting. Worthy of a compliment and definitely not something out of a can or a carton from the deli. Completely surprised, she said, "I've never personally known a male cook. That sounds totally sexist, but it's the truth."

"In one of my past lives," he confided, "I was a chef in a large institution. Later, when I could afford better ingredients, I took up cooking again." He shrugged. "A hobby."

"Better than knitting baby sweaters that have to be hand washed." Worn once before being wrapped in tissue and tucked in the back of a drawer.

"I'm sorry about your friend." He dove right in as though he needed to clarify the reason for his visit—this was a condolence call, nothing more. "Had you known her long?"

"Rose? Just nearly forever. We were next-door neighbors when our kids were little. Best friend, mentor, spiritual advisor, sister, Obi Wan Kenobi, that was Rosie, all rolled into one petite fireball." Surprised at her own forthcoming, she absently stirred the soup with her spoon. "We'd only been in our house for a week when my mother came to help and was watching the neighborhood kids play in the dirt." No grass, not for another year. "And my mother said, 'What a cute bunch of kids.' She didn't realize one of the kids was actually the mom."

He gave a polite chuckle and glanced around the room as if he couldn't recall where he was, and she wondered if he'd heard anything she'd just said.

"Forgive me," she sighed. "I've forgotten your name. Sue's always warning us that *names are the first things to go*."

"Ed Johnson." He studied her face. "Not as ordinary as Jim Smith, but close. There must be at least five thousand Johnsons in the Salt Lake directory."

But this man wasn't ordinary at all. She guessed he'd had trouble of his own, because his polite manner was cautious, almost wary, and he chose his words carefully. His jaw was strong, and he had a thick head of white hair and frank blue eyes. It was difficult to imagine him dishing out scoops of mashed potatoes or overcooked peas; he was too well spoken.

"So," he continued, "Rose Kimball was a close friend."

"Sisters with different mothers," she said, which seemed like a silly thing to say. Feeling embarrassed for making such a mundane remark, Maggie wished he would leave.

"You were lucky to have her as a friend. Men don't make friends that easily. We don't confide or share our stories with other men. We're more likely to compliment a friend on his tee shot or a twenty-foot putt." When she didn't respond, he asked, "Do you have other family? A sister with the *same* mother?"

"I did. She was older than I am. Ten years older."

"Nieces? Nephews?" It was a safe question to string out a conversation.

"One. My sister married when she was older and only had one daughter, and that daughter married when she was older and only had one daughter. Two generations of only children who've grown up believing the sun revolves around them." She found herself smiling. "My niece lives in Northern California and her first husband died," she said as though the two things were connected, and the husband had succumbed to a pine-related fungus. "She remarried a man with three children, and I haven't heard much from her since." She didn't intend to criticize her niece, but her tone implied that the situation was difficult, which was something she didn't know but only surmised. Maggie tried to take a more positive stance. "Her little girl is as sharp as a tack. Caroline. Goodness, she must be almost seventeen or eighteen."

She'd said too much, rattled on without saying anything worth knowing, whined about an inattentive niece, spread ridiculous gossip about people he couldn't know. She closed her eyes and visualized this tall man walking out her door. And then he shocked her by saying, "Let's get out of here tomorrow night. You and me. Walk over to City Creek and people watch. Maybe catch an early dinner?"

"I work at a yarn shop on Thursday evenings." She sat a little straighter.
"Tomorrow's Wednesday."
She felt like a dope. She'd lost a day and her excuse.
"We could go early," he said, "and be back by seven or eight?"
Maggie amazed herself by responding, "That would be nice."
And then he left, almost abruptly.

Other than the occasional visit with her bishop or the heated exchanges with Mr. Padilla about his barking dogs, Maggie's conversations with adult males—of more than twenty words—were limited to five first dates in thirty-four years. Former friends had advertised her as "shy but lovely" and lined her up with a variety of willing men, but after a couple of evenings of awkward exchanges, those willing men rarely called a third time. In her twenty-five years at Bethlehem Trucking, two or three hundred truck drivers had stopped by her desk for paychecks, messages, or forms for medical leave, but none had ever approached her to suggest a cup of coffee, or a movie, a stroll through the park, or to escort her to her car in the parking lot in this industrial side of town. Nothing. One afternoon her boss had sauntered in from the back office and said, "Maggie, it wouldn't kill you to smile once in a while."

"This is my minimum wage face," she'd said. "This is what comes with a two-dollar raise," and she'd flashed him a thousand-watt smile and an exaggerated wink.

"You just got your raise," and he'd laughed, backing into his office, "but dial it back a bit or we'll be knee deep in truckers in front of your desk."

When he'd left, she'd rested her head on her desk and squeezed her eyes shut. Some days smiling just wasn't in her repertoire—until she moved to the Eagle Gate, until she entered this third act of her life.

So this whole male-female chitchat thing felt rusty, and she couldn't believe she'd just spilled out several hundred words in one sitting. Dinner? She was disinclined. She'd call him in the morning with a headache or a loose tooth or an age-related irrational fear. There must be some phobia that would fit, a fear of crowds—but he'd seen her on South Temple. Or a fear of heights—but she loved staring out her window at the miniscule people strolling along the sidewalk. Or a fear of germs—that wouldn't get much traction, because the inside of her apartment wasn't too scrubbed. The muscles in the back of her neck started to constrict. She hated lying. It might be easier just to go with him. She started to think about what she would wear.

An hour later, with her face washed, she sat on the side of her bed clutching John's picture with both hands, staring at the handsome face that never aged, and whispered, "I miss you every single day. Why did you leave me to be old alone?" She touched her finger to his lips.

Chapter Fifteen
ICE IN HIS VEINS

SITTING ON THE DIRTY MATTRESS, Carly tugged on a hangnail. There wasn't much to say. There wasn't much to do. Nolan, the quietest of the *compadres*, had been caught on a surveillance video at City Creek stealing a customer's phone in the Apple Store, a pricey necklace in Nordstrom's, *and* a fleece hat in Brook's Brothers. What was he thinking? Did he want to be caught? There was a fuss, and mall security had rushed in like he was a member of the Mafia or pedaling drugs to little kids who'd been let loose by the fountain. A horrified Lemon had watched the arrest from his vantage point on the skywalk, at least that's what Lemon said. Carly had her doubts. If Nolan had wandered off the reservation, why was Lemon there watching him? Why didn't he stop him? Why didn't he post bail, bring Nolan back here to add another story to the mix? Another near miss, except it wasn't a miss. It was an arrest—according to Lemon.

She wasn't there. She'd been walking along Second South, missing the cracks in the pavement to spare her mother's back, when a bare-legged girl in cheap high-heeled boots spoke out of the blue. "Hey, are you crashing in that skanky apartment with Lemon?"

Carly stopped and eyed the skinny girl who was almost blue with the cold. "Not for long."

"That's what you think." The hollowed-eyed girl gave a half-hearted laugh, exposing all the wonders of childhood orthodontia. "I used to be you. As dumb as you are." One hand on her skinny hip, she gave Carly a knowing smile. "Get out while you can." A green Forester pulled up to the curb and the window rolled down with a mechanical whir, exposing a nice-looking man wearing a puff parka vest, maybe forty. He looked faintly like Carly's dentist at home. Negotiating her price in a five-word exchange, the girl opened the car door and called over her shoulder, "I'll be watching for you. The name's Michelle."

***

That night Carly sat on the mattress, not moving. It was like she was frozen—scared stiff. Who could you trust? No one. Slouching against the wall in the corner,

Bill watched Lemon and then he turned toward Carly. Her skin crawled like tiny ants had invaded more than the closet-sized kitchen. The guy had ice in his veins. All he had to do was walk into the room and any safe feeling went up the vent. Cruelty was written all over his pug face. It was all she could do to sit there and listen to Lemon's next lie.

"There were a couple of outstanding warrants, so bail would have been outrageous. And cash flow's a problem of late." Lemon sniffed loudly and pinched the bridge of his nose. He was a nose toucher, feeling the lengthy exterior when deep in thought. Carly watched him and wondered how Lemon could possibly know what bail would be.

Burt was sniveling quietly. She'd contaminated every flat surface in the apartment with her germs, and maybe he'd caught this bug that was making her miserable, or maybe he was genuinely depressed. She'd heard them mumbling in the shadows late at night. Nolan was Burt's friend and perhaps a step-nephew or a half-brother, or both. Days ago, Terry had whispered that Burt and Nolan were extraneous males from one of those huge polygamous families on the Utah-Arizona border. They'd been dumped in St. George by their stepfather or cousin-once-removed or an uncle. The official designation was "lost boys" according to the article she'd Googled at the library. *Happy eighteenth birthday*, she'd thought. *You're homeless.* The screwie mishmash of families was a mystery to her, and those towns on the Arizona border were a place to avoid, but Burt's grief was real. She wasn't sure if she should hand him a clean tissue or say something reassuring. *Don't worry. He'll be out of jail by next Christmas, and maybe they'll teach him a trade.* But she kept her mouth shut because Bill and Lemon had just exchanged a wary look, and then Lemon flicked the end of his nose and cast an eye on her.

"Give us a status report on your auntie."

"I went back to the shop on Saturday. And this knitting," she waved at the plastic bag on the counter, "is a mess."

"Excellent. That mess will require more of Auntie's time. Time you will use to become a sympathetic knitting devotee. All those latent maternal instincts need to focus on you before she discovers your true identity."

In addition to being kicked off the Star Wars set—questionable—she wondered if Lemon had tried his hand at screenwriting before he got a master's degree in bilking old ladies and taking advantage of abandoned kids and runaways. "There's a problem," she said. "She wasn't there Saturday or this morning."

She and Terry had taken the cash she'd begged from Lemon for more yarn and gone to Five Dollar Monday at the Cineplex. Terry had bought a single ticket and then held an exterior door open for her to slide through when no one was in the corridor. They'd gone from one holiday blockbuster to the next, eating discarded boxes of super-sized popcorn. She'd surprised herself. Eating popcorn abandoned by strangers with filthy fingers would have revolted her a year earlier, but not now.

Today it was a bonus—a freebee, a popcorn feast, particularly if it was buttered. It was wonderful to be out of the cold and sitting in a padded recliner so comfortable that she had almost forgotten how badly her head ached.

"There was a big deal Friday night at the apartment building," Burt said.

"And you're just mentioning this now?" But Lemon had been gone for two days—an uncharacteristic absence—and there was no one else to tell.

"Fire trucks and an ambulance and a hearse." Burt nodded enthusiastically, which was probably the wrong thing to do. Bill's eyes narrowed.

"Just this morning," Carly jumped in, "I asked the shop owner why Maggie was gone. There was a death. Her friend."

Lemon grinned. "Emotional vulnerability. The timing is perfect." He reached over and patted her on the head. She flinched. "We're going forward. The next opportunity is Thursday night. Correct?"

But he already knew that, of course he did. Thursday was Knit Night. Everything was noted in that cagey brain of his, his plan for stealing from the rich and giving to himself—and of course, Bill.

"You'll tell your aunt who you are, and then on Saturday, when all that lovely pre-Christmas feeling is floating in the halls, you'll pay Auntie a surprise visit. See what's what and who's who—which doors are locked and which old ladies are choking on diamonds."

"Won't that seem a bit contrived? 'By the way, I'm your long-lost niece, *great-niece*, who's living on her own in a big city with no visible means of support.'" Carly's eyes were dry, and she was feverish. Terry got a glass of water to ease her coughing, and then she said, "If my aunt has any common sense, she'll drop-kick me out the front door and run the other way."

"But you're sick. And such a pretty little thing. She won't turn her back on you."

"What if she calls my mother? What if she calls the police?"

Bill shifted and pocketed the knife he'd been using to pare his fingernails. "Why would she call the police?" It was the first noise he'd made all night. The rest of them averted their eyes and didn't move.

"I don't know. Maybe she'd be suspicious."

It was odd that Bill could speak and none of the muscles in his face would move, like maybe they weren't attached. "Don't act suspicious," he said. "Be convincing. Is there any part of this you don't get?"

Carly mumbled, "I get your drift."

"Cash and jewelry. That's what we need. Stones we can pop out of a setting and sell to a jeweler who isn't afraid of a bargain." Lemon paused and touched her forehead, before he started talking again. "And we don't want a sudden cure. You can't quit being a biohazard overnight. Maybe you should snooze near the open window. Bill has something to help you sleep."

I'm sure he does, she thought, and then next thing she knew, she'd be the shivering addict walking the streets at two a.m. wearing not much of a skirt and platform heels. "Thanks all the same," she mumbled, "but I'm really tired."

But she didn't sleep. After Lemon and Bill left and before Lemon, their keeper, returned, she and Terry whispered back and forth.

"Nolan's as dumb as a post," she said. "You think he'd lift a necklace at Nordstrom's? Expensive fakes? Not a chance."

Terry didn't answer. He was listening to Burt's steady breathing, and when he was convinced Burt was asleep, he muttered, "They'd never take a chance on Nolan being tossed in jail and talking to the police or a DA." They'd spent summers watching *Law and Order* in her basement when her mother was at work and had a good idea of how these things went down. Terry shook his head. "Nolan's a liability." He shrugged. "Who knows why?"

"Maybe he knows too much. More than we do." She wondered if he'd known Michelle, liked Michelle, that girl on the street. Was she someone he knew? A former *compadre*?

Terry grasped her hand. "Do you think he still knows anything?" He said it like he thought by now Nolan might be an unnamed body in a dumpster at a truck stop in Nevada.

Burt sat up. He'd been faking sleep, clearly waiting to see what they knew, what they'd say. "He was never arrested for nothing. No outstanding warrants. It's all a big lie."

His voice startled Carly, but not what he said, because they were all thinking the same thing. No fingerprints on record. Probably not a birth certificate. Those midwives in Arizona never recorded a birth with the state. It was like Nolan had never existed.

"He just wanted to go home," Burt mumbled. "That's all he wanted, to see his mom and his little sisters at Christmas. He thought he could sneak into town and see if the elders would take him back and let him work construction. He hates Lemon."

"There's a tsunami coming. We need to head for high ground," Terry whispered as though Lemon might be listening in the hall.

Carly nodded. "One phone call. That's all it will take, and I'll have a plane ticket out of here."

"But what about me?" Terry groaned. "No one wants me back, and you know it."

"We'll figure it out. I promise." She felt hollowed out, and there was no time.

"They're watching us," Burt muttered. Something in his face pulled tight. "You never see them. That Bill, he's good. Ten years in juvie for cutting his dad."

"Tell me you're kidding." *Please,* she thought, *tell me you're making this up.*

"He sliced his dad's ear off when his old man was asleep. You think you can just head to the airport? He'd jump you before you get ten feet."

Carly couldn't breathe. She couldn't think. Even in the library, hiding back in the stacks, she'd felt something, something evil reaching for her, breathing on the back of her neck. "Someone's been following me during the day."

"Bill." Burt nodded. "If this deal with the old people falls through, they're going to pump you full of drugs and sell you both. I heard them talking."

For a moment Carly sat terrified and quaking like a dry leaf. She wanted to scream and run out in the hall and down the stairs into the frigid night. But where could they go? The homeless shelter? That's the first place Bill and Lemon would look. She imagined herself running into the blade of Bill's knife or sinking into a snowdrift and slowly freezing to death or dying of the pneumonia she was sure she had. But she didn't move. This drafty, filthy studio apartment, this garret, was a horrible place, a dangerous place, but she'd stay here for a day or two, waiting. She sat for an hour, a petrified lump, before she snuggled next to Terry until she was close enough to whisper in his ear without Burt hearing.

"We're going to outmaneuver those jerks. They're snaked-eyed monsters, but we're smart and they're dumb. In another month, we'll be in San Diego in the sunshine, walking on the beach. When it's safe, we'll make a few phone calls and tell Salt Lake PD everything we know. This nightmare will just be a bump in the road, a bad memory. We'll have a dog-walking empire of our own, and we'll never have to look over our shoulders or be hungry again. That's a promise."

Eyes wide, Terry looked at her and shook his head, but he didn't speak.

Chapter Sixteen
TRIPLE-WORD SCORE

"Funeral's on Saturday," Jan said. "They always are." Whenever the funeral was, the residents of the Eagle Gate would be out in force. The entire building would clear out, carpools would be arranged, and money would be collected for a floral display—daisies and roses. Something large with a purple ribbon that said *Friends Forever* in gold glitter.

"Forty-three direct descendants," Sue said, passing Jan a silver bowl of cashews and candied almonds. She placed the wooden tiles on the board. "Zither," she said, "Triple-word score."

Sue had called Maggie early that morning. "One o'clock. Bring the board." She didn't say, *we're having the Rose Kimball Memorial Tournament*, but that's what this game felt like, and Maggie couldn't look at the empty chair without tears clouding her vision.

"Do you know what you're going to say?" Sue asked, fingering the black cord around her neck, her med-alert button, the building's new status symbol.

"Five minutes is two pages double-spaced. Not much time at all. One visual memory. That's about it," Jan said with a sigh. "I was the clean-up speaker at graduation every year. If you need a poignant poem, I've got a dozen."

Maggie nodded. A visual memory. Which one? She had years and years of memories of Rose: A laughing young mother planting petunias in the backyard. A middle-aged Rose giving it to Maggie straight. A white-haired Rose growling with a furry puppet raised above her head and an audience full of children giggling. Rose's children and grandchildren would all miss her. At least twenty had arrived Thanksgiving morning—was that only a week ago? With a great deal of hilarious uproar and Rosie calling the twin three-year-olds *little whipper snappers*, they'd escorted their grandmother out to the waiting caravan of Escalades, Navigators, and minivans heading south to Rosie's son's magnificent home in Alpine. She'd returned home that night as exhausted and confused as if she'd spent a dissolute weekend in Wendover.

Sue reached across the board and placed three tiles on Maggie's tray that Maggie had forgotten to draw. "The idea is to say something that will comfort the family. It doesn't have to be true. Embellish."

"And whatever you do, write everything down." Jan gave her a serious look. "Even if you think you've thought it all through, you'll get ten inches in front of the mike and your mind will be as blank as a whiteboard."

Maggie smiled at her friends. "I'm lucky to have you."

"Yes, you are, Dear." Sue nodded. "We've got your back." She rearranged the tiles on her tray several times. "After the service I'm going to wander around at the luncheon looking for ancient Sigma Chi's. *Ah, Mr. Richards, tell me, how did you know Rose? A college friend of Carl's? She died in the basement searching for a picture of you.*"

"We'll never know what she was trying to find." Jan sighed. "Best to let it go."

The last bits of afternoon sun were shining through the window. The shortest day of the year was just a week or two away.

"V-A-C-U-L-T-Y." Sue smiled. "I think that puts me two hundred points ahead."

"I was going to use that Y," Jan said. "Why does it always feel like you're cheating?"

"Because I'm so amazing." Sue popped a cashew in her mouth, then she wiggled her fingers over the tiles until she selected six new letters. "My fingers are clairvoyant."

Both palms pressed down on the table, Maggie blurted, "8-B brought me soup last night."

"No," Jan said, wide-eyed.

"And we're walking over to City Creek to have an early dinner tonight."

Tiles slipped through Sue's fingers and clattered on the board. They both stared at her as if she'd suddenly started spouting Greek.

"Well, well." Sue raised a single eyebrow. "A December romance."

"It doesn't feel that simple." Although after thirty-four years of being a widow, Maggie wasn't sure what she felt or what simple meant. "I don't know what to think."

Jan laughed. "Think *free dinner*. Order anything you want."

Sue enunciated each word as her voice rumbled, "Winner, winner, chicken dinner." For the first time in days, they all laughed, which felt oddly disloyal until Maggie realized that wherever Rose was, she was bent over giggling too.

"He just stood there holding a pot of soup in one hand and his cane in the other, but he was impatient like maybe I hadn't answered the door quickly enough. And he didn't say much, but his face was calm and together, like the visit was something he needed to cross off a list." She stopped for a breath. "Seeing me was somehow incidental."

"You're not making any sense." Jan slid H I E F under the T on Sue's *zither*.

"You think you're a project?" Sue gave her a sideways look. "My French diplomat was always trying to save his American ex-pat," she touched a palm to her ample chest, "from exposing her crass materialism at formal soirees." Sue huffed. "I was being taken in hand, which was really rather lovely on a sleepy afternoon, but I did tire of having my pronunciation corrected." She tapped a manicured finger on the tabletop, and the sparkle of a couple of magnificent diamonds was hard to miss. Every piece of art on her walls, the Persian rugs on the floor, and the overstuffed circular ottoman were all perfectly arranged in restful colors. Lounging in Sue's apartment was like waking from a nap happy and rested.

Maggie nibbled the candy coating off an almond. "All the single women in this building have baited their traps for this poor guy—except the three of us—and he knocks on my door? What's the logic there?"

Jan shrugged. "You're slender and not stooped."

"I wasn't fishing. I think it's strange."

"That's all very well," Sue said, "but what are you going to wear?" She nodded toward her bedroom. "I have a silver jacket that would set off the color of your hair perfectly."

"Maybe you're right," Jan said. "Maybe there's a list. Maybe he's interviewing acceptable women with all of their teeth or at least well-matched implants. What if he's starting on the seventh floor and working his way down to two?"

Sue laughed. "And next week he'll be visiting Jan, and then he'll meander down to 7-F where I'll be waiting for him—just like a spider—with a pot of soup of my own and an application."

"For what?" Jan gave Sue a look over the top of her glasses as though she already knew what Sue was going to say and was just playing the straight man.

"The position of husband number six. Or seven. I can't remember if that rugby player was ever official."

Jan handed Sue an almond. "Eat this to keep up your strength."

"Maybe he wants something else. Companionship?" Maggie knocked on the tabletop. "I'll tell you what. Maybe he wants to be Rosie's replacement in the Scrabble game."

"No men," Sue sang. "They all think they have to win."

And Jan rolled her eyes.

***

Maggie should have met Ed in the lobby. His knock on her door alerted everyone on her floor because every door had been purposely left ajar, and Sue, the minute Ed's back was turned, stepped out of her apartment and waved a white handkerchief at Maggie. Surrender without a fight? Maggie was relieved to leave the building and all those eyes with or without cataracts.

It was a clear night, and she could see her breath—it had to be ten below. Everyone had been complaining earlier about the weather and treacherous black ice. Mr. 8-B used his cane, but his gesture was concise, a pleasant rhythm—like he'd grown up watching Fred Astaire movies—as they strolled down the sidewalk, making their way through the crowd. Masses of bundled families hurried across the crosswalk to Temple Square, then the light changed and the road cleared, and in few minutes, another group hurried across to join the throng. Had all the inhabitants of Salt Lake Valley converged on Temple Square on a Wednesday night?

"They must be auditioning," she feigned a laugh, "for the mob scene in *Ben Hur*. They're filming a remake right here in the heart of the city." The remark wasn't one she'd rehearsed, and the moment she said it, she regretted sounding stupid. He laughed, a small, obligatory chuckle, but at least he didn't do an about-face and walk her back to the Eagle Gate.

"Maybe," he said, dodging a stroller so loaded with blankets and mittens that the baby inside was buried up to her nose. "We should have dinner first and avoid being crushed." They made a deliberate left into the City Creek Mall and encountered an army of shoppers with bags of wrapped presents clutched tightly in their hands. Christmas music, lights, shoppers checking their cell phones, garlands with gigantic sparkling bows; it was overwhelming.

Standing in front of the fountain, a man dressed in a shabby jacket with *Rudy's Repairs* sewn to the chest had two children, maybe six and four years old, tugging on his sleeves. The man was missing a front tooth and much of his hair, and his face was as worn as his coat. The trio seemed to be the only shoppers without bags, and maybe the fountain was their destination and not the stores, but the sight of the three brought a lump to Maggie's throat. Children with tangled hair and dirty faces had that effect, particularly if the weather was freezing and they had no mittens.

Perhaps she'd sent Ed a telepathic message or perhaps the sight of the unkempt children wrenched him too, because he said, "Stay right here. I'll be back in minute." He approached the man missing the tooth, spoke with him for a few moments, and then oddly, Ed touched the man's arm before he scribbled a message on a business card and slipped it into the man's hand. With a puzzled expression, the man glanced at Ed in disbelief as if good fortune was not something he normally experienced. Ed circled the man's shoulders with the arm unencumbered by his cane, and Maggie heard him say a quick "Merry Christmas."

His gentle touch on Maggie's arm turned her away, and they walked the length of the mall with the artificial stream on their left and the shops on their right. He paused for a minute, took a small spiral notebook out of his breast pocket, and made a quick entry before he spoke. "He'll never get a decent job without a front tooth. My dentist does implants. Really excellent work." He winked at Maggie and said, "I have a reservation at the Cheesecake Factory."

Handing out free dental care was a strange thing to do, and she almost commented about what she supposed he had done, but instead, "They don't take reservations" came out of her mouth. She knew because Sue always insisted on reservations and didn't take kindly to the Cheesecake Factory's policy.

"They do for me."

Maggie raised her eyebrows. Tall, well dressed with a duck-headed cane, he looked so conventional, but clearly he was not.

"I know people." He laughed. "My second wife was a pastry chef."

If the woman had died, Maggie hoped it had been with a glob of butter cream frosting in her mouth. "She worked here?"

He didn't answer.

They entered the restaurant, bypassed the queue and the display case full of delicious-looking cheesecakes, and with a nod at a perky girl, Ed led Maggie to a booth at the rear of the dining room.

If Wife Number Two wasn't dead, maybe they'd run into her. Maybe Maggie was a prop; maybe she was Ed's way of saying, *See? I'm not alone. And I don't miss you.* Had Maggie been invited to dinner to make a strategic point just like one of those rebound maneuvers she'd read about in tragic novels? "Does she work here?" she asked. "Making the cheesecakes?"

"Nothing's made here. It's all shipped in frozen. I met Number Two in an innovative food court in Denver. I think she's still working there. I had a pulled pork sandwich concession."

"Pulled pork?"

"Pork Barrel Pig, subsidized sandwiches. Your government dollars at work."

"Pretty catchy."

He laughed. "They were really good. I got up at five every morning to be ready for the lunch crowd. We were in an old warehouse downtown, and we'd get mobbed every day at noon. By six o'clock, we were done."

"We?"

"All the guys who worked there. It was sort of a group deal for a few years."

A silence fell between them. Gaps in dating conversations in college could be filled with *what's your major.* Since she had changed her mind every week about which career she didn't really want, majors were a constant source of fresh material. Of course, once a person passed seventy, it was like their car had been permanently put in reverse, and everyone craned their necks looking backwards at the minor mistakes, the raised children, the homes and the jobs and the risks that hadn't worked out and the ones that did. She wasn't sure how much she wanted to know about Mr. 8-B. This dinner might be the end of the beginning. So her next question was safe and frequently asked in polite conversations she overheard at church.

"Have you completely retired?" Because about half the residents at the Eagle Gate had a little something on the side, a part-time this or that, a few hours consulting, a seat on a board of directors, a not-so-silent partnership in a family business, or a position as artist-in-residence at a yarn shop.

"Done," he said. "I sold everything last year, closed the door, and said good-bye to the headaches and the phone calls."

"And what did you do?"

"Well, my last stop was in plastic fabrication."

"Toys?" She was thinking Legos or knock-off American Girl dolls.

"Water bottles. I talked some guys into lending me start-up capital in 1980 to buy a business that was failing. And then, low and behold, the bottled water craze hit, and I was cranking out bottles twenty-four hours a day. I caught the crest of a wave. Water's the second most popular beverage in the United States."

"That was lucky." Bottled water. Who could have predicted that?

"You make your own luck, and the work was so consuming it cost me Wife Number Three."

This man was starting to sound like Sue. So many ex-wives that they didn't have names or faces, just assigned numbers. Mass-produced wives in addition to plastic water bottles. Maggie inhaled and glanced down at the menu, but before she could make a choice, the waitress hustled up, an electronic device in hand.

Ed spoke over the clink of silverware and glass, and the noisy commotion of a hundred people escaping the hordes to enjoy a holiday meal. "Shrimp Scampi," he said. "Two." He turned to her quickly. "You're not allergic? To shellfish?" And then, as if he were in therapy for being overbearing, he explained, "It's the best thing on the menu."

They'd skipped the line of hungry diners to race through the menu? What next? In, out, a brisk walk home, and done?

"I'd prefer something else." She gave the menu a cursory glance. "I'll have the rib eye steak with mashed potatoes and the vegetable medley. And the house salad with ranch dressing on the side. And a sliver of that raspberry cheesecake." She nodded at what a woman at the adjacent table was eating. It looked delicious, and Sue's voice was whispering in her head, "*Winner, winner, chicken dinner.*"

She glanced over at 8-B. Why was this man bothering with her? She had all her own teeth, but other than that, she wasn't what anyone would think of as particularly appealing. Sitting here next to him, she felt like an item in that little black notebook in the breast pocket of his very expensive camelhair coat. If that's all she was, a name on a list about to be crossed off, she might as well enjoy herself and have a little gossip to share with Sue and Jan. So she asked him, "What about Wife Number One? And is there a number four or five?" Were they locked in a closet perhaps? For just a second, Maggie's sense of wellbeing started to sour.

"Bluebeard?" He winked, but it didn't cover his discomfort.

"It did cross my mind." She locked her gaze on her water glass so her eyes didn't start rolling involuntarily.

He loosened his tie and took a sip of water. "Wife Number One was a storybook princess. She was the only daughter of a wealthy man highly thought of in elite business circles. His name opened a lot of doors. But you know what happens when things go south?" He shrugged, intimating that he was about to tell her something she already knew, as though it were common knowledge, as though everyone was invited to public beheadings on Tuesdays. "They take those errant sons-in-law to the top floor of the Wells Fargo Building—twenty-four stories up." He mimed giving a body a shove and then waved as though he could see his younger self flailing through the air before he splattered on Main Street, and then he started laughing at the expression on her face.

"Oh dear. What a mess." Who was this man? Without looking, she twisted her napkin into a skewer. How long could it take the kitchen crew to fix shrimp scampi and a rib eye steak? She inhaled deeply before she breathed out. "No kids?" He'd obviously survived the fall.

"No kids. Maybe that was the problem. One of the problems."

"And wives number four and five?"

"No number four. It's just me. No kith, no kin."

Chapter Seventeen

A WAIF IN THE SHOP

THURSDAY MORNING JAN ARRIVED BEFORE breakfast, before Maggie had brushed her teeth or made her bed.

"Bluebeard. You honestly said that?" Laughing, Jan collapsed on the couch. "I can't believe it."

"He said it. Not me."

"Nevertheless." She laid her head back on the cushion and laughed until tears trickled down the side of her nose. "What else?"

"Dinner, which I was not allowed to choose, but I outflanked him and ordered a steak. We walked through Temple Square so packed with people that there were moments when the crowd just picked us up and moved us along." Ed had clutched her arm, and they kept each other vertical. "My feet weren't touching the concrete. Changing direction would have been impossible."

Jan nodded. "Like after a football game."

"Exactly. We finally peeled away from the crowd and staggered into the Assembly Hall like a couple of religious refugees. A high school choir was singing carols, which was nice if you shut your eyes."

"Let me guess: sparkling hot-pink dresses and the boys wore matching bow ties."

"Not last night. It was all school colors and borrowed graduation gowns—silver for the boys and green for the girls with wide white collars that looked like they'd been starched nearly to death. Maybe they were going for a church choir look. I don't know." She'd rested in the pew like a bump on a log, trying to smile but not saying much.

"You weren't impressed? With him? With the singers?"

"Maybe a little. The singing was lovely with their young voices." She and Ed had shared a quick look, a knowing smile, and then a laugh as the soloist, a plump girl with braces, warbled the high notes beautifully. They'd smiled listening to *the weather outside is frightful.* Ed had leaned in and said, "Well they got that part right."

Before they'd given up their seats on the bench, they'd sat through a charming rendition of "I'll be Home for Christmas," a song that always poked at Maggie's heart.

"I've got to get Sue," Jan said. "She needs to hear this."

"No, no, no." Insert Sue? Not a chance. In less than three minutes, Sue would be planning a small but elegant wedding in the party room off the lobby. It would have thirty or forty guests, very exclusive: the Scrabble crew, close family, and other women deemed worthy. Sue would haul silk dresses out of her closet, looking for something in an icy lavender or powdery blue, for Maggie to drape on her tired body. No thank you.

"You know how this feels?" Maggie said. "It feels like I'm putting beans up my nose."

Jan covered her mouth and shook with laughter.

"If my mother hadn't told me not to, it would never have occurred to me to put beans up my nose or in my ears . . . but after she made quite a point of *no beans in nostrils,* suddenly my little fists were full of beans that had nowhere else to go."

Jan brushed a tear off her cheek with the stray dishtowel drying on the back of a chair. "For an entire summer," she said, "my friend's daughter had chronic allergies, dripping and sneezing, until they took her to an ENT. Guess what he found? A rotting bean up her nose that had started to sprout. Roots almost to her sinus." Jan had a wealth of stories about troubles borne and lessons learned and chances that hadn't panned out.

"Rotting and sprouting? At the same time?" Pinching her top lip, Maggie said, "I don't believe you."

"I swear it's true. Every word. My friend would never lie."

Maggie leaned forward, smiling. "No beans. No more old men. No more high-risk behavior. Just one unwritten talk."

In less than forty-eight hours, Maggie would be standing at the pulpit in a chapel in Bountiful delivering a five-minute memory that she hadn't written. A notebook in her lap, the blank pages looked up at her like an angry accusation. She loved Jan, but this morning, she needed quiet and space to get something, anything, to coalesce in her mind. The tapping of her pencil on the page became more insistent. "I'm worried about this talk."

Jan sat up a little straighter. "Tell me anything you remember hearing in church three weeks ago."

"Why?"

"Because in three weeks, no one will remember what you say. No offense. It's just a fact of life."

"I'll remember, and this is for Rose."

But Jan was enjoying herself too much to hear the quiet insistence in her friend's voice. "Men are so crazy. The last fight I had with my husband was about driving a rental car. We were going on a long weekend with friends, and I made the arrangements, but Ralph, the other husband, said he'd reserve the rental car, and I thought, *No big deal.*" She shook her head. "Huge mistake."

Talking about her husband was something Jan never did, and Maggie had no idea how he'd died—if it was a burst aorta or an accident or a lingering bout of cancer— but Jan was not to be hurried. "If Ralph rented the car, Ralph was going to be the driver. I couldn't imagine it would make a difference, but the driver is the man in charge. No question. Can you imagine what either one of those men would have said if I'd insisted on driving?"

"That explains 8-B perfectly. He's an alpha male, a driver." Maggie wasn't the least bit sure that she wanted or needed an alpha male in her life. After all these years, she was finally comfortable paddling her own canoe in this slow-moving stream. But last night, he'd slipped the exhausted waitress a hundred-dollar bill when he thought Maggie wasn't looking. Who was he?

She erased the lengthy doodle she'd been drawing on the side of the page. "Maybe I'll say something about Rose and Carl. They had such a lovely marriage. He pretended to be shocked by the outrageous things she said, and she pretended he was a stuffed shirt." Maggie surprised herself by laughing. "Maybe I'll tell stories about her kids."

"You'll come up with something." Jan was still smiling at the memories tucked inside her head.

A grin on her face, Maggie made a line of loops across the top of page. "I've got to get going on this."

But at that moment, an envelope slid under the door, not a typical occurrence, and Jan snatched it. It was small with an unsealed flap, and a strong hand had written across the exterior, *Second chance?* Jan pulled out a printout of tickets to the symphony's Christmas concert. She held the folded sheet scissored between two fingers. "Look out. This guy's tenacious."

***

Typically, Thursday Knit Night was slow, but not tonight. It was nearly half-past seven before the crowd started to thin, before the bells on the front door quieted, before Maggie stretched out her tired legs under the table in the back room and ruminated about the memories she was delivering Saturday morning. The interior of her head felt crowded. She could hear Isabelle laughing with a male customer in the next room, when the girl came up behind Maggie so quietly that she nearly leaped at the sound of the girl's voice.

The girl muttered reluctantly, as though each word came at a cost. "I've made a mess of this." She held out the plastic bag with needles and yarn in a sloppy tangle. The girl's cheeks were flushed, and her clothes smelled musty, like old wool left too long in a damp closet.

Pulling the knitting out of the bag, Maggie whipped out the stitches, rolled the yarn back into a ball, and laughed. "Sometimes it's better just to start over with a cup of tea." She ignored the girl's cough.

The poor child's cheeks were hollow, and those pretty green eyes were lifeless, almost vacant. So young to be so defeated, and yet she'd walked here on a cold night with a ragged hole in the fabric toe of one shoe. She was obviously hungry, so why was she learning to knit?

Maggie set the tea and some crackers on the table before she cast on forty stitches and knit a few rows. The girl wasn't watching her. She'd fixed her gaze on a knitted Santa propped on the mantel across the room.

"You'll have to forgive an old woman's faulty memory, but I don't remember your name." She pressed a palm against her chest. "I'm Maggie. Maggie Sullivan. But we're not formal around here, and *Maggie* will do just fine."

The girl turned slowly as if the effort to keep her head upright on thin shoulders was more than she could manage. "I'm Caroline. Actually Barbara Caroline." And then she waited, watching Maggie's face, her hands twitching in her lap. "I was named after my grandmother, but everyone calls me Carly."

Maggie stopped knitting. Somehow nothing in the moment felt entirely her own, from the words in her head to her practical shoes braced on the floor, from the hand that grasped the knitting to the bifocals that were slipping down the bridge of her nose. Caroline.

She took a deep breath and felt her heart flutter. "Why don't we give this another try?" Gently, she wrapped the girl's chapped fingers around the needles, but the girl didn't grasp the soft yarn.

Maggie had lived long enough to know that life is full of bizarre coincidences, but the fleeting thought that this girl could be the indulged—okay, *spoiled*—plump, only child of a niece Maggie hadn't seen in years, and that by some strange happenstance, this great-niece had wandered into a yarn shop on Eleventh East where Maggie worked was just too crazy.

The girl nodded toward the front of the shop. "That other lady told me your best friend died. I'm sorry. My best friend died too. My dad. Four years ago." The girl was well spoken, but she mumbled so softly that Maggie had to lean in closer to hear. The "I can't believe he left me" she said next sounded a bit scripted. Then her delicate frame shook with a rumbling cough that lasted too long.

Maybe this was the wrong time for a religious platitude, but it was all that came to mind. "Heaven exists. I know it. Your dad hasn't left you. Never." But Maggie understood abandonment and desperation that was so overwhelming she couldn't begin to see the end of it. Suspicious or not, she wanted to rest her cheek against the girl's head—just a touch, just a moment of comfort, human to human—but instead, Maggie lifted the yarn and waited. The girl wasn't watching her fingers, something beginners normally did; she was glancing furtively over her shoulder at the dark windows as if she expected to see a specter peering in at her, but not her father.

Maggie had read somewhere long ago that dogs can smell fear, which she thought was extremely odd at the time, but sitting next to this girl, Maggie intuitively knew the girl was terrified of something or someone hiding in the frigid cold, waiting for her beyond the squares of light from the shop windows.

Between bites of crackers mounded with cheese, the girl gradually mastered moving the yarn up through her fingers and over the tip of the needle as the hands of the clock over the mantel moved slowly.

Maggie whispered, "You've got it. Once you master knitting, purling is easy." The girl looked at her, eyes watery, and smiled. Maggie's dead sister's smile, the older sister who had braided Maggie's hair, taught her how to tie her shoes, quizzed her on the multiplications tables after breakfast, and scolded her for eavesdropping on her phone calls. It was as though Barbara's eyes were staring up at her, hopeful, waiting, wanting something, but what?

Everything felt both fast and slow. Maggie shook her head. Her imagination was in overdrive. She was tired, worried about the talk for Saturday, confused by the attentions she didn't understand of a wealthy gentleman, and now this poor child was tugging on her heart.

Isabelle turned off the light in the front room, and after the noise of the cash register drawer opening and closing, she stuck her head around the corner. "Can I give you a ride home, Maggie?" This was a question that didn't need to be asked because Isabelle always gave Maggie a ride home on Thursday nights. The question was a message that it was time for the girl to leave.

Maggie' was nobody's psychic, but she could have sworn she felt a nudge, a literal nudge, as if she'd been shoved from behind by an invisible hand, and she reached for a bit of scrap paper in the waste basket and jotted down the number of her landline. "I'm around all weekend if you need help with your knitting. My friend's funeral is Saturday at noon, but then I'll be home. This is my phone number. I live downtown at the Eagle Gate." The girl's shy smile was a reflection of Barbara's, no doubt about it. "You shouldn't be out this late at night. Can we drop you somewhere? Give you a lift?"

The girl dropped her gaze. "No thanks. Someone's waiting for me."

Someone, not *a friend.* Not a shy boyfriend who entered the shop, smiling, hat in hand, waiting for a pretty girl in filthy clothes.

While Isabelle locked up, Maggie watched out the front window as the girl walked down the sidewalk, glancing right and left, until a shadowy form stepped out from behind a parked car and started walking beside her.

Chapter Eighteen
A FUNERAL FOR ROSE

KRISTEN STOOD SHAPING HAMBURGER, CHOPPED onion, and breadcrumbs into meatballs for dinner when a serious-looking Blake walked in early with a newspaper clipping in hand. She read the news—when she had a spare minute—online. Print news was a relic, an anachronism from an earlier age, and she glanced up when Blake placed the obit on the counter and then came around the kitchen table to hold her.

"Rose died day before yesterday," he whispered. "Your mom's been trying to reach you. She didn't want to leave a message. She finally called me at work. There was some kind of accident in that catacomb in the subbasement. Pretty terrible. No one found her for most of a day." Meatballs forgotten, Blake held her close as she sobbed, chest heaving and mopping tears with a dish towel for nearly an hour. During a break in her storm, he whispered, "The funeral's Saturday at noon. We can drive up that morning or Friday after work if you'd like, but we need to go. Your mother's one of the speakers."

She put her hand on her heart. Her mother speaking from a podium was something she couldn't visualize, couldn't imagine, because she'd never seen her mother speak at church, not once since she was a little girl, hair braided and dress starched, sitting on the second row in primary. No farewell talk before they moved from Bountiful. No let-me-introduce-my-adorable-family address in the Fremont Park Third Ward. It just wasn't something her mother did. Other mothers wrote poems, ran auxiliaries, canvassed for the Republican Party, volunteered at the food bank, produced reams of genealogy, or cared for refugees, but not hers. Not long-suffering Maggie, the martyr.

Rose was dead. Kristen was aware that Blake was stroking her hair, but everything else was a blur. Rose. Dead? Rose, who was everything her mother was not, had died? Sniffing loudly, Kristen wiped her hands on her stained apron. And Rose had loved Maggie, absolutely loved her for over forty years. Kristen grabbed a paper towel off the roll and blew her nose. None of this made any sense.

***

Leaving Jenny in charge with a list of instructions a page long, Blake and Kristen buckled seat belts at seven on Saturday morning and began the four-hour drive to the city. Blake had allowed an hour to spare as he hustled her out of the bathroom and into the garage. "Extra time to comfort Maggie," he said, "before she has to speak. This will be hard for her." Kristen trained her gaze on the dash to keep from making a snarky remark. Her hair felt damp. She knew it would frizz, but today was not about her. Today was for Rose. As a kid, she'd secretly wished she could call Rose *aunt* and fantasized about edging her way across the backyard to Rose's red brick house. She could gradually take her possessions over one stuffed animal at a time, and then one night she'd just sleep there and be adopted, and that would be that. A permanent member of a functional family.

Maybe she'd dozed off, or maybe she was just tired, but as they were driving past Fillmore, that endless stretch of I-15, so many memories were clamoring in her head that one made its way out of her mouth.

"Chris Thorndike was the only kid who came to Henry's ninth birthday party," she mumbled. "The only one." One scrawny kid with mustard hair and more freckles than skin. He was thrilled to be included in anything: flu shots, the entire class being kept in for recess, remedial math, anything. He was that kind of desperate. Other neighborhood moms had kept their precious darlings away. *Hush*, she'd almost heard their whispers. *We have to go to grandma's, or the mall, or the zoo, or the roller rink, or to a play date that can't be cancelled.* With heads averted, mothers had driven past the helium balloons tied to the mailbox under a Hawthorne tree. "Henry just sat and waited." The two little boys wore newspaper pirate hats, one boy had a corny grin splashed on his face and the other stared at his feet planted on the concrete front step.

Nine-year-olds are too old to cry, but eventually Henry's bottom lip quivered and his eyes watered. The ice melted in the orange punch. The plastic pirate swords sat untouched next to the party paper plates. Games weren't played. Favor sacks filled with chocolate doubloons waited untouched by the door.

At the time, it didn't occur to Kristen that, all things considered, a pirate-themed party might not be the best choice. Any suggestion of *theft* should have been avoided, but no one was thinking straight. A doe in the headlights, her crumpled mother sat next to Henry on the front step and patted his leg with her limp hand while Chris was like a puppy with a bad case of the wiggles. Kristen, her skin a blotchy red, had run out the back door. She dashed across the grass to Rosie's kitchen door and didn't bother to knock.

In a matter of minutes, Rosie's four sun-tanned boys, Dusty, Johnny, Jason, and Phil, were marching across the back lawn carrying hastily wrapped, discarded treasures—a Star Wars blaster, a set of Legos missing the instructions, and a Red

Sox baseball cap stained with sweat. They'd gulped cake and sang loudly. They'd joked with Henry and Chris and, in hearty junior high voices, mimicked swarthy pirates and staged sword fights that had everyone laughing.

"Rose came over later to help us clean up. She was absolutely seething," Kristen continued. "Rose stuffed the paper plates and cups into a garbage sack. She wadded up newspaper hats into a tight ball. Of course, none of it was Henry's fault. Rose was itching to punch in the phone numbers of those nasty mothers with their noses in the air. Clean their clocks. When Rose was on the warpath, her words could raise a blister."

Kristen pushed her bangs off her face and glanced over at her husband who had one hand clenched on the steering wheel. "I was cleaning up the cake crumbs. I flipped off the vacuum to move a couple of chairs, and I heard my mom say, 'He's tainted. We all are.' You know what Rose said? 'Baloney.' Rose was my mother's spine."

Without taking his eyes off the highway, Blake reached over and touched her hand.

"Rose made us leave those balloons tied on the mailbox." To prick consciences, to remind children of what they'd done. "And then Rose asked my mom if my dad was coming. And you know what Mom said?"

Blake shook his head. Not much else he could do. This story was just one of the many buried under her skin that he'd heard dozens of times.

"Mom said, 'John doesn't do disaster,' which was what our life had become."

The interior of the car was quiet, windows rolled up tight, and the snow and the low clouds reduced the landscape to a blur of white and gray. Blake squeezed her hand, flipped on the turn signal, and passed a UPS eighteen-wheeler, probably loaded with gifts and good wishes.

"I didn't know your mom said that," he said. Each retelling added a new detail, filled in the picture, worsened the pain.

Why would he know? She'd never told him. But a spasm of irritation raced through her like a chill. There was a piece of her that resented him for not knowing, for not understanding, for having such a bland, ordinary childhood and well-attended birthday parties. At least once a month, those differences landed like a concrete barrier between them that neither of them could breach.

"There's a lot you don't know." It whistled out of her mouth like a high-pitched accusation.

The poor guy nodded, and then he tried to smile. "I always wondered if you'd just materialized spring quarter, the world's prettiest redhead, in front of the student union like I'd willed you into existence. A girl for me to love."

Pretty talk. She rolled her eyes. *Blake is a pro.* She wanted to love him for trying, but it felt like condescension, like Blake was talking down to her from his lofty perch, from his upbringing that was all about normal. He couldn't begin to understand.

"It was like you didn't have a past," he said, and then, because he knew he was irritating her, he quit talking. He didn't prod. He didn't tell her how she should feel or that lancing that abscess in her brain would free her. He just kept following I-15 north through rounded mountains frosted with snow.

The day she met him, she'd expunged her own past, the official record made clean, but now, this morning like so many others, her past was filling the car, front seat and back. It was like there was no room left for oxygen and the windows wouldn't roll down. She was starting to panic. Not enough air.

"My dad killed himself," she said as if she were making a point. "He drove his BMW into a tree going ninety."

"Sweetheart, I know."

"He abandoned us." Melting into a mess of tears might make her feel better, but her eyes were as dry as a stale bit of bread. The flood of words came out in a series of pants and gasps. "He took everyone's money and promised them a ridiculous return. Grandma. Mom's sister. All the neighbors. Everyone. And not just nickels and dimes. Everything they had. We're talking life savings. Second mortgages. Two families on our cul-de-sac lost their homes."

Checking his mirror, Blake pulled off onto the shoulder of the road, stopped the car, and reached for her. "Your father abandoned you." He was trying to speak calmly, but there was an unsteady tremor in his voice. "I can't imagine what was going on in his head when he pushed down on that accelerator, but Kristen, I will never abandon you. Never." He didn't need to promise; she knew it was true, but it didn't slow the gush of words flowing out of her severed artery.

"We had to leave our pretty house and my friends and move to a horrible neighborhood where Henry was tortured every day at school. I love Henry. He was my baby. He liked me best. He held my fingers when he was learning to walk. And now he doesn't want to have anything to do with me. Like this whole disaster was my fault." Betrayal, the glue that held her together, was dissolving.

"No, no, no." Blake held her face gently in his hands so she couldn't turn away, and he looked into her eyes. "Henry's done the same thing you have. He's tried to build a new life. You're part of that old life he's trying to forget."

She glanced at the clock on the dash. "We need to go. We'll be late."

"Then we'll be late." He turned the key in the ignition. "It doesn't matter."

She reached down into that black core inside her and pulled out the final piece. "Davey," she said. "If I close my eyes, I can still hear my mother wail. Twice in one year. Too much, just too much."

Blake's chest heaved, then his arms tightened around her as she spewed every furious thought, every pent-up resentment, the cruel details, the injustice, the false friends, until there was nothing left, no more words, nothing left in her stomach. He waited for another dry heave, but she was spent, exhausted. *Here we are, parked on the gravel shoulder of I-15 while I choke out my childhood,* she thought, *yet again.* If he was impatient, he didn't show it. He just stroked her hair and kissed each of her fingers.

"I love you," he whispered. "More than you know."

***

A half an hour late, they arrived at the Bountiful Fourth Ward as the flock of small grandchildren was assembling in the front of the chapel to sing *Families Can Be Together Forever.* She and Blake had missed the eulogy, but not the sight of little Rosie Number Two—all of three and a half—belting out *they are so good to me.* The small blonde clone of her grandmother made every face smile. And for a moment, Kristen forgot to be miserable until her own mother stood and walked unsteadily to the pulpit and touched the microphone tentatively with one hand as if it might rear up and bite her.

Maggie's voice wavered, too soft to be heard. Her hands trembled. People sitting in the last pews leaned forward to hear. She stopped and began again, louder. "Rose. We all love her. We all need her." Then Maggie paused, seemed to gather herself, stood a little straighter, and quit fussing with her pages on the podium. "I'm pretty sure she's with us right now. She's straightening little Rosie Two's hair ribbon. She just brushed Billy's bangs off his forehead. She's got her arm around Jason's shoulder." She glanced down at Jason sitting with his flock of children in the second row. "Which is something of a miracle, because on a very cold January afternoon, I thought she was going to kill Jason, the instigator of World War III, a battle fought on multiple fronts in the neighborhood. I seem to remember snowballs being the weapon of choice. Your mother pulled into the driveway with a car full of groceries and three police cars on her tail." Jason's brothers laughed.

"Of course, everyone in the neighborhood remembers the day Sister Obermeyer thought she felt a burning in her bosom, but it turned out to be smoke inhalation because the field behind her house had been set on fire by Dusty and Phil launching their potato rocket." More laughter.

"Life in the Kimball household was never dull. I used to stand at my kitchen window in amazement at the endless energy required for Rose to shuttle her boys to Little League, Jr. Jazz, soccer, orthodontist appointments, piano lessons, and everything in between. I don't remember ever being in the Kimball home when someone wasn't playing the piano, planning an assault, or building a science fair project. It was like that red brick house was a factory designed to manufacture kind-hearted, hard-working men. And at the epicenter of that operation was a loving marriage. Carl and Rose. Team Kimball."

Maggie took a deep breath and smiled. "Darling Rose was a gift to us all." Her voice caught, and then she began again. "She'll stay with us today until we leave the cemetery. When we come back here for a lovely lunch, Rose will turn away from us to find Carl."

Blake leaned into Kristen and whispered, "Don't look now, but I think the authentic Mary Margaret Sullivan is speaking at the pulpit."

"What?"

"If you peel off the layers of poverty and depression, this is who you get." He nodded toward the front of the chapel at the slender woman wearing a dark-red cardigan and a tender expression.

"The talk's a collaboration. I'm sure Jan and Sue helped her write it."

"I don't think so. They don't know those stories."

Kristen shrugged and leaned forward to listen to her mother speak.

"Not long after Rose and I became neighbors again—at the Eagle Gate—she called me one morning. It had snowed all night long, but when the sun rose, the sky was that beautiful crystal blue and the fresh snow was sparkling. Rose called Brother Entwhistle down on the fifth floor and borrowed a couple of sets of ski poles because she thought we should go for a tromp in the snow. Her well-intentioned children hadn't confiscated her car keys yet, and I said, 'Rose, do we really want to drive on snowy roads?' but she just laughed and said, 'Maggie, we grew up on this stuff,' and off we went, sliding more than a few times, to Millcreek Canyon." Maggie took a deep breath. "It was just so breathtakingly beautiful. Every twig decorated with snow and branches bowed down making an enchanted canopy. Ski poles in our hands," and she gestured as though she were planting a pole with each step, "we set off."

Kristen could see them. Rose in sturdy snow boots, her mom wearing goulashes over a couple of pairs of wool socks. Two old ladies bundled in coats and hats, laughing like kids making angels in the snow.

"We hiked a couple of miles until we came to that elbow in the road. Cross-country skiers passed us, and we tossed snowballs for a golden retriever puppy, but then we were alone. The only sound was the river flowing through mounds of snow and over rocks sheeted with ice. And then Rose stopped." Maggie stopped too, a dramatic pause, before she continued, speaking more slowly. "Rose said, 'Carl is just around that bend—waiting for me.' And perhaps he was. But Rose stayed with us a while longer because we all needed her. I certainly needed her.

"When we climb into our cars today and leave the cemetery, Rose won't be with us. She'll be walking up that beautiful snow-covered road into the mountains. The ice crystals will float down around her until she comes to that bend. Her wonderful Carl," and Maggie looked down at the congregation, "your grandpa, is waiting there for her—at the bend in the road—so they can walk the rest of the way together, holding hands, forever." Maggie swallowed a sob. "But we will miss her. Oh how we will miss her."

For one uncomfortable moment, Kristen thought her mother might cry, but she didn't. She just touched the tip of her nose with the tissue balled in her fist. "I thank God every day that Rose was in my life."

Maggie sat down and a couple of granddaughters rose to play a violin concerto, and Kristen waited for Blake to take advantage of a teaching moment and prod her into forgiving her mother with a *Rose understood your mother better than anyone*, or *You have to respect that kind of love*, or *Love heals all*, but he didn't. He just grasped her hand more tightly and whispered, "I will always love you, and I'll never leave you. Not ever." And she knew if he were killed in a car crash on the way back to Cedar City or died of a lingering disease, it wouldn't matter. He would be with her, watching, waiting, just out of sight.

Kristen glanced at her silver-haired mother wearing her lovely hand-knit cardigan, sitting on the stand, alone, her hands clasped in her lap and her eyes focused on her hands. What was she thinking? Was Kristen's father waiting somewhere for her mother? She hoped he was.

Chapter Nineteen
WRUNG OUT

AFTER LEAVING THE CEMETERY, TWO hundred people arrived at the Bountiful Fourth Ward building for lunch. Fifteen-foot-long tables covered in butcher paper filled the cultural center as ladies in low heels and dressed in Sunday best served plates filled with slices of ham, cheesy funeral potatoes, and green Jell-O. Excited cousins raced between the tables and voices echoed in the din. A lit Christmas tree stood in the corner and a lone poinsettia sat in the center of each table. Dark suits and somber ties were a reminder of the occasion that brought them together, but the visit to the cemetery was over, and if Rosie wasn't forgotten, she had certainly been pushed gently to one side.

Looking wrung out and dangling a fork between two fingers, Kristen sat on Maggie's right. Blake sat across from her not looking much better. Kristen could be difficult, and Maggie wondered if they'd had an argument in the car, but she wasn't going to ask. She used to think she had a special right to be useful, but not anymore. Their business was their own.

Leaving a cluster of chatting relations, Melony Kimball, the first daughter-in-law to intrude into Rose's tight family circle, found Maggie. She leaned over and draped her plump arm around Maggie's shoulder. "Thanks for taking my side—too many times. You were the only one Rose ever listened to." She planted a soft kiss on Maggie's cheek and then drifted away.

Kristen said, "What was that about?"

"Turning down the volume on things that don't matter." Maggie patted her daughter's hand. "Children aren't possessions."

Blake lifted a brownie off the dessert cart and passed it across the table. "Good job with your talk. The walk in the woods nailed your relationship with Rose. Nicely done."

Of course she thanked him. Blake was unfailingly kind, but she was tired and needed to go home, back to her couch with the split cushion, back to her knitting and the comforting rumble of traffic seven stories below. She hesitated before she spoke, "You're welcome to spend the night. They're predicting another storm." *Be safe* was her message. *Five children need you.* "We could blow up that air mattress," she said, and stopped herself before she added, *and borrow a couple of extra pillows from Rose.*

Relief was all Maggie felt when Blake declined. "We're staying at The Little America. Maybe we'll do some Christmas shopping or see a movie. Can we take you out to dinner?"

The surprise on Kristen's face said the night at Little America was unplanned. An unscheduled luxury. Maggie hoped it wasn't a peace offering, but in any event, their evening shouldn't include a cumbersome third person.

She toyed with the potatoes on her plate, and Blake leaned forward to hear her say, "Too much food for one day, but you kids go on. Enjoy your night alone." She didn't want to do the classic mother-in-law routine, *Don't worry about me. I'll just sit here alone in the dark,* because that's not how she felt.

Arching her neck, she glanced around for Jan and Sue. That morning, Sue had retrieved her green Mercedes from cold storage and driven the three of them to the funeral in style, but now Sue seemed to be missing. As he made his way to where Maggie was sitting, Mr. 8-B—she was beginning to think of him as Ed—dodged a flock of two- and three-year-old cousins darting between tables and scrambling under metal folding chairs. His charcoal suit was perfectly tailored, and the tie he'd chosen was a splash of red against his white shirt. Why had he come? He didn't know Rose.

"Sue had an appointment at two thirty and asked if I could give you a ride home," he said, "unless you have plans with your daughter, because that's obviously who this must be." So charming and elegant with his plaid woolen scarf and his camel coat folded neatly over his arm, and he was walking without his cane. He rested one possessive hand on the back of Maggie's chair. Caught off guard, Kristen stared at her mother with her mouth open like an oven door left ajar. If the two women shared a resemblance, neither of them could see it.

"That's so kind of you, Ed" Maggie said, enjoying the expression on Kristen's face. "I'd love a ride home."

Blake pushed back his chair and extended his hand. "I'm Maggie's son-in-law. Husband to the good-looking redhead." Interesting that such a simple gesture eliminated the need for awkward introductions. Maggie reached for her purse and her navy coat on the back of the folding chair.

Who nudged 8-B? she wondered. She doubted it was Rose, more likely a conspiracy of two well-intentioned friends. And this man was certainly complicit. She'd noticed him chatting with Sue in the foyer while they were stomping the snow off their feet. Sue had been explaining the advantages of a private graveside service as she kept her balance with one hand touching a heat register, and Jan had been glancing around, not making eye contact, as though she were an innocent bystander in an armed ambush. The three of them were part of an unspoken agenda. Maggie wondered again if Mr. 8-B was angling for the vacant fourth spot at the Scrabble game.

Heading for the parking lot, her purse in her hand, Maggie overheard Kristen. "Ed? Who's Ed?"

Blake shrugged.

"She's seventy-four." As though loneliness could be canceled out by the onset of Medicare.

He extended his palms.

"What's his last name?" Kristen demanded.

"I didn't catch it."

Maggie took a last look around the gym filled with Rose's smiling relations. A chapter was closing. Quiet tears had been shed. In a matter of days, Rose had become a disembodied collection of memories, most happy, but some not. Rose's least favorite daughter-in-law looked relieved as though she'd survived a polio epidemic, and Maggie smiled. *Who even remembered polio?* In a month or two, in the bustle of dance classes and Little League and primary lessons and meetings at work, who would remember Rose?

Sitting in the front seat of Ed's car, an expensive something-or-other in a dark shade of blue, without any warning, she started to cough and sputter. Rose was gone. Was Maggie trying to cough something out of her chest? The pain out of her chest? The pain and tightness out of her throat? Tears leaked from her eyes. Ed fumbled across her, reaching to open the glove box, reaching for a box of tissues that wasn't there. He bumped her purse sitting on her lap, and the contents spilled on the floor mat. The clasp had broken years ago. Snow was falling, thick and fast. The wipers were on high. Leaning over, she scooped her wallet, her lip-gloss, a couple of ancient receipts, and a comb into her purse. No tissue.

One hand on the wheel, he glanced at the smear her face had become, but he didn't speak. He turned into a gas station, opened the door, and nearly slipped on the pavement. He returned in a couple of minutes with a bottle of water, a box of Kleenex, and a Rice Krispies Treats bar wrapped in blue cellophane grasped in his hand. His other arm was extended to keep his balance as though he were tiptoeing across a high wire. If Rose had been sitting in the back seat, they both would have collapsed laughing, but she wasn't in the back seat. Rose was dead. And that was all Maggie could see, the shriveled facsimile of her Rose painted a sick shade of orange with her hair arranged in tight curls like a Madame Alexander doll laying in a blue satin box. A casket.

Maggie hid her face with the tissue Ed offered and rested her forehead against the cold window. She'd held it together, but now she was falling apart. She had no desire to speak. It took five minutes for a stray tear to dribble down her neck. She called out, *Rose, Rose*, but only in her mind.

"Let's get you home," Ed mumbled softly. "This is a lot for one day."

She didn't know what he'd expected. Perhaps a polite comment or two about riding in such a quiet car. The dashboard was covered with enough screens and gadgets to fly a fixed wing aircraft. It must be electric. Something he plugged in like a vacuum cleaner or a hand mixer, and then the crazy thing called him on the phone, and he spoke into the steering wheel to his dentist as easily as if he were reclined in an exam chair.

"I did give him your number. He's not lying," Ed said. "Send the bill to me."

Send the bill to me? Who says that? No one. It's a line from a movie, a play, a punch line from a joke, but not something ordinary people said. Who did he think he was kidding? She sighed heavily, audibly, but she'd quit coughing. That was something. She took a bite out of the Rice Krispies Treats bar and broke off a piece for him, which felt oddly intimate, but he'd only bought one. It would be rude not to share. The snow was coming down faster, sticking to the asphalt, an inch or two deep, but the car didn't slide. Maybe it was a hovercraft.

"Does this vehicle have a name?" she asked.

"It's a Tesla."

"Elon Musk? I read about him in the doctor's waiting room."

Ed took his hands off the wheel for a moment and laughed. "It steers itself, but maybe not in a blizzard when it can't read the lines on the edge of the road."

Resisting the urge to examine her face in the mirror, Maggie daubed at her eyes and sat up a little straighter, her feet planted on the floor the rest of the way home. They turned into the parking garage, and neither of them spoke more than a few cursory words as Ed tossed his keys to the attendant and held the back of her arm as they skated down the incline. They stomped the snow off their feet as they came in the front doors. Residual flakes melting in their hair, they stood silently in the elevator. She unlocked the door to her apartment and took a step inside. Fully intending to desert him in the hallway, she thanked him for the ride and apologized for her unseemly behavior, but he ignored the social cues and followed her, shrugged off his coat, and barged into her kitchen. She stood, dripping snow on the carpet, haunted and bewildered, as if she were walking in her sleep. It had taken a week for the truth of Rosie's death to penetrate her core. On Monday and Tuesday, it had been just a few days since they'd talked, laughed in the hall, shared half a donut. That face in the casket wasn't her Rose. The real Rosie was gone, and she wasn't coming back.

What was this man doing? Intruding into a woman's kitchen was like an assault. Maybe men thought kitchens were impersonal, like a car engine or a printer next to a computer, but that kitchen with her paltry possessions was private terrain. She heard the faint hum of her second-hand microwave.

He dropped something, something heavy. Maybe an old mug. All her mugs were old. Nothing she owned matched. He'd figure that out if he opened a couple of drawers. The contents were clean and worthless. Bare essentials. She thought she'd put small indignities behind her years ago, but this felt like someone had opened her favorite purse and discovered it was empty. The change purse empty. The lining frayed. The clasp still broken. He should leave her alone and take the elevator back up to his penthouse on eight. She didn't need his charity or, worse, his pity. Lips in a firm line, she took a few steps toward the doorway when he said, "Herbal tea?" He banged a cupboard door. "Found it."

He favored his left leg awkwardly as he walked toward her, managing the mugs by the handles, his hair flattened and damp against his head, his self-assurance spent. He handed her the mug that said *MOM* and kept *Seattle World's Fair* for himself. *He doesn't want to be here,* she realized, *any more than I want him here.* He looked as tired as she felt. Home was one floor up where he could slip out of his shoes, turn on a basketball game, lean back in his leather recliner, and close his eyes. Forget the day.

"Thank you," she said. "I know you're tired too. It's been an exhausting afternoon."

The tea burned her tongue, and she couldn't keep her hands from shaking. She set the mug on a magazine so it didn't leave a ring on the table she'd polished too many times. Without being invited, he sat down on the couch in her favorite spot. She waited, sitting on the straight-backed chair, and then the question that had been bothering her all afternoon stole out of her mouth.

"Why were you at the funeral? You didn't know Rose." Perhaps it sounded as if she were accusing him of trying to ingratiate himself like a friendless eighth grader in a new school, and she were the mean girl putting up a barrier, a warning, a reminder of *not for you.* It wasn't something she would ever say or scribble on a sheet of paper taped to her door, but it was true nevertheless.

He made an empty gesture as though he were reaching for his cane that wasn't there. "I knew Rose's husband." Was that simple answer all he needed to say? The hollows under his eyes almost maroon, he fingered the stuffing exposed by the split in the cushion and stared out the window. "Carl talked about Rose endlessly before he finally asked her out. I was home a year later and went to their wedding." He held the steaming mug in his hands but didn't take a sip. "I was at their beginning. I thought I should be there, you know, at the end." A silent witness. Not a disinterested bystander. "I saw Rose at church the first Sunday after I moved in. I thought she might remember me, but she didn't."

But Rose had known a piece of memory was missing. There are things some women agree on or don't agree on when they've lived side by side most of their lives—what can be discussed and what topics are under lock and key—but not her and Rose. Without saying a word, Rose had been in the basement searching for a bit of her mind that had been misplaced, a key to something Carl had mentioned. Casual pillow talk or a dark rumor? It was something Maggie needed to know.

Chapter Twenty

NOT HENRY

SHE AND ED SAT, NOT speaking, their mugs of tea untouched and cooling. Staring past her shabby furnishings, Maggie watched the snowflakes falling outside the sliding glass door. The overhead light in the kitchen was on, but the living room was dark and felt cold, unwelcoming. She should stand up and turn on a lamp.

In any other living room in any other apartment in this particular building, a single woman her age would have been delighted with the attentions of an affluent stranger with an amazing Christmas tree lit in his penthouse for the entire world to see—but not Maggie. An alpha male, made slightly less alpha by age and a bad hip, still made her wary. Other conversations might begin with a smattering of benign chitchat. Polite inquiries. Do you have grandchildren? (Maggie already knew he didn't.) Winter travel plans? Sunny locales? Perhaps a holiday cruise on the Rhine? Christmas shopping completed? Staying home for the holidays? What about pets? Fish? Hamsters? A faithful dog, long since dead? That's what Lillian Hollingsworth— she lived on the fourth floor—would be asking. And compliments. Lillian would be complimenting Ed. Lots of compliments and funny stories. Lillian was big on funny, self-deprecating stories. She wrote a blog about aging that got a thousand hits a month. At least, that's what she claimed.

Maggie didn't feel chatty and wasn't eager for company. She needed to sit alone in the dark, mull over the day, remember her Rose, watch the snow fall, and see the lit windows in the Alta Club across the street shining through the storm. If she stood next to the window, she could look down at miniature people seated at tables in the formal dining room on the second floor. Maybe a Christmas party. If this man would just leave, that's what she'd do. She'd stand next to the window, feel the chill, watch her shadowy reflection in the glass, and step into one of her imaginary lives. Wearing elegant clothes, maybe something black with sequins, she'd arrive at that party through the front entrance. Mingling with the guests, she'd toast Christmases past and present with sparkling apple cider in a crystal flute, while appreciative friends smiled at some clever observation she'd make, maybe some astute opinion about the commercialization of Christmas or some prediction she'd borrowed from Forbes about market directions in the coming year.

But Ed didn't leave. He was settling into her couch, adjusting a pillow under his hip, moving the knit afghan to one side as though he were colonizing a favorite spot in her living room and was determined to monopolize the entire evening. He reached for a photograph sitting on the end table of Henry's little girls. On one of Maggie's rare visits, she'd braided their long brown hair and crossed those braids around their heads, creating little crowns. She'd gathered a handful of spring flowers and decorated the braids, then a laughing Henry had taken a half dozen pictures. A beautiful day. He'd sent the best one to her, but that was years ago. Now the girls were teetering on the far edge of childhood, nearing adolescence.

"Bessie," she smiled. "She's a rascal. The little one's Meg." Ed passed the picture to her. Framed little girls frozen in time. She dusted them once a week and sprayed the glass with Windex, but even so, she never tired of looking at the little girls with flowers woven in their hair. She exhaled through her nose until her chest felt hollow.

"They belong to whom?"

"Henry. He lives in Virginia."

"And this is?" He touched another framed picture.

"That's Jenny. She's my oldest granddaughter." Maggie was about to mention Jenny's lead in the school musical—the missed school musical—but realized it would sound trivial to him. It was just one minor injury in a lifetime cluttered with events no one could recall—no one except her—and certainly insignificant compared to the water bottle revolution.

"Did I meet her parents today?"

"Yes. Blake and Kristen."

He nodded, setting the picture in the exact spot where he'd found it. Maggie had the pictures arranged at an angle, so they were all facing her, greeting her, when she walked in her door.

"Blake seems like a nice guy," he said.

"Very nice, kind, thoughtful." A bishop twice over who never seemed inconvenienced or rushed. "They live in Cedar City."

"Shakespeare's second home?"

She laughed. "Exactly."

Ed was a slender man, and his breadth didn't cover more than one cushion, but his presence filled the room and brought to mind a Christmas when she and John had been engulfed by a bushy tree that had looked reasonable on the lot, but when fixed in the stand, it had filled the living room. Edging past boughs and ornaments to get from the front door into the kitchen, they'd laughed for days until the tree dried out and the pine needles turned prickly. Maggie was a private person, loved by just a handful of people, and this man on her couch felt like an intrusion, an oversized tree filling the middle of her room.

She could starve him out, but given his previous behavior, he might forage in the kitchen and witness the scant offerings in her cupboards and fridge. Always prepared, Lillian Hollingsworth would be ready with a tub of hummus and crackers, or something more intimate, chocolate mousse with a handful of wild strawberries that hadn't been sliced, but Mr. 8-B didn't seem to be in any hurry to vacate Maggie's couch. She should offer him something, but she didn't have a tin of stale Christmas cookies or a stray box of chocolate mints left over from Scrabble afternoons. The best she could do was a tuna sandwich on last week's bread and a single apple cut in quarters to share.

"Can I get you something?" And he said yes before she could detail the options.

An opening between the kitchen and the living room, a window without glass, allowed conversations between the cook and her guests, and she was mixing a bit of mustard and mayonnaise in a glass bowl when she saw him take that same slim notebook out of his pocket and jot something down with a stubby pencil. His notebook returned to his pocket, he sat quietly, and then in a moment he picked up a picture of Davey, all smiles, wearing his Little League Oakland A's uniform. When Ed stared at the picture too long, she wanted to snatch it out of his hands. Then he picked up a baby picture, Davey the wobbler starting to take a few steps. Brown eyes wide, Davey had been afraid of his mother-turned-photographer waving a stuffed chicken behind a tripod and was about to tear up when she'd clicked the shot.

A plate in her hand, she stood in front of Ed, offering him a ruffle of flattened lettuce and a glob of tuna between thin slices of bread, the best she could do, but he didn't look up. It was as though he were alone in the room, and that wouldn't have been such an extraordinary thing, except it was her room, and the picture in his hand was of her precious son. Ed's presence shrank, withered to the size of a single old man sitting on a battered couch. He reached for the sandwich, before he whispered, "Who's this?"

She turned away, returned to the kitchen, fussed with the dirty bowl and a bit of apple core in the sink, before she spoke in a voice loud enough to hear if he strained a little. "That's my son." Leaning against the refrigerator, she took a bite of the sandwich she didn't want and had a hard time swallowing. She wiped damp palms on a dishtowel before she carried her sandwich back into the living room.

"Not Henry?"

"No. Not Henry."

They sat in silence, eating tuna on toasted sourdough bread and watching the storm. She noticed the tremor in his hands when he carried his dish to the kitchen. His limp was more pronounced.

"I'm assuming this boy is an adult now," he said after sitting back on the couch. "Where does he live?"

Maggie knew he was lying; she didn't know how. Was he interrogating her or extending his visit for reasons she didn't understand? With eyes fixed on her face, he reached across the throw pillow and touched her hand, a simple gesture, but it didn't change the truth.

"Davey is dead." She didn't pull her hand away, didn't notice his gesture, because her mind was on Rosie and a promise they'd made not long after Greta Vanderhoff slipped away in the night. If Rose died first, she promised to find Davey, wherever he happened to be. In some little outpost in heaven or some little celestial valley. Rose would find him and give him a hug from his mother.

"I'm sorry," he said, watching her closely.

"Thank you." But what she wanted to say was *Why? Why are you here? Why are you sorry? You didn't know my little boy.* Hands in her lap, she sat staring at the storm outside the window and was so tired, so very tired.

"What happened?"

Her chest tightened. "He was in the wrong place at the wrong time with the wrong people." *Foolish people*, she thought, *who didn't know Davey.* She walked across the room and touched her palms against the window, felt the cold, and watched the flakes drift down from a cloudy sky. No stars. The tentative pressure of his hand on her shoulder surprised her, and she smelled the musky cologne he was wearing and just a hint of starch in his shirt.

Nodding toward the bright windows across the street and the people inside milling around tables draped in white cloths, she said, "What do you think they're doing?"

"Not much. Boasting about portfolios. Making connections. Hitting friends for contributions. This and that." He stood a little straighter, perhaps relieved to have such a simple question to answer. "I'm a member." He cleared his throat. "We could go over for dessert. Cheesecake or a chocolate torte. I can't remember what else. Not much choice." He shrugged. "The pastry chef went back to Vienna without notice."

"I thought you just moved to this neck of the woods." A week or two wasn't long enough to make friends with the pastry chef.

"I had a home in Park City. I've been a member of the Alta Club for years."

She wondered if he was one of the elegant people she'd watched from her dark perch seven stories above.

"Why did you move?" This was absolutely none of her business, but she was curious, and his hand on her shoulder felt like permission granted to ask personal questions.

"I like the city. People bustling around, bumping into each other. I thought this would be a more convenient place to live, where everything was already familiar." His eyes flickered away. His story sounded plausible, but a piece was missing, something he wasn't admitting. He said, "So what about that peppermint cheesecake? A calorie load at the end of a long day."

"I don't have the right clothes." She raised a hand to her collar.

"You look great." The half-smile he gave her wasn't convincing. "An inch of makeup and expensive clothes don't cover much. We wear what we are."

And what was he? Besides being profound in a pinch.

He grabbed his coat from the back of the couch. "Let's go. Why not?"

"What if it's slick?" she said.

"Someone's been out shoveling and sprinkling rock salt. Members are litigious."

"Do you want to stop and get your cane?"

"I'll just hold on to you. If we go down, we'll go down together. Cause an uproar."

The thought of the two of them landing in a snowy pile of camel coats and scarves and sturdy shoes shouldn't have made her laugh, but it did.

"A million years ago," she started, "they set up a hidden camera outside the student union and caught kids falling on the ice. Someone edited it, and it was the short before the main feature on Friday nights. Funniest thing I've ever seen."

"If you're into sadistic bone breaking."

"Kids bounce back up." She remembered sitting next to John, sharing popcorn that was too salty, but neither of them cared because blood pressure wasn't a concern. They were just two kids young and in love and laughing at students, arms and legs flailing, losing their balance and books on a sheet of ice. When Maggie could crest that terrible barrier in her memories and look back at their life together, laughter is what she remembered, laughing with John. So much happiness, so much hope. Her pictures of him weren't part of the array on tables in the living room. Pictures of John were in her bedroom where only she could see them, and their wedding album was tucked under her bed, close at hand.

She buttoned her navy coat up to her chin and covered her hair with a scarf. No bows on the toes or heels crusted with rhinestones, her black shoes looked like a prescription from a podiatrist. "Lead on, Macduff." She smiled.

As they left the building, the frigid air stole her breath, and they slid once on black ice in the intersection, but they clung to each other and entered the Alta Club without any serious mishaps. Walking through the heavy oak door, Maggie thought she'd stepped back in time, and maybe that was the club's charm. The whole building was an antique, a Victorian Christmas card with pine garlands on the banister, candles on a tree, and the stink of cigars wafting out from the lounge. A uniformed girl said, "Good evening, Mr. Johnson. What do you think about this weather?"

The maître d' greeted Ed by name and showed them to a small table by the fireplace blazing with a couple of logs; obviously, these people weren't concerned about spewing carbon into the atmosphere. Seconds later, the waiter arrived on cue as if he were making an entrance in a BBC production. Ed made two choices without consulting her, but she didn't care what he ordered; she'd just choked down a tuna sandwich on dry bread. The waiter produced the cheesecake with a flourish. In a few moments, a gentleman stood from a table nearby and came over to greet them. "Johnson, good to see you. Glad to see you survived the move."

After a quick introduction, "This is Mrs. Sullivan," the man returned to his table. As if she'd been sitting too close to the fire, warmth flushed her cheeks. What if he'd introduced her as Mrs. Memmott? The holiday bubble would have burst in a collective horrified gasp, and she would have been bustled out the front door like a rat chased out of the dining room with a broom.

She glanced across the white linen tablecloth at this man whose shirt never wrinkled—and how was that possible?—and tapped her fingernail on the table. Who was this guy hiding under a tidy white beard? A cook, a plastic bottle magnate, a dispenser of free dental care to strangers, and a determined intruder into her life, her inconsequential, happy existence, her contented third act. Something here didn't make sense. Did he think she held the key to some secret? She pressed the tine of her fork on one last sugary crumb, before she asked, "Who are you really? FBI? Retired CIA? Santa Claus?"

He leaned toward her until he was inches away from her face, and she couldn't escape his eyes. "I thought you'd have me figured out by now, Maggie," he spoke softly, a pensive smile on his face. "I'm a thief."

Chapter Twenty-One
A STRAY PUPPY

CARLY HID IN THE SHADOWS, avoiding the streetlights as icy crystals from yesterday's storm whipped down South Temple and felt like glass shards piercing her bare ankles. The Eagle Gate, lights glowing, stood across the plaza. She didn't know if Bill worked at being tough or if he was just born nasty, but his sour breath lingered in the darkness as he snarled final instructions. "Don't touch anything. Not a book of matches. Not a quarter under the couch. Not a cookie or a piece of cheese. Nothing that isn't offered." He shook her arm roughly as if to make his point clear. "They need to trust you. Don't make them suspicious by doing something stupid."

Wearing his long coat, Lemon nudged her other side and huffed into her ear, "Think of yourself as a stray dog. Better, a puppy. A hungry, pitiful, little motherless dog. Adorable, but needy. That's what you are: needy. Can you do needy? No one likes a dog with an attitude. Those growling, flea-bitten mongrels. No one likes them. If you act like that, you'll be out in the cold in a minute. And cough, but not too hard. You don't want to scare them. Don't act contagious for heaven's sake. Cover your mouth when you sneeze." Unlike Bill, Lemon didn't seem worried. He seemed impatient—chiefly with her—but, on the whole, rather pleased with himself. His straggly pale hair fanned out in the wind. This plan he'd concocted was in play.

Pitiful. Hungry? She knew all about hungry, and her skin burned. Every joint and hair follicle ached. She was so dizzy all the streetlights had halos. When Bill poked her side, she groaned, "I hear you."

"We'll be watching," he muttered. "Don't blow this." He shoved her toward the front entrance, and she limped across the plaza, a loose pebble cutting the ball of her foot—one of Lemon's great ideas. She scratched at her neck as though she were wearing a collar and Bill was jerking on the leash. She had to get out of here. Leave. All she needed was a little money. Two bus tickets. One for her. One for Terry. That was all. Why didn't she take that doctor up on his offer? Beg him for a ticket for Terry? Too late.

Pulling open the door against the wind took all her strength, but then it was quiet. Still. Muted silence. And warm. The vestibule was warm. She'd left the wind outside. Feeling lightheaded and weak, she leaned against the wall, her forehead touching the panel, and tried to breathe. Running her finger down the list of electronic names, she finally pressed the button next to M. Sullivan, and in a couple of seconds, she heard Maggie's voice. "Yes?"

"Maggie," she said, trying to keep her voice even, "It's Caroline. I met you at the shop last week. I'm having trouble with my knitting." She clutched her plastic sack in one hand. "Do you have time to help me?" *Please say yes. Don't send me back into the cold.*

"I'll buzz you in. I'm on seven. 7-B."

Lemon had already scratched the number on her palm.

The heavy door clicked. The unlocking mechanism performed smoothly, as if it were a willing accomplice. She gave the handle a shove, and she was in. This was too easy. An overstuffed couch against the far wall wasn't covered with stains or rips or grime. She gravitated toward it. She needed to sit, just rest her head for a moment or two before she found the elevator. Touching the cushion, she lowered herself gingerly as though contact with her filthy jeans might leave a dirty reminder, evidence. Her hands were freezing, but her head was on fire. Cruelty wasn't a thing she recognized in herself—not until now—as she was about to abuse a bunch of old people, rifle through their belongs, steal memories saved for years, rummage through treasured human debris. But she didn't have a choice. Bill had Terry.

Her head resting in her hands, she started to cry. No wrenching sobs, just a spattering of tears and a dripping nose. She was so miserable. And exhausted. It was time to give up. Go home. Then she remembered poor Nolan with acne so disgusting it looked like a Halloween mask and Terry with a trail of needle marks on the inside of his forearm, and she cried harder, which required a fair amount of energy she didn't have. She leaned over and untied her shoe and nearly passed out on the carpet. No one was in the lobby. No one was watching. She collapsed on the cushions. Saturday night, eight o'clock, a stupid time for a problem with knitting, but Lemon had been adamant, waving his arms and prancing around the apartment like he owned the stage in an amateur theatrical. "Spend the night. She won't turn you away."

She couldn't lift her head. Too sick. Too tired. A chill passed through her and then another. She coughed and couldn't stop. Every breath was an effort. She was going to die sooner or later. Why not here? Why not now? The lobby was quiet. Warm. The ceilings were high. The lights were low. One eye closed and then the other. Sleep was a blessing. Her breathing slowed.

She sensed his presence before she saw the blurry pant leg. A thread of drool on her cheek, she tipped her head back to search for a face, a face horrified at finding a nearly dead carcass in his lobby, a mess he'd have to shovel into a black plastic garbage bag and toss in the dumpster. She closed her eyes and groaned.

"Can I help you?" The blurry face belonged to some guy, not much older than she was, who crouched down beside her.

She mouthed, "I'm dying." But he didn't understand, so she whispered, "I have a rock in my shoe." A ridiculous thing to say. Not a plausible excuse to be comatose on his couch.

He eased off her shoe and caught the sharp pebble in his palm. Her foot started to bleed, red drops on the carpet. With hands that were gentle, he lifted her dirty foot a couple of inches and examined the cut. "I have a first aid kit in the office." He staunched the blood with a tissue. Suspicious, his brown eyes traveled over her face. Pushing thick glasses up the bridge of his nose, he spoke in a scratchy voice, "I'll be right back."

Take your time, she thought. *It doesn't matter. I'll die before you get back. Right here on this nice couch. A stray bit of garbage no one will miss.* If she quit breathing by the time he came back, would he do CPR? Cover her mouth with his and puff air into her lungs while he thumped her chest? She pinched her nose with one hand and pressed her lips together. Didn't work. She couldn't fake being dead any more than she could fake being skinny when she was a kid.

"This will sting."

He was back. She'd missed her chance. She was still breathing. And it felt somehow inappropriate to just up and die in front of this person without a proper introduction. His warm hands on her icy foot, she felt the angry cold of the alcohol swab and the quick press of a Band-Aid. His fingers lingered on her skin, adjusting an edge that wouldn't adhere. A patch was sewn on his navy shirt, *Security Resources*. Security. In-house cop. Great. If he knew what she was, he'd chuck her out the front door onto the snowbank. She pulled her foot away.

He touched her cheek, brushed the hair off her face. "You're burning up," he said, his hand on her forehead. "Who are you here to see?"

Blinking, she tried to focus on the potted plant behind him. "Maggie." She couldn't remember the last name. "Maggie something or other."

He squeezed one eye shut and studied her face. "I'm taking you to the ER."

"No. Please," she begged. Not in the game plan. No hospital. No clean white sheets and officious doctors asking difficult questions. She thought of Terry, the absent hostage. She hadn't seen him all day or yesterday either. Maybe panic showed in her face, because the uniformed guy glanced over his shoulder through the heavy glass doors that kept out the night. "Please," she whispered again, "just Maggie. She's my great-aunt."

"Okay." He sighed. "Maybe you're not as sick as you look. And you can't stay here. Not in the lobby."

Why not? she thought. *Cremate me and put me in a little pink jar on the end table. That would be better than what's waiting outside in the cold.*

"Can you put your arms around my neck?"

She moaned at the thought of being jostled, of leaving this very soft couch, but she did what he asked. He lifted her, struggled a bit, and made his way to the elevator. His stiff shirt scratched her cheek. Her nose under his chin, she inhaled the clean odor of shaving lotion. She hoped he hadn't ruptured anything when he lugged her off the couch. *Good deeds never go unpunished.*

He backed into the elevator and hit the button with his elbow, then set her gently on the floor, one strong arm around her shoulders, supporting her as the elevator rose. He leaned down, his warm breath by her ear. "Did you say something?"

She didn't know. Maybe what she was thinking had tumbled out of her mouth, maybe she was delirious, but she mumbled a soft "No." The elevator door opened, and a worried Maggie was standing there, ready to descend and scour the lobby for her visitor.

"Caroline," she said. "What on earth?"

"She fainted on the couch. Out cold."

Carly wobbled a step or two before her knees buckled. His grip on her shoulders saved her. Without him, she would have crumpled on the floor. She thought, *Smile,* but her mouth wasn't connected to her brain.

Maggie stared down at the single bare foot as though the missing shoe might be some sort of explanation. Carly felt a pinch of humiliation at the lines of dirt under her toenails and thought of all those pedicures in her past life, little dots and flowers painted on her big toes, but now when her feet actually mattered, her toes were revolting.

"She's got a fever." The guy sounded official. "She says you're related."

Maggie didn't speak; she just maneuvered to Carly's right side. Between the two of them, Maggie and Mr. Security Resources hauled Carly down the hall—past a gawking mouth-opened woman—and deposited her on Maggie's couch. The apartment smelled like cinnamon, like Christmas and wassail, but there was no tree, just a paltry string of colored lights around a sliding glass door. Dozens of blurry faces in frames stared at her, accused her. They knew why she was here. A younger version of her mother, pre-Dale-Call-Me-Dad, shook a warning finger in her face. Carly's head swam. She was losing it. Three people stood above her. She glanced from one grim face to another, and then her eyes closed without any warning. She was in the building. She'd done her part. Now she could sleep.

The soft chatter morphed into a dream about warm weather and birds making a racket outside her bedroom window at home, but the dream didn't last because she felt awful, and now a fourth face was inches from hers, examining her as though she were an endangered species. This woman had Carly's wrist in her fingers feeling for a pulse, then touched Carly's throat with icy fingers. No sleeping through this. She started to cough.

"We don't know what we're dealing with. Maybe an infection, maybe pneumonia. I hate to say it," the woman glanced at Maggie and then spoke with conviction, "but this might be a drug overdose." Tortoise shell glasses balanced on the end of her nose. The woman's skin looked like a thin layer of plastic stretched over good bones.

"Sue, let's not go looking for zebras." The no-nonsense woman speaking had short, spiky hair, but her voice was calm. "You've never dealt with kids." She lifted one of Carly's eyelids and peered inside. "Her pupils aren't dilated."

Maggie lifted Carly's head gently and arranged a soft pillow beneath it. "She had a mean cough last week when I first met her." The two women glared at Maggie.

"What do you mean *when you first met her*? I thought she was your niece's daughter." Sue's fruity perfume turned Carly's stomach.

"Okay. I should have said *when I met her again*. At the yarn shop."

"She wandered into the yarn shop?" Spiky Hair whispered. "She didn't know who you were?" The unspoken accusation hung in the air like a bad smell. "Seems like a stretch."

"Serendipity," Maggie said, averting her eyes.

"Fate," Sue responded. "This waif needs a friend. But I sense a positive aura. I'm sure you're related. If not now, certainly in a past life."

"Paulo, how did you find her?" Spiky Hair was in on the cross-exam.

Maggie interrupted, "I buzzed her in."

"But Paulo found her."

Jittery, his arms crossed tightly against his chest as if he were protecting his vital organs, he watched the ladies across the length of the room. He rocked back and forth, his toes to his heels. "I get a beep when the doors open, and I check the screen." He shrugged. "She was crying in the lobby and had a rock in her shoe."

"Some rock if it made a girl this old cry." Sue pulled a wooden chair near the couch and plopped down as if she needed to join the small circle for an extended length of time. The Band-Aid was noticed and examined but not touched.

"Jan, do you have a thermometer?" Maggie asked. And the spiky-haired woman left and returned in a moment. She touched a palm-sized device to Carly's left temple and gasped, which startled everyone, except Carly, who already knew her death was imminent.

"It's a hundred and three."

With a light touch, Maggie smoothed the hair off Carly's forehead.

"I'm calling a doctor." Sue pulled a cell phone out of the pocket of her chenille robe. "That's all there is to it."

"They don't make house calls. That went out with hand-cranking car engines." Maggie bit down on her lip.

"This one will." Sue raised her eyebrows. "Dr. Carlyle, chief of internal medicine at the U. One of a long line of nephews waiting to read the fine print in my will. Just you wait and see. A little greed goes a long way."

Carly was starting to feel like a specimen, something unique and wiggly on a petri dish, not a girl, not a girl with an attitude and a grade point average that always surprised school counselors who had a bias against tattoos. These elderly ladies were peering at her like she was just a lifeless exterior and couldn't hear a word they were saying. Like maybe closed eyelids meant her ears had closed too.

She glanced over at Paulo—she liked his name; she liked his looks—and they exchanged a bleary glance, a secret between them. He was fond of these ladies. That was clear. Little girls played house, but little old ladies played hospital. Carly was sure that's where she was—she'd jumped right down the rabbit hole onto the set for *Grey's Anatomy*. Bill would clean them out in a minute, and no one would notice. She closed her eyes, and a wave of sadness hit her.

Sue mixed ginger ale with orange juice while the other lady—her name was Jan—went for an aspirin substitute after a brief discussion about pharmaceuticals. Paulo departed for the lobby to wait for the doctor/nephew to arrive, and at nine thirty-five—they all knew the exact time because Jan kept announcing it—Paulo and a fortyish man, wearing a tux with a stethoscope hanging out of his pocket, arrived.

In such a small space, six was a crowd. No one seemed inclined to leave. The low buzz of conversation about who she was, the cut on her foot, the fainting, the high temperature, and the weather outside didn't include where Carly was living or if anyone had called her parents. *Thank heaven,* Carly thought. That she was Maggie's great-niece seemed to be enough of a family connection, and everyone deferred to Maggie's opinions, particularly when she suggested the medical exam be conducted in the privacy of her miniscule bedroom.

Sheets that smelled like lavender were such a cliché, but Maggie's bed did. And the sheets were clean and fresh, and the bed was soft. Dr. Carlyle was kind. He warmed his stethoscope between his palms before he asked her to take a deep breath. He didn't ask many questions, just how long she'd been sick, how the sickness began, and how it had progressed, but he looked like he already knew her answers before she spoke them.

"Pneumonia," he said, one hand on her forehead. "This girl needs to stay quiet until her fever is gone and her lungs clear. A day or two in the hospital with IV antibiotics and fluids, and she'll start to feel better." He sighed as if it had been a long night and he'd been rounding on nearly dead patients instead of schmoozing with donors at a holiday gala.

Carly was ready with her whispered spiel. She squeezed a few large tears out of the corners of her eyes. "My dad died in a hospital. He was sick a long time. Please, Aunt Maggie, can I just stay with you?"

The doctor and Maggie exchanged a quick look, and he cleared his throat before he spoke. "The hospital is what I recommend, and if your temperature doesn't come down, that's where you're going." He turned toward Maggie. "I'll call you first thing in the morning, and I'll come back on Tuesday after work." He unfolded a blank prescription he took from his wallet and jotted a couple of lines before he stepped back into the living room.

Carly strained to hear the muffled conversation. Someone needed to go to a twenty-four-hour pharmacy, not the doctor—he'd already done his part and needed to return to the party—and Paulo couldn't leave the building, but Jan and Sue volunteered, their voices low. Carly heard them leave with the doctor who was saying, "You must call me right away if she doesn't improve."

Standing next to the bed, Maggie wiped Carly's face with a damp washcloth. "Just sleep," she whispered. "I'll be right here if you need me."

Chapter Twenty-Two

A SICK NOVELTY

STARTING ON THE BACK ROWS, a ripple of concern made its way through the pews on Sunday morning, ending with Lillian Hollingsworth who always sat front row and center. Rose and her funeral were momentarily forgotten because an extremely sick girl had arrived the night before, been buzzed in, and promptly fainted on the couch in the lobby, something that had never happened before. Headline news. Maggie Sullivan, a thin woman with meager resources, and this girl, this abandoned baby in a basket, were connected. A granddaughter? A great-niece? A second cousin once removed? No one was sure. The suggestion of a communicable disease infecting the entire building was something of a concern. Many of the residents of the Eagle Gate had compromised immune systems, but curiosity and innate kindness overcame their fear, and by one o'clock on Monday, people were knocking softly on Maggie's door with sound advice and a plate of cookies, a loaf of fresh bread, or a container of soup. Some items were purchased at the deli at Harmon's, but other papery, veined hands remembered what they thought they'd forgotten and kneaded and mixed baked goods from scratch. Maggie didn't know she had so many well-intentioned friends.

A sick child was a novelty, but most of the women who lived inside the yellow brick walls had been mothers, mothers who nursed sick children through the measles, the mumps, rubella, assorted broken bones, young adult addictions, and the occasional bout of pneumonia. They were a seasoned crew and knew enough to be quiet; the girl was still sleeping.

On Tuesday morning, with a plastic bag of trash in her hand, Maggie was about to head to the garbage chute hidden in a utility closet, when Rachel Murphy came, balancing a humidifier on the front of her walker. Her swollen ankles turned in at an uncomfortable angle, Rachel was inching her way down the hall with brisk determination.

"I thought we could make a steam tent for your girl." Her voice came out in a breathy mumble, having exerted more than she was able. Rachel was a hundred years old. If not for problematic feet, she could easily pass for ninety. Meals on Wheels delivered what she ate, which was not something anyone—a hundred-years-old or not—would consider re-gifting, so Rachel's offering was mechanical.

"Billy nearly died of pneumonia when he was just three, and old Dr. Randall told me later I'd saved his life with a kettle and a tent. That was the difference. That's what he said."

Maggie hefted the Vick's Warm Mist Humidifier—guaranteed to drink two gallons of water and regurgitate steam for several hours—next to the kitchen sink.

Rachel pushed her walker into the living room and started repeating what she'd just said. "I saved Billy's life with a tent and a kettle. My little boy. Not more than three."

Interrupting the old woman with a kiss on her wrinkled cheek, Maggie said, "He was lucky to have such a wonderful mother. This will save Caroline too. If you can just wait here a minute, I'll run next door and see if Jan has a card table."

And because Jan seemed to have one of just about everything, she and Maggie fashioned a tent over the couch and a couple of chairs, turned on the humidifier, and stuck their heads inside to judge the effect. Bending over and inhaling deeply, Rachel bumped the leg of the table, upsetting the works, and the sheet, chairs, and table crashed down around her. Buried her.

For five seconds, Maggie and Jan stood, not moving, hearts pounding. The room was silent. They'd killed the delightful old woman who everyone loved. Her dead body was under the rubble. They were afraid to look, afraid to see a fatal bump swelling on the side of Rachel's head or blood oozing out of her nose, then Maggie heard the old lady laugh. A deep, throaty chuckle that made them laugh too. Maggie and Jan both found an arm and hoisted her up on her arthritic feet. They were in the process of straightening Rachel's clothes and resurrecting the tent when a yawning Carly emerged into this world of women.

The sunshine spilling in the windows made her squint. For the past two days, Maggie had nudged her awake every four hours to take her pills and check her temperature, but other than those few interruptions, Carly had slept almost non-stop since Saturday night. The cotton nightgown the girl was wearing made her look like a child playing dress-ups in her grandmother's clothes. Maggie smiled in a relieved sort of way.

"You're rejoining the living." Jan grinned.

"Breakfast? Pancakes? Scrambled eggs?" Maggie offered.

"Coffee?" Carly said. "Caffeine?"

"Food is what you need." Jan reverted to her high school principal self, and for a minute Maggie was afraid the girl would take offense, but she just glanced at the three of them standing beside the card table with two collapsed legs, a sheet piled on the floor, and a flipped-over walker.

"I heard the commotion." She smiled. "Are you all okay?"

This precious foundling left on the doorstep had a voice and was capable of concern. Maggie had done the math in her head Saturday night. The girl—she didn't think of her as Carly—was nearly eighteen. "We're making a steam tent for your lungs. The air here's so dry."

"It saved Billy's life. A kettle and a tent," Rachel started in with the story churning in her head since Sunday afternoon.

"Great," Carly said. "Maybe a bath first and some food? Then the tent all afternoon." She clutched the doorjamb as if just remembering to feel a bit wobbly. Her color hadn't improved much, and her hair, a light-brown tangle, was limp. Maggie wondered if she'd cut it herself without using a mirror. But deep inside Maggie, something else was taking place. A wealth of memories was bubbling to the surface of a sister who braided Maggie's hair, taught her to play hopscotch in their one-car garage, and listened on the phone years later while Maggie poured out the contents of her broken heart. Barbara, Maggie's only sister, had been dead for over ten years, and her ashes were scattered in the Albion Basin. Even though this girl was grimy and sick, she resembled Barbara. That heart-shaped face and green eyes? She was family. No question. Her sister's only grandchild.

The clothes the girl had been wearing on Saturday were so filthy, Maggie had put them through three cycles in the washer, and when she gave the jeans a shake before she tossed them in the dryer, most of the color was gone. She hated to let the thought enter her mind, but the minute she'd handed the girl the nightgown in exchange for the clothes she'd been wearing, Maggie knew the girl was homeless, living on the streets. The thought broke her heart. How had Caroline found her? Divine intervention? Had a guardian angel guided the girl? Had Barbara guided her? Why had Caroline feigned such an interest in knitting? How had she found the adorable yarn shop on Eleventh East? Maggie would settle her in the tub where she couldn't escape and put the questions to her. That's what she'd do. Then she'd call Caroline's mother and make a plan for the girl's return. It was the only responsible thing to do.

Rummaging in the kitchen, she called out to Rachel, "Stay for a second breakfast," and then she whispered to Jan who was mixing pancakes, "I'm calling her mother."

Jan sliced a finger across her throat. "She's running from something, and she'll run again if she thinks she has to go home. Have you met the stepdad?" She raised both eyebrows nearly to her hairline. "Kids don't run if everything's great. Kids run for a reason."

That unpleasant thought hadn't occurred to Maggie. Thank heaven for Jan. "I haven't met him. I knew Caroline's father, of course, before he died." A good-natured professor a little on the plump side. "But this new man? He's a mystery. My sister died before the remarriage, so no insights there."

"Not Caroline. Carly," Jan corrected. "That's what she calls herself."

Maggie nodded. "I'll go run a tub."

"Let her eat first."

"Of course." So much had happened in the last week or two that thoughts in Maggie's head continued to tumble. She couldn't keep things straight, couldn't work through a problem in a linear fashion, couldn't make two and two add up to four. She rested a damp palm on her chest and took a deep breath. "The skillet's in the drawer under the oven, but I don't have any syrup or jam." Luxury items she couldn't afford.

"Sue will. She has everything. Let's make it a party."

***

Sitting on a yoga mat in a shaft of wintery sunshine, Sue was doing a seated twist, but when Maggie barged into her apartment and gave her an update, Sue stood. She raised her palm as if signaling for peace, then she slowly lowered her arms. "Thirty seconds in Mountain Pose." Then Sue almost bounced off her mat, "Okay, let's do this."

Wearing a purple tunic, she loaded Maggie's arms with a bottle of gourmet maple syrup—no Aunt Jemima for her—and two bottles of Stonewall raspberry preserves. "How delightful. A party. This early in the morning?" She studied Maggie's face. "How are you doing old friend?"

"To tell you the truth, I've been better. I'm feeling a bit scattered."

"Of course you are." She patted Maggie's arm. "And Rachel Murphy is having pancakes with us and not her dead relations? It looks like Rose stole her place in line."

For the first time in days, Maggie laughed, not just a polite chuckle, but a laugh that shook her body. "What we need around here is a little more uproar. Maybe an 8.7 earthquake. Honestly, what else could happen?"

Their eyes met before Sue spoke, "What indeed?"

"I just tempted fate?"

"Yes, but no time for that now."

Maggie nodded and hurried down the hall.

"I'll be there in a minute," Sue called out her door.

Carly was on the floor, her head inside the tent, and Rachel sat on a chair beside her, coaching her on how to breathe. Jan was flipping pancakes in the kitchen. Paulo had materialized after his night shift—something he had never done before—and now he was setting mismatched plates on the table, which had been cleared of Maggie's clutter.

Still wearing her yoga garb, Sue arrived with a fuchsia bag in her hand. She'd collected her bottles of hair product, scissors, a comb, and a hot air brush that looked ingenious, something Sue had discovered in Paris, no doubt.

What was it about love and attention? Carly's lips were still tinged with blue, but there was a bit of light in her eyes as though someone had flipped a switch. One plate in his hand, Paulo was telling a funny story about wading through dozens of Cheetos bags to reach the computer terminals in their office, and a pretty trill of a laugh was coming from Carly—like the sound of a silver bell ringing. The girl could have been Maggie's sister rising from the dead to find a place at the table. The girl had been absolutely round as a toddler, her little green eyes just slits above plump cheeks. But now it was as though Barbara were sitting here at Maggie's table, cutting a pancake with the side of her fork, smiling and chatting with the group of old ladies as though they'd all been transported from this table to a high school cafeteria.

Paulo gave up his seat for Sue and stood near the window in the morning light with his arms folded neatly across his chest. With an odd expression on his face and his glasses at an angle, he was studying Carly eating pancakes as though she were a question he couldn't answer or a problem he couldn't explain. Maybe the girl felt the young man's eyes on her back, because she straightened the cotton nightgown and glanced at him over her shoulder, but she didn't smile.

A familiar rap on the door sounded. Maggie looked up and Ed was standing in the doorway. The surprise was the collection of bags he held in his left hand. Green ribbons and bows and boxes wrapped in brown paper peeked out. Maggie dropped her shoulders and rolled her eyes. What next? Reindeer? A couple of elves?

Who was this guy? A thief? The other night, sitting at the table after he'd made his strange confession, she'd smiled pleasantly and nodded at him to continue. She'd waited for the rest of a funny story, some exaggerated tale about not delivering a pulled-pork sandwich on time or transporting a crate of leaky water bottles across state lines, but no explanation was forthcoming. It was as though someone in the adjacent room had pushed a mute button. Ed just sat there watching her like she was a textbook he needed to study because a pop quiz was coming. She'd been so startled she hadn't spoken until they were waiting at the traffic light with his gloved hand grasping her arm. The snow had stopped falling, but the air had been so cold that each breath chilled her lungs and ice crystals hung in the air. "Really?" she'd finally said. "A thief?" He'd spoken softly as the semaphore changed. "Everyone makes mistakes."

And that's when she knew; somehow he'd discovered her married name. She'd been Googled, or worse, he'd hit the Tribune archives online and read about the scandal dozens of reporters had examined under a microscope. The worst Ponzi scheme in the history of the state. Had his awkward revelation been his way of telling her she wasn't going to hold her past against her because *everyone made mistakes*? Was he kidding? Suicide was a mistake? Suicide was a disaster, a complete heartbreaking disaster, the ultimate punishment for the people left behind, the gift that never quit giving. Not ever. She couldn't get across the street fast enough.

She'd avoided him the last few days, which was hard to do. The Eagle Gate was such a small town, and he was only one floor up, but she'd been successful, until now, until Carly gave him an excellent excuse to pop in for a quick visit. Here he was, ready to share an impromptu breakfast, deliver his gifts, and invade her small home. And the man was absolutely beaming, like a ten-year-old who'd just scored a home run.

"I thought we could celebrate Christmas a couple of weeks early," he said.

Jan called out from the kitchen, "Pull up a chair and have a pancake."

Maggie vacated her spot next to Sue who was suddenly all winsome smiles and fluttering eyelashes. *This flirting business must be innate.* Maggie retreated behind one closed eye.

When she opened it again, Ed was handing one of the bags over to Carly who stared wide-eyed at this bearded man she'd never seen before.

"I thought you might need a few things." He shrugged and smiled pleasantly.

A few things? Carly ripped open the first box and found a strange pair of pants with a drawstring waist. Ed must have gone to REI and told the clerk he needed to outfit a young girl—that he'd never laid eyes on—for an arctic expedition. Out of wrapped boxes came boots, fleece mittens, four pairs of Smart Wool socks, a couple of Ski Utah sweatshirts, and a florescent orange puff parka that would stop rush-hour traffic. Carly glanced around as if this were some kind of a trick or a bear trap lined with money, and Maggie gave her credit for looking chagrinned. Something simple—a pair of high-tech gloves, a couple of movie tickets, or an afternoon at the spa—would have been an appropriate gesture, an understated act of kindness, but this? He was like an ex-father trying to purchase his children on the stock exchange when prices were low.

Ed was laughing, head back, at something Sue said. "If you buy the display, you'll never go wrong." Carly was holding up the orange parka as if it might scorch her fingers while at the same time making a concerted effort to smile.

Buy the display? He'd purchased half the store, Maggie thought.

"Did you go to the REI with the climbing wall?" Sue asked as though she'd been there days before to repel her way down and up. "On Thirty-third South."

"That might be the one."

"Tell the truth," Maggie spoke above the breakfast din. "You told that car of yours what you needed, and it drove you there. *Look, Ma, no hands.* You can't believe his car. Humans are incidental."

"What?" Carly almost shrieked. "You drive a Tesla?"

He feigned a quick bow with a mouth full of pancakes.

Was he some Robin Hood who'd been beamed in from some previous time slot?

He glanced up at Maggie and spoke softly, "Are we still on for Wednesday?" She felt dizzy. Her heart thundered in her chest. Wednesday was the symphony, the Christmas concert.

Sue answered for her. "Of course. She's delighted. Chris Tomlin is the guest artist." No way to decline. Jan was calling out for seconds, Sue was giggling like a sixteen-year-old with an oddly wrinkled neck, Rachel was mumbling about Billy and steam tents, Carly was balling up wrapping paper, and a concerned Paulo looked like a man who arrived at the correct address only to discover the house was missing.

This was too complicated. Maggie wanted them all to leave. She needed a nap. She needed her knitting, worsted wool in her fingers, something she understood. She didn't mind being Ed's friend, but not a beneficiary, because symphony tickets and gifts this expensive invariably came with attached strings. But what could he conceivably want from her?

Chapter Twenty-Three
DANCING WITH OUR FEET

CARLY COULDN'T REMEMBER EVER SPENDING so much time around people this wrinkled. Nothing had prepared her for these zany women sitting in Maggie's miniscule bathroom and brushing color over cheeks dotted with age spots—like it would make a difference. She bit her tongue to keep from saying, "Really guys? Would you decorate a prune like you do an Easter egg?" But she didn't, because they were having such a good time poking fun at Maggie, serious, reluctant Maggie, who claimed she didn't want to go to the symphony with Mr. Fabulously Wealthy 8-B but was in a total freak-out mode getting ready. How many million times had she heard her mother say, "We talk with our feet"? And what were Maggie's feet saying? Carly could almost hear those feet complaining about being shod in orthopedic, rubber-soled shoes while there was still some dance left in those toes.

Jan sat on the edge of the bathtub laughing. Sue had tried to turn the top of Maggie's head into an elegant froth of silver curls, but Maggie looked like a handful of miniature springs had been stolen from a bin at Home Depot and wired to her skull seconds before she'd stuck a fork in a socket. Sitting on the stool, Maggie didn't open her mouth because Sue had a firm grip on the red-hot curling iron as she fussed with a few errant strands around Maggie's ears. It was a miracle no one was burned, no thin skin sizzled, since the curling iron in Sue's hand was used more like a baton she waved to make a point. *This is just like a group installation in sophomore art,* Carly thought, avoiding Sue's dangerous backswing but not wanting to miss all the fun. "Close your eyes." Sue shot a stream of perfume at Maggie's head.

Maggie batted the bottle away. "I don't want to smell like a brothel." Maggie couldn't possibly know what a brothel smelled like, but Carly thought it was a hilarious thing for anyone to say, particularly strait-laced Maggie.

"Come on, Maggie," Jan said. "Have some fun. Enjoy your third act. Think of everything you'll miss if you stomp out of your life at intermission."

Sue squirted more perfume above Maggie's curled hair. "Scents should be released when you move, turn your head, remove a scarf, or unbutton a coat. Forget daubing the stuff behind your ears. By the time a man gets in close proximity to that part of your body, the battle's already lost—or won."

Jan wiggled five fingers at Carly's reflection in the mirror, then she lifted her chin and said, "Husbands. She knows whereof she speaks."

Maggie put up a tentative hand and touched the curls. "Here's the unvarnished truth: he irritates me. He thinks he can buy approval, and that's impossible."

Carly rolled her eyes. "Maggie just landed in that last spaceship inbound from Mars."

Jan started laughing again, slipped, and nearly landed in the tub. She was saved from disaster by grabbing the soap dish.

"Listen," Maggie said as though she might not be heard in a space that small, "He's a very nice man, but we're just not in sync. Everything feels forced."

Sue brushed more pink sparkles on Maggie's cheekbones, stood back and brushed on a little more, and then she rested her hands on her hips, surveying Maggie in the bathroom mirror as though her friend were a canvas nearing completion. "'I tell you, she that can lay hold of him shall have the chinks.'"

"Shakespeare," Jan said.

"No kidding. Romeo and Juliet." Carly grinned. "I've watched it at least four hundred times." That got everyone's attention.

"I'm impressed." The expression on Jan's face said she truly was.

"Chinks," Maggie whispered softly. "Never enough chinks." Their laughter vanished like a layer of soap bubbles down the drain. What had changed? Had the temperature in the bathroom suddenly dropped ten degrees? Carly didn't understand. What did these ladies know that she didn't?

Sue unplugged the curling iron and left it next to the sink.

Maggie sighed. "What would Rose say about all this?"

"Sweetheart," Sue whispered. "We all miss Rose. And no one's suggesting you sell yourself to this man for financial security. Certainly not me."

This pre-date production hadn't started in the bathroom at five o'clock. The entire day had been devoted to prepping Maggie for her date, which was what they had all decided it was. That morning Sue had insisted they all soak their feet in buckets of hot water before they sanded rough skin off their heels and painted their toenails an iridescent blue. Jan thought it made their toes look gangrenous, but Carly had just laughed.

"It's the style now. Purples and blues and even black."

Painted digits that didn't show were one thing, but Maggie refused to have her fingernails painted black, blue, or even a sensuous pink. "That's just not me. Remember I go to work Friday morning." And all the silly urging couldn't budge her, not even Jan saying, "Even an old barn looks better with a fresh coat of paint."

Jan ducked when Maggie tossed a pillow in her direction. "No old barn. No blue paint."

Carly knew they were being silly for her benefit, entertaining her, pulling her inside their tight circle, or maybe they were pretending to feel young again, forgetting aches and pains and disappointments. Whatever the reason, Carly sat in the midst of their laughter and thought, *This must be what it would be like to have a grandmother, a fairy grandmother,* a person she missed. She could use a woman with a magic wand—and soon. She sat watching Maggie and felt so many things at once. Maggie wasn't particularly tidy—there was always a pair of shoes kicked off by the front door and books and junk mail scattered on the table, but everything was clean. Towels in the bathroom and the sheets she used to make up Carly's bed on the couch smelled fresh. Spills on the inside of the refrigerator were wiped up before they got sticky. Carly sighed. She couldn't stay. In a day or two she'd have to disappear, but she would miss Maggie. So much.

At six thirty, Jan and Sue left. Perfumed and coiffed, Maggie was fussing in the kitchen. "There's clam chowder, half a carton of broccoli salad, some ravioli Mrs. Wellington brought over on Tuesday." Maggie didn't waste a thing, not a crumb, not a half cup of soup, not three stale chocolate chip cookies, or two slices of leftover meat loaf that Mrs. Nielsen had delivered, smiling, on Wednesday. Nine months ago, Carly wouldn't have understood, but she did now. Going hungry day after day wasn't all that fun.

Maggie straightened when she heard the knock of the cane, but she didn't hurry to the door. She turned and studied Carly with an unspoken question on her face.

"It's okay." Carly leaned over and kissed Maggie on her sparkling pink cheek. "I'll be here when you get back." Maggie's face relaxed, and she opened the door. Sue and Jan called him Brother Johnson to his face and 8-B behind his straight back. Maggie typically skipped over his name, but in a crunch, she called him Ed. One syllable. No smiles.

He took in the curled hair and the trace of paint on Maggie's cheeks and the pink gloss on her lips, and he winked at Carly. "Does she have a curfew?"

The guy was a charmer, no question. "I'm thinking eleven at the latest." She tapped a non-existent watch on her thin wrist. "She needs her sleep."

He held Maggie's coat, which made her look more uncomfortable, if that were possible, and then they strolled down the hall.

Carly fidgeted on the couch and knit a row or two until she felt certain Maggie wasn't coming back to fetch a glove or her purse or the handkerchief she'd ironed that afternoon and forgotten on the counter. Hugging the wall as though a passerby might be able to see through the window on the seventh floor, Carly stole into Maggie's bedroom. She nudged open the top drawer in Maggie's dresser, examining the socks and slips and underwear, before she reached beneath the contents. There wasn't much there, certainly nothing hidden, and then the faded velveteen box almost leaped into her palm. It contained a ring, an antique for sure, with three tiny diamonds. Returning the ring box to the drawer, she reached into the back corner for the little pouch with a drawstring. It rustled. Two fives and a handful of twenty-dollar bills, folded twice, were tucked inside.

Under the crocheted doily on top of the dresser, she noticed a letter, actually a printout with a penciled note on the bottom and today's date in the upper right-hand corner. No envelope. She opened the sheet folded in thirds, scanned it, and inhaled a mouthful of air. "Poor Maggie." She grasped two handfuls of her short hair and tugged her head back and forth. She stood up, sat back down, and bit her bottom lip. Where will Maggie go? But Carly couldn't think of that now, couldn't let bad news distract her. There was no time. She and Terry were in serious trouble. She sat on the edge of the bed and counted the money out loud. She gasped. Smoothing the bills with her hand, she counted again. Almost five hundred dollars. It was a rainy-day fund, but all Carly saw were two tickets to San Diego where Bill and Lemon would never find them—and that was something to think about.

She fingered the bills, counting them for a third time, when Maggie's landline rang. She'd only heard it ring once before, and the noise jerked her back into the present. She picked up the bedroom receiver.

Terry's voice. "Carly. Buzz me in." He was probably at the front door.

"Are you straight-up nuts? Anyone can see you."

"We've got to talk."

"Are you alone?" Stupid question. She knew he wasn't. They'd watched Maggie leave.

"It's just me," he lied.

"Get out of there. Loop around to the west entrance. Don't go straight. Wander around." She sounded like Lemon. "I'll meet you in ten minutes. If anyone's parked in the loading zone, wait in front of that dry cleaners."

She stuffed the bills back in the pouch and shoved the drawer shut with her hip.

***

Shivering, slouched against the yellow brick wall, Terry stood waiting. A bruise on his cheek had turned that sickly yellow tinged with green. She yanked him inside. "Look down. Away from the camera." Adjacent to the exterior door was an unlocked janitorial closet. She and Terry dodged inside, closed the door with a firm click, and flipped on the light. The stench of industrial-strength chemicals hit her full on. A commercial vacuum and a bucket with a wringer didn't leave much room for standing.

"Gag," she whispered.

"What happened to your hair?" he said.

"One of the old ladies trimmed it. They think I'm about ten."

The closet was muggy, but he couldn't stop shivering, his thin arms crossing his chest, his hands tucked in his armpits. "I found Nolan's backpack under the sink in the kitchen." His eyes were huge, and he looked ready to cry. "No one's come around asking about him. Police don't care. You'd think they'd match up his face with surveillance videos or something." Terry wasn't making sense. Who would miss Nolan?

"Why didn't Lemon chuck it? The backpack?"

"They wanted me to find it." He shrugged. "Some kind of screwed up warning."

The vacuum and mops crowded their feet as they stood in the silent closet, unsure what was waiting outside. The chemical stench in the confined space made her nauseous. She touched his bruise with the tip of her finger, and his cheek twitched with pain, but he didn't look at her face because his eyes were closed with his neck stretched back as if he might be sending a prayer through the ceiling.

"Do you think if I'd been as thin as a stick and you weren't gay, we'd be in this mess?" She couldn't stop herself from saying it. "Or if your dad were a human and my dad weren't dead."

"Geez, Carly, now's not the time to get introspective. We're in a load of trouble. More than you know."

She started to sweat. The massive pipe behind her was making horrifying gulping noises like it was swallowing sewage. She skirted a disgusting-looking drain in the middle of the floor. Terry finally spoke. "If your dad hadn't died, I'd have moved in with you guys. He was everything my dad's not."

She hadn't thought of that before. That she was a stand-in for her dad. A rescuer. She stood a little straighter.

Terry worried a cold sore in the corner of his mouth with his thumb. The scab had cracked.

She inched away from the pipe before she inhaled. "Maggie's got enough cash in her drawer to get us to San Diego, plus a deposit on a room—nothing fancy, but who cares. It's warm there." She'd need that ring too. Pawn it for food money. "We can make up some flyers for people with dogs on Coronado Island. They're loaded. There's a dog beach. We can walk the dogs to the beach—everyday if they want—and let the pups play. Tire them out." She'd been thinking about this since October. She'd even sketched a couple of flyers on the back of paper she'd snatched out of the recycling bin.

She'd been there once. Strolling down the beach in front of the Hotel Del Coronado with the sun in her face and its heat on her shoulders. She'd been surprised by hundreds of dogs—and not a single fight or even a growl. They were just so happy, chasing balls and sticks, running in and out of the waves. Dogs, all breeds and sizes.

Tails wagging. A couple of dachshunds were wearing orange life vests. Dog Heaven. Owners stretched out on the beach chatting in the sunshine. She'd been there on a girls' weekend with her mom, a therapist's suggestion, and left Dale-Call-Me-Dad smoldering at home with his three obnoxious brats. She and her mom had eaten Mexican and seen a couple of movies, but that dog beach was where Carly wanted to be. With all those happy mutts playing in the water and wagging their tails as if life were simple.

Terry leaned the mop in the corner, turned the bucket upside down, and sat down hard. The metal scraped on the concrete. "We'll never get past them." He'd given up, caved in. "It's like I've got a tether around my ankle. Lemon's a human fly—he sees in every direction at the same time." He grabbed her hand. "We've got to do what they want. Let them in here." His face was ashen. "Think about Nolan."

"I am," she snapped. "I think about him, about Lemon, about this whole mess, all the time. I dream about it." She pressed her fingers against her temples like her head was about to explode. "But they're not going to beat us, not you and me."

"They think you're holding out, pretending to be sick. You've been here a week." He grasped her hand more tightly. His palm was sweaty. "They want their money."

"It's not their money. What did those slugs do to earn anything?"

"They think it's theirs. That's all they do—talk about how they're going to spend it."

"So how did you get away tonight?" No question: Terry was a messenger. Lemon and Bill were probably waiting around the corner, and Lemon was smoking one cigarette after another and flipping the butts down the storm drain.

She opened her mouth, ready to tell Terry about the tunnels, an underground maze lined with immaculate yellow brick tile connecting the buildings on Temple Square, the perfect exit, the perfect escape, but mouth open, she stopped. Right now, it was best not to trust Terry—love him, but not trust him. She had to keep a clear head and think for them both. She and Terry could tunnel out, so to speak, right under Lemon and Bill's eyes. She and Terry would have tickets to California in their hands before it would even occur to those two creeps that they'd been outfoxed.

"How can I get a hold of you?" she whispered.

"You can't. I don't have a phone." It was like they'd cut out his tongue. "You'll hear from me in a couple of days. Maybe Sunday or Monday. The first of next week." She wasn't the only one planning.

"Okay, Terry. They'll send you back here. And when they do, you've got to be ready for anything. Flexible is what I mean, 'cause I'll have a plan. Trust me?" She put a hand on his shoulder and looked in those exhausted brown eyes. "We're going to spend Christmas on the beach this year. You and me. Sunny San Diego. Hold that picture in your head, Terry. It's going to be okay."

But those brave words coming out of her mouth decided something for Carly. She could not steal from the women on seven or even Mr. 8-B. She couldn't start a new life on something so ugly and rotten. She couldn't turn into a Lemon. She'd borrow Maggie's cash, but she'd pay it back, every nickel, the first chance she got. She'd leave a note in Maggie's drawer, an IOU.

Chapter Twenty-Four
WHO ARE YOU?

CARLY PUSHED THE EXTERIOR DOOR open with her shoulder, and Terry slipped out into the glare of a streetlight. He reeled as the harsh cold hit him. His coat was thin. He didn't look back, didn't say good-bye. She didn't see Lemon, but she knew he was there, just out of sight.

She felt the frigid rubber mat beneath her bare feet as she watched Terry slink away. Her clean toes painted blue felt like a betrayal, like she'd stepped into a world with plenty of food and a safe place to sleep and abandoned Terry to fend for himself in a pack of mangy wolves. And it was cold, bitterly cold. She hadn't been outside in a week, but she could look out the window and see ice on the sidewalks and piles of snow that didn't melt. The heavy door shut with a whoosh, and she scampered down the hall, caught the elevator, and was back up on seven, but her head was still on the first floor, huddled in a closet with her only real friend.

Tunnels. Their existence wasn't a secret, but it wasn't common knowledge either. An escape route for Terry and her could also let in the rats, but according to Sue, who seemed to know everything, those tunnels were always well lit with florescent lights. There were security cameras and kind, beefy guards constantly patrolling. "The tunnels save the bigwigs from the weather and the groupies," Sue had confided. And maybe those tunnels could save Terry. She'd have to find him a white shirt and tie so he'd blend in with the clean-cut troop marching beneath the streets.

Back in the apartment, too nervous to sit, she wandered over to the bookcase against the wall, one of Maggie's fixer-uppers. "Lost causes," Carly whispered to herself. Someone's garbage wasn't always a treasure. Maggie had painted the whole business a dusty shade of blue and filled it with an odd assortment of houseplants and a dozen second-hand classics with dog-eared corners. With the novel *Rebecca* in hand, Carly cocooned herself in Maggie's afghan and was just starting down the road to Manderly when she heard an urgent, business-like knock on the door. She expected to see Jan checking on her with a donut as an excuse, but instead there stood Paulo Ferrante wearing his starched uniform like a suit of armor. And the guy wasn't smiling.

"I need to come in for a minute." His voice sounded official.

She stepped aside. She'd been here a week, but this was his first solo appearance. Something about the set of his shoulders made her anxious, and she waited for him to say something nasty, because in her experience, that's what guys did.

He crossed the room and stood in front of the sliding doors, framed by the Christmas lights, like a man enclosed in a marquee. She didn't think he was posing, because he didn't seem like he had a huge ego, but here he was anyway, gorgeous and tall in spite of thick glasses, wearing that navy uniform that announced what he was, *Security*. Why was he here, on the seventh floor, staring at her? Logic insisted not all straight guys were jerks—there was her dad for instance—but she'd been shoved against lockers and tripped in the hall too many times to count. The cafeteria at school was a minefield of snorts and mean laughter. Harassing overweight girls was politically correct, socially acceptable, and cruel every time. She curled her frigid toes under the afghan.

He cleared his throat. "Are you okay?" This was a dumb thing for him to say, and he knew it.

She thought she'd help him out. "Do you want something to eat? The fridge is packed. Mrs. Abernathy brought cookies, and they're to die for."

"She lives down on three, and she's a sweetheart. They all are." There was a defensiveness to his voice that sounded like he was leveling an accusation at her, like maybe her offer of a cookie was a ruse. He didn't move, didn't speak. Were his feet stapled to the carpet? What next? She swallowed hard and clutched the book to her chest.

When she was a kid, she had a life-size cardboard cutout of Han Solo in her bedroom. She loved him. He had a blaster in one hand, and he didn't talk, didn't lurk around, didn't rifle through her stuff, didn't compete for her parents' attention, didn't bug her about what she ate. Pretty much perfect. Maybe Paulo might be made of the same stuff—cardboard. Good to look at, but not particularly chatty. And then the cardboard bent in half and sat right there on the couch, next to her, with not so much as a blink behind those dark rimmed glasses as he glared in her direction.

"Who are you?" he said, which struck her as odd because she was the same person she'd always been. Inside her head, she was still the fast talking plump girl, but he wasn't here to ask about her dress size. He'd seen something. She opted for a distraction she'd overhead once in the cafeteria when a cute blonde was being excessively cute and explaining her name.

"I'm Barbara Caroline Maughan. Named after my grandmother." She gave him a smile she hoped was winsome. He didn't respond, so she kept on going. "But no way could I say Barbara when I was learning to talk, so I started calling myself Baba, which wasn't okay with my dad because he never liked the Beach Boys, and me saying my name sounded like *Ba Ba Ba Bababarbara Ann*, at least to him." She paused for a breath but Paulo still wasn't saying a word. "Dad decided I should go by my middle name. So then at school, I became B. Caroline which was a real problem because it turned into a joke. Be Caroline. Like maybe I was trying to *be* someone else, because who in their right mind would want to *be* me?" She'd said too much, something she did when she was nervous, but this guy, Mr. Security, was sitting close enough for her to see a tiny red line by his left ear. He'd nicked himself shaving, but no scab. She looked down at his hands. They were amazingly clean, no dirt under those pristine fingernails. What was it about this place? Was there some dirt alert device in the ceilings?

"What are you?" He cleared his throat. "I guess that's what I should have asked."

"What kind of a question is that? What am I?" She wanted to cry, because clearly, he already knew what she was, but she spoke up instead, "What are you?"

"I'm a guy who tries to keep a bunch of old people safe."

"Right. That's your job." He wasn't sitting here on the couch because he was interested in sharing a cookie with her. He wasn't here to flirt or get her non-existent phone number. He wasn't going to suggest a burger or a movie when the bacteria finally exited her lungs. When she'd done the whole fainting routine a week ago, he'd carried her snug against his chest with her weak little heart galloping along at a hundred and eighty, but maybe he hadn't felt that tug in the center of his being like she had. Did he think about that ride up the elevator a million times a day, his warm breath in her hair, his brawny arm circling her shoulders keeping her steady? She did, but maybe it was just all in a day's work for him. Maybe rescuing was old news. She should have known. All guys are trouble.

She scratched the back of her neck with her blue fingernails and coughed a little cough, before she nodded at the door. "I guess what I am right now is tired."

"Come with me." This was no invitation. His gruff voice felt like a tractor beam. "I want to show you something."

Like maybe a train looking for a place to jump the tracks? That *something* was going to be Terry covered in blood by the exterior door or Dale-call-me-Dad waiting downstairs with the police. She could feel something bad coming, and she would have held back, but sitting there on the couch, Paulo reached over and touched the back of her hand. Her knees turned to jelly, and her ankles weren't trustworthy either. He did it again, that warm pressure on her thumb, as they marched down the hall and onto the elevator. He hit B and down they went, her stomach right under her heart.

The basement hall was dimly lit. They passed a couple of offices, doors closed, and kept walking until they came to a sign that said, "Security Personnel Only." The door, which had a smudged glass window, was open. The room was dark. A couple keyboards and five screens in a semi-circle sat on a large desk, monitoring the outside entrances. From the looks of things, the lobby was empty and so was the west entrance and the swimming pool. Not much happening on the plaza or on the walkway into the garden. A whiteboard listed the names of the residents next to three straight columns labeled *Here, Out of Building,* and *Out of Town.* The colorful magnets next to M. Sullivan and E. Johnson indicated they were out. Not very original, but the message was clear: Mr. Security kept track of everyone.

The minute she walked into the office and saw those screens, she knew she shouldn't have come. He was setting her up. "What do you do when everyone's tucked in for the night?" she asked.

"I relax and start studying."

With one eagle eye on the screens. Any mention of Paulo, and Jan always chimed, "He lives with his mother," as though that were a commendation of the highest order, but he spent his nights here and went to class in the mornings, and for an hour sometime between four and six thirty p.m., he must hit the gym to tone up those manly biceps. Did he head home in the late afternoon to nap and shower? Lucky him.

Aleph's mess, Cheetos bags and maybe the remnants of a burrito, had been balled up and stuffed in a garbage sack. A week ago she would have been tempted to scrounge for a couple of leftover bites or a stray chip or two. Not tonight.

Leaving her standing, Paulo dropped into the rolling chair and typed a couple commands. The center screen jumped back an hour in time. She inhaled and squeezed her eyes shut, but not for long, because there were three guys standing in the shadows across the plaza: Lemon, who never wore a hat; Terry, who looked pained; and the other person had to be Bill facing away from the camera. Clever Bill. On screen one, Lemon gave Terry a rough shove, and then Terry walked unsteadily across the plaza under the hazy lights. Screen two. Terry punched in the number for 7-B and talked into the microphone, but there wasn't any audio. He hung up the house phone and went back outside. Enter adorable Carly on screen number three. Barefoot, holding the west door open for Terry, she glanced around like the guilty person she was. She and Terry vanish into the janitor's closet, and the little digital clock in the corner of the screen clicked away as Paulo watched the closed closet door—for the second time that night.

"Who's the guy?" His eyes traveled over her face and down to her white-knuckled hands clutching the edge of a console.

"He's my best friend," she muttered. "He's gay."

A gap was about to open—he wanted to believe her. She could feel it.

"Why let him in the side door? Why didn't you just buzz him in?"

"I don't know." She bit down on her lip. "I thought you might see him," she confessed to the linoleum.

"I have seen him. Plenty." He tapped a few keys, opened another file, and clicked through twenty stills—various times of the day and the night. Terry and Nolan waiting by the bus stop. She gasped. There was Nolan, not dead, but the pictures didn't stop; they kept rushing by on the screen. Burt straggling behind Maggie and her friends heading down South Temple. Loveable Terry with a fresh haircut scanning people coming and going at lunchtime. Terry and Lemon standing at the edge of the plaza—watching. But no pictures of Bill, just a grey blur, just a shadow, just a nondescript guy with a hat pulled down low on his forehead and thick eyebrows that joined in the middle.

"Aleph and I have been watching these guys for a couple of weeks."

Her chest rose and fell. She was breathing through her mouth. In and out. Now was not the time to panic, because she couldn't duck past him. He filled every square inch between her and the glass door.

"And then out of nowhere," Paulo said, "a pretty little girl arrives, down and out, sicker than sick, probably homeless. Low and behold, she's Maggie's long-lost niece. A Christmas miracle." He tapped the surface of the desk with his index finger. "What are the chances?"

She shrugged and wondered if he had handcuffs in that backpack sitting in the corner.

"You arrive, and this whole building comes to life. People smiling, hopeful. Interested in living again. Trading bits of news. *How's that girl up on seven today? Is she feeling better?* Maggie's turned into a celebrity because somebody actually needs her."

She felt sliced down the middle, flayed wide open. "I love Maggie," she whispered, more to herself than to him.

"Give me a break." He leaned forward in his chair. "Who are you really? B. Caroline, or Carly, or whatever your name is? What are you doing here? It better not be what I think it is." His finger was out and right in her face. "A scam."

Too bad she'd already played the fainting card, but her throat still felt raw, and it was hard to speak. "Maggie is my grandmother's sister, her only sister. That's not a lie." He was staring at her, eyes hard as flint. "I went into a yarn shop to learn to knit, and there she was. She looked like my grandma, had the same voice, used the same words. She was kind to me from the first day I met her."

"Knitting?" He rolled his eyes. "You've fooled those ladies on seven, but you haven't fooled me."

Maggie Sullivan was the only good thing that had happened to her in years, and he was turning it into something ugly. And maybe it was. She looked over his shoulder at the photo display that kept zipping by. Lemon, Burt, Nolan, and Terry.

"Hey," she protested, "have you ever tried it? I can actually make something with my hands." But the blue nail polish called her a liar. "We sit on the couch— knitting—and watch mysteries on Channel Seven. And she tells me stuff about my grandma. Stories. Things I never knew." She was scrambling hard, but he wasn't buying it.

"I can hear it in your voice. You were a privileged little girl." He drummed a pencil against the table. "The forty-year-old you—who's going to be waiting tables—is going to hate the eighteen-year-old punk who stole all her chances. Cause that's where you're headed, that or jail."

She hated the way *punk* came out of his mouth, like a slur.

He stood. The chair hit the desk, rollers spinning. He grabbed her shoulders roughly. "You're tossing your life down the drain." She couldn't duck, couldn't squirm out of his grasp. His face was inches away from hers. Was he going to kiss her? She jerked her head to one side. His jaw grazed her cheek, and suddenly all the anger and bluster left him. She didn't recognize the girl she saw mirrored in his soft brown eyes.

"You're really a mess, aren't you?" He shook his head.

"You could say that."

"I can help you." And she knew that he meant it.

"No," she said, "actually, you can't."

He touched her cheek with a hand that was calloused but warm, and then his mouth found hers, and he kissed her, softly. His lips were chapped, and he tasted faintly like Cheetos, but she didn't care. His hands on her waist, he lifted her onto the console so they were eye-to-eye. Gently cupping her face in his hands, he kissed her again before he whispered, "Why am I doing this? I must be out of my mind."

If she had been expecting him to say anything, that wouldn't have been it, but she hadn't been expecting anything. This was all new to her. She'd never been kissed before—not once. She'd been groped on the bus and shoved in the hall, but she'd never been kissed. Not like this. Whispered softness.

Moving slowly, he touched her face and then traced the outline of her mouth with his fingertip as though he were blind and this was his only way of learning who she really was. She buried her face in his chest. She wanted to cry, wanted to tell him everything, wanted to beg him for help, but behind Paulo, Terry flashed by on a screen.

"Please don't be what I think you are," he muttered, "because if I have to choose, I can't choose you."

Chapter Twenty-Five
AN ARROW MARKED UP

As she was exiting symphony hall, Maggie knew she was being morbid, and maybe if she'd started out calling him Edward, things would have been different, but in the back of her head, *Ed* sounded like *Dead*, and the feeling this relationship would not end well had dogged her for days. A couple of weeks ago when he was still the mysterious Mr. 8-B, she'd been sort of intrigued, but now she had an odd sense she was somebody's project, like *Re: Maggie* on the top of a memo, or *Ms. Sullivan* named in a codicil in a will, or *M. Memmott needs saving* in that little notebook he kept in his breast pocket. There was an agenda at play here, but no one had invited her to the planning sessions with a therapist or an attorney.

It wasn't that Ed's color wasn't good, because it was. He was the picture of robust health other than his significant limp and the duck-headed cane in his hand. When they'd left The Eagle Gate, she'd floated along beside him just like a smiling actress in a Celebrex commercial—two blissful seniors holding hands and gazing off a cliff at the ocean—waiting for the right moment if their knees didn't give way and the cliff didn't crumble beneath them. But even if their knees, hips, and the ledge cooperated, that moment wasn't going to arrive anytime soon, because she wasn't some cracked china vase that could be purchased in Bertoni's Antiques on Third South. She was a woman with a mouth and a brain crammed with tough memories and thoughts of her own. Years ago she'd taken a turn being a pretty girl on a handsome man's arm, and what had it gotten her? A twenty-seven year sentence living in Fremont Park and children who ran the other way when they saw her coming.

Earlier that evening, she'd eaten scrumptious food on Ed's dime. Dinner at The Roof was an upgrade from The Cheesecake Factory. Twelve stories up, she'd sliced succulent bites of prime rib while she'd stared the Angel Moroni right in the eye through the plate glass windows. For a hundred and twenty-six years, that angel perched on top of the temple had watched the trees and the city grow beneath him without breathing a word, but now she needed the statue to give her a nod or wink to suggest how she should feel, but he didn't move either one of his golden eyelids, not once. She offered him a spoonful of her crème brûlée, but he wasn't tempted, he just held that trumpet to his lips as though letting her know he'd seen it all from on high, and the only thing new in this world was the history a person didn't know.

The symphony had been lovely, and she and Ed crossed symphony square with *God Rest Ye Merry Gentlemen* still playing in her perplexed head. They didn't quarrel or spar. She didn't question him. What was the point? She knew he was a good man, a generous man. Their laughter was polite and good-natured. They just came at life from different directions, and that was what she meant to tell him: *Thank you, but no thank you.* No more awkward dinners where she felt like she was chewing on cash, dinners that cost more at one sitting than her food budget for a couple of months. She'd refer the elegant Mr. 8-B to Lillian Hollingsworth on the fourth floor with her cheese ball and her elder blog and her generous hips. Maggie would tie a red ribbon around Ed's neck and stuff him under Lillian's tree, because Maggie was just too old to take any more risks. Her heart couldn't endure more hurt, and in seventy-four years, that's what she'd learned. Love was followed closely by exquisite pain. John, her children, and even Rose had abandoned her. Something must be terribly wrong with Maggie Sullivan. She'd known it for years. She didn't deserve love. It was as simple as that.

Only the brightest stars outshone the city lights, and Maggie's and Ed's breaths puffed white as they walked along. *Do the right thing*, she told herself. *Make the stern pronouncement.* For no reason that made any sense, her eyes started to water and her nose started to drip—not the refined look a person needed for making a serious rejection—and she discovered she didn't have a handkerchief in her pocket. Being discreet, she wiped a drip from the end of her nose with her mittened thumb, and Ed pretended not to notice.

"Christmas isn't Christmas if you're not spending a fair amount of time freezing." And he smiled. "My parents emigrated from Norway before I was born. Converts. All their Christmas memories included stories about near-death experiences on frozen lakes and being high-centered in snowdrifts. I tried to spend the holidays in Hawaii one year—couldn't make it work and came home early. It was just too warm and humid."

If he wanted a real change of pace, she thought, *he should have visited Fremont Park for the holidays. Christmas creepy.*

"Hawaii?" she said. "Hard to imagine being unhappy on a trip to Hawaii."

He opened his mouth and shut it before he decided to laugh. "Have I offended you? New money?"

She shrugged. "New money, old money. People make silly distinctions. It's all just money to me."

"Did I overdo it with Carly?"

"Maybe a little."

"I didn't mean to offend."

She patted his arm. "It's okay."

Walking along in an easy rhythm—step-cane-step—neither spoke as they passed Temple Square and the millions of lights twinkling in the night sky. They were both slender and tall. Her hand fit easily in the crook of his arm. He paused in front of the statue of Brigham Young as though he were posing and said, "I was the kid whose parents jabbered in broken English. Parent-teacher conferences were torture. I wanted to hide under those little tables and chairs. It was hard for my parents too. When I was ready to start high school, they pulled up stakes and moved back to Norway."

"What did you do?"

"I was fourteen. I went with them. Then I was the kid no one understood."

"You must have grown up hearing Norwegian."

"Sure, but those garbled words never came out of my mouth. I was Ednar, the poster child for assimilation, until I turned fourteen. Four miserable years, and then I was on a plane heading west with a scholarship to BYU in my hand."

"To the land of the free and the home of the brave?"

"To the land of opportunity. That freckled-faced kid with clunky glasses married a well-connected girl and set about making money as quickly as humanly possible."

"You were a Viking coming to pillage and plunder." She raised her eyebrows.

He laughed and brushed a stray flake of snow out of her hair. "Something like that. If there were any ladders in the vicinity, I climbed them." He tapped his cane against the concrete and glanced away from her. "If you hold a penny close enough to your eye, it's all you can see." He was quiet then, glancing at the frozen pond across from the temple doors.

An odd thought from a man who enjoyed spending money more than anyone she'd ever encountered. Was he under orders to spend the way he did? Sealed orders? Penance or a mission assigned from . . . whom? She stretched her head back and gazed up at Moroni who seemed unfazed by the cold. Where was that nod, that wink, or a drone note from on high to let her know she was dancing in the right direction and not teetering near the edge of some cliff in a TV commercial?

The Eagle Gate was a block away, a reassuring mass of windows and yellow bricks, and up in the penthouse, a Christmas tree was blazing with hundreds of flickering white lights.

"How long did it take you to string all those lights?"

He gave her a dutiful smile. "I hired a decorating service."

"You're kidding. Services to string lights on trees?"

He nodded his head as they skirted a patch of black ice.

Why go to the trouble and make all the phone calls? She pictured him standing aside as a troop of elfish decorators invaded his quiet with garlands and sparkling bows and oversized ornaments. Was he planning several large parties, catered affairs for the city's elite, all those friends from the Alta Club where she didn't belong? Just thinking those thoughts made Maggie realize her legs ached. Her ankles were swollen, no question about that. She tightened her scarf with her free hand. Her ears were freezing. Time for the handoff to plump Lillian on the fourth floor, but as they turned to stroll along South Temple in the chill breeze, Maggie clutched his arm more tightly. He smiled at her touch and circled her waist with his left hand, pulling her close. She didn't pull away. They walked into the wind without speaking until they arrived at the west door. She forced herself to think about Carly. Was the girl asleep on the couch, had she made any phone calls while Maggie was away, and what would the girl like for breakfast? Her mind had conveniently turned the page into tomorrow. Standing in the elevator, she wasn't surprised when Ed asked, "Would you like to come up and see the view?"

She'd love to see the view—Temple Square in miniature and all points west— but she whispered her refusal, "Too tired."

"Another time." And he left her at the doorway.

Carly was asleep, one arm flung over the edge of the couch. Her clothes were scattered on the floor, and a dirty bowl and spoon sat where the girl had left them on the end table. She looked so peaceful and young—a little girl maybe ten or eleven— and Maggie resisted the urge to tuck the blanket around her and plant a kiss on her forehead. She mustn't get attached. This girl, healthy and well, was ready to fly back to wherever she'd come from or perhaps land someplace new. And she would be missed.

Her shoes in one hand, Maggie sat on the side of her bed and massaged the ball of her foot. She glanced toward the mirror wondering how her corkscrew curls had survived the evening, but her eyes stopped at the dresser. The top drawer was ajar. Not more than a half-inch, but enough to tell her what she didn't want to know. A couple of irregular beats, and then she felt her heart shrink. Her hands trembling, she couldn't see properly and wasn't sure she was awake. She unbuttoned her coat, let it drop on the floor, and recognized the navy puddle it made at her feet, but she didn't pick it up, didn't hang it carefully in the closet.

Grabbing the knobs, she gave one quick tug and the top drawer opened. Her neatly arranged clothes were mussed. The bills she'd folded so painstakingly were stuffed willy-nilly inside the pouch. She flattened them with her hand and mumbled the count. She thought of hours spent knitting dozens of hats, the cables turned, increase, decrease, slip-knit-and–pass.

She placed the pouch next to her socks and opened the faded blue box cautiously as if it might snap shut and cut off her fingers. Her mother's wedding ring was tucked in the velvet crease. Covered with age spots, Maggie's hands pressed against her chest, her heart slowed, and she wondered what to do. Her feet wouldn't budge. To the ceiling she muttered, "I am no longer myself." For the first time since moving to 7-B, she felt wary, unsafe, like she should check the closet for glassy-eyed strangers. A practical second opinion, that's what she needed. She'd visit Jan, but Jan had a rigid schedule, a ten o'clock bedtime that never varied.

Careful to close the door softly and forgetting her shoes on the floor, Maggie walked out of the apartment and made her way down the lit hall to Sue's apartment but received no response to her knock. She called, "Sue," in a loud whisper, but Sue wasn't there. Maggie ran her fingers through her hair, uncoiling the curls. What now? There was no need to panic, but she rushed down the hall as though she were being chased, arrived at the elevator door, and pressed the arrow marked *up*.

Palms sweating, she didn't ring the bell—if he was asleep, she'd leave—but the tap with one fingernail was answered so quickly he might have been waiting for her behind the closed door, except his starched shirt was untucked and he was missing his shoes. They stood in the dimly lit entry, two mature people in their stocking feet, not speaking for several long minutes, until he said, "You came to see the view?" Which was just a nice way of asking if she'd lost her mind or left her frontal lobe in his pocket after dinner.

"I hoped you might still be awake."

He glanced at his watch. "Almost ten thirty." Good to know. Maybe.

"I feel violated," she blurted and felt heat rise in her cheeks.

His look passed concerned and went straight on to startled. She could see wheels turn in his mind, reviewing his evening's behavior.

"It's not about you." She swallowed the sob in her throat. "It's Carly."

"Come on in, Maggie," he said quietly, as if he'd been expecting the visit, and he held the door open.

Entering the room filled with chrome and soft leather, she almost gasped. It was perfect, austere but perfect. Her toes touched an ivory fur rug so soft she almost forgot she was frightened. The ceilings were high, probably ten feet, and in front of the window stood the tree that shimmered.

"When I was a little girl," she mumbled softly, "my sister and I used to crawl under the Christmas tree, lie on our backs, and stare up through the branches."

"Would you like to do that again? It might take us a while to get old knees to bend, but we could do it." He laughed, but he looked as tired as she felt, so she sat on the edge of a chair and began her story.

His eyes never left her face as he nodded and muttered in all the right places, but as she spoke, she realized that nothing had been taken, no crime had been committed, and the thought occurred to her and perhaps to him that in her excitement about the symphony and her new hairstyle, she might have left the drawer ajar. Except, and the *except* was large in her head, her small reserve of cash—and it must seem paltry to him—had been handled and stuffed in the pouch.

Tracing a finger along the polished chrome, she knew she must sound pitiful, and she felt ashamed, sorry she'd come. She stared at the Christmas tree and wished for a miracle, nothing too difficult, just a quick blink that would beam her back home.

He inhaled loudly and got her attention. "How do you want this to look on the other end?"

"What do you mean?"

"Her visit isn't long-term. In six months or a year, how do you want Carly to feel about this time spent with you?" His smile was so gentle. "You've taken this girl in. My sense is you love her. She's your sister's only grandchild." He readjusted his hip against a cushion and a quick grimace crossed his face. "If she skips out with your money, she'll feel like a petty criminal, and you'll never hear from her again. Or she'll leave you feeling valued. I'm not sure how you'll go about making that happen."

"Maybe she was just curious."

"Maybe. But I doubt it."

Maggie hadn't come anticipating a handout, but she waited for the response he'd led her to expect, a hefty check made out to Carly, but he didn't speak. He was too busy studying her. She couldn't tell him about the letter on the dresser that said the paltry stash was needed for more than a jar of lemon curd or movie tickets for matinees at the Broadway. Her pride wouldn't allow it. Instead she nodded.

"Thank you," she whispered. "I appreciate the advice. It's very wise."

With a slight tremor in his hand and a look of sadness on his face, he reached over and touched her arm. "Are we friends, Maggie?"

"Yes. I think so."

"Good. Will you let me know how this story ends?"

"Yes," she murmured.

"If my bum hip cooperates, maybe in a week or two, we can figure out how to wiggle under the tree and look up through the branches. Or maybe we could just have dinner and enjoy the view. Have I ever mentioned I'm a gourmet cook?"

"Once or twice." She stood to leave. "Maybe four times."

***

Back on the seventh floor, Maggie heard the elevator door open and hesitated by her apartment, her hand on the doorknob, as Sue sauntered down the hall.

"You're just getting home from the symphony? It was over hours ago." She wagged a finger at Maggie. "Old," Sue raised a suggestive eyebrow, "but not dead, not by a long shot."

"Not what you think. Not at all," Maggie sighed. "And where have you been?" Sue was wearing a politically incorrect full-length mink coat.

"Family Christmas festivity. Didn't I mention it? Deer Valley? I love to go and watch the nieces and nephews sniffing at my wallet."

"Sue, do you have a silver chain you don't wear anymore? Something you don't need?"

"I'm sure I do. Come on down. We'll have a cup of hot chocolate and do a post-mortem on the evening."

Part Three

Chapter Twenty-Seven
THROUGH ME TO YOU

THE NEXT MORNING WITH HER hair still wet from the shower, Maggie rubbed the tarnish off Sue's necklace with the edge of her damp towel, grabbed a dry washcloth and rubbed again. The links were delicate, probably sterling. Of course sterling. She slipped the necklace through her mother's ring, and snapped the box shut. She didn't look at the ring, didn't caress the faded velveteen box with her thumb. She just sat on the edge of her bed with damp hair and invented reasons to worry.

An hour later, the bright sunlight flooding the living room woke the girl. Maggie stood silently in the kitchen spooning steaming oatmeal into a bowl. She forced a smile at the sleepy face above the white nightgown before she dropped a glob of honey into the bowl and passed it through the opening from the kitchen to the living room.

"Your color's better. No more blue lips," she said.

"How was your hot date?" Carly dribbled a thread of honey onto her tongue.

The muscles in Maggie's shoulders ached like she'd been lifting a backpack full of rocks, and she felt so defeated she needed to sit. Last night's holiday symphony? It was the last thing on her mind. "He's a thoughtful man. He means well."

"No spark?" Carly gave her a sly wink.

Maggie forced a laugh, but all she felt was a twist of guilt at her own reluctance. She was about to do the right thing—her hand grasped the velvet box in the pocket of her apron—but she couldn't force the words out of her mouth, so she stepped out of the kitchen, sat in her spot on the couch, and watched Carly eat.

"I have something for you," she said. "An early Christmas present. Actually, it's not from me. It's from someone else. Through me to you."

Carly abandoned the oatmeal, and hesitated for just a moment before she sat down beside Maggie on the couch covered with pillows and tangled sheets and quilts, her makeshift bed. *She knows*, Maggie thought, *that I know she was looking through my things.*

"I've had this for years—since the morning she died—but I want you to have it." Maggie opened the box, and silver links fell through her fingers. "It's your great-grandmother's wedding ring. She never took it off her finger," Maggie paused, "for sixty-three years. I've worn it when life's been difficult to remind me of her." To feel the quiet presence of her mother.

Carly sank back against the pillows as Maggie rested the delicate chain around Carly's neck, touched the warmth of her young skin, and saw the shame in the girl's eyes.

"Oh, Maggie, are you sure?" she mumbled. "You've got granddaughters." The girl understood the value of the gift.

"You're my mother's oldest great-granddaughter. It should be yours." Maggie smiled. "The chain's long enough to hide the ring under your clothes where no one will see it." They were silent. They both understood how easy it would be for a rough hand to snatch something this precious and break the connection.

"I won't lose it." A single tear rolled down Carly's cheek.

"I know. I wouldn't give it to you if I thought you were careless." Not completely true, but Maggie had done the right thing, not the easy thing. But it was this next part that was going to be truly difficult. She picked up a fabric wedding album, fifty-four years old, and rested it on her lap. A slight tremor in her hand, she opened the front cover. Two young faces smiled from the page, so delighted, so happy. Sure they'd won the marriage lottery, they'd danced across the grass in their finery while the wedding photographer snapped photos. Maggie inhaled until her chest rose. She ran one hand up the back of her neck until it reached her hairline. She felt the stiff ache in her elbow.

She turned back a page. "This is John the week before we got married." She touched the picture. John wasn't alone. She stood beside him all shy smiles and soft brown hair.

Her throat constricted. Her words lost. She pulled out a half-dozen snapshots tucked in the back cover. One picture was of a plump baby with curly brown hair and large eyes. Carly waited, reluctant to look at the snapshot, until Maggie began talking. "He loved baseball." It wasn't a fatal sport. Nothing that put him at risk.

Carly moved closer to Maggie and gave her a hug before she whispered, "And he died. My mom told me."

"It didn't need to happen. It was a stupid, stupid mistake. The consequences so unfair, because Davey was such a good boy, always a good boy." Maggie felt a little frantic. "But life turns on a dime. One slip and it's like a U-turn you can't correct and can't unwind."

Carly rested her head on Maggie's shoulder. She smelled the floral sent of shampoo in the girl's cropped hair. Carly whispered, "It wasn't his fault."

"No, it was mine." There, she'd said it. Finally the truth. "My husband died—"

Carly silently unwound the aged fingers balled in a fist.

How could this young girl understand suicide by car crash in the middle of the night, and the police ringing the doorbell, hats in hand, and the terrible screaming that filled her ears? And the surreal realization that she was making the noise, making the horrible sound that filled the house, every room, every corner. Scream after scream.

"Bad choices are like an avalanche or a rockslide, and once they get going, they just hurl down the mountain, no stopping them." Her precious John had been lured into a vicious scheme that was too good to be true. At some level, she'd known. She'd whispered misgivings that should have been shouted. "*How can you promise an eleven percent return, year after year?*" And he'd said he didn't know; he was just the salesman declaring great tidings, the clean-cut face offering the glossy prospectus. He didn't do the investing. He left that to Will—a man she'd met once—the financial genius whose father-in-law's name opened doors like an enchanted key. Granite Financial Consulting, a weighty name for such a young group of men—of *crooks*—listed in the Tribune along with their ages and pictures and warts. Worst Ponzi scheme in years, most profitable Ponzi scheme in years, and Maggie had never heard that word before, *Ponzi*, didn't know what it meant, didn't know more than the names of the men who designed the disaster. How could she not know? She should have known, should have stormed around the kitchen and stopped the whole crooked mess. *But the money*, she thought, *lured them all in.*

With one hand, she touched the girl's hair softly as though she were shaping a cloud. Her other hand rested on the album, John smiling up from her lap. "When his dad died, Davey was on a mission in Paris." The mission name was lost, the official title, words on an envelope were erased from her head. "They were so close." The world's greatest dad, the baseball coach, the charming man who'd become a charmer with a corporate credit card—one of the first on their street. "Davey was depressed. He couldn't function and needed professional help, so they sent him home." Poured him into a suitcase. The mission president, a kind man, walked him onto the plane, clicked the seatbelt, and then called Maggie at home.

"He was kind of a zombie." Maggie whispered. "We were losing our house and had nowhere to go. Not the best homecoming a boy ever had."

Carly just nodded.

"There was a wedding. Another boy in the ward, not much older, had been back a year. Davey and his high school friends were all invited, but those other boys didn't speak to him." They sat beside him, talked around him, over him, but never included him. "They were headed for a weekend of waterskiing at Bear Lake." Happy chatter about a basketball game on the driveway, pretty girls, a barbeque, plans for the future, plans for next week, and classes to take in the fall. "Would it have been that hard to put an arm around Davey?" But their family was stained by a premature death and a scandal with a price tag in the millions.

"I would have included him." The girl snuggled next to Maggie. "I know what it's like to be left out."

"It stung. Of course it stung, but that didn't stop Davey." He was so tall and good looking and an All-State second baseman. "He got a job right away." He filled the house with his plans. Kristen started to smile again. Henry would wait up to see him. And he'd talk to Maggie when the house was quiet night after night. What could they do? Where would they go? *Don't worry, Mom. We'll figure it out.*

"There was an accident when he and some kids were coming down Big Cottonwood Canyon. The driver had had a few beers. He missed a turn and went into the river. No one else was hurt, only Davey. He drowned." The kids were shocked and tossed in total darkness. No one knew Davey was trapped. Maggie gave the girl a hard look, and the girl looked down at her hands. "I'm telling you this for a reason," Maggie said. She needed to scare her. "There are no second chances. Not for mistakes this big." Her feet felt heavy, detached from her legs. "No one sets out to be a disaster. You need to be careful."

"Davey wasn't careful?"

"Not that night." She grasped Carly's hand. "You're so young, and I'm guessing you're in some kind of trouble. I don't know what you've done or why you ran away, but you can reverse this. You've got time to make things right. You can go to college and have a good life. Don't make mistakes that will start the rockslide."

The girl sat not moving like she'd forgotten to breathe.

"If you want—and I don't want to push you—I'll call your mother. Help figure this out."

The girl didn't shake her head, didn't look at Maggie. She just muttered, "Please don't."

Maggie didn't tell Carly her mother was suffering, staring at her computer screen, checking her email, keeping her phone in her hand day and night hoping for a text, a message, something, anything. There was no happiness in the home Carly had left, no Christmas joy, not a bit of it. If the new husband had crossed swords with Carly, he was paying a price. After seventy-four years, Maggie had learned something about people.

"We don't have to do anything today, and you'll always have a home here with me. Always." The sunshine coming through the window couldn't lift the weight of confessions, but Maggie tried. "Sue thinks you have an uncanny sense of style and your own pink aura. *Shimmering* was the word she used. Jan says you're college material—no question."

She released the girl's hand before she reached into her pocket. "This is a little something to tide you over." She pressed her bit of money into the girl's palm and closed the girl's fingers around the bills. It was everything Maggie had. "This isn't a loan. I don't want it back. No strings. This is a gift." She stood. "I need to get ready for work." She'd be late, probably a half hour late, but that couldn't be helped. "Would you like to come with me? Isabelle could use extra hands. You could man the gift wrap table." And they could sit together knitting if there was a pause, a few un-busy minutes. Share a peanut butter sandwich at lunch. The thoughts of a young companion on the bus eased the tightness in her chest.

"Maggie," Carly said, "You can't give this to me. You need your money. What about that letter on your dresser?" No shame on her face for being nosy.

Maggie had read the letter a half-dozen times, wept a few tears, and read it again. She should have shoved it in a drawer or burned the scrap of rotten news.

"I'll be fine," she lied. "Years ago, I discovered that happiness is a choice. It's not an address." She didn't believe the words coming out of her mouth, because she'd been so happy in this yellow brick building. *The best years saved for last,* she'd told herself too many times to count. It was too late to make new old friends, but that's not what she said. "You're the future kiddo. That's all that matters."

Carly gathered the nightgown around her knees. "Maybe I'll stay here and finish *Rebecca*. Mrs. Danvers is up to no good. Could we have dinner tonight? Maybe invite Jan and Sue or that hunk from upstairs."

Maggie tried to laugh, her smile fading, as she walked into the bedroom to fluff out her hair.

***

Maggie's breath fogged the bus window. She'd unleashed a tangle of memories she'd been so careful to confine in a cardboard box in the basement. For years she'd pushed them to the back of her mind as though chicken wire separated the lobes in her brain. Now those memories crowded back. Her purse in her lap, Maggie stared out the window at the blur of houses and passing cars, the snow piles and the sounds of traffic. Had Carly understood what she'd tried to say? She rested her hands in her lap, but desperation clung to her like a musty smell. She needed to help the girl, but she didn't know how.

Chapter Twenty-Seven
A FRESH START

NO LAPTOP, NO CELL PHONE. Carly was hiding out in the Dark Ages. Standing at the window, she watched Maggie cut across the plaza and catch the ten fifteen bus. Her silver hair stood out like a beacon. And the precious woman was old. And her feet hurt at night. And she never quit hoping for a better day, not Maggie. Carly glanced around at the dozens of pictures, but those faces weren't snapshots, not anymore. Each one was a memory trapped under glass in a cheap frame, and the memories weren't all that nice. *They're weighing Maggie down,* she thought. Each picture had an outstretched finger beckoning Maggie out of the present and back into her gloomy past. Carly wanted to dump those pictures in a cardboard box and stuff them under the couch.

Maggie needed a break, a fresh start, sort of like a Christmas present. Carly thought about calling the guy upstairs and giving him a head's up. *The woman needs help. Something to live for. Take her on a Rhine river Christmas cruise or a trip to the Bahamas.* Maybe that's just what she'd do—call Mr. 8-B and make a couple of pointed suggestions. Maybe to those ancient eyes, Maggie was a real looker. Hard to know.

Though Maggie was carrying a heavy load, Carly'd been set free. With Maggie's cash in her fist, she felt like a little girl with brand new shoes, and she could run faster and jump higher than any kid on the block. She tossed the cash in the air and laughed out loud. A twenty-dollar bill floated past her nose and landed on the beige carpet, and she realized in that moment that she was a selfish brat, something Dale-Call-Me-Dad had shouted at her too many times to count. She bit down on her lip. She could start over, but Maggie? Maggie was too old to pack her bags and say good-bye to her friends, but—truth be told—five hundred bucks would only delay the inevitable. In Carly's hands, those dollars would save Terry's life.

No question, she'd pay Maggie back, unless Maggie and 8-B tied a loose knot, which seemed like a great solution, a practical solution, and who knew? Maybe that's what 8-B had in mind. He'd certainly been hanging around. Carly scooped the cash into a neat pile. She loved Maggie, but she couldn't worry about her now.

She needed to move fast and make a disaster-proof plan. She needed a phone—one that would work. She needed the internet. Google. She shook both fists over her head. How did people live without texting? If Maggie wanted to ask Sue a question, she marched down the hall. This was so third world.

She picked up the receiver attached to a corkscrew cord, but the thing just buzzed in her ear. Not helpful. She needed information about buses and schedules and the price of two tickets to San Diego and sunshine. She couldn't risk a quick trip to the library; Lemon would pounce in a minute. She couldn't borrow a laptop from Jan or Sue without a well-intentioned *someone* peering over her shoulder. A frown on her face, Carly plopped onto the floor. Time to think clearly about Terry and getting out of here. Not the time to worry about Maggie or handsome Mr. Building Security and soft kisses in the half-light. No time to be *crazy*. Her un-tethered heart fluttered around in her chest, but she cleared her throat in a business-like fashion, as if she could easily banish Paulo from her mind.

"Stay in the basement where you belong," she cried to the empty apartment, but it didn't help. Every word Paulo said, every touch, every gesture, each kiss replayed in her head, one continuous loop. Staring off into space, she started editing, imagining her heartfelt confession, enlisting his help, the two of them rescuing a grateful Terry, but that's not what she'd done. Heat rose in her cheeks. There was nothing heroic about wiggling off the console and bounding to the elevator without a single coherent word. How could she have been that stupid? What had she mumbled? *Got to go.* So lame. He'd never speak to her again. Who could blame him?

She picked up the phone and stared at the keypad. O for operator. Why not? Give it a try. What was she out? She punched zero and waited. After a few seconds and a couple of clicks, a recorded woman's voice asked if she was "experiencing difficulty." *Why were these voices always women? Siri? The obnoxious voice on the GPS? If you were really in trouble, wouldn't you want to talk to a burly man, like maybe a security professional?*

She wanted to call Paulo and ask him to find the bus terminal and the departing times for San Diego, but he'd fire right back with too many questions. He'd want to call the police, but hanging out on the plaza wasn't a crime. Nothing had been stolen. No one could be arrested. And if the police stopped by that ratty apartment—with serious questions—it would mean trouble for Terry. Big time.

She listened to the recording suggest she call 911 or stay on the line and an operator would assist her. *No kidding?* she thought. *A real live person is going to listen?* Her request was pretty simple. "No emergency," she said. "I'm calling from a landline, and I just need a phone number for the bus terminal in Salt Lake City, Utah."

"Directory assistance is a service no longer available."

"Please," Carly said. "Just one number. I won't make a habit of doing this. I promise." She launched into a description of the fictitious care center she was visiting that didn't have Wi-Fi, and she'd misplaced her phone, maybe left it in the car. It was a series of small lies, but the voice believed her and gave her the magic number.

In a few quick minutes she had the location, 600 West and 300 South, which was a serious problem. For a mile they'd be on surface streets with no cover. Maybe with a head start they could make it, but if they didn't, Bill would be lurking at the terminal. Nasty, nasty Bill, who probably tortured kittens when he was three.

Sinking down on the couch, she started to cry, but this was no time to fall apart. No time for tears. Wiping her face with her sleeve, she strode to the window and watched stragglers heading to work, heading to Trax. Trax. A block away. Bingo! They could head out through the tunnels, exit through the Executive Office Building and grab Trax to that mega hospital in Murray, then catch the Front Runner heading north. The info person hadn't given her the address for the Greyhound station in Ogden, but how far could it be? Lemon and Bill might search for them in Salt Lake or maybe even Provo, but Ogden would never cross their minds. It was the total wrong direction.

Bill and Lemon were coming. Maybe tomorrow. Maybe tonight. She'd need to grab Terry and run. Her mind clicking along at a hundred miles an hour, she raced across the room to have a shower.

Her short hair a mass of dribbling curls, she pulled on her jeans. She needed to map the tunnels. When push came to shove, there was no time for dead ends. She thrust her feet in Maggie's slippers and edged down the hall past Jan's open door.

The elevator dropped to the uncarpeted basement, and she slinked down the hall, uncertain of the direction she should take. Obviously west was the way she wanted to go, but all the halls ran north and south. There were no printed diagrams on the walls, no emergency exits, no handy little arrows pointing to freedom and fresh air. "Dad," she whispered, "or Great-Grandma," and she grasped the necklace touching her skin, "I could use a little help." A bit of good luck. But what she got was a head-on collision with Paulo rounding the corner. She took a step back and shook her head. *Awkward,* she thought, but "Sorry" was what she said. The word stuck in her throat, but she forced herself on, "Shouldn't you be in class?" She'd never learned to be demur in a crisis. Not in her skill set.

"Test week was over last Friday." Blushing, he pushed his glasses back up his nose. "I was coming to find you. What are you doing down here?"

No plausible reason to be searching for the tunnel entrance, at least none she could share, but what had the guy just said? He was looking for her? Her heart started to bounce between her neck and her knees.

"Me? Why are you looking for me?" A drip from her hair trickled down her neck.

"To apologize for last night." His voice was gruff. "I don't want you to think I lured you into the basement under false pretenses."

"False pretenses aren't necessarily bad," she muttered, as her stomach unclenched and her shoulders relaxed. The brown eyes behind those thick glasses softened, and they stood for a good sixty seconds not saying a word, just staring at each other, staring at the floor, staring at the walls. "You don't need to apologize." For the next five minutes she forgot about Terry and exits to tunnels, and for no reason that made any sense, she felt safe for the first time in years. "It wasn't sexual harassment or anything." His warm hands on her neck, he was pulling her close when he touched the necklace and lifted the ring from under her shirt.

"What's this?" He frowned. "A prior commitment?"

"It's my great-grandmother's wedding ring. Maggie wanted me to have it."

He raised a single eyebrow.

"For luck." She touched the tip of his chin. "Or to ward off evil. Maggie was sort of vague about the details." Then Carly remembered her previous life, the one that existed before she collided with Paulo. "Poor Maggie. Her son died. And her husband. And now she doesn't have enough money, and she has to move." The ring hadn't saved them.

Paulo held her at arm's length. "No one's supposed to know Mrs. Sullivan's moving. It's nobody's business."

She squeezed one eye shut. "I know all about it. I read the letter." The penciled note on the printout from the building manager detailing the arrangement with Mrs. Kimball who had been subsidizing half of Maggie's rent—hundreds each month—for seven years, and then Mrs. Kimball had inconveniently died without making any provision for Maggie. "I swear, Maggie didn't know anything about it, which is hard to believe, but it's true, because Maggie is so honest, and she'd be humiliated if anyone knew she was receiving charity, and so she won't ask anyone for anything." Thinking of her own domestic situation, she spoke with authority. "She'll just move to some ratty studio apartment with bad smells and strange people coming and going at odd hours. But that's not the worst of it." She took a deep breath. "She told me about her son Davey, a returned missionary who made a tragic mistake. She didn't tell me the rest of the story because she's so heartbroken, even after thirty years, but I guess you'd never get over something like that."

Thoughts shot out of her mouth as if she were a machine sending tennis balls over a net too quickly for anyone to return. Only his gentle kiss interrupted the torrent of words.

She'd wondered over the years how people could breathe and kiss at the same time, but it wasn't hard at all. Her knees felt wobbly, but at that moment, he took a step back, but not far.

She knew the numbers. Cure rates for foodies. Only a measly sixteen percent didn't take the plunge back down the black hole to large. She shook her head. Maybe she'd get lucky, but size six or size four double X, it never mattered to Terry. He was her best friend and never said a word about her penchant for donuts. But what about Paulo? Was he thick or thin? He was almost drinking her face in with his eyes, his glasses smudged and askew. And then Paulo took a deep breath and broke the spell.

"And . . . why are you down here?" he said with more suspicion than she thought she deserved—all things considered.

She shook her head and sprayed them both with droplets of water. What could she say? She was looking for him? But he was a surprise. "A computer," she improvised. "Maggie's not connected to Wi-Fi." Not much of a lie, but what next? She opened her mouth, but nothing came out, at least not for a few seconds, then her brain kicked in. "I remembered that bank of computers in your office. I thought maybe Aleph would let me check the Trib's archives to look up Maggie's husband and son. I know that's cyber stalking, but she was so sad that I want to know more. You know, so I can comfort her if it comes up again."

He wanted to believe her—she could see it in his face—but he didn't, not for a minute. She needed to be careful, not tip her hand. Not say anything totally dumb about tunnels.

He held up a finger, sign language for *wait right here*, and he went to retrieve his backpack. Her knees had had enough, and she slid down the wall until she was sitting on the ice-cold linoleum, her head on bent knees. She counted to three between each breath, but before she could calm her rampaging heart, he was back again, all six feet of his wonderfulness, sitting next to her on the floor.

"Be still my heart." This was a totally stupid thing to say, a line from a melodrama she'd seen as a kid, but Paulo laughed out loud as he opened his laptop and moved the curser with his finger.

"You get thirty days for free," she whispered as though a corridor in the basement required hushed voices. "Access to the Trib's archives," she added as explanation.

He nodded, typing in *Davey Sullivan*, but she corrected him, "David Memmott. Maggie uses her maiden name. Try the late eighties' obits." A listing of articles, maybe three or four, popped onto the screen. He clicked on the first one. Up came a staged yearbook picture, a handsome young man in a jacket and tie. Most likely to live—but now he was dead. Carly shuddered. The hallway was frigid and dimly lit. She wiggled closer to Paulo, but she was still freezing.

After a short lead, the next article devoted four column inches to Davey's father—a rehash of the story still on everyone's lips. Death by drowning didn't have the same appeal—no scandal, just one tragic drowning, not much to say. The driver was barely above the legal limit. If the accident had occurred in August when water levels were low, Davey might have stumbled away with a few cuts and bruises. The story's angle was family because David was a Memmott. Each subsequent article was worse than the last. The driver was convicted for vehicular manslaughter, and Carly felt her stomach shrink until it was touching her spine. There was a picture of a much younger Maggie. "What does it say?"

Paulo scanned the page. "Maggie spoke at the sentencing hearing. She wanted the kid released. Give him back to his mother. Sending the guy to the Point of the Mountain wouldn't bring her boy back. Wow," he whispered. "Maggie was a hero."

Carly swallowed hard. "How old was Davey?"

"All of twenty-one. A year younger than I am."

"So sad." She rested her chin on his shoulder and read the article herself. It rehashed the worst Ponzi scheme in the history of the planet. In an attempt at being evenhanded, the journalist quoted several attorneys, but her implication was clear: Maggie's plea for forgiveness was a ruse, a dramatic ploy, to generate sympathy for her family in the civil suit yet to be tried.

"That's just not true. They didn't know Maggie."

"It's harsh." Paulo kept summarizing the article as though Carly were visually impaired. "When the Ponzi scheme imploded, the man with the Midas touch got immunity for delivering his friends—everyone else involved—on a platter. He got a couple of years in a country club prison outside Denver, and the rest of the guys got five to ten years at a federal penitentiary." He looked away from the screen. "Rough duty."

She started to shiver and couldn't speak. How could Maggie talk, or walk down the street, or sleep? No wonder she changed her name. And now the poor woman was going to be evicted, in a very nice way, from the seventh floor and her friends. Sue or Mr. 8-B could make up the difference in the rent without even blinking. A few hundred a month was pocket change to them, but Maggie's pride wouldn't allow it. What to do? She hated the thought, but the answer seemed clear.

"I'll take care of her," she mumbled, because she loved the old lady. She'd have to be careful, but Carly knew how to lift a wallet out of a diaper bag or pluck a billfold out of the pocket of cargo pants. She'd send Maggie cash in a plain envelope. Terry could start the dog walking business while Carly worked crowds at LAX. Travelers headed out for vacation were ripe, and they'd be on the non-stop for Paris before they'd realize what they were missing—their cash, credit cards, and IDs.

Without speaking, Paulo closed his laptop. He squeezed her hand and leaned over to kiss her, but she ducked. This guy was the promise of a life she couldn't have. "Are you around tonight?" he muttered as she'd obviously lost interest. "I don't work until ten."

"Sure." She waved one hand toward the intersection of three halls. "Where do they all go? No apartments down here."

"Mechanical stuff. Water pipes. Electrical." He pointed. "That one heads to the tunnel that connects us to Temple Square."

She swallowed her smile.

Chapter Twenty-Eight
FITS AND SPURTS

LOOKING IN THE MIRROR IN the yarn shop's half bath, Maggie thought she'd gone from being a youthful seventy to barreling down the road toward eighty in less than twenty-four hours. *Age is a funny thing*, she thought. *It occurs in fits and spurts*. At the end of the long day, a tube of lip-gloss raised in one hand, she stared at the bags under her eyes and wondered, *What's the point?* and slipped the lip-gloss back in her pocket. The silvery bells on the shop door announced another customer, no doubt a woman needing an elegant handmade gift that could be whipped up in an hour or two. Maggie thought she'd direct the customer to Hip and Humble to buy one of her adorable hand-knit hats. She straightened her shoulders, rounded the corner, and there was Ed Johnson. More than a little surprised, she swallowed a gasp.

Always impeccably dressed, he was wearing a gray puff parka and a pressed pair of jeans—he must send everything to the laundry—as he stood in the entry of Blazing Needles as though he were an abandoned husband who had lost his car keys or his wife and wasn't certain where to find either one. Thinking he was a man in need of a gift, Isabelle started around the counter. "Can I help you?" But he spotted Maggie and a warm half-smile played on his lips. He took three steps across the unvarnished wood floor as though Isabelle hadn't spoken and didn't exist.

"Your apartment's occupied for a couple of hours, so I thought I'd give you an explanation and a ride home before you interrupt a candlelit dinner."

Laughing at the confusion on Maggie's face, Isabelle nudged her. "Introduce me to your friend." After the introductions, Isabelle followed Maggie into the kitchen/office to collect her coat. She discreetly closed the door. "Who's the silver fox?"

Maggie indulged her with a deliberate sideways smile. "A nice man from the eighth floor." With a hovercraft instead of a car and an obscenely beautiful Christmas tree, and now, evidently, a secret, maybe more than one. Maggie sighed as she left the shop she'd come to love with its cheery Christmas decorations and the smell of cinnamon and the musty odor of wool.

She was sitting in the heated passenger seat with her seatbelt clicked before he explained, "I had an unexpected visitor this afternoon."

"And who was that?" If the police had come to arrest Carly, he wouldn't be smiling. He was obviously pleased with his bit of good news, and she was ready to hear something happy after her sleepless night and a day choked with worry.

"Paulo. We spent a couple of hours talking, and then at about three, we adjourned to the kitchen."

"Curious. Do you know him that well? Odd that he'd seek you for a cooking demonstration." It was more than odd, but not more perplexing than Ed arriving at Blazing Needles on a frigid December evening with a fedora in his hand.

"No, I don't know him, but the boy knows us. All of us. He sees us coming and going. He knows the outward details of our lives, and I think he feels responsible, somehow, for our well-being. He feels terrible about Rose Kimball's death."

She couldn't talk about Rose, not yet, so she said, "You cooked?" The two of them in his stainless-steel kitchen? She tried to imagine a football game blaring in the background or maybe classical music, Handel's Messiah or a Rachmaninoff concerto piped in on Spotify.

"We slow cooked chicken in a tarragon cream sauce. And we made a salad, of course, with pickled beets and goat cheese over spinach and lettuce that he'll finish off with a splash of vinaigrette." Clearly pleased with this food recitation, he said, "And bread pudding with raspberry puree." The car's turn signal must intuit when it was time to blink, because she didn't see Ed move his hand before he turned left, but the last fifteen minutes had gotten so strange that in comparison, this high-tech car almost seemed normal.

"Sounds like a fun afternoon, but I've been on my feet for the last eight hours, and I need to go home." But that wasn't quite true, because she was surprising herself; she was actually enjoying the attention.

"Well, that's the catch. The young man's in love. Head over heels." He reached over the control panel and touched the back of her hand. "With your Carly."

Paulo in love with Carly? The frail would-be thief who slept on her couch with tiny holes poked in her face, minus the hardware for the time being, but of course, all that could change. As difficult as the last twenty-four hours had been, she felt the tension unwind in the back of her neck.

When she didn't speak, Ed said, "He wanted to take her to a movie and then get a burger, but she made a silly excuse about not being able to leave the building because she's still contagious, which is preposterous, but she wouldn't relent, so he came to see me."

Why would Paulo go to see Ed? And Carly wouldn't leave the building? Why not? What devilish game waited outside? What was frightening the girl? Maggie clutched the knitting bag in her lap. Why was the world so dangerous for people she loved?

Ed, still rambling about food, was relishing the part he'd played, but his smile was tentative, which didn't make sense. "Sue lured Carly away to have a grapefruit pedicure—not sure what that involves—while Paulo's setting up dinner in your apartment."

Sue loved a conspiracy better than most, and the pedicure was probably stretching into a bubble bath and an egg-white facial. Maggie could reconsider her own tired feet, but it was the thoughts of relative strangers coming and going in her pitiable apartment searching for silverware and candlesticks she didn't possess that made Maggie extremely uncomfortable. Her poverty flayed open, her penury exposed.

"They're going to watch *Gone with the Wind* after dinner," Ed hurried to say as though she might leap out of his car the minute they arrived at the Eagle Gate. When Blockbuster Video went under, Maggie bought two dozen old movies for a quarter each—a treasure trove of film legends—that she watched when nights stretched long. Certainly, her VHS player was the only one still functioning in the entire building, something Ed and Paulo had probably discovered when they were plowing through her belongings. If she was a person who snorted, that's what she would have done, but since she wasn't, she didn't.

Perhaps he sensed her discomfort, and before she could speak, he said, "I'm not surprised he's fallen in love. We've all grown a soft spot for your niece from the moment she arrived. She's funny and quick and such a pretty little thing. I don't understand why she won't leave the building, but we can give them an evening and cross our fingers for a little Christmas magic. Paulo might be the detour she needs. Deserves."

Maggie didn't say, *And what about me?* because his news delighted her; but nevertheless, she was bone weary, and her heart stumbled along, missing every third beat. She needed her head on a pillow, her weight off her feet. Sue was going to a glittering fundraiser for one of her many curious causes. If Maggie could get home before Sue locked her door, she could borrow Sue's couch for three or four hours, an elderly babysitter for Sue's empty apartment. A small price to pay if Carly was pleased.

She exhaled audibly. "A little romance might be just the thing." If life were only that simple, but perhaps this man who'd been married three times was blessed with a cross-eyed optimism Maggie didn't possess. She glanced at the watch on her wrist. Six thirty-two. The pedicure was over, and Sue was long gone. Carly and Paulo were probably in the midst of their first course, sliced beets and goat cheese. Maggie's stomach rumbled.

"I thought," he said, ignoring the sound, "perhaps you could spend the evening with me."

Stupidly tired, sitting in the dark, his car softly purring, she stared at the Christmas lights strung on eves and front porches and glimpsed lit Christmas trees through front windows—and wondered how many Christmases she had left.

"Sure," she said, resolving to be pleasant. *What are my options?* she wondered. *The couch in the lobby? The bench by the elevator? Arriving unannounced at a friend's door on the third floor for a four-hour visit?*

She looked longingly at the elevator buttons as they passed seven and stopped at eight. The elevator doors opened. She stood a little taller, stared straight ahead, carried her purse by the strap, and held her knitting in her left hand. He'd left Spotify playing a medley of classical Christmas music, and *The Little Drummer Boy* was concluding as she entered his apartment and stared. Polished silver stood in attendance on each side of a Spode Christmas plate, roses and holly decorated the center of the dining room table, and Waterford crystal caught the light from the tree. A stage had been set, but for what? She was long past the age for staged romantic seduction, although this felt more like an ambush.

"You didn't need to go to so much trouble," she whispered before she remembered her manners. "It's all very lovely, but this effort is wasted on me." But she was tempted to run her toes through his fur rug and rest her head on the Santa pillows arranged on his couch.

He hooked his cane on the back of a chair and spoke over his shoulder. "Put your feet up. Make yourself comfortable. I'll grab a quick something out of the fridge."

She caught the scent of tarragon as she folded her coat neatly over the arm of an upholstered chair and dropped down on the couch. She slipped off her shoes, but the smell of tired feet assaulted her nose. Shoving swollen feet back inside worn orthopedic lace-ups required a bit of doing. And then Ed was back with squares of pumpernickel and smoked salmon nestled in parsley on an appropriately festive tray.

An hour later, the only remnants of dinner were dirty dishes on the table. Blue and gold flames flickered on the gas log. Staring beyond the Christmas tree at city lights, Maggie sat on the couch, balancing bread pudding on a plate. Ed had spent his afternoon polishing silver, arranging roses and holly on the table, whipping raspberry puree, and coaching Paulo in the kitchen. She didn't want to get lulled into a relationship with this man, but she enjoyed his attention. She liked the feel of his hand on her elbow when they skirted a patch of ice on the sidewalk. His tone of voice was low, comforting. He listened more than he spoke—unusual in a man. He was attentive when she spoke, as though what she said were important. He was a good man, a kind man. She was sure of that.

Bing Crosby was dreaming of a white Christmas, and she was so comfortable and sleepy that the lights in the distance started to weave and blur. Ed reclined in a chair with a pillow wedged beneath him.

"This hip's a real problem." His low voice sounded oddly rehearsed. Trying not to yawn, she smiled instead and watched words form slowly on his lips surrounded by his white beard and mustache. "When I couldn't play tennis anymore, I was surprised at how quickly my doubles partner quit calling. Same thing with my golf foursome."

He was about to say something important, so she gave her head a quick shake and sat a little straighter. He took a bite of bread pudding before he continued. "A couple of years ago, I got a less-than-pleasant diagnosis from my doctor, and I realized I didn't have anyone to call who'd want to listen. No one to talk to except my therapist." He wasn't fishing for pity—his voice was too matter-of-fact. "There I was alone at home in Park City. I have hundreds of acquaintances but not a single real friend." He dipped a bit of bread pudding into the raspberry puree, and then he silently laid his fork on the dish. "I wasn't connected to anyone."

She didn't know what she'd expected but certainly not a declaration this personal. Her life had been one of scarcity and trying to empathize with a stranger surrounded by luxury was a stretch. He'd had choices most people wouldn't dream of having. She watched him frame thoughts with his hands, and he seemed as distant as one of the talking heads she watched on TV delivering the news.

"If you move," he spoke softly, "you'll lose your connections with these people you love. Even if you find a place in the lower Avenues, an apartment or a room to rent, it won't be the same."

Startled awake, she glared at him and set her pudding on the glass tabletop. The evening felt poisoned. "Oh," she cried, "that's no one's business but my own." She reached for her purse. "And who told you?" But the answer was obvious, Carly. She'd read the letter tucked under the doily on Maggie's dresser. Maggie started to stand, but her tired legs wobbled.

"Please don't leave." He reached around the back of the chair for his cane. "Carly's worried about you. That's what Paulo came to tell me. He's a good young man. Open hearted. He's handing me the chance to make a difference. To pick up a loose thread Rose never intended to leave behind."

Loose thread? Maggie knew something about loose threads—if you tug on them, you can end up standing there naked. And that's how she felt, all her lumps and bumps exposed. "I know you mean well," she pressed a flat palm against her chest, "but I'm not a nonprofit begging for donations." She grabbed her coat from the back of the chair. "Two healthy young people have been alone in my apartment for the past three hours, and I don't think Carly needs more knots in her life right now. She needs to figure out who she is all on her own." Maggie felt like her brain had vacated the building—she was that kind of tired. "Might be just the moment for a timely intervention." *Hello, Kids. An old woman needs to take back her flat.*

She kept praying for life to offer her a reprieve, but not this. Not charity from a stranger. After seventy-four years of moderately good behavior, wasn't time-off for that good behavior deserved? Why all this trouble raining down on her head? Why did she outlive Rose? Where was the sense in that? Why didn't her children need her? Why was the only way out of humiliating poverty a check with so many strings attached she couldn't begin to count them? She felt like a wounded deer, cornered and desperate. Riding the bus that morning, she'd convinced herself that renting a room in a kind woman's house might not be so bad. Now here was this man telling her if that's the choice she made, she'd lose her connections to the people she loved. No more ordering pizza on a whim with Sue and Jan. No more spur-of-the-moment Trivial Pursuit games at the table until ten. No more kicking through fall leaves on the way to the grocery store or water aerobics in the pool off the lobby when the weather turned foul. And the laughter? Gone? Did this man think she didn't understand this left turn she was taking? She didn't want to curse God and die; she just wanted to slip quietly away in her sleep. No hard feelings. This was no one's fault.

"I know you mean well," she said, "but please allow me a little dignity. It may not have much value to anyone else, but it means a lot to me." In the time it took him to rise, her hand was on the doorknob.

"There's more." He was speaking to her back. "Our stories are connected, Maggie."

Her head jerked around.

"Moving here was no coincidence. It took me eighteen months to find you. It didn't occur to me you'd take back your maiden name. I was sure you'd remarry." He stole a deep breath. "When I found you, I moved here so we could get to know each other—hopefully become friends—before I hit you with the truth."

She hadn't been lost, misplaced, or remarried. She had sidestepped the line of fire because she'd been clobbered with the truth enough for any lifetime. No more revelations.

His smile was genuine and kind, but confident, always confident, like he was a car dealer and she was an easy sale. Now she understood, she was a name in the notebook he kept in his pocket. An item to scratch off a list. She couldn't speak, but the warmth in his eyes nearly made her lose her balance.

"I didn't think I would feel this way," he said. "Knowing you, caring for you, understanding your life is making it impossible to forgive myself for the unforgiveable."

Chapter Twenty-Nine
CHOICES

STANDING BY THE DOOR, MAGGIE turned slowly on her heel, swollen feet forgotten. *Are you kidding?* didn't come out of her mouth, but it must have been spelled out on her face, because in less than two seconds, his face became so haggard and anxious that she almost whispered, *Whatever it is, it can't be that bad,* but maybe it was. Some intuitive undertone had been pinging her since that first time she crashed into this man on South Temple. The tree shimmering with a thousand white lights, chicken doused with a tarragon cream sauce, and even the raspberry puree suddenly felt like bait in a trap ready to spring. A past connection . . . between the two of them? Something he knew that she didn't? He'd been playing with a full deck while she sat at the card table empty-handed.

She returned to his leather couch, laced her fingers together, and waited with both tired feet planted firmly on the fur rug.

"Let's have it," she said. "Give it to me straight."

That confident demeanor crumbled, his face seemed to sag, and there was pain in those eyes. After a couple of false starts, he began a scripted preamble, and it wasn't hard to imagine him staring at his reflection in the dark windows rehearsing this speech.

"When you hear the word *cancer,* it's like mortality hitting you in the face." He paused. "I'm resigned to dying alone," he began again, his voice lowered. "It's no one's fault but my own. Poor choices landed me here."

That was a sad and lonely event to contemplate, but millions of people died solitary deaths, and Maggie thought of poor Rose breathing her last in the bowels of this building. If her guess was right, Rose was in the basement searching for the lost connection this man was about to divulge. If he'd been forthcoming a month ago, her Rose might be very much alive downstairs on seven enjoying a laugh with some of the neighbors. Contriving his stage, for whatever this was, had been more important. More important than Rose? Never.

When she didn't speak, he faltered, but only for a few seconds. "I don't need my name on a brass plaque on a library or the keys to the city or any of those things." He brushed the thoughts away with the back of his hand. "But before my life ends, I need your forgiveness. That's why I moved here. So you'd know the man I've become. The man I want to be now." He took a deep breath. "If we were friends, I thought I'd have a chance. It's taken me a long time to unwind some pretty horrendous mistakes, but you're the last, Maggie."

She huffed. "I don't think of myself as a mistake that needs to be unwound."

"That's not what I meant. Not your mistake. Mine. What I've done to you."

She was happy to mourn with those who mourn, but this man was afraid of his own history. Everyone made mistakes—large and small. What did he think would happen if he told the unvarnished truth, laid it out on the glass coffee table? She was too tired to keep up the pretense of cautious manners. "Can we talk about this tomorrow? When we're not so tired?"

He shook his head and started to speak slowly. "I spent two years in prison." He was so matter-of-fact he could have been telling her he'd been to the dog park on E Street.

She collapsed against the cushions. Her chest started to ache. "What does this have to do with me?" But the question she knew she should ask was *What does this have to do with my husband?* because that's where this was going. She didn't know how she knew it, but she did.

Ed shook his head deliberately, and a lock of snowy hair slipped down his lined forehead. "I was at a minimum-security facility. One of those federal country club prisons for white-collar crime. I worked in the kitchens."

"Cooking," she said. Of course.

The mention of food loosened his tongue, and his story progressed in a linear fashion into the shadows and out again as the tall Christmas tree silently listened and Maggie sat wondering where this strange tale would end. Pulled Pork Barrel Sandwiches, funded by a federally subsidized program to rehab convicts, became a food truck in downtown Denver, and that single truck grew into a fleet, which Ed sold. Serious cash in his pocket, he returned to Utah and gambled on a fluke, a plastic fabrication business in bankruptcy that Ed turned into a multi-million-dollar water-bottle bonanza. *Old King Midas*, she thought. His forty-five-year-old self had ridden the cusp of a trendy wave to his beautiful home in Park City inhabited with a stylish third wife but no children. And now, here he was in the heart of the city, thousands of bright lights on the horizon, and resigned to dying alone.

"What does this have to do with me?" she whispered. Her life was a small one, not of much consequence to anyone but herself. "What exactly am I forgiving?"

"My middle name is Wilhelm. Ednar Wilhelm Johnson. Will Johnson." He searched her face for a hint of recognition. "Rose's Carl introduced me to your husband. Carl and I were in the same fraternity."

She shrugged. This felt like an absurd case of mistaken identity, and then something pricked in the back of her head. She was right. This man sitting across from her was the memory Rose couldn't find in the basement.

"When you bumped into me on South Temple," he said, "I recognized you right away. For a couple of years, I saw you every day. Your picture on John's desk, that is. You were wearing a light-blue dress, and your hair was down, the sun behind you. Some mornings there were snapshots on his desk, you smiling with a trio of little kids at the beach, at Lagoon, or clowning around in the Albion Basin. The guys were all a little jealous. We wished we had a marriage like John's. He measured every decision by what Maggie would think, what Maggie would say. Everything was about the life he wanted to buy for you. Cars and a big house. Travel. Clothes. College for your kids. And then it fell apart." Imploded. She knew. She was there.

"Will Johnson," she muttered, her breathing shallow.

He nodded.

John made such a point of leaving work at work. In sleepless nights filled with teary hindsight, she understood why. There was too much he didn't want her to know. But now she remembered Ed's strong face at a Christmas party. No tidy white beard, but dark wavy hair and an extravagant tan. Lean, fit, cocky, and incredibly handsome. Will Johnson. Her face felt numb. She thought she knew what death was—she'd experienced the memories so many times flashing back when she least expected them—but never before had she confronted the man who'd killed her husband's will to live. And now he was here, sitting before her in his expensive chair with tears trickling down his cheeks and wetting his beard.

"Two years and then a new life," she said, her voice constricted. Seemed like a paltry consequence to her. She stared at him. He was the one, the incredibly selfish mastermind who'd bailed on his partners. He'd made a sweet deal with the prosecuting attorney. Sold out his friends for a cushy sentence. His partners got ten long miserable years, divorces, and estranged children. Where were those men now? Those children? Those wives? "How can you live with yourself?" came out of her mouth. Because his sin was that he hadn't quit living. He was living well and had been for years. Sitting across from her, he was easy to hate.

He didn't speak. He just studied his hands as though they were the face of a clock.

"Did John know?" she whispered. "In the beginning?"

He looked up. "In the beginning there was nothing to know, nothing to hide. We weren't doing anything wrong." His jaw flexed. "We were working hard. Three of us were investing and churning options. There were a handful of accountants and staff. John was selling. The whole thing was magic; we couldn't go wrong, couldn't misstep. We were so arrogant and young."

She didn't have to close her eyes to see John's face because there he was, his warm brown eyes looking right through her.

"Then we had a bad year. Everyone did. I was terrified we'd lose our investors and the business would fail, so I kept paying dividends, inflated dividends, with cash on hand. The more we paid, the more we needed. New investors. New money. The pressure was on John—on all of us. That's how it started. We weren't crooks. It was a terrible mistake, but we didn't design some monster Ponzi scheme. It just got away from us."

His father-in-law's name opened plenty of doors, but surely Ed understood John was the face of the fraud. John Memmott was the one who'd convinced family, friends, ward members, strangers, anyone who would listen, to invest. He'd been the one to promise ridiculous returns. Not Ednar or Will, or whoever this guy was propped on a pillow in the leather recliner.

He was handing her a simple explanation that didn't include her precious husband smashed against a tree. "Two years?" she muttered. "That was it?" Not much of a price. Nothing compared to what she had paid.

"No. That wasn't all. I knew what happened to your family and the others. I tried to push it aside, but it was always there. What I'd done." He spoke slowly. "I felt terrible about John. He was my friend. You and I have spent the last thirty-five years grieving, but yours was the grief of the innocent. Mine was the grief of the guilty. It was all my fault. My feelings are nothing compared to yours, but I've never forgotten. Not a day, not an hour. I'm not the selfish, greedy person I was thirty-five years ago. I've tried to be a better man."

Right. She didn't know what to say. Meager words couldn't begin to express the pain she was feeling. The moment was awkward. Something flickered briefly across his face, tightened the skin between his eyes, and was gone again. For over an hour, he'd been talking nonstop about his mistakes, about his convoluted, self-absorbed feelings. He was a little late coming to this party. After an absence of thirty-four years, this guy popped out of a hat with his credit cards, his fancy car, his Christmas tree in the penthouse, and now he had the audacity to expect something from her? She extended empty palms. "What do you want?"

"Forgiveness, Maggie. I need you to forgive me."

Forgive the architect of her misery? Rooted to the couch, both sweaty palms flattened on the cushions, she stared at the floor. Was she the same woman she'd been an hour ago? Twinkling lights on the tree were a blur. Nothing had changed and yet everything was different. She waited in stunned silence before she lifted her head. "I can work at forgiving you, but I can't be your friend. Not a chance." Even to her, her voice sounded different, strangled and unfamiliar. She stood and gathered her things.

Recoiling as though he'd been slapped, his eyes watered, and he ran his fingers through his white hair. "Before you walk out that door, please listen. Just for a minute."

She was trapped between his memories and her own, but she eased back down on the couch. He'd taken an hour; she could give him two more minutes.

"Five years ago, maybe six, my third marriage was in free fall. I was incredibly wealthy and incredibly unhappy. I ran into a neighbor at the grocery store. Maybe he'd been stalking me. I don't know, but it turned out he's my bishop. Long story short, until he moved, we became friends. My story came out when we were riding a ski lift. Amazing what a little kindness will do."

"No kidding."

No pause in his story. It was like she wasn't there. "It was one of those crystal-blue days. Perfect snow. The guy pushed his goggles up on his forehead and looked right at me. He said everyone makes mistakes and that I'd certainly made some beauties, but this is what struck me: he asked me how much time I spent thinking about myself. Pretty simple idea." A tremor in his hand, Ed toyed with the fork on his plate. He couldn't meet her gaze. "He was right. I'd been drowning in self-pity. Beating myself up for all the things I did wrong. So I quit and started looking for people to help. A big check to a foundation didn't do it for me, but slipping a tired waitress a couple of hundred-dollar bills sent me home happy. I was leaving the post office one day and saw a woman with a couple of kids get in a beat-up car with cardboard duct-taped on the back window. I followed her home, found out who she was, and a couple of days later, I was walking down her street when a new Subaru was delivered to her anonymously. One of the happiest days of my life. I've given away twenty-six cars since then." He studied her face like a teenager desperate for approval.

"Ed," she said, "that's a beautiful story. I'm glad you've found some peace—"

It was the right thing to say, but he interrupted her as though he was afraid she'd escape before he could finish. "I decided restitution was part of my equation, and that's what I was going to do. So, I've humbled myself, humiliated myself a couple of times, and gone on my knees to most of those investors and partners—not an easy thing to do—but what happened to John was in the back of my mind. Always."

She raised both hands shoulder level. "What a fairytale. Let's leave my husband out of this." He winced, but she couldn't listen to another word. Plus, she knew where this was leading—to a certified check with a lot of zeros. That was next.

"You're the last, Maggie. The one I hurt the most. The one I couldn't find. Maybe I was afraid of finding you. Couldn't face the damage I'd done. A husband and a son." He covered his mouth with his hand, and those pale blue eyes teared up again.

She shook her head. Unbelievable. Most of those cheated investors were in their late eighties, lost in nursing homes or cemeteries, or they'd become ashes scattered in the mountains. "What about my mother? My sister? Did you send them a check?" Maybe he'd tucked a handful of cash behind their headstones.

His time and the effort required to move here—to the Eagle Gate—were wasted, and he knew it. The realization stood out on his face, but he soldiered on.

"I don't have much time left. A few years if I'm lucky. Months if I'm not. I've given most of my money away, but what's left, I'm leaving to you. Nearly four million dollars for you and your kids. No strings. No handholding at my bedside. I don't want anyone else to know. Not until I'm gone."

Four million dollars. Hers? Unbidden, her sleep-deprived brain dashed down State Street, and there she was, standing under the bright lights in the fruit and vegetable aisle in Harmon's grocery store. She could put three or four boxes of raspberries in her cart without that constant tally ringing up in her head. And she could buy comfortable shoes with nice, thick soles, maybe two pairs. And a new coat. And a set of tumblers that matched; she knew just the ones she wanted. And college for her grandkids. Forget student loans. And college for Carly. Maybe she'd take Kristen and Henry and all their kids on a Disney cruise. She could imagine them laughing, splashing in a pool, joking with Buzz Lightyear, building sandcastles on a private pristine beach, but then she realized the little faces she kept inside her mind had arrived at adolescence. The kids were too old for anything Disney. It was too late for breakfast with Minnie Mouse and Goofy. It was too late to make another life. For a second or two, she'd been racing down that road to affluence, and now she skidded to a complete stop.

"No," she said, her voice wavering. "No." Her heart pounded, and her lungs felt like they'd been turned inside out. "Your money would corrupt my children. Give it to the food bank or the zoo. I don't want it."

Maggie would never tell her children she'd refused a gold mine. She didn't want them to live out their lives in that frustrating land of "what ifs." And what would she do? Shoulders straight and head held high, she'd move out of the Eagle Gate with a smile pasted on her face. She'd quietly move into an upstairs bedroom in the home of a lovely lady on Third Ave, an arrangement her bishop suggested. And she would be happy. Maybe she and the lady would be great friends. Perhaps the lady was an accomplished knitter. Anything was possible.

"I'll try to forgive you." It was the best she could do. "But you can't buy penance. Not from me." She left him sitting in his recliner—the blood drained from his face as if she'd fired a last, fatal shot right through his heart—and closed the door quietly behind her.

She needed to feel angry, get a good burn going, stomp down the hall, yell at the injustice, but all those feelings just petered out. She was so tired, and thirty-four years is such a long time. "Money," she muttered. Money had stolen her life. Her husband. She leaned her shoulder against the elevator wall. Ed was perched on a pile of money, and it was worthless, trash. It couldn't buy him more time, fix his hip, change what he'd done, or deliver grandchildren to love him.

She stared at the elevator door without seeing. Thirty-four years. The months after John died, her life was about going forward one step and then another, not falling all the way down a mine shaft to rock bottom. She didn't think about changing her life; her life had already been changed. She just needed to survive it. Then one day she realized she was still alive. Breathing. And Henry and Kristen were alive too, and she needed to look up at the sky and love the living and not just the dead.

Standing there in the elevator, her skin started to tingle. She felt someone behind her. And then she heard a man's voice, inside her head or next to her ear. It was John. "Let it go, Maggie." She jerked her head in the direction of his voice.

"John?" She could sense him, smell him, almost feel his hand on her shoulder. He was right there beside her, and then he was gone. She'd needed him so many times. Why now? Why did he come to her now? Her knees started to buckle, and she grabbed the safety rail.

The elevator doors opened and closed—three times. She kept hitting the button. *Let it go?* What did that mean? Did John want her to go back up to eight? Her finger hovered above the up arrow. Comfort that guy? Take his hand in her own? Forgive him? She wanted to punch Ed. Right in the face. "I can't, John," she whispered. "I can't forgive that man."

The fourth time the door opened on seven, laughter drifted down the hall. She was drawn to it and stumbled forward. Her apartment door was open. Paulo was standing at her sink washing dishes, and Carly was at his side, snapping a dish towel. She wasn't drying anything. She was chattering a mile a minute, and all Paulo could do was laugh. Maggie stood watching. They were so young.

"You have no idea what it's like to be a fat kid," Carly said, a grin spread across her face like raspberry jam. "Summer camp was a nightmare." She waved the striped towel like a flag. "Most kids go on hikes, right? But at fat camp, they took us on forced marches, left us in the woods to survive on nuts and poisonous berries. And forget water. We'd be gasping for a drop of fluid to drink—we'd murder each other for a can of warm soda—but the counselors would do anything to sweat off a few pounds. The first day, when the bus unloaded us, we got weighed in and our luggage was checked for contraband candy. Every night we got weighed—our tonnage was on this graph in the dining room—and when we dropped ten collective pounds, they'd pay us with these tacky little piggy coins we could spend at the trading post."

Paulo turned around with his back against the sink. A smile stretched across his face, and his glasses were smudged.

"For a couple of piggys," Carly gestured extravagantly with her hand, "you could buy an extra carrot, which doesn't sound like a big deal, but it was for us because we were starving to death. I swear, the counselors got paid by the percentage of body fat we lost in three weeks. A racket if ever there was one." She was so engrossed in her story that she didn't notice Maggie standing in the doorway until Paulo pulled his eyes away from Carly's face to give Maggie a wink.

Maggie felt so dizzy the wall receded, and she grabbed the refrigerator door to steady herself.

"Are you okay?" The girl kissed her cheek. "Too much excitement for one night?" Her arm around Maggie's waist, she half-carried Maggie to her favorite spot on the couch. "Come and sit down."

The smell of tarragon lingered in the air. Crumbs of bread pudding were scattered on the tablecloth next to candle stubs. *John,* she thought, *let what go?* Maggie wrapped her arms around the girl and hugged her. "I need you to be happy," she whispered in Carly's hair.

"Are you kidding? We just watched three hours of one disaster after another. *Gone with the Wind*: Atlanta goes up in smoke. Melanie dies a lingering death. Scarlett's a witch. What a downer." But nothing in the girl's face said *down*. She was euphoric. Completely, deliciously in love.

"Mostly she's been talking," Paulo said and made his hands quack like a duck.

"As if?" Carly laughed. "You were the one who wanted to hear about Dale-Call-Me-Dad."

"Dud. Dale-Call-Me-Dud." Paulo laughed. "Walk me down to the office." He grasped her hand. "I'm late for work." And off they went. The room fell silent.

Maggie glanced past the dark window and sighed. All these years she'd been climbing up Mount Olympus backwards—no matter how many steps she took, she never reached the summit. Until now. She had the whole story, but all she could see was Ed's face framed in his doorway, so desperately sorry. And what had she done? But honestly, who would blame her?

Chapter Thirty

THE CURSED SPINDLE

Somewhere in the last few months, Carly had wiggled out of the only body she'd ever known. Flexing her toes under the blankets on the couch, she pictured her former self in her head as though she were sidestepping a snakeskin on a dusty mountain trail. *So done with all that.* She stretched her arms above her head and felt lusciously content. Adorable, that's what she was. Sitting on the couch watching *Gone with the Wind*, Paulo had told her that in about twenty different ways. He was pretty cute himself and smart and capable. He'd confided to Mr. 8-B about Maggie's hassle with the rent, and now Maggie wouldn't have to move. She was going to be thrilled. Problem solved. Carly hummed softly, *Merry Christmas to you. Merry Christmas to you. Merry Christmas, dear Maggie, your rent isn't due.*

A relaxed grin across her face, she rolled onto her back and stared up at the ceiling, imagining Paulo's face in the drywall. "Thanks, Dad," she whispered. Every good thing in her life was attached in some fashion to her father, because he was watching out for her and had delivered, on cue, one handsome prince in a starched Security Resources uniform. Of course, last night Paulo left his uniform in the office on a hanger and wore a flaming-red University of Utah sweatshirt as though it were an advertisement for a future they were going to share. She could quit being the kid with a "'tude," a dozen piercings, and a bright-blue Mohawk. Enter a semi-serious student, a pretty girl with a *boyfriend*, walking to class, studying in the library, eating fruit and raw vegetables. Brave new world.

In an hour or two, when she got dressed, she'd run down to the security office and confess absolutely everything. She'd promise to return in the spring—maybe sooner. If all went well, Terry could handle the dog walking business without her—he was great with dogs. And Lemon and Bill? She had a plan for them too, but the timing was tricky, because no harm no foul. If nothing had been stolen, no crime had been committed. And poor Nolan? No body. No questions. She fingered the empty holes in her ear lobe.

This last week in those groggy moments between sleep and consciousness, she'd imagined herself not as the unfortunate, much maligned step-daughter but as a princess locked in a pristine tower with a solid yellow brick fortress surrounding her and a corps of elderly soldiers keeping her safe. She rose on one elbow. But how could these loveable relics with white hair and age spots protect her—or themselves—from people like Lemon, the scarecrow; or Bill, who was so terrifying a nickname wouldn't stick? That crew of scheming jerks would be coming. Today. Tomorrow. Soon. That realization, that momentary lack of faith in her new skinny life, that disastrous crack in her universe, allowed fear to get a toehold and grasp her in a vice-like grip. Waves of cold shot down her spine. She stared out the window at two inches of new snow on the roof of the Alta Club, which meant slick concrete and ice on the steps. Her gaze settled on the landline. It started to buzz. She was in telepathic communication with trouble. "Nooooo," she mumbled, her fists clenched.

The buzz wasn't a call from her adorable Paulo. The irritating noise told her someone was waiting in the vestibule seven floors below. Someone who wanted entrance into the building on a Sunday morning. She kicked the covers aside. She hadn't escaped, not yet, because her past life was roaring back to claim her.

Her heart thumping in her throat, she sat motionless on the couch. Maggie was in the shower. If Carly didn't answer, whoever it was would buzz again, and Maggie would pick up the phone. Then what? She tapped her finger against her closed lips. She'd call Paulo. He already knew something was up, and he was taking Aleph's shift this morning. Down in the basement.

The phone buzzed again.

She held the receiver next to her ear, but she couldn't make herself talk.

Terry's voice mumbled, "Let me in Carly. I'm freezing." No skin on those bones, no insulation, and probably a knife at his neck. She reached out a single finger as if she were Sleeping Beauty about to touch the cursed spindle, and then she paused. She knew what came next. She'd watched the movie a dozen times, dancing the dances and singing the songs, but that didn't stop her, she pressed the button that opened the front door with an electronic click.

"Terry," her words gushed, "go straight through the lobby. There's a party room. No one will see you. Use a house phone on the south wall. Call me right back. I've figured this out."

"You don't get it," he whispered.

"Oh yes, I do. Hurry." She needed to get Terry out of the building fast before she called the police to nab Bill and Lemon in the act. Put those thugs away forever.

Carly's finger was poised on the button to signal Paulo when Maggie walked in, toweling her hair. "Did someone want to be buzzed in? On a Sunday morning? Who was it?"

"Someone hit the wrong name. A nothing," Carly muttered. No time to explain.

"Have you thought any more about calling your mother?" Maggie eased down on the couch.

Eyes wide, Carly stared at the silent phone that was going to ring any second. No time for a chat. "Nope."

"Maybe later?"

"Doubtful." Conversation over. Maggie couldn't be sitting here when the phone rang again. She watched the dear lady shaking her head as she walked, so slowly, back down the hall. When her bedroom door closed, Carly snatched the phone and punched SECURITY, but no answer. She slapped her cupped palm over her mouth repeatedly. *Paulo, pick up.*

The phone started to ring. She grabbed it.

"They're in," Terry whispered. "Five of them. One in the basement. You've got to hide."

It hit her like a fist to the gut. They were inside the building. Probably in stupid disguises, hats and ski masks, coats padded with stuffing, a bright scarf, an orange pair of gloves, costumes Lemon devised. But none on Bill. A cap pulled down low, facing away from the cameras; he was a vampire with no reflection. His image couldn't be caught.

"No exodus of old folks leaving the building," Terry's voice hammered her ear. "They're furious you didn't warn them." She was supposed to call Lemon at midnight while the building was asleep? One last step in his elaborate scheming? "Can we get out of here, Carly?" Terry whispered. "To San Diego?"

"I have money. Enough." She bit down on her thumbnail then whispered, "Where are you?"

"That room off the lobby," his voice rushed. "Why didn't they leave at nine? The old people?"

Stupid question. They lived here. Outside was a layer of treacherous snow. *One fall and that's all.* How many times had Sue said that? "There's another sort of meeting. At ten o'clock. A stake conference, but nobody's going. Too slick." Lemon hadn't checked the weather and the meeting schedules. Not as clever as he liked to think he was.

"Listen," she murmured softly. "Get off the elevator on the fourth floor. Away from the cameras. I'll be there. Waiting."

She slipped into jeans and a T-shirt, grabbed her orange puff parka and the backpack stowed under the couch. She was on her way when she heard Maggie open her bedroom door. Carly didn't shout good-bye over her shoulder, didn't make lame excuses. She just ran, as though she were being chased, and stood by the elevator doors, panting. *Not saying good-bye is awful. But what are the choices?* The elevator was too slow. Turning quickly, she pushed open the fire escape and sprinted downstairs. Painted cinderblock walls and metal railings were cold to the touch as she raced down three floors. Her ear against the door covered with a large *four* painted in red, she waited and waited. This was no good. She nudged the door open a crack. No Terry.

Where was he? She dropped to the floor, the toe of her shoe holding the door open a crack, and her eyes glued on that opening—and she waited.

Quivery voices drifted down the long hall. Wearing rubbery galoshes and coats, each button fastened, three or four women walked toward her. She pulled back out of sight onto the landing and let the door close. The stouthearted were braving the snow to get to their meetings with plenty of time to spare. If old people weren't ten minutes early, they thought they were late. The elevator was slow, but it finally opened. The ladies stepped inside, and the doors closed behind them. Carly chewed on a fingernail. Where was he? She glanced at her watch. Terry wasn't coming. Not to meet her.

She inched the door open and peeked at the numerals above the elevator. It went down, and moments later up it came. Each number lit for a couple of seconds. No pause on four, but when the elevator stopped on seven, Carly's heart stopped too. Unsuspecting Maggie was fixing her hair, touching her lips with pink gloss, calling for Carly, who'd slid out the door. Maggie had nothing left—her paltry stash was deep inside Carly's backpack. Sue was the target. And maybe Jan. And the Badgers at the end of the hall. And that tiny little woman who only spoke to Maggie. Bill would scare her right to death. Hold a knife to her throat and her Depends wouldn't be so dependable. And good-hearted 8-B. They'd go after him. Mr. Intermountain Plastics was loaded, but he couldn't move fast, not anymore.

"Help me, Dad," she whispered. "A miracle would be handy." Back in the stairwell, there were fewer surprises. She could hide, wait for trouble to exit the building, but instead she tucked her backpack in the corner and started to climb. She was past the sixth landing when the lights flickered and went out. She stood in blackness so thick she couldn't see her hands and waited, listening. She wasn't the only one listening; it was as if the very stairs and the cinderblock walls were listening too. The pipes gurgled once or twice and then total silence, except for the sound of her own ragged breath.

Afraid to put out her hand in case it touched nothing, she waited. Then, groping empty space, her hand found the handrail. She took one step and then another, but she was unsteady in the dark. What waited ahead? Emergency lights blinked on and strips glowed on each riser. Hands trembling, she exhaled. The large red *seven* appeared. She rested her head against the door and wondered what on earth she should do. She heard noises. High-pitched protests, fear in their voices, all except Sue, who scolded in a shrill voice that carried above the rest. She couldn't hear Maggie, but Maggie wouldn't yell, not a sound. Maggie would just collapse in on herself, go to that sad place in her head and shut down.

Where was Paulo? Why didn't he call the police? He wouldn't be fooled by Lemon's stupid disguises. He'd know in a minute these guys were the ones he'd been watching for weeks. Where was Paulo?

Moving slowly, softly, she pressed the door lever, the metal icy beneath her fingertips. The door opened a sliver, exposing a slice of shadowed hallway. The only light came from the narrow window at the far end. She heard Lemon's voice barking orders at poor Terry lost behind a huge floral arrangement, carnations and daisies with sprigs of holly and one gigantic red bow. They'd spruced Terry up in an immaculate FTD deliveryman's uniform. Brilliant.

"Get that guy up on eight. Bring him down here. And don't be stupid. Grab his phone before he knows what's happening." Then Lemon turned his back.

The power was off. The closer Terry got to *Exit Stairs,* the smaller the sliver she could see, but one of his eyes was puffy, not more than a slit, and Band-Aids couldn't cover the scrape on his forehead. He'd been beaten, and badly, not long before.

She knew what they had done. Hiding behind the ridiculously large floral arrangement, Terry had stood in the building's vestibule and buzzed her. He'd waltzed into the lobby under the eyes of the cameras, and Paulo thought nothing of it? Really? Flower deliveries didn't happen on Sunday, and that would have occurred to Paulo, no question. Why didn't he call the police?

Her thoughts were flying. While she'd been waiting for Terry to call back, he'd been holding a door open for Bill and Lemon, and who knew who else? Three other guys? Paulo must have seen them slink past on his screens. But what if some deft hand—the boy in the FTD uniform—tossed his jacket over the camera on the west entrance. Terry. Sweat dribbled down her hairline as she waited. Her underarms were sticky.

His arms full of flowers, Terry opened the door a crack and then thrust his way in with his hip. He was inside with one foot on the first stair when she scared him spitless.

"Shush." She tugged on his pant leg. "I'm right behind you."

Water sloshed out of the vase as he set the flowers on the concrete. "Carly?"

"Who else?" she hissed and dropped down on the metal step. "What's going on?" But she already knew. The long-awaited robbery, the elderly heist.

"Things are a mess. No one planned on dealing with actual people. Not this many. Lemon thought they'd be at church." He crouched down beside her. "There are seven witnesses crammed in your aunt's apartment." He nodded toward the stairs behind him. "Soon it will be eight. Not good."

"I've got five hundred bucks in my backpack waiting on the landing on four. You and me. Time to be gone." She signaled with both fingers like a soccer referee. "We'll be out through the tunnel and on Front Runner heading north before anybody knows we're gone."

He shook his head. "They'll kill me. Twenty minutes to get down seven flights. Their guy in the basement will flip on the power. The elevator will beat us, and they'll be waiting for me with baseball bats." In the eerie glow, she watched his terrified face.

"Get Ed. Bring him down here. That will buy us some time. Don't tell him what's up or he'll do something stupid. Lemon and Bill will be busy stealing and making sure no one slips away. They'll think you're ransacking Ed's apartment, and we'll take off. We can make it." Maybe.

"They know you're in here somewhere. They're furious with you like you're some kind of traitor."

"I don't care," she said, which wasn't true. She was trembling all over. And Paulo. Where was he? Dead? "Once we get to San Diego, I'm writing letters to the Salt Lake PD. I'll tell them what they did to Nolan."

"Lemon and Bill?" Terry laughed. "They'll be long gone. They've got plans too. Each day it's different. They'll vanish into thin air." He picked up the flowers and trudged up the stairs. She was right on his heels.

"Leave Ed in Maggie's apartment and tell them you're going back up to eight. Then we head down. It's the only chance we've got. They're not going to hurt a bunch of old people."

He nodded. Waiting, she listened to him announce himself at Ed's door and heard Ed's husky voice. "Flowers? Who's sending me flowers?"

Terry's voice rushed, "Hey, I must have dropped the card. The elevator's out."

"The power's out."

"I hauled this arrangement up seven floors." Terry faked a laugh as though he were fishing for a tip. "Let me check my clipboard." He glanced down. "It looks like your old employees are wishing you a Merry Christmas."

"I thought the building had an emergency generator." Ed sounded worried. "No elevators? That's no good."

"You're telling me? Christmas gremlins. What can I say?" Terry returned his cap to his head. "Some deal's happening on seven. The paramedics are there. A lot going on. Some lady got sick. That's all I know. Maybe they're using the elevators."

"Which apartment?"

Terry shifted his weight. "I'm not sure."

"Can you give me a hand down to seven?"

"Yes, sir."

Leaning heavily on his cane, Ed walked toward the stairs. "You get in a fight, son?"

"With a truck," Terry lied.

Chapter Thirty-Two
CARLY'S GONE

MAGGIE HAD ONE MORE THOUGHT, one more gentle nudge to persuade Carly to call her mother. She opened her bedroom door and started down the hall. She kept her voice light.

"What if we invited your mom for a weekend? No pressure. We'd agree to that before she comes. Just shopping? Lunch? Maybe the symphony? Or an Indie at the Broadway?"

Carly didn't answer. Carly was gone. The front door ajar. All that fresh energy? Vanished.

Of course, she'd always known the girl would leave; it was just a matter of when. Maggie touched the indentation in the pillow where Carly's head had rested not twenty minutes before. Carly was here, and now she wasn't. Maggie stuck her bare toe under the edge of the couch to feel for the grimy backpack the girl secreted there. Gone. Someone had called from the entry, and Carly bolted.

Sitting down heavily on the rumpled pile of sheets and faded quilts, Maggie inhaled the sleepy scent of the absent girl and wondered who'd called. She wasn't surprised to find the girl missing. She knew time was short, but what unfinished business had called the girl away without a good-bye? She sighed. People vanished out of her life without much warning. She expected to feel something, but her senses were dulled. Numb, as though loss was akin to bad weather, like a sleet storm that caught her unawares. When she'd turned away from the fierce wind and water, people she loved had been swept away. John, Davey, Rose, and now Carly.

As she added years with each passing birthday, she found she rarely cried, but conversely, when she experienced terrible loss, she couldn't talk either, and that presented a problem, because at that precise moment, her phone started to ring. She glanced at her worn watch—almost nine thirty. Expecting to leave a cheery Christmas greeting, her son would be surprised to hear her voice, because of course it was Henry, leaving his obligatory, five-minute message she looked forward to hearing each Sunday when she returned home from church. She gulped a dry sob before she lifted the receiver and struggled to speak.

"Mom," he said. "The craziest thing happened. I have four hundred thousand frequent flyer miles in my Delta account. Obviously a huge mistake, but Delta says it can't be reversed. Long story short, we're coming for Christmas."

The sensation she experienced was something like falling. "Here?"

"Or maybe Cedar City," he said. "I found the mistake yesterday. Isn't that crazy? I'll call Kristen after I talk to you."

She tried to smile, thinking of the penciled note Ed tucked in his pocket that night she fixed him tuna on rye. She'd mentioned Henry, and Ed had jotted down a name and a reminder in that little notebook of his when he thought she wasn't looking.

"Trust me," she began. "It's no mistake—" but Henry corrected her. He'd emailed Delta and received a solid reply.

"An intentional error or an anonymous donor?" she repeated. That described Ed exactly. Not hard to imagine him smiling as he transferred the miles, but she couldn't explain Ed to Henry. Not over the phone. And *Let it go.* How could she explain his father's voice? He'd think she was crazy. Her son couldn't begin to understand how complicated her life had become. She tried to concentrate on what he was saying: skiing at Brian Head and caroling on Christmas Eve with Kristen's crew, and beneath the surface, the wheedling price he'd paid to convince his wife that a family Christmas in the mountains was a memory their girls should have.

She felt light-headed. "Carly's gone," she blurted.

"Mom, did you hear what I said? We're coming for Christmas? Caroling? Skiing? Turkey dinner." Pleased with himself, he paused for a minute. "Okay. Ally's daughter has run away again? Maybe that's just her MO."

Even to her, her voice sounded garbled as she recapped the convoluted story she'd explained the previous Sunday about the girl who'd arrived with pneumonia, a girl with Maggie's sister's cheeks and chin and the soft texture of her dead sister's hair.

She surprised herself by saying, "What if she comes back and I'm not here?" Momentarily out of the frigid air, Carly standing in the vestibule waiting and waiting, pushing the button for 7-B, and no one would let her in, no one would love her, or give her a home because Maggie had moved to Third Ave.

Henry wrongly assumed she was worried about Christmas. Not the right moment to tell her son she was moving, but the truth slipped out of her mouth in a gush of words. Rose hadn't meant to die—it was a terrible accident—but nevertheless, she'd been subsidizing Maggie's rent for years, and now Maggie was moving to a lovely room that would be perfect if it weren't for Carly. Third Avenue was just a stone's throw away. She didn't mention Ed up on eight or their shared history because there was nothing to be done. She just simply would not take his money or Henry's either.

"You're moving? I don't understand any of this. You're not making sense." Henry's voice rose. "Leave the girl a note or have the manager give her a message. Have Jan or Sue let her in." He paused as if scratching his head. "When are you moving? Why are you moving? Does Kristen know about any of this?" His voice was insistent. She held the phone away from her ear. There was too much he didn't understand.

A ruckus in the hall grabbed her attention. Jan—all the color leeched out of her face—staggered into Maggie's apartment without knocking. An extremely tall person who looked more like a Halloween costume than an actual human being was standing behind her, a filthy red ski mask covering his face, and Jan's elbow clenched in his fist.

Gaunt with wisps of straw-yellow hair framing his mask, he barked at Maggie, "Drop the phone. Now." Then he waved a snub-nosed pistol—a pitiful little thing— in her direction. It looked like a cheap toy, but he was acting so tough, it must be real. Sue shrieked in the hallway, and the phone left Maggie's hand, clattering onto the table. Henry's tinny miniscule voice shouted, "What's going on?" She lifted the receiver and dropped it in the cradle as though she were positioning herself between her child and trouble. One hand behind her touching the spindles, she eased herself down on the ladder-back chair, her bare feet on the beige carpet and her silver hair damp from the shower.

Floundering in the doorway, hands grabbing the doorjamb, Sue stumbled into the apartment, shoved from behind. Her colorful caftan was more of an announcement than she wanted to make, but it was too late to wear something appropriate for a kidnapping. Because what else could this be? Eyes wide, the Badgers tottered in next and then old Mrs. Clarke, a small mouse of a person with loose folds of skin where her neck used to be. She skittered across the room as though hiding under the couch were an option for someone so close to the floor. Herding them in, a second man, eyes heavily lidded, kicked the door closed as though Jan or Sue might make a break for the hall. A tattered bandana covered his square face, and a cap was pulled low on his forehead. All her years living in a rough section of Fremont Park hadn't prepared Maggie for such a pitiless expression on another human's face. She shuddered. She couldn't help herself. She was suspended upside down in a very bad dream.

The blond stick of a person gestured with his gun before he nervously squeaked, "You get all the cell phones, pagers, devices? Anything electronic?"

"Down the garbage chute." The other guy snickered as though he'd done something clever, as though elderly people plowing through slops and trash for expensive electronics were some magnificent joke.

The blond tugged on the edge of his mask, and the two exchanged a quick look. "Okay." He hit his phone, a prearranged signal, and Maggie's radio, broadcasting the Tabernacle Choir, was silent. No power. "That will keep everyone in their apartments, but we've got to be quick. Send Terry up to eight. Bring Johnson down here." The blond shouted down the hall, "Terry, get Johnson."

Johnson. Ed. Mr. 8-B. The mastermind of all her life's troubles.

Carly's departure was not incidental. She was part of this, whatever this was, probably a robbery, but Maggie had already given the girl all she had. There was nothing left, nothing to hide, nothing to produce to put in the ratty gym bag grasped in the fingers of the thug wearing the bandana.

Maggie stared at Jan's and Sue's faces; they were all she could see. The rest of the apartment had become a bizarre backdrop that felt vaguely familiar as she tilted her head. The walls were moving, the couch seemed small, the kitchen, detached from its moorings, floated above the linoleum floor with pots and pans shuffling slowly on the counter as if they were fixing refreshments for invisible guests. She was losing her grasp on what was real.

Always a couple, the Badgers huddled in the corner clutching each other, trying to be brave. Mrs. Clarke had stumbled into the only comfortable chair. Maggie's two friends stood in the middle of her living room, certainly thinking they'd rather be at church singing Christmas carols or dozing through talks. Actually, they'd all rather be anywhere but here with this frenetic person waving his toy gun like a flag in the hand of a child on the Fourth of July. Maggie hadn't invited Sue and Jan over for a robbery, but there they both were. She stared at them. They were so precious. Shaken and rattled, she needed this to be over quickly, so her friends could meander down the hall and propose cooking Sunday brunch together, something they routinely did. With rough hands and foul breath, the man in the bandana jerked the rings off their fingers. Sue's eyes narrowed, and Jan put a hand on her arm.

She heard the uneven gait in the hallway. Ed with his cane and a young man, with an FTD logo emblazoned on his pocket, came through the doorway and brought the body count up to ten. No one spoke until a mouth opened in the ski mask and all seven eyewitnesses turned instinctively toward him.

"Is his door unlocked?" He spoke to the uniformed young man with a cap in his hand, but oddly, nothing covering his face.

He nodded. "He didn't lock it." The boy faded back down the hall.

Startling them all, Ed spoke in a gravelly voice. "My credit cards are on the dresser. My pin number is 3315. That will give you access to thousands." His eyes looked up as if he were searching the inside of his head for a password or a signal to save all their lives. "Take me with you. Take my car." He gestured toward the residents of the seventh floor crammed in the living room. "We're old. Our stuff's just a burden." He was dressed for church, and his expensive clothes called him a liar.

"Oh please," the blond snarled. "Don't think we're stupid. We pull more than a thousand out of your account, and all the bells and whistles will ring. Bring the cops down on us. And that car of yours. That Tesla? You'll give it a code word, and the car will lock all the doors and drive us to the nearest police station."

"Take him hostage?" The guy wearing the bandana lifted his chin.

Maggie felt like she was looking at the future from the bottom of a dry well. What if they took Ed? Abandoned him by the side of the road, but not just abandoned. The car door would open, and he'd be given a hard shove. Into the snow. At night. Hurt or shot at close range. On a gravel road in the mountains. Who would find him? Animals? She wished she'd forgiven him. Three little words. I forgive you. Done.

What if they took Sue? But who in their right mind would take Sue? If she were to be believed, her relations would send the kidnappers a thank you note on bonded stationary. *We received your kind offer to return our ancient aunt for five million dollars, but after careful consideration, we must decline. Best wishes, yours truly.*

Maggie must have telegraphed her fears, because Sue started speaking, her voice operatic. "I have ten thousand dollars in my kitchen. In cans that look like Campbell's cream of chicken soup and a couple that have peaches on the label. I ordered them from a Sharper Image catalogue years ago. The tops pop right off. Simple." Her tone said, *Even for dopes like you.*

Jan snorted.

"Well it's true. You just never know." Sue paused. "And my jewelry is sitting on my dresser—it's insured for half a million. Take it all. I don't care. Just leave us alone. Go back where you came from." *Under a rock* is what she implied. "The Badgers' don't have much, and Mrs. Clarke is nearly a hundred. Her kids cleaned her out two years ago." Not particularly accurate, but Sue was convincing. "You already know about Maggie from that nasty little girl you planted in our lives." Sue twisted her neck around. "Where is she? The girl on the inside?" Sue knew, they probably all did, why Carly had come. It was clear; the floor they'd chosen to rob was no coincidence. But Carly was gone.

In a quick motion, the blond shoved his gun under Sue's chin. "One more word, you stupid old broad. That's all it will take. *Pop.*"

Maggie sat, not moving, barely breathing, her feet pulled under the chair and her hands grasping the wooden seat as if she might lose her balance and topple onto the floor. She looked up. Ed was watching her. *Let it go.* She should have gone back last night. Now it was too late.

I'm sorry, she mouthed. What would a little forgiveness have cost her? Nothing. What if these moments were their last? He stared into her face, then he turned away. He'd taken the measure of these wicked boys trying to be men, and he'd chosen not to be afraid. He'd lived among thieves and knew who was dangerous and who was just stupid. *Maybe,* she thought, *if you're marching down the road toward cancer, a brat with a gun isn't all that frightening. Maybe Ed's personal demons are worse.* She listened to breath fill her lungs, and she wished she'd been kind. She wished she'd forgiven him with an ounce of sincerity. Why was it so hard to let the past go?

"Terry!" The blond scarecrow waved his pistol and called to the boy whose eye resembled a ripe plum. "Head upstairs." But the boy was gone.

"I don't keep cash in my apartment," Ed said.

"Sure you don't." The blond nodded toward the hallway—Sue had been more than just loud; she'd been persuasive—and the other man left. "Everybody sit. No talking. Not a word. Not a peep." The blond scratched the side of his face through the ski mask, then he checked the safety on the gun. Agitated, he wandered over to stare down the hallway. Like a strange bird, maybe a crane, he hoped from one foot to the other. He strutted across the room, stepped into the kitchen, looked around, and then tapped his watch impatiently before he stared down the hall again.

The clock on the stove ticked past ten. Time was dragging. Jan fidgeted with her finger missing the ring that had been jerked over her knuckle. Old Mrs. Clarke's high-pitched mew ratcheted up everyone's blood pressure. Sue was starting to hyperventilate, red splotches on her skin—and that's when Maggie noticed that thin black cord around Sue's neck.

Wide eyed, she blinked at Ed, then she stroked her throat, starting at her jaw line moving down to her collarbone. She stroked her throat again. Barely nodding at Jan, she repeated the gesture, stroking her throat three more times. Sue stifled a gasp. A half-smile crossed Mr. Badger's face, but Maggie shook her head. Old Mrs. Clarke clutched the buttons on the front of her dress as if they were the ripcord on a parachute. As the scarecrow glanced down the hall for the fourth time, Maggie held up three fingers. *On the count of three,* she mouthed, raising her eyebrows, and then she dropped one finger, and then two, and then the third. They grabbed their Med-Alert devices beneath their clothes and pressed the buttons. There was silence in the apartment, but an alarm at the local fire station was ringing. Five distress calls arriving simultaneously. She held up one silent thumb. Five minutes, that was all it should take before the United States Marines burst through the door, or at least a few paramedics, and hopefully the police.

Ed grasped his cane more tightly and inched toward the edge of the couch. *Not the time for heroics,* but nothing came out when Maggie opened her mouth.

Chapter Thirty-Two
FAT OR THIN

WITH THE STRAPS ON HER backpack tightened across her chest, Carly sat wedged into the corner as far back as she could go and chewed on her knuckle. Glancing down the gloomy stairwell into seven floors of darkness, she shivered against the cinderblock wall, the solid concrete cold beneath her. She couldn't stop shaking. Seven floors and then the basement. One false step, one slip, and splat. Broken ankle. Wrenched knee. Game over.

Terry needed to come like right now. The minute the lights came on, the elevator would be running, and Bill and Lemon, loot in hand, would be racing to exit the building, but not before they took a quick minute to silence forever some messy details, like a couple of runaways who knew too much. She thought she and Terry could make it to the tunnels before they turned on the power, but the goose bumps on her arms told a different story.

She heard footsteps sprinting down the hall. She braced herself. Terry burst through the fire door, his good eye wide open and the other bloodshot, not more than a slit. A grim reminder there was no time to waste.

"Go!" She grabbed the railing and sailed down the stairs. Terry behind her, they plunged into cold air and darkness, the only light the faint emergency strips on each riser, but it was enough.

She'd never been much of a runner—exercise wasn't her thing—and this sprint burned her lungs, and her legs ached, but she didn't slow down, not for a second. The chill air smelled stale and tasted metallic, but she didn't care. Terry huffed along beside her. Someday they'd laugh about this, but then again, maybe not. Hard to say. Their pounding steps echoed up the shaft. Her knees screamed with each footfall. At last, the basement level. Bending almost in two, she sucked in air. The heavy door painted with a large red B stood in front of them, their portal to freedom.

Gasping between breaths, she questioned Terry. "Did they station someone down here?" New desperate recruits found on the street or seasoned pros employed specifically for this job?

"A guy I've never seen before. He cut the landlines and turned off the power. Two other guys are on five and six, but not Burt. He vanished Thursday." She thought of poor Burt hitching his way south. He'd escaped just in time.

"When we open the door, it'll be black as night," she whispered. "No windows and lots of intersecting hallways. There's a tunnel." She leaned against the wall, afraid to leave the stairwell, terrified of the stranger waiting in the dark.

Breathing hard, Terry nudged her. "Let's go."

But her feet wouldn't move. It was like they were encased in the concrete. All was still, quiet, too quiet. Lemon and Bill thought of everything—except stake conference—so no doubt there was a plan for Paulo. What had they done to stop him from sounding the alarm or calling the police? Desperation drenched her like a wave of ice water dumped over her head. Above her, a muffled sound grumbled through the ceiling, a series of soft rhythmic thuds.

She clutched Terry's arm. "Go right and then left. Keep going. The entrance will be well lit. Yellow tile. When you get there, stop running. Just walk like you've got all the time in the world. There will be people. Not many. White shirts and ties. Going to meetings. Just smile and nod." She hugged him tightly. "Get to the Joseph Smith Memorial Building. It's marked on the wall. Go up the escalator and out the front entrance. Trax is right there. Head south to the IMC hospital. Lemon won't look for you there. That's where you pick up northbound Front Runner. It will take you to Ogden, and the Greyhound Bus will take you to San Diego."

He stared at her. "You're coming with me." The inflection in her voice had said she wasn't. "We're in this together."

She repeated, "Trax, Front Runner, bus. Simple. But you've got to hurry."

He grabbed her shoulders. "We're going together." Panic shook his voice.

"I'm right behind you. I promise. But I know my way around here, and you don't." She couldn't leave. Paulo might be in the security office. Hurt. Needing her. "You've got to go," she whispered loudly. "Now. I need to get to a phone and call the police before Bill and Lemon get out of the building. They need to be caught red-handed. Locked up. If we ever come back here, I don't want to be looking over my shoulder every second." She reached in her backpack and pulled out the roll of twenties. She tucked some cash in his pocket and a couple of bills in the side of his shoe. Funny, the precautions against petty theft she'd picked up working for Lemon. "There's a ton of stuff I haven't told you. What's the plan for the security guy?"

"I don't know. Bill wasn't saying."

She didn't know what was on the other side of this door. A beginning or an end? Terry's face was full of worry and fear, and she took his hands in hers and held them tight. Her heart lurched in her chest. "Go. No time to talk. The dog beach on Coronado Island. Stay safe. I'll find you. It might be a few days. Email me from the library."

"The police will track me."

"Not a chance. But if they do, we're only seventeen. Worst case is six months in juvie. Come on." She pushed her hip against the door. It opened a crack. The emergency light from a bulb in a metal cage didn't shine far. She hugged him again. "You're the best friend I've ever had. Fat or thin." Then she gave him a shove in the right direction. Jogging down the dark corridor, he looked back over his shoulder, his good eye crying.

She'd made her choice, but watching him vanish was more than she could stand. *Fat or thin.* That's what they'd said to each other when things at home and school got rough. *The Gay Kid and the Fat Waddler* is what cruel kids called them, and those names stuck from the third grade into high school. Terry never—not once—talked to her in solemn tones about her food addiction. Nope. Not Terry. He just rode his hammered bike over on hot afternoons to race through the sprinklers and chat with her dad.

Her eyes searched the dark hallway in the opposite direction. Paulo. Where was he? The security office was down there somewhere. No signs of life. No light. She clung to the wall as she spider-walked her way down the corridor. She finally clutched the doorjamb of the security office. Broken glass crunched under her feet. Someone had trashed the office. The chair rollers spun, but no damaged body lay inert on the floor. No body. Period. No Paulo. Where could those jerks hide a person his size? She tripped over the upended chair, then caught herself with her palms on the floor. Pain shot through her hands, but she didn't cry out. She picked sharp splinters out of her skin and felt blood ooze from the cuts.

Touching the wall, she inched her way down the unlit corridor. How long since she'd buzzed Terry into the building? She'd been staring into the darkness nearly forever. Something rustled behind her. Waiting for Lemon's bony fingers to pinch her, she stopped dead on the linoleum floor. A pipe rumbling, a person breathing, or maybe a mouse skittering past a heat vent? She couldn't see her hand in front of her face. Her palms slippery with blood, she fingered the mace canister in the side pocket of her backpack. Not much good if the guy lurking in the room labeled *Mechanical* had a gun. How long would it take Bill and Lemon to rifle through the apartments on five, six, and seven? And eight. That was the prize. No time to waste. *No time, no time,* she muttered to herself.

Terry must be through the tunnels and on his way up the escalator by now. She crept back to the stairwell and the single light. She sprinted up one floor to the lobby—and then she stopped cold. That sound, that steady thump, was louder. It stopped. She waited a few seconds, and it started again. Something in the back of her head said, *Pay Attention*, but she couldn't wait. She had to get to that phone in the party room on the far side of the lobby to call the police. She pushed the door open a crack. Wind whistled outside, but the lobby was bathed in fresh morning sunlight like nothing was wrong, like robbers could never breach a fortress this steadfast. The light was bright. She stepped back into the shadows to let her eyes adjust. She pushed the door open again. The exterior doors to the plaza and freedom were only thirty feet away. She could dash outside and get help. But how long would it take her to flag down a driver and borrow his cell phone, or pound on the service door of the Alta Club until the kitchen help heard her? By then Bill and Lemon would vanish.

She took a deep breath, slipped off her shoes, and sprinted across the empty foyer. Her heart ricocheting inside her chest, she stood with her back against the draperies in the party room to catch her breath and wiped the blood off her palms on the fabric. The room, the size of half a football field, was washed in shadows and hushed silence. The phone waited on the wall behind the grand piano. She raced across the room, grabbed the phone, punched 911, and waited for a voice that didn't come. The phone was dead. She'd forgotten; the lines were cut. What now? She wanted to bawl.

Any second, the power would come on. The elevator carrying Lemon and Bill would rumble down the shaft and arrive right here, next to the lobby. What if Bill glanced in and saw her? No police, just one handy hostage to torment—forever. She couldn't stay here. She couldn't duck behind the drapes. Skinny or not, they'd see the bulge.

That irritating sound started again. *Thump, thump, thump.* And then it hit her. A sound this measured wasn't mechanical. It wasn't a thief—they avoided noise like the plague. This was a human, probably an eagle scout sending out Morse code. And the sound was coming from the hall by the west entrance. That janitor's closet.

She fished the purse-size mace out of her backpack. One night in Pioneer Park, she'd tried it on a hostile tomcat that attacked the last bite of her baloney sandwich. Very effective. She clutched the canister in her fist and tried not to think about her knees turning to jelly as she crept across the room and inched toward the west entrance.

The doorknob on the janitor's closet was quiet, but the hinge squeaked loudly enough to wake the dead. Stepping into the dark interior, she shoved a rag by the bottom hinge to hold the door ajar. Something moaned behind her, and she jumped, a vertical leap a foot in the air.

"Who's here?" she hissed, one finger poised on the nozzle. No response, just another groan. She held the door open wider, and a sliver of light exposed the shadowy outline of a man with his arms extended over his head as if he were reaching for something on the ceiling and had frozen in place. His hands were cuffed over a horizontal pipe. Paulo, although the realization was slow coming because duct tape— wound twice around his head—covered the lower half of his face. She shoved her mace back in her pocket. He'd been kicking the huge vertical pipe that gurgled even now. That was the noise, the thumping, she'd been hearing.

Her left hand extended, she reached for his curly hair and that cheek she loved. "Paulo?" she whispered standing on tiptoe. Her fingers traveled over his face as though his features were a lecture in Braille. Another moan escaped. She searched for the end of the tape and felt dampness, gooey dampness, on the back of his head. Blood. Her nose close to his face, she sniffed the coppery smell.

"Oh, Paulo. Are you hurt?" *Stupid question*, she thought. *Generally, blood equals bad news.* She kissed his chin.

His arms flexed against the restraints.

"Hold on," she muttered. "Let's get this off first."

She didn't know much about duct tape, but she knew removing a Band-Aid was best done with a quick yank, not a prolonged tug one hair follicle at a time. Channeling her father's comforting voice, she said, "This might hurt a little." Just a bit of intense pain to distract him from the wound on his head. Tape off tape took some muscle, but it was the duct tape stuck in his hair that jerked his eyes open.

His mouth finally uncovered, he coughed in her general direction and fresh blood rolled over his collar. "This is your doing," he mumbled. "You and your friends."

She felt cold and bruised and wet as she studied the expression on his face. Too spent to speak, she strained to inhale and thought, *I'm drowning in my own sweat.*

"Get out," he said.

She shook her head. "No." She shoved a stepping stool beneath him so he could sit and ease the strain on his shoulders. "They're robbing the building. And looking for me."

But he turned his head away, not much, but enough to communicate, *You're part of this.*

Just strangle me now, she thought, *and get it over with,* but that's not what she said. Instead she tripped over her words. "Long story short, I made a big mistake, but I'm not in on it now. I'm here, Paulo." She struggled to free his hands, which was a ridiculous waste of time. She'd need an acetylene torch or a bolt cutter.

"I wanted to run away, but I didn't. I didn't leave. I came to find you. I thought you might be hurt." Another stupid thing to say. He *was* hurt. While she talked, she groped along the shelves for anything that could free his hands. "Maggie and Ed are in serious trouble. We need to do something, like fast." She tipped over a bottle of solvent and the fumes scorched the inside of her nose. "I need to call the police, but the landlines are cut, and I don't know what to do. If I go outside the building, I can't get back in."

He wanted to smile at her. She could tell he did, but his head had to be killing him, so she jumped up with the can of mace in her fist like some kind of a candle.

"A fire alarm," he huffed. "By the elevator in the lobby. Break the glass and give it a yank. Then scoot back here and barricade the door."

"How did you get here?"

His story was quick. He'd watched Terry arrive behind a wall of fresh flowers and then the west entrance camera went blank. Not a good sign. He should have called the police right then, but he went to check the west entrance himself. Big mistake. Next time he'd listen to his gut. Something cracked the back of his head, and when he woke up, he was trussed in the closet like a side of beef with the headache to end all headaches.

"They trashed your office. I couldn't find you. I thought you were dead." She stifled a sob as she daubed the back of his head with a Kleenex.

"I'm not dead. Not even close. You've got to hurry."

"I think maybe I love you," she whispered in the dark. "I've never felt like this before, not ever." Not the best time, but she had to say it.

"I know," he muttered. "Let's talk about it later." If they had a later. The lights flickered on and off a couple of times and then came on full strength.

"They're coming," she whispered, peering down the empty hall.

"Don't go. Forget the fire alarm. It's not safe."

"I have to," she whispered and pushed the door open.

Chapter Thirty-Three
LOVELY REPRODUCTIONS

IN ADDITION TO HER NON-STOP mewing, old Mrs. Clarke clutched her Med-Alert button in her fist like it was a diamond necklace she thought she could hide. The others discretely let theirs dangle inside their clothes as they waited, not moving, listening for any sounds of help on the way. Just one siren, maybe two, that's all they wanted. Maggie turned her wrist slowly and watched the minutes click past on her watch. She remembered the endless suggestions Sue had made over the years: *Breathe in through your nose. Breathe out through your mouth. Listen to the air exit your body.* Watching Sue, whose expression was almost beatific compared to bug-eyed Jan who looked like she was about to launch into orbit, Maggie decided from this moment on, she was going to pay more attention to Sue's advice on lowering blood pressure.

Stretching her long neck, Sue made a couple of graceful side steps and took a gander out the window, then she smiled at Mrs. Clarke before she hummed the line "The Yanks are coming" from the song *Over There*, which meant everything to the captives but nothing to their blond captor. Ed still had a firm grip on the handle of his cane, but he nodded at Sue as if trying to determine the part he needed to play. Mrs. Clarke collapsed into the faded wingback chair as though she had become viscous and soaked into the upholstery fabric. The sudden quiet after ten minutes of the centenarian's pale whimpering caught Lemon's attention. The climate in the room had obviously changed, and he sauntered over to the window to glance down at the plaza.

"Company," he screeched, panic raising his voice an octave. "Bill!" If he'd been holding a cup of coffee, it would have sloshed all over the floor; instead, he jiggled his gun dangerously in one hand. "An ambulance and two cop cars!" But no sirens. He ran out in the hall and shouted again. "Bill!"

Mr. Bandana hustled back through the door. "She was telling the truth. About the cash and the jewelry."

Sue grinned as though she'd just received a compliment from a new admirer.

"Is Terry back?" He glanced over his shoulder as he pulled an empty Nordstrom's sack out of his gym bag, plus a rope of pearls, a couple of diamond dinner rings, a huge star sapphire, and handfuls of earrings, bracelets, and sparkling baubles, and plenty of loose cash. He stuffed the cash and jewelry inside two zippered bags typically used to carry triple-combination scriptures.

Had these thugs perused the aisles of Deseret Book searching for believable props? Maggie wondered.

He dumped the contents of Jan's purse on the table, grabbed the cash from her wallet and several coins. They were as dedicated to their greed as a band of hedge fund managers living on Park Avenue.

The blond yipped, "We've got to get out of here."

"Carly. Any sign of her?"

"Nope."

As he tossed Jan's purse on the floor, Maggie gave Mr. Bandana's face a quick once-over, and her eyes rested on his filthy hands, a rim of dirt under each fingernail. "Carly left this morning."

He zipped the scripture bag shut. "No. She didn't." He coiled the pearls and stuffed them deep in his pocket. "We'd have seen her leave. She's somewhere in the building."

Maggie made a fist to stop her hands from trembling. Carly wasn't helping these men. She was hiding, hiding from them. If they found her . . . What? What would they do? She held her breath. Police cars on the plaza. Help coming soon. The thieves didn't have time to search for Carly. She wasn't a part of this. She couldn't be. She was just a kid.

Without disturbing his bandana, Bill shrugged off his ratty parka to reveal a relatively nice sport coat, a starched white shirt, and a striped Christmas tie. Sunday best. He barked into his phone. "Cops in the building. Leave. Now. Head to the elevator. If you get stopped, say an old lady on three had a heart attack." He made a second call. "Turn on the power." He nodded toward Lemon. "Go. Quick." Crossing the room with one scripture bag in his hand and the other under his arm, he muttered, "What idiot didn't take all the cell phones?" Med-Alert hadn't occurred to him.

At that moment, the choir resumed singing on the radio, something about angels on high, but Maggie wasn't sure. Her mind focused on Carly, she prayed the girl was safe, but where was she?

His gun in his left hand, Lemon tugged on his jacket's zipper with his right and called after Bill, "What about Terry?"

"Can't wait." Bill headed down the hall. "Let the cops have him."

She saw the collar of the blond's starched shirt, and then his zipper stuck, caught in his jacket's frayed lining. He took a few steps toward the hall and stopped, yanking at the zipper. Her eyes flitting between Ed and the blond, Maggie couldn't believe what she was seeing: Ed grasping his cane more tightly, his knuckles white as he edged off the couch. Was he crazy?

In one quick move, Ed swung his cane down on the young man's exposed wrist. The bone cracked. Lemon screamed. His ski mask was in place, but she could see the shape of his face contorted in agony. The gun flew across the room, a pop fly shooting past third, and landed at Sue's feet. In a move that could only be called nimble, Sue dropped into a partial lotus position, sitting on the gun like a goose squatting on eggs in a nest. The look on her face said, *And what are you going to do about that?* She'd clearly had enough.

Lemon jerked his good hand across his body, ready to backhand Ed, but Maggie was on her feet. Swinging her phone like a rock in a sling, she connected with the back of Lemon's head, surprising herself and certainly surprising Lemon. He yelled and flipped around to face her when Ed's cane struck him above the left ear. He stumbled against the couch.

Bill reappeared at the door yelling a string of curses. "What are you doing? We've got to get down before the cops come up." He yanked at the zipper on Lemon's jacket then shoved the blond scarecrow through the open door. Favoring his left arm, Lemon shrugged off the mask and his jacket as they sprinted down the hall. The muffled sound of their feet on the carpet was such a relief. The phone dangling in her trembling hand, Maggie stood not moving. "Oh my goodness."

"He's not going to get far with a broken wrist," Ed said. "That's how they'll catch him."

Jan stuck her head out the door. "They stuffed their coats and masks in that Nordstrom's sack." She pulled her head back inside and flipped the deadbolt, which made Mr. Badger smile at locking out thieves who'd already stolen all their cash and jewelry and peace of mind. Even Mrs. Clarke's ancient wedding ring had been ripped off her plump finger. "Those jerks are going to pass themselves off as church-going citizens who shop at City Creek Mall," Jan said. "They thought of everything."

"Hurry!" In three steps, Maggie crossed to the sliding glass door and splayed her hands on the cold glass. No EMTs pulling gear out of the ambulance. They must be in the building, but where? Did the Med-Alert buttons give an exact location? Was help laboriously climbing seven flights of stairs?

Under an unforgiving sky, snow whirled across the pavement. Head tilted and talking into the microphone on his shoulder, a solitary policeman strolled across the plaza. A knitted cap was pulled down over his ears, and his parka had SLPD stenciled on the back in florescent yellow. Maggie pounded on the glass. "Look up!" She pounded again. Mr. Badger and Ed stood next to her, looking down, but it was Sue who pushed them aside and unlocked the sliding glass door.

"Really, we can do better than this." She stepped onto the two-foot ledge waving her arms in the bitter cold. "Officer! We've been robbed!"

Mr. Badger edged out behind her and added his voice. "We've been robbed! Up on seven!"

After a few precious seconds, the officer looked up. He raised his shoulders and lifted both gloved hands. He couldn't hear voices lost in the chill breeze.

"He can't hear us. Not in the wind. We're too high," Mr. Badger yelled. Snow crystals swirled around them.

"Those creeps are taking the elevator down while the police and the paramedics are climbing the stairs," Jan said. "They thought it all out."

Ed glanced at Maggie. "Paper," he said. "And a marker."

She didn't own a printer, so there was no stack of pristine paper within easy reach. The best she could do was the ward newsletter sitting under the phone. She handed him the black felt-tip marker from the top drawer.

Robbery in progress. Gang wearing Sunday clothes exiting west entrance. Ed crushed the note into a ball and tossed it to Mr. Badger who fired it off the ledge. Holding their breath, they watched the ball sail through overcast light, catch an updraft, and lodge in the bare branches of a tree. They all gasped.

"More paper?" Ed asked.

Her eyes did a quick search around the room, but loose paper wasn't something she had. Then she remembered the yellow pages tucked in the drawer. She been chided too many times about being the last human on the planet to actually own a phone book, but now she was glad. She ripped out a page. Ed rewrote his message, folded the page around a tangerine from a bowl on the table, and lobbed it to Mr. Badger.

Intrigued by a couple of old people waving on the balcony—one firing missiles— the officer caught the tangerine with two hands, read the paper, and gave them a quick thumbs up.

With Sue and Mr. Badger still outside and the rest of them pressed against the glass, they watched the officer speak into the microphone attached to his shoulder.

"He's calling for reinforcements," Jan called out as though dozens of onlookers filled the room behind her. "Will they get here in time?"

They waited. Mr. Badger and Sue stepped back inside, frail Mrs. Clarke sat in her chair, and the rest of Maggie's friends stood, not speaking, as though they were doing an emotional inventory of their body parts and brain cells—and remembering to breathe. The power went out. No more choir. The thugs had arrived in the lobby while the paramedics were still climbing the stairs.

"If they have more guns," Maggie said, "that young officer won't stand a chance." She wondered if he had a wife waiting at home on a Sunday morning and maybe two or three little kids and toys wrapped under a tree.

"Well," Sue announced, blowing on cold fingers as if she'd just painted her nails, "the jewelry they stole—all fakes. Lovely reproductions. The real stuff is in a safety deposit box at Zions. I'd love to see their scrawny faces when they try to hawk that diamond bracelet." In a deft motion, Sue retrieved the gun from where it slid under a chair and clicked on the safety. She held it out in two fingers like a rank bit of garbage, rose to an upright position, and carried it out to the sink. Maggie exchanged a look with Jan when they heard the tap water running. Then they heard a watery plunk.

"She's drowning the gun," Jan said with a hysterical laugh.

"What about the cash?" Ed called into the kitchen. "Was it real?"

"Unfortunately," Sue's voice sang out.

His white hair mussed, Ed sank down on the couch. Jan walked over to the sliding glass door circled in Christmas lights and stared at the gray morning. No sign of pale sunshine on the pavement. Clusters of curious people stood on the sidewalk, gawking at the emergency vehicles until cold air forced them inside or scurrying down South Temple. The policeman kept talking into the microphone on his shoulder. Sirens blaring, a third patrol car careened through the light traffic as though the driver were auditioning for a role in a blockbuster movie.

"I bet they got away," Jan said. "Took off in six different directions."

Sue walked over beside her, her arm resting on Jan's shoulder. "We got off easy. I was afraid they'd want a hostage, and of course, I was the obvious choice, just from the standpoint of general agility and name recognition."

Chapter Thirty-Four
SOMEONE TO BLAME

"WAIT, CARLY. STAY PUT." PERCHED on the stepping stool, Paulo muttered, "I mean it," with all the force he could muster. His shoulders and arms, stretched over his head, had to be killing him. In the harsh fluorescent light, she could see growing circles of sweat darkening his shirt and blood stains around his collar. "The power's on because they got what they wanted, and they'll leave." He tugged against the handcuffs. "Turn the lock. Push those boxes in front of the door. We'll get the police when they're gone."

"You don't get it," Carly said. "Maybe not today, and maybe not tomorrow, but they'll come after Terry eventually. He knows too much." And they'd come after her and other girls like her, stupid runaways too naïve to know predators lurk in blind alleys, or in grassy parks, or on street corners near bus stations. Maybe here or maybe in another city, Bill and Lemon would keep turning young girls into petty thieves or, worse, emaciated addicts to sell to pimps. They'd never stop. Wolves, that's what they were, predators preying on lost kids. Kids like her. Boys like Terry. Boys like Nolan.

Ignoring Paulo, who was frantically yanking on the handcuffs, Carly pushed the door open and stole a quick look down the hall. Pale light flooded the lobby. After spending a half hour in the dark, the light made her feel stupidly euphoric. She blinked at the brightness. Her eyes teared, but she shook her head and straightened her shoulders. She could do this. She turned back toward Paulo.

"I've been bullied all my life," she said. His hands stilled, and Paulo's eyebrows rose. "Enough." Standing on the second rung of the stepping stool, she kissed him hard on the mouth, jumped down, and charged out the door.

Her hand skidded along the wall as she sprinted down the hallway, and then she saw it, a small red box ten feet from the elevator doors. She grabbed the glass door and jerked the lever. Nothing happened. She slipped the mace into her pocket. This was a two-handed job. She pushed on the lever, and the glass tube shattered, but there were no alarms or loud sirens. *What's up with that?* She was counting on a total racket. *Is the alarm disabled?* She glanced up. No water showered from the tiny spigots in the ceiling. *This whole place is defective.* And that's when she saw emergency vehicles parked just off the concrete steps, but no police. No uniformed guys. No fire trucks beamed in by her tug on the lever. And no noise at all until she heard the sound behind her: elevator doors opening.

"Carly."

A chill shot up her spine. She recognized the voice that sounded like the screech of a tire. Pivoting on one heel, she faced them, Lemon and Bill. Their clothes surprised her. Sunday best. And fresh haircuts and clean-shaven cheeks. The perfect disguise. But nothing could mask Bill's eyes, narrowed and looking at her with a hatred that felt like the prick of knife at her throat.

Lemon's swollen left hand made an awkward fist that he tucked against his chest. His good hand protected his left. Beads of sweat shone on his forehead, and his face twisted in a tight grimace. The elevator doors closed behind him as he babbled, "Why? Why weren't they at church? They're always at church. That's what they do. We should have had two hours." He spoke as if he'd been outmaneuvered by someone more devious than he was, that some dirty trick had been played specifically on him, and he needed someone to blame. Lemon the victim. His eyes were teary. That was something new, but Bill wasn't paying attention. He was glaring at Carly and then past her at the emergency vehicles parked on the plaza.

His hand shot out and grabbed her arm roughly. This was the first time he'd ever touched her. His grip was ironclad. She kicked at his leg, but it was like kicking a cement post. He didn't feel a thing. He just dragged her down the hall toward the west entrance, his scripture bags in one hand and Carly—struggling and yelling—in his right.

Three steps behind, Lemon whimpered, "Why didn't you tell us? That was your job." Bill's scripture bag grazed her leg and nearly tripped her as she stumbled beside him.

"Where's Terry?" he barked.

"Gone. Where you'll never find him." She hated them both, hated them for beating Terry, for what they'd done to poor Nolan, and for what they had planned for her, but she didn't have time to scheme. So she screamed. A gut-piercing shriek louder than any siren. Bill slapped her. Her head jerked to one side, and she tasted blood. The light started to flicker, and her feet quit supporting her weight. She shook her head. No time to faint. This monster was going to kill her because she knew too much or not enough. A piece of her was terrified, but there was also that other side of Carly, the brat that always got her in trouble. She quit moving her feet. Bill was lugging dead weight. He hit her again, harder. Blood sprayed from her nose.

"You can kill me," she sputtered, "but you'll still be stupid and ugly."

Bill dropped his precious bags. Furious, he seized her left ear, ready to smack her again, but the sound of Paulo yelling startled him. He glanced toward the closet door. In that one spare second, she grabbed the canister in her pocket and flipped the safety lever with her thumb. With blood streaming down her lip, she pushed the red button and shot pepper gel in Bill's face.

Screaming, he let go of her, and she squirmed away. Tears gushed down his cheeks as he frantically rubbed his eyes. He gasped and staggered blindly toward the lobby.

Lemon twirled around, searching his pocket for the gun that wasn't there. She blasted him too. He dissolved in a heap on the floor. His skin strangely mottled, he sputtered to breathe and rolled back and forth on the carpet howling.

Carly looked down at the canister. *This stuff is magic*, she thought. Stunned and sitting on the floor in front of the west entrance, she was trembling, but she also decided this was the best moment of her entire life. Payback for almost everything; plus, she wasn't dead.

She heard footsteps in the lobby. Her arm shot up, finger poised on the button. Three more guys were loose in the building, but what she saw was a single policeman holding a very serious gun in both hands. He was stocky with thick thighs, and she recognized his stance from TV.

"There are more," she said, wiping the blood on her face with her sleeve. "One in the basement who keeps throwing the circuit breaker. And two on five and six robbing old people." She inched her way slowly up the wall until she was standing. "You should probably call for more help."

But he was already talking into the mike on his shoulder. He asked her, "Pepper spray?"

She nodded.

"It works for about thirty minutes," he said as he cuffed Bill who loosed a string of thorny curses, but Bill had turned into a blind wolf and wasn't so scary after all. Lemon writhed on the floor, and he screamed so piteously when the officer grabbed his wrist that she almost felt sorry for the guy, but the officer wasn't deterred and jerked Lemon's hands together. Her nose gushing blood, she stood, tenderly touching her jaw and feeling for loose teeth. But a loose tooth was nothing compared to the payback Bill had planned for her. She was a lucky girl, and she knew it.

The officer was tense, his gun on the ready, waiting for three more bad guys to surface, but suddenly the hall darkened and the elevator doors closed. The power was off again. "The jerk in the basement's still busy," she said. "Those other two might be coming down the stairs."

Maybe he could read her mind, because he said, "I won't leave you here alone."

"Thanks. I don't know how many squirts are left." She held up the canister hooked to a key chain.

"Typically five. It won't stop an army." They both turned their heads toward the sound of a siren.

"Yes," she whispered with a raised fist.

"Who are you?" the officer asked.

"That's a good question. I've asked myself the same thing more than once." She cupped the side of her jaw with her hand pushing the sleeve of her orange parka under her nose and paused before she spoke. "B. Caroline, a repentant accomplice." Her voice was muffled. He didn't smile; he just gripped his gun more tightly and glanced toward the stairs marked *Exit*, which was okay. Maybe these police types didn't like jokes. "There's a security guy cuffed to a pipe in the janitor's closet. It's around the corner and down the hall. Unless he's chewed off his hand trying to get free."

The officer didn't relax, not for a second. He was young. Not much older than Paulo.

"You know," she said, "like wild animals caught in a trap." She was feeling loopy and a little unnerved by Bill and Lemon, arms behind their backs, trussed like a couple of stuffed pigs waiting for the oven. Bill was eerily quiet, but Lemon was moaning and rolling from side to side.

The young officer gave her a nod, but that was about it. She'd played a part in all this, and they both knew it, but he didn't question her. That would come later. The mike on his shoulder started to chatter, and he grumbled directions to incoming officers. The commotion was probably driving Paulo crazy. Paulo. He didn't know which side was winning, hands over his head, strung up in the closet.

Suddenly a dozen policemen arrived, and maybe it was the headache and the blood seeping down the back of her throat, but to her, they looked like blowflies buzzing around dead animals. They arrived just in time to nab two more clean-cut guys with bad teeth exiting the stairs on their way to church with scripture bags stuffed full of cash and jewelry.

A youngish man she'd never seen before spoke up with feigned concern, "An old lady up on three is in real trouble. She's clutching her chest in terrible pain. We gave her an aspirin and called 911, but there's no cell coverage and the power's out." They were talking fast, but not fast enough. Busted.

No pepper spray for those two guys. They could actually see the exterior of the yellow brick fortress as the police shoved them into the backseat of a patrol car. Bill and Lemon couldn't see anything. Their eyes were weeping and swollen, and she could make out Lemon's theatrical protests of innocence and his demands for immediate medical attention. He'd been assaulted by some old duffer, and he was going to sue. *Good luck with that,* she thought and would have laughed if her nose weren't full of blood clots.

The police searched for the guy flipping the switch in the basement, but he got clean away, probably out through the tunnel. She hoped he was scared straight, because that's how she felt. Her sticky fingers washed clean forever. Another officer, an older guy with a very serious expression on his face, took her elbow too tightly as he marched her to the couch in the lobby. He handed her a compress for her nose, but before he could pummel her with a hundred unpleasant questions, she said, "Paulo. The security guy. He's handcuffed in the janitor's closet." She nodded in the general direction of the west entrance. "By now he's probably dislocated both shoulders. I'm not talking until someone takes care of him."

The man in charge nodded at another of his uniformed crew. She worried out loud about finding a key to fit the hand cuffs, but the officer cut her off. "Who are you, and what are you doing here? This isn't where you live." He was working hard at being nice, and maybe he had kids of his own who weren't allowed to watch TV, but she'd grown up with a daily dose of *Law and Order*, plus all the spin-offs, and so she moved the compress away from her mouth. "My role in this charade is a little dicey; plus, I'm underage, so I'm going to need an adult relative or an attorney before I answer any questions. Sorry."

The cheesy smile on his face didn't mask the officer's irritation. "If you haven't done anything wrong, you don't need to worry."

"Right," she said and sat without speaking.

"How about the names of your parents or guardian?"

She thought about that for a moment or two, and then she gave him the answer that anyone in the building could supply. "Maggie. She's my great aunt. She lives in 7-B."

Chapter Thirty-Five
CONFESSIONS

WIDE-EYED FRIENDS IN 7-B CLUSTERED around the sliding glass door and stared down at the plaza as police hustled four clean-cut young men—hands cuffed behind their backs—out the front doors and into patrol cars.

"What time is it?" Jan asked.

"Who cares?" Sue gave her a one-armed hug. "We're alive."

"They caught them," Ed muttered. "Red handed."

"They'll be here in a minute. The police. To question us," Jan said. They stared at each other as if they'd somehow been complicit in the robbery.

"Carly's only seventeen." Pulling her sweater tightly around her chest, Maggie turned away from the south windows. If an officer loaded her darling Carly into a patrol car—like a common criminal—and carted her off to the police station, Maggie didn't want to watch. She couldn't bear it. She couldn't stop thinking about the girl, how she came to be in the yarn shop, and how she looked so different from the plump little niece smiling in photographs, and yet she was one and the same.

"What will happen to her?" Sue asked.

"They'll question her and discover the part she played." Jan sighed. "Find out about this guy named Terry. Call her mother. Maybe book her. Maybe refer her to juvenile court. Maybe let her go." Clearly there was more to being a high school principal than just making announcements about dances and ball games on the PA every morning at eight.

"They won't keep her," Ed said. "She'll be back here by five. Maybe before that."

"Maybe." Jan shrugged and was silent.

A sharp knock on the door and they all froze like actors in a silent movie. Mr. Badger closed his eyes, but Maggie could see his lips moving. Ed's fingers tightened on his cane. Straightening her caftan, Sue faced the door, a determined expression on her face. The morning's violent interruption had unsettled them all. Four thieves were caught, but the guy in the bandana had been talking to someone. Who? The door was locked, but what if a desperate straggler was back, searching for a place to hide? With a gun. They were anxious, fearful. *Who could blame them?* Maggie thought.

A second knock. Louder. An unfamiliar voice said, "Police."

But no one moved. Police? Or another clever disguise? Maybe a thief in a stolen uniform—with a jittery finger on a trigger—stood on the other side of the door. The exterior entrances were manned. Did the person knocking need elderly hostages, a human shield to get him outside and protected in a stolen car? Maggie slapped her cheeks with both hands. *Turn off the TV in your head.*

Ed shouted, "Slide your ID under the door."

"We're the police."

"Great. Side your ID under the door."

After a fair amount of muffled grumbling, a worn pocket-sized folder appeared.

Moving awkwardly, Ed bent down on one knee and held up the badge. He turned the deadbolt, and the door swung open. "Detective," he spoke as the man stepped inside, "we've had a rough morning."

"So I understand." The man wearing an inexpensive parka, government issue, glanced around the room at seven exhausted faces. He was average height, average weight, with a simple gold band on one finger, but his inflamed nose in the center of his face was ready to sneeze. "Which one of you is Maggie Sullivan?"

No mention of Memmott. Thank Heaven. Maggie took a deep breath and raised a limp hand.

"Are you related to Carly Maughan?"

"You found her? She's safe?" Maggie's shoulders relaxed, and she rested one hand on her chest. "She's my great-niece."

"She's downstairs with an officer. I need contact information for her mother."

Maggie didn't reach for an iPhone; she reached for an address book covered in paisley fabric. It was slightly dog-eared, but that didn't matter as she flipped to the correct page. The detective snapped a picture.

He pulled the scripture cases out of an evidence bag and spread the contents on Maggie's kitchen table. They each identified pieces of jewelry, except Maggie and Ed. They had nothing to contribute.

"We'll need each of you down at the station," the detective passed out business cards as he spoke, "tomorrow morning. We'll need statements about what happened today. And last week." He glanced at Mrs. Clarke asleep in the chair. "We can arrange for an officer to come and get you. Not a problem."

Sue waved one hand in an expansive gesture. "Ed and I can provide transportation. Ten o'clock?"

"Carly's a sweet girl." Maggie needed to say something, anything.

"No doubt." The detective turned to leave. "Glad you're all safe."

Maggie wanted to ask this man a hundred obvious questions, but she sighed instead. Tomorrow would be soon enough.

Jan walked over to the sliding door circled in Christmas lights and stared at the overcast morning. The policeman they'd watched earlier was still talking into the microphone on his shoulder. A third police car rolled slowly, easily off the plaza into light traffic as though this story weren't going to be the lead in the six o'clock news.

"Would they have gotten away?" Jan said. "You know, if it hadn't been stake conference?"

Sue stood beside her. "We got off easy."

"You think? I'll be having nightmares for days. But Lillian Hollingsworth is going to be furious that she missed the whole thing. We'll be celebrities. Blog worthy." Jan smiled. "Take our stuff. Who cares? Possessions are nothing. Things don't define us. We are our stories, and you can't steal another person's story." She shrugged. "Maybe we don't know each other's beginning chapters and that doesn't matter. We're here for each other now. For the conclusion."

That felt a bit morbid, like the covers of a book were about to slam shut, but Jan was looking a little unhinged, her hair in white spikes. No one made a move to leave. No one collected this morning's experiences like a jacket or purse or a loaned book before edging out the door. No. They needed to process what had just happened and the parts each had played. Joined forever by this unnerving violation, they needed to laugh at Sue settling her expressive backside on a loaded weapon. They needed to remember their paralyzing fear, where they'd been standing, and what the thieves said, and finally, they needed to remember Ed's angry rebellion against infirmity and the thieves' contempt for advanced age.

"They've been watching the building. Checking us out," Ed said. "E. Johnson isn't much to go on." The implication wasn't lost on anyone, certainly not Maggie. The thieves had insider information and had been cataloging potential loot for days. Carly? What part had she played? Eventually, feelings of betrayal would morph into heartache, because Maggie knew they all loved her, the teenage foundling left on their doorstep.

"They saw that car you drive," Maggie muttered, shifting the guilt that was an arrow pointed straight at Ed. No help needed from Carly. Maggie rested her head against the wall. "The minute you saw those guys, you wanted to whack them." She peered at the ceiling and then she lowered her gaze. "What on earth were you thinking?" She spoke as if she and Ed were alone in the room.

He shrugged, his face scarcely moving.

"Well, I'm selling the Mercedes," Sue said. "My next ride will be something small. A Honda Civic. Something white. Maybe I'll run into the concrete pillars in the parking terrace and dent a few fenders. A little rust. Incognito affluence—"

Frowning at Ed, Jan interrupted, "You didn't know how many guns they had. You could have been shot. Pretty careless move." And any one of them could have caught a stray bullet—in a face or a stomach or a descending aorta—collateral damage or a death sentence for a person their age, but her accusation missed its mark.

"What's the worst that could happen? I could have been shot? I could have died? I've got cancer." Ed's expression hardened. "One thing you learn in prison—if you let yourself be a victim, you're done."

No one took an actual step back, but horrified silence drew a cautionary ring around Ed. This elegant, well-spoken gentleman had a significant past?

"Prison?" Jan whispered.

"Two years."

Ed's revelation wasn't the proverbial last straw, but it wasn't information they could assimilate easily. Mrs. Badger's mouth made a round O. One of their own wasn't whom they'd assumed, wasn't a prize, or a new friend worth making. And this wasn't the moment for a long-winded confession. No one had enough energy. They were exhausted.

The room was silent. Ed gazed out the window at the wintery quiet before he began. "It's not just my story. It's more about Maggie." His lips formed a line across his face, and his jowls sagged. He waited for her to speak.

Why was he doing this? Drawing her into his story? Or was this a calculated gesture, served up like a plate of tarragon chicken left over from last night? Or did he need to distance his own spectacular brand of thievery from these crooks of such a small caliber? She pressed a damp palm against her forehead. Her heart fluttered in her chest, and a couple of butterflies were running relays in the pit of her empty stomach. This was too much for one Sunday morning a week before Christmas.

"Maggie?" he spoke softly.

Her mouth formed words, but there wasn't much volume. "You don't want to be a victim, but neither do I." Sue started to speak, but Jan elbowed her.

Maggie had fashioned a new life for herself, a respectable life with interesting friends who valued her company and opinions. She was charitable in her dealings with other folks' failings and endlessly patient with beginning knitters whose fingers stumbled doing slip-knit-and-pass. And now this man wanted her to plunge headfirst into that old swamp named The Tragic Life of Maggie Memmott? Confession was good for the soul and perhaps that's what he needed. He hadn't gotten enough mileage from last night's self-flagellation, and now he had a bigger, better audience for his humble revelations, but his choices didn't obligate her.

Her friends had a glimpse here and there of her previous life, a simple black line drawing that Mr. 8-B wanted to embellish with splashy colorful strokes. He'd turn her into a pathetic scandal, an innocent victim; but it was a story worth repeating, nevertheless. One that would bounce down each floor until she landed headfirst in the basement. She'd probably be the subject of Lillian Hollingsworth's blog. And goodness knows, it was a lovely story. After thirty-plus years, a multi-millionaire seeks a woman he wronged, and certain she could never forgive him, he takes up residence in the building where she lives to woo the unsuspecting woman with gourmet meals and

Christmas concerts and the suggestion of love, thus ensuring her heartfelt forgiveness. It was a story so romantic—and sweetened with money—she'd be painted right into a corner. The residents of the building—her community—would expect flowery absolution, the only acceptable climax in this charming work of non-fiction, because after all, the penitent was dying. But Maggie wasn't dying, not technically, not yet.

"I'm not up for this." Maggie raised her finger in a gesture telling him to halt. Other than Mrs. Clarke, who'd fallen asleep with her mouth hanging open, the other sets of eyes were fixed on Maggie's face, but she was staring at Ed and couldn't see anyone else.

"Maybe a cup of something hot," Sue suggested as though she could loosen Maggie's resolve with a stiff shot of chocolate. "We're all a little anxious. And rightly so." She fussed in the kitchen, opening drawers and cupboards, filling the teakettle. Finally, clinking spoons against china, she waltzed around the corner with mugs on a tray.

"I just sensed a crack in our collective consciousness. Something we should pursue for the good of us all." Sue passed out the mugs, then inhaled long and loud, almost a lesson in breathing. Ignoring Maggie, she looked pointedly at Ed. "Let's have it. The story." She moved Carly's pillow and settled herself on the couch as she crossed her ankles neatly, a steaming mug in one hand.

"Maggie?" Ed asked.

"My story is my own," Maggie said, steel in her voice. "That's all there is to it. I'll take it with me when I go." As in *die*. They all understood.

She sat a little straighter, but everyone else slouched as though they'd paid for excellent seats for a blockbuster movie, and after the opening scene, the projector malfunctioned, leaving the audience waiting, disappointed in the dark. No one spoke.

Choir music returned, as the lights flickered on, and for a moment, a mellow voice distracted everyone in the room.

"And thus at this season of the year, we all need to remember the birth of our Savior."

Sitting without speaking, Jan, Sue, Maggie, Ed, and the Badgers listened to the message they'd heard hundreds of times—each through the filter of his or her own life—while Mrs. Clarke slept. Maggie's humble room was shrouded in pale winter light. They heard the sound of her refrigerator starting to hum, and the furnace kicked in. Whatever any of them had planned for the rest of the day seemed oddly anti-climactic, not worthy of mention, not a reason to jostle one another or fold up the quilts. They were relieved to be fixed in the moment. And even if they'd learned safety was an illusion, this morning they'd survived a brush with danger.

Ed was examining the new crack in his cane. "It's not meant to be a weapon, but I didn't think it would break at the first sign of trouble." He gave Maggie a sad wink and mouthed, *I'm sorry.*

"You need a knitting needle," she said. "More resilient."

And that's when it occurred to Maggie—suddenly, a Christmas epiphany—that Ed wasn't confessing to lift some weight off his soul; he wanted to share who he'd become and what he'd learned through seventy-two years of painful lessons. That's what he'd been trying to tell her in his awkward way last night, that hiding from mistakes is a just another kind of prison, one of your own making, and shame creates the bars.

Sitting on her straight-backed kitchen chair, she realized what Rosie had known all along, that Maggie had wasted too much of her life stagnating in a past that couldn't change. She glanced around the room at this small collection of people she'd grown to love, these random residents of the Eagle Gate life had thrown in her path. She knew why the last seven years had been so happy; she'd lived inside each valuable moment, found delight in new friendships, discovered happiness in the laughter of children at a puppet show, enjoyed pleasure in a teaspoon of raspberry jam, and felt worth in helping strangers learn to knit. It was enough.

"I'm thinking brunch might be just the thing." Sue exhaled. "We're all famished."

"I'll whip up my signature eggs." Ed announced. "Cheese, peppers, olives, a little onion, eggs, and a pinch of oregano and kosher salt."

"Scones," Jan said. "Apple scones. I'll grab my apron." And she headed to the door.

"Cindy and I make a great tomato smoothie," Mr. Badger offered. "I'll collect the Vitamix and be right back."

The moment he turned down the hall, Mrs. Badger whispered to Sue, "He flips the switch and thinks he's cooking." They all laughed, not a rowdy laugh, just a simple laugh at Mr. Badger's expense, a man they admired. The laughter expelled the tension in the room, as though the sliding glass door had been opened and a breath of Christmas replaced a foul stench.

The smell of onion and peppers and eggs scrambling in a pan woke Mrs. Clarke, and to everyone's relief and professed envy, she didn't remember any of the morning's events. Maggie didn't worry about the state of her kitchen or the age of her utensils or her mismatched dishes in the hands of friends. They all raved about the eggs, the scones, and a tomato concoction that had to be disgustingly healthy. Around noon, anxious adult children arrived to shepherd the Badgers out of the building as though it had suddenly become infectious and an immediate rescue was the only prudent course a responsible child could take.

After announcing the time of her Delta flight Monday morning, Carly's mother kept Maggie on the line and had plenty to say, a mixture of relief, betrayal, and anger, none of it pleasant to hear. Taking their collective consciousness with them, Sue and Jan departed at one forty-five to attend a Brahms's concerto in honor of Christmas at the Assembly Hall. *A mental health break* was what Jan called it. And Mrs. Clarke? She thanked Maggie for a lovely morning and returned to her apartment having enjoyed a good nap.

Ill at ease, Ed stood, leaning gingerly on his cane as though he were afraid it would break and he'd land on the floor. Maggie kept her back to him. He was taking a few ungainly steps in Maggie's general direction when an overwrought Paulo burst in the door.

"Where is she?" He looked frantically around the room. Dark stains covered the collar of his wrinkled Security Resources shirt, and the back of his head had been shaved and looked oddly pink around a circular bandage. He'd taken a serious crack to the head.

"Sit." Maggie gestured to the chair Mrs. Clarke had vacated minutes before.

Paulo didn't move. "She can't go back. Her step-dad's a five-star jerk. One of two things will happen: she'll slip back into her old ways or she'll run away again, and we'll never find her."

"What happened to your head?" Maggie whispered.

"I'm fine. That's not the issue," the boy almost shouted. "Can't she stay here with you? Stay out of trouble?"

"Of course she can. But I'm not her guardian. I don't have a say."

Paulo continued as if she hadn't spoken. "He hates her. She's smarter than his kids. You can just bet she gives him plenty of attitude. Going back there is just an accident waiting to happen. Can't you do something? She's almost eighteen."

"I can try," Maggie said. "I'll do my best." She didn't mention her own precarious situation, but wherever she landed, Carly would be welcome, even if the girl had to sleep on the floor.

"Sit down," Ed said in a voice that couldn't be ignored. "Your head's got to hurt."

"It won't for an hour or two. They deadened it up before they started sewing."

"Does your mother know where you are? She'll be seeing all this on the news."

Paulo shook both his fists at an imaginary enemy. "I'll call her, but what about Carly?" Maggie didn't hear the elevator door opening, but Paulo did, because he turned and sprinted down the hall.

With Ed standing beside her, Maggie stood watching.

Carly's face was a mess. She had a purple bruise blooming on one of her cheeks, and her nose and lip were swollen to twice their normal size. That florescent orange parka was spotted with blood, but Paulo didn't care. He grabbed her, pressed her head to his chest, and stroked her hair.

"I heard you scream through the door. I thought they'd hurt you." The skin on his wrists was rubbed raw.

They were both laughing and crying at the same time. Carly pointed to her nose. "He did hurt me. I'm hurt. I can't breathe through my nose."

Paulo leaned forward to kiss her, but she pulled away. "Not my lips. I have a loose tooth."

Ed touched Maggie's shoulder. "They don't need an audience." Maggie ignored him, but then the phone rang and redirected Maggie's attention. A relieved Henry called to say Kristen had texted him that the ruckus at the Eagle Gate had hit Facebook. Thank you, Lillian Hollingsworth. While Maggie spoke to her son, Ed cleaned up the kitchen with an efficiency that was no longer a surprise.

He held up the Seattle World's Fair mug after Maggie hung up the phone. "More chocolate or do I wash this?"

"No chocolate." Maggie shook her head. "She'll want to stay here to be near Paulo." She desperately needed the girl to be happy.

He smiled. "Young love."

"I was their age when I fell in love with John. Nearly eighteen. All those wonderful feelings hit me like a truck."

He turned the empty mug in his hands before he spoke gently, "Oh, Maggie, I'm so sorry. I know how badly I hurt you and your kids. I'd do anything if I could turn back the years and erase those mistakes."

"I can't talk about all that with you. Too painful." She shook her head and was silent for several long minutes. "Was Carly protecting someone?" She stumbled over the words. "That boy. Terry?"

"Give it time. It will all come out, the whole story." He set the mug on the counter and studiously arranged the damp dishtowel over the back of a chair as though something that simple actually mattered, then he joined her on the couch without disturbing her knitting. "He was beaten pretty badly. I'll talk to Carly. We'll find the boy and give him all the help he needs. That's a promise."

The unintended weight of his words settled on her, and she almost said, "We?" but she paused instead, before she answered, "Of course. I know you will." Terry's name would be written in the little notebook in Ed's pocket. Maybe underlined twice.

He closed his eyes, and Maggie wondered if he'd fallen asleep. His breathing was quiet and even. The soft yellow wool slipped through her fingers as she deftly managed four double-pointed needles; she was knitting a cuff. The time on the clock clicked by. The room slowly darkened as the afternoon passed. She reached over to plug in the strand of Christmas lights around the sliding glass door.

"If I don't open my eyes," he spoke softly. She leaned closer to hear what he was saying. "I'm a kid again. This apartment smells like home. Feels like home." Was he giving her a compliment or nudging open a door? She rested her knitting in her lap, her hands not moving.

"If I wrapped up forgiveness in Christmas paper and a red ribbon," she said quietly, "and put it under your tree, what would be inside that box when you opened it on Christmas morning?"

He studied her face and considered what she'd just said. "Forgiveness? What does it look like?" He clasped her right hand. "One thing for sure, I'd want the fourth spot in the Scrabble game on Tuesdays. All that laughter, I need that in large doses. Do you think you could swing that for me?"

"We've never considered including a male."

"Sexist?"

"Absolutely." She smiled. "But I could give it a try. Sue's easy, but Jan will be a hold-out."

He nodded and grasped her hand more tightly. "One more thing—and don't say *no* out of hand. Think about it for a minute. I want to arrange a modest annuity, enough of a monthly stipend for you to stay here comfortably for as long as you like."

As long as she lived. She knew what an annuity was.

"Maybe a two-bedroom with room for Carly." He didn't stop. "You're happy here. You don't want to leave your friends, and they need you. Let me do this one little thing. Please." He reached for her other hand and held it so she couldn't escape this face-to-face moment. "Let me do this for John." He faltered. "I loved him too. He was my friend."

Forgiveness. What was forgiveness? Accepting small acts of kindness? An absence of anger? Freeing the past? Letting it go? She didn't know, but what she felt in this one quiet moment was peace.

He released her hands, and she settled her knitting in her lap. The look on his face said he was afraid he'd offended her. She slid the needle into a stitch, and then another, and another. She gave the yarn a tug, and the ball bounced off the couch. They both bent to retrieve it and nearly bumped heads. She just laughed and winked at him. "What would you think about a hand-knit sweater? Something in a light blue. To match your eyes."

She understood what he'd been, but she also knew what he'd become: a good man, a kind man.

He gave her an inquisitive look. "We're not quite done yet, are we?" He sighed contentedly. "Maggie, you and I get to write a few more chapters."

"The third act." She smiled as he slipped off his shoes and rested his stocking feet on the ottoman. She knew without saying a word that the years when her children were small and life was fresh had been the best, but these years, these last years that stretched before her, would be filled with love and friendship and triple-word scores. She patted the back of his hand.

About the Author

WHEN HER FAVORITE AUNT MAEDAE moved into the Eagle Gate Apartments, Annette Haws became a frequent visitor. Those visits and the people she met became the inspiration for *Maggie's Place*.

A native of a small college town on the northern edge of Utah and a people watcher from an early age, Annette examines the tribulations and the foibles of characters playing their parts on a small stage. After fourteen years teaching in the public school system, she set aside her denim jumpers and practical shoes to pursue her interest in writing fiction. Her first novel, *Waiting for the Light to Change*, won Best of State, A Whitney Award for Best Fiction, and the League of Utah Writers award for best published fiction. Her second novel, *The Accidental Marriage,* was released in December of 2013. She's been published in *Sunstone and Dialogue*. She is the mother of four above-average children and is the spouse of a patient husband.